THE DYING ROOM

Tim tried to run away, but it wasn't any use. He closed his eyes, to keep from seeing, but that didn't keep his feet from following one after the other toward the room he didn't want to visit.

Ahead of him he heard the door creak open, and the light that came out was so blindingly bright he could see it red through the living blood of his closed eyes.

And the sound that he heard was a silence so powerful it felt like the sound of the world shaking against its foundation. And the air that pressed against him felt like the fevered air that rises from an open oven.

And the thing he smelled was a thing he never smelled before. It was the scent of a man about to die.

Tim gasped, and opened his eyes before he realized what he'd done. . . .

BOOKS BY ALAN RODGERS

BLOOD OF THE CHILDREN
FIRE
NIGHT

NIGHT

Alan Rodgers

BANTAM BOOKS

NEW YORK • TORONTO • LONDON • SYDNEY • AUCKLAND

NIGHT

A Bantam Spectra Book / November 1991

ISBN 0-553-28971-3

Published simultaneously in the United States and Canada

*Bantam Books are published by Bantam Books, a division of Bantam
Doubleday Dell Publishing Group, Inc. Its trademark, consisting of the
words "Bantam Books" and the portrayal of a rooster, is Registered in
U.S. Patent and Trademark Office and in other countries. Marca
Registrada. Bantam Books, 666 Fifth Avenue, New York, New York
10103.*

PRINTED IN THE UNITED STATES OF AMERICA

OPM   0 9 8 7 6 5 4 3 2 1

DEDICATION
For Dad and Alexandra—
comings and goings that mark this book.

ACKNOWLEDGMENTS

Lots of folks helped me with bits of this book—some of them by reading the manuscript and talking to me about it; others by supplying information that I couldn't've begun to find on my own. I'd like to thank them for their effort: Ralph Vicinanza, Lou Aronica, Rob Simpson, Jennifer Hershey, Amy Stout, Charles Conrad, Jerry Oltion, Sandy Willard, Ginger Booth, Stephen Dorato, and Sarah Collier.

There are others I need to thank for help on *Fire*, where (despite intention) I forgot to include a note like this one: Tom McComb, Clayton Walnum, and Dan Moran.

ONE

Grandpa's lawyer called early Sunday morning, while Tim sat sipping at his coffee and staring at the headlines on the bulging Sunday paper. Staring at them, not reading them; it was still too early in the morning for the letters to resolve themselves into words.

He knew that call was trouble from the moment he heard the first ring. Not that he had reason to know; it wasn't like he'd never gotten a phone call early on a Sunday. But reason or no, Tim's heart tried to force its way up into his throat when he heard the phone. And it stayed there, pressing and lurching against him, all through the call and for a long while after.

"Could I speak to Timothy Fischer, please?"

"Yes?—That's me."

"Mr. Fischer? I'm William Rhine, your . . . grandfather's attorney."

"Yes?" Grandpa was actually Tim's grandfather's grandfather—his own great-great-grandfather. But explaining that was usually too complicated a thing, and Tim didn't see any reason to correct the man.

"I have some bad news for you, Mr. Fischer. Your grandfather . . . has passed on. You're aware, aren't you, that you are his heir?"

Tim managed to force a sound out of his throat that sounded something like "Um."

The man on the other end of the line didn't seem to notice Tim's discomfort; he went on and on about the provisions of Grandpa's will. About instructions that certain things be conveyed to Tim promptly. About the details of Grandpa's death—in a car accident on a highway somewhere in the Great Plains.

And Tim heard it—or heard most of it. With half his mind. And all the while the biggest part of him screamed soundless to himself *no no no no no*. Screamed not because he loved his Grandpa—even though he did— nor because he'd miss him—though he knew he would.

Tim's heart raced and his ears rang and his sweat slicked up all over him because his Grandpa had died and left the fate of the world in his hands. The biggest, strongest chamber of his heart—the piece that had lain dead or sleeping these seven years since the horror with Jill and Mom and Dad and worst of all Tim's daughter— the biggest chamber of his heart shuddered and throbbed and beat out a pulse of fear for the first time in seven years.

Though it was a thing he'd spent two-thirds of his life bracing himself to carry, he knew beyond any ghost of a doubt that he wasn't ready to lift the burden he'd been born to bear.

The lawyer's office was in a tall building downtown—a sleek, glassy, newish building that contained nothing but floor upon floor of offices and two or three street-level shops. And Sunday morning it was all but entirely deserted, just as the whole of downtown Tampa was empty on weekends. Except for the bus stations, in fact, this part of town got hauntingly empty by six in the evening on weekdays, too—no one lived here. So far as Tim knew no one lived within twenty blocks of the attorney's office, unless you counted West Tampa, on the far side of the river. But West Tampa was another world; its old wooden houses had long since begun to rot away in the sun and the humidity that are anathema to wooden buildings, and the people who lived there were so poor and so hungry that it made Tim ache to look at them. He had a hard time imagining that anyone who worked downtown would live in West Tampa.

Except maybe the maintenance man who waited in the lobby of the lawyer's office building—a friendly, grey-haired black man who looked Tim over carefully, asked him his business, and had him sign a register before he let him get on the elevator.

Which let him out on the twenty-sixth floor, in a lobby with polished walnut walls. Above the empty reception desk were gold letters: RHINE MILLER & SMITH. Off to the left, sitting in one of the plush waiting chairs, was a man in a navy three-piece suit. He looked up from his neatly folded paper when the elevator opened. Spotted Tim and got up to greet him.

"Tim? Tim Fischer? Yes, I thought that was you." The man smiled a fatherly smile and held out his hand to shake Tim's. "How are you feeling, son? Are you going to be okay?"

Tim nodded and said he'd be fine, which was a lie. Somewhere on the highway between home and here grief had hit him, and he'd begun to mourn the loss of his Grandpa, and now that was mixed with the fear and the responsibility that was more than he could cope with. Heaped on top of all of that was shame—shame that he was wrapped up in his own concerns when it was Grandpa who had died. All of it together left Tim badly shaken—shaken enough that he couldn't imagine things ever being fine.

"We need to go back to my office," the attorney said. "To go over papers. Ordinarily that could wait until Monday. Could wait all week for that matter, if need be. But there's a packet your grandfather insisted I give you *immediately* on his passing. It didn't seem wise to me at the time—grief can leave people in no condition to deal with anything too directly—but he was adamant. And he was sure that you'd understand the need to hurry."

Tim nodded. Now they walked down a wide, white hallway. A hallway carpeted in thick-soft beige that looked clean and new enough to have been installed the day before.

At the end of the hall an open door led into an enormous corner office. William Rhine led Tim inside, and he saw that the outside walls were glass from floor to ceiling. Tim didn't have any particular fear of heights, but that broad a view from the twenty-sixth floor was enough to bring on vertigo all the same.

"Sit down," Rhine said. "Sit down. Make yourself comfortable." He pointed toward a well-padded armchair as he walked around his desk. Sat, and opened a thick manila folder already laid out on top of his desk's blotter. "These first of all," the lawyer said. And handed Tim two manila envelopes: a very small one that clearly contained a key, and another, wide, thicker, that held some form of manuscript. Tim had known the contents of each of them before the attorney had even sat down at his desk. Grandpa had told him to expect these things years ago.

The key was the key to Grandpa's house—an enormous place that was nearly as old as the city itself. The other envelope was more of a mystery; Grandpa never told Tim exactly what the papers inside it had to say.

If it was anything he'd wanted me to know while he was alive, Tim thought, *he would have had me read it before he'd died*. Followed that idea just a little farther, and shuddered. Whatever it was that Grandpa couldn't tell him until it was absolutely necessary—whatever it was, it wasn't anything Tim wanted to know.

Not that there was any choice. He had a responsibility; a responsibility he'd been born with. It wasn't about to go away just because Tim felt faint of heart.

"These are the things your grandfather wanted me to give you immediately," Rhine said. "There's other business we need to attend to, also—but it's a good deal less pressing. Are you feeling up to it? If need be we can leave it wait until later in the week. . . ?"

Tim frowned, distracted. "We might as well get it out of the way," he said. "But give me a minute. There's time, isn't there? I need to look this through—"

He had the larger envelope halfway open before the lawyer had a chance to nod. And then Tim had the paper out, and he was skimming through it, and the world and the height and Grandpa's lawyer all faded away.

Part of the package was instructions.

Part of it was advice.

At least ten pages were family history; just glancing

over those pages made Tim feel . . . warm. Like he belonged.

But the thing on top—the thing that made Tim's blood pound and rush in his ears until it made a sound like the ocean in a storm—the thing that was the worst of it was a letter from his grandfather.

It was supposed to be a comforting note.

It was a letter from a man who'd seen his death waiting for him decades before his end. It told Tim not to worry; told him that Grandpa was resting inside the hand of God, and that even if the old man had loved his life death was fine because another, more important life waited beyond this one. It told the circumstances of Grandpa's death in a depth that was at once easy and comforting. Grandpa had known long ago what his death would mean to Tim, known that Tim would never honestly believe he was ready for the responsibility. And Grandpa left this letter behind to comfort Tim, and to reassure him.

There was only one problem with that letter.

Just one.

Every detail—every intimate and gentle detail that described his grandfather's death—was absolutely and unmistakably incorrect.

Just plain wrong.

And that was when Tim knew that someone had murdered his grandfather.

And that the end was at hand.

Tim was five years old the first time.

He was five, and it was Christmas season, halfway between Thanksgiving and Christmas day, and his Mom and his Dad went north to the mountains for the weekend.

And left him with his Grandpa.

Which was cool. Real cool, and more than cool; Grandpa was just about Tim's favorite person in all the world. A whole weekend alone with Grandpa was just about the neatest thing a five-year-old Tim could ever think up. And he hadn't even had to think it up! Mom and Dad had thought of it for him, and they gave him barbecue and corn on the cob for dinner on Friday night—like they were trying to make it up to him, if you could believe that. Like they felt *guilty* for leaving him with Grandpa for a weekend. Well, Tim wasn't about to tell them otherwise. If they knew he was looking forward to it, they might not give him barbecue and corn on the cob next time. Or have ice cream for dessert.

So after dinner while Mom was packing Dad drove him out to Grandpa's enormous old place. And dropped him off, and when he said he was sorry Tim sure didn't bother to tell him that there wasn't anything to be sorry for. Not him.

When Dad was gone, Grandpa frowned at Tim and shook his head. Not like he was *really* angry or anything, but like he was kind of maybe a little bit disappointed only he was going to get silly about it and tease Tim instead of letting on that he was upset.

Well, that was Grandpa for you. Kind of like they always say about Santa Claus—about knowing when you've been bad and good and being good for goodness sake and all that. Grandpa always knew what was going on. Whether you knew it or not, whether you told him or not, whether you wanted him to know or not. It didn't seem especially remarkable to Tim; he'd known Grandpa as long as he'd been alive, and that was what Grandpa was like.

"That wasn't too nice of you, was it, Tim?" Grandpa asked.

And of course it wasn't especially nice. But there were ameliorating circumstances, to Tim's way of thinking. He had to protect his supply of barbecue and ice cream, after all. So he kind of cocked his head and didn't answer, and waited for Grandpa to go on.

"It wasn't, Tim. Your poor Dad is worried sick. You've never been away from your folks for a whole weekend before, and he's going to spend most of the next ten hours thinking about how you're getting on. All because you played your cards close to the chest."

Tim was beginning to feel just a little uncomfortable. Yeah, it was wrong, all right. And he'd known what he was doing, and known then that it wasn't right. But it wasn't *that* wrong, was it?

He shrugged, trying to act like it wasn't like it was. "Mom wouldn't have made barbecue if she'd known I was looking forward to coming to see you for a whole weekend. She never makes barbecue anymore. And I never told them any lies. They just kind of made them up themselves."

Grandpa sighed.

"You. You're a rascal, all right. And cute as a button. But you're not the only person in the world, Timbo. Your Mom and Dad are people with feelings, just like you are. You wouldn't want to be left to feel like that, would you?"

And that hit home, all right. Hit a lot harder than it would have just a few weeks back, since lately Tim had been thinking about just exactly that idea: what it would be like to be somebody else, and standing in his shoes, and feeling his feelings, and how come they all felt like that anyway?

"Sorry, Grandpa." He couldn't think of anything else he was supposed to say. But he sure didn't feel any good.

Grandpa picked up his suitcase and started carrying it up to the guest room. "Don't take it that bad, Timmy. It isn't the worst thing any little boy ever did—not by a mile. Besides, your Mom and Dad won't be gone for another hour. Plenty of time to call before they go."

Well, that was Grandpa for you. Mom and Dad, when they found him up to something he ought not to be doing, would get stern and harsh and wag their fingers. And maybe they'd even slap his hand, mostly depending on what kind of a mood they were in and exactly how bad a thing he'd done. But Grandpa—he never got harsh. Not that Tim ever saw. Never got certain. Sure never raised his hand to hit you. And somehow he always found Tim exactly where he lived. It was enough to make Tim start considering ways to avoid getting Grandpa disappointed in him in the first place.

Anyway, after Grandpa unpacked his things he put on popcorn and they called Mom and Dad, and to help them feel better Tim acted like he was having a really good time, which he really was even if Grandpa had got upset at him, so it wasn't a lie. It wasn't good to tell a lie even if it was for a good reason—that was another thing Grandpa told him. (Grandpa did allow as how there were a goodly number of times when there wasn't any sense in coming out with the truth—lots of times people just weren't up to coping with it. It was the sort of thing, Grandpa said, that you had to use your judgment about. But all that was more in the category of keeping your mouth shut than it was about honesty.)

And they took the popcorn out to Grandpa's living room, and Grandpa turned on the TV to channel 44, and they spent a long time watching old Christmas movies and eating popcorn and playing Parcheesi. All in all, it wasn't the kind of night you had at home with Mom and Dad.

Sometime in the middle of the second movie they both sort of wandered away from the Parcheesi game and got caught up in the picture. And a little while later Tim found himself losing interest again, because the movie was *Miracle on Thirty-Fourth Street*, and he'd just seen it Wednesday afternoon on channel 10. And he got up off the couch and wandered off to explore Grandpa's house.

Which was another of his favorite things.

Grandpa's house was a really enormous place. *Really* enormous. Three storeys tall, at least, and more rooms than Tim could even begin to count at the age of five. And Tim had the run of it. Well, not the run of it, quite—Grandpa let him go anywhere he pleased on the first two floors. The upstairs upstairs was off limits. And that was just fine by Tim.

'Cause there was something up there on that third floor. Something that made him ache anytime he got near the stairs that led to it. Tim thought of that thing—whatever it was—as Grandpa's Secret. Deep in his heart someplace he knew that it had something to do with him. Which was maybe the reason why his desire to avoid it was more powerful than his curiosity. There was something about that thing, it seemed to Tim who'd never seen it, that made him think of cough medicine when he was sick: it tasted gross and it made him feel all pukey and even if Mom said it was needful Tim didn't see how it did anything but make him feel sicker.

So Tim got up off the couch, and headed off toward Grandpa's den, and as he did Grandpa called to him and reminded him not to get himself hurt.

The den was one of the neatest places of all. Grandpa's books were there, and so was his desk. Which was okay, when you wanted to play with things like that, Tim guessed. But the cool part was the models all over the place. Models of dinosaurs, and of sailing ships and cruising ships and warships. Models of the world, like that big globe beside the desk that stood in its frame taller than Tim could on tip-toe. And a globe of the moon, too. And other stuff that was even neater. Tim had spent lots of afternoons in that den of Grandpa's, and while he was there the evening spun by like a silent carousel, or the stars spinning round in the sky overhead. Till bedtime, when Grandpa came to get him, and carry him up to his room on the second floor.

Morning was almost as much fun as the evening before had been; Tim spent it playing cat and mouse with Grandpa's old tom, Ben Franklin. Sometimes Tim wasn't completely certain which of them was hunting and which the hunter—maybe they were taking turns. Or maybe the cat had a different game in mind than Tim did. Sometimes animals were like that. Minds of their own, and they'd get ideas in their head and not bother trying to make themselves clear to you. And if a boy like Tim didn't get the point, well then that was his problem, so far as Ben Franklin was concerned.

Well, it didn't matter that much if they were playing different games. Tim had fun, and that was the point, wasn't it? It was.

He had so much fun playing with the old tom, in fact, that when Grandpa came in a little while before lunch and told Tim that he needed to go to the store, Tim barely even gave it any thought.

"So," Grandpa said, "are you going to tell me which one of you is the cat and which one's the mouse?"

Tim laughed. "I am!"

"You are, huh? You are what—the cat or the mouse?"

"I am the *cat*!" Tim said, and he ran to his Grandpa and gave him *such* a hug. And Grandpa lifted him up and hugged him up in the air just the way Tim would've hugged his stuffed Teddy bear.

"I'm out of cigars, Timbo," Grandpa said after a while. "Got to run up to the corner shop. You want to come along? Or are you and Ben Franklin too caught up in cat and mouse just now?"

Tim frowned. Rubbed his nose which was all itchy-tickly from breathing cat hair. He shrugged. "Play, I guess?"

Grandpa nodded. "I thought so. You sure you're going to be okay by yourself for half an hour?"

"Uh-huh. '*Course* I am, Grandpa."

Grandpa set Tim down, shaking his head. "All right, then. Just remember: don't play with anything sharp. Don't try to pick up anything heavy enough to hurt you if you drop it. And don't even think about going up to the third floor."

"I won't, Grandpa. Don't worry about me." And Tim honestly meant it: he had too much sense to try to make a toy out of something that could hurt him. And he sure wasn't going anywhere near the third floor.

Tim really and truly believed that when he said it. It wasn't a lie, and if it was a promise that he ended up breaking, it sure wasn't one that he broke on purpose.

"See you in a bit, kiddo," Grandpa said. And he patted Tim on the head. And he left.

In the front room, Grandpa's enormous old AM radio was playing Christmas carols.

The other part didn't start right away. For a good five minutes Tim stayed down there in the parlor, teasing old Ben Franklin and getting teased right back. Listening to the radio with half his mind as someone sang about the Baby Jesus having to be born in a barn and how it was kind of special anyway.

And then he began to hear it.

Not loud, at first. Not even so he noticed it, what

with the cat and the music on the radio. But even if it
wasn't loud enough to recognize, it had an effect on him
right from the first. A peculiar effect, too; it got him
thinking about church. And about how Grandpa was so
mindful of church, and not mindful about it at all. Like
for instance Grandpa said mean things about Father
Thomas, and they always made Tim laugh because he
could hear the truth in them, and Grandpa almost never
went to Sunday Mass. But when he talked about church
there was something awfully special in his voice. And
there was a crucifix in Grandpa's bedroom, hung square
on the wall above the head of his bed.

Crucifix.

Tim always hurt when he saw that crucifix. It wasn't
like most of the crosses you saw here and there. It had
Jesus right there on it, bronze long-haired Jesus with the
nails through his hands and suffering. . . .

And that was when the sound got loud enough to
hear.

Well, not a sound, exactly. Sound was the radio,
where a chorus was singing: *"God rest ye merry,
gentlemen—let nothing you dismay; remember Christ
our Saviour was born on Christmas Day—to save us all
from Satan's power. . . ."*

There was something about that carol that always
gave Tim the creeps. Mostly because whenever he
thought about the word "rest" being used that way he
thought about people resting in their graves—

There. That was it. Not a sound at all, but something like a sound. A sound like you hear it with your
heart and feel it . . . kind of behind your stomach.
Almost like a tickle, and almost like you touched an
electric wire, and scary, too, because what was there
inside you that was like an electric wire?

At first Tim looked around for whatever made him
feel that way. Glanced around the parlor, because he was
curious and not really because it was pulling at him.
Which it was. But gently. Gently, then, some kind of a
pull but so soft it was hard to say which direction it
meant to take him.

There was no sign of it, of course, in the parlor. Tim

shrugged off the pull and the unease and tried to go back to playing with Ben Franklin—but the cat was gone, or maybe he was hiding, and Tim just didn't have it in him to hunt after the thing. . . .

Then the siren call grew loud enough to move him, whether he wanted to follow after it or not. And that was when Tim finally figured out that the feeling in his gut wasn't just trouble, it was something more than trouble. Much, much worse. Trouble, as far as Tim was concerned, was a thing that got you in bad with other people. The thing that drew him step by step across the parlor, into the front room, and up the stairs had nothing to do with anyone but him.

He tried to stop in the second-floor hallway. Focused every iota of his heart and his head, and paused, actually made himself come to a halt right outside Grandpa's room. Turned his head to look in, trying to think about anything else at all in the entire world but the thing that drew him up, up. . . . Looked at the sheets still rumpled where they lay on Grandpa's bed. The bureau, tall polished dark wood with its top still so high above his head. The tile floor, and the throw rug lying pretty-pretty even now that it was threadbare— and looked up at the wall. Which was a horrible, horrible mistake.

For high on the wall hung the Lord Jesus on his bronze-cast cross, dying—

And the sight of him sent the thing in Tim's gut sliding toward his heart easy as the blade of a razor cuts flesh. And his will went slack, and he was in the hall again, walking toward the far end where the stairway started.

The stairway that he'd never ever climbed before. The stair that he'd always avoided with every fibre of his self.

Downstairs, in the front room, a man with a deep voice was singing "We Three Kings of Orient Are."

And as Tim set foot on that ultimate stairway, the radio launched into the song's third stanza. Which, in Tim's book, was about the creepiest Christmas carol he could even imagine.

Myrrh is mine—its bitter perfume
Breathes a life of gathering gloom.
Sorrowing, sighing; bleeding, dying
Sealed in the stone-cold tomb.
Star of wonder, star of night. . . .

Was all he heard before he reached the head of the stair, and once he was there there was no way he could hear anything at all but the searing throb behind his gut.

Down a strange, dark hall with closed doors on every side. At its far end a final door—half-open, and shining from it light that was neither daylight nor the light of any lamp that Tim had ever seen.

He tried again to turn and run away, but it wasn't any use. He closed his eyes, to keep from seeing, but that didn't keep his feet from following one after the other after the other, slow and steady toward that room he didn't want to visit. Ahead of him he heard the door creak open and the light that came out was so blinding bright that he could see it red through the living blood of his pressed-closed eyes—

And the sound that he heard with his ears was a silence so big and powerful that it felt like the sound of the world shaking against its foundation. And the air that pressed on him like wind wasn't wind but the fevered air that rises up from an open oven. And the flavor in his mouth was the flavor of his own blood, or someone else's, and it had to be someone else's because he hadn't bit his tongue.

And the thing that he smelled was a thing he'd never smelled before. And still a thing he knew for certain, recognized though he'd never been near it before.

It was the scent of a man about to die.

Tim gasped, and opened his eyes before he realized what he'd done.

And saw the Lord Christ Jesus dying on His Cross.

It was a great, tall, rough-wood Cross, made of crude-hewn beams. Here and there upon it the Lord's blood stained the splintered wood to a color that was neither brown nor red but darker than either, and slick.

There was pain on His face—pain like nothing Tim had ever seen before—and worse because it wasn't like watching someone else in agony. No. Looking at the Lord Christ writhing and suffering, Tim could feel that pain in his own heart. . . .

There were nails through His wrists, pounded down into the great wide beam-arms. Nails almost the size of railroad spikes.

The Lord was strangling.

Strangling. Tim could see that, because he'd been born with a careful eye: There was no way the Lord could breathe when His body hung slack from His wrists. Hanging as He hung there pulled tight the muscles in His chest that drew air into His lungs.

As Tim watched Jesus pulled His shoulders tight and lifted Himself against the pain in His wrists to breathe. And as He eased down, and the life sagged out of Him again, Tim heard Him speak in a language he'd never heard and could not understand.

And somehow he knew what God had said, even though he had no way to know the words.

MY FATHER, JESUS SAID, WHY HAVE YOU ABANDONED ME?

Tim was crying. It wasn't a thing he meant to do. Nor understood—not really. He was scared out of his mind, and he hurt for the God he couldn't help but love, and—

There. On His side. Just above the loincloth at His hip: a wound. Wide as a man's fist, and deep; looking at it Tim somehow knew that the gash went nearly to the Lord's heart. And knew that the wound would kill Him long before He grew too weak to lift Himself to breathe.

And he wondered if maybe—just maybe—that wound was someone's way of being kind. And shuddered because the idea chilled him down down into his deepest heart.

Tim took in a deep, self-conscious breath. Closed his eyes. Swallowed. Forced himself to be brave enough to open them again.

And what he saw was different, now. Not that anything had changed, except inside Tim's heart. Christ's agony was everywhere in the air, like an impossible mist made of light or spirit. But it was quiet agony; suffering without bitterness or hate or blame. Almost as though divine purpose was behind it, tempering and intensifying it.

It only took him another moment to realize what that purpose was. *His agony holds our sins. Every sin ever committed, and every sin yet to be.*

And knowing that, Tim began to feel God's love. And he knew that Jesus loved him, and loved every man, woman, and child ever born to the world—loved them powerful and true, in spite of and because of and completely without regard to everything they'd ever done. Would do. And were.

And everything changed. Sudden as though He'd never been, Christ dying on His Cross was gone, and where He'd suffered lay a bloodstained ancient fragment of a wooden beam.

And Tim recognized it. Recognized and knew those bloodstains by their shape, because he'd seen them before.

Only a moment before.

Christ's Cross.

Christ's love for man, made whole and tangible in the world.

The three-foot shard of wood lying before him on the bare tile floor was all that remained of the True Cross. And trapped inside that shard, now and forever, was the agony of the death that He'd died so man could live.

And that scared Tim most of all. It broke the trance that held him and sent him running out of the room, back down the stairs, to the ground floor, and he was going to run right out of Grandpa's house and never come back—

But he never got that far. Because down in the front room, standing beside the now silent radio, Grandpa stood waiting for him. And looking at his eyes, Tim knew that the old man knew what had happened. Had known that it would happen. And had intended it, just so.

It isn't likely that anyone who saw Tim Fischer walking through the airport that Sunday afternoon was especially

impressed. Certainly no one with a careful eye for
character. Tim was thirty, but he looked and acted like a
man ten years younger: his body hadn't yet begun to
bend under the weight of time. And his manner—the
fact was that he acted self-absorbed as a teenager. Which
maybe was appropriate, since by heredity he could
expect to live a long long life indeed. There's a reason,
after all, why young men and women spend so much of
their hearts' attention dwelling on their selves—there's
so much they don't yet know about themselves and their
destinies that nature bends them inward and presses
them to learn.

But for all his youthful vanity there were facts about
Tim Fischer's heart far more telling. Watch, here, as he
gets off the bus from long-term parking. Above him a
sign reads ARRIVING FLIGHTS—BLUE—DELTA. Behind him
is a big family. Five children, father, mother. He doesn't
even think about helping with their bags, but he does it
all the same—gratuitously, almost. He's hardly aware of
what he's doing, and even still he ends up loading most
of their luggage onto the hand-truck.

But that's inconsequential in the scheme of things.
More important is the fate of the family's youngest son,
the toddler. Watch him, here, slipping out the bus past
his harried mother, past his father all but blind to the
comings and goings of small children. Past Tim, turned
away, stooped down to set three heavy duffels into the
Red Cap's cart.

Past them all and into the drive. Where cars fly by
in the outer lanes at highway speeds. And what toddler
can resist to watch fast cars up close where no mother
would allow?

And the tiny boy runs out into the traffic.

Tim sees this the moment it's too late. He shouts—
screams!—but it makes no difference. The boy is out in
the second lane already, running faster and faster because he knows his mom'll be on him in a minute.

The taxicab in the third lane is doing forty, at least.
In a zone where there are SPEED LIMIT 10 signs every thirty
feet. There's no way it'll stop in time, nor even see the
child till it's much too late.

Tim has seen this before somewhere. In his dreams he's watched this boy die a thousand times while he stands here helpless

(or perhaps it isn't déjà vu, but something similar, a sense not of repetition but of staring into an inevitable future of the child's death. watch the pulped strange-bent childbody fly up into the air, watch the tiny corpse land all floppy broken bloody on the sidewalk near his mother's feet)

watching

Again, Tim doesn't think, but acts. A great stride toward the child. He still has one suitcase in hand—there hasn't yet been time to set it down. But right this moment that's just as well, because now he can let it go flying back, use its departing mass to give him forward motion.

Two more strides—

—wide, long, unbelievably fast strides, not super-human but *exactly* human, strides so mercuric so broad that only hysterical strength could drive them—

—fast as fire though to Tim it seems he's swimming slow motion through clear lead—

—two more strides and he's there beside the toddler just above the line that marks the beginning of the third lane.

The taxicab is half a dozen feet away. Its driver hasn't seen them yet.

Nor has the tiny boy yet realized that he's put his life in jeopardy. When Tim reaches down, grabs him, and heaves him back (as just a moment before he heaved the suitcase) the boy screams indignant, violated. Angry!

Not that it matters. Furious or not, the boy is safe.

Not so Tim, of course. Heaving the boy backward has thrown him faster and more irrevocably into the bumper of the taxi.

He was perfectly aware of this before he did it. And aware that saving the boy would more likely than not mean sacrificing himself. Neither fact gave him even a moment's pause—if either had the boy would now be dead, flying off the bumper of Tampa Yellow Cab number 121.

But neither is Tim so fatalistic as to spend the last instants he has waiting to die. Instinctively he pushes his torso up, away from the ground—it takes considerable effort, since he stooped to throw the boy out of harm's way, and that thrust him low, almost into a somersault. Up, up, and he tries to jump high enough to miss the now (*finally!*) braking cab. It isn't much use, of course; Tim is in good shape, but he's no high-jumper. His leap carries him two feet, three feet into the air—

And it's enough. Just barely enough to save him. The grille of the taxi catches the back of his ankles—hard enough to bruise but not so hard as to break bones—and Tim lands at an odd angle on the taxi's hood.

Lands hard jarring bonebruising *thwap!* on the hood of the taxicab. But alive. And fine. And unbroken, for all the spectacle collision between his back and the hood. The bruise on his left ankle is real, more substantial, but not so substantial as to make him limp. And anyway Tim heals quickly by nature; he'll be halfway to Omaha before he worries about his ankle, and when he checks the bruise he'll find it already healed.

The taxi driver climbs out of his cab furious and screaming that Tim is a fool, demanding to know why he decided to attempt suicide at the driver's expense. Tim rolls off the hood of the taxi, brushes himself clean. Tries to explain exactly what happened. But there's no reasoning with the man, no way even to force a word edgewise into the conversation. So after a while he shrugs, and turns away, gets his own baggage, and heads off to meet his plane.

As he passes, the toddler's mother and father thank him—he can see in their eyes as they speak that they want to do something to show their gratitude. But they're too stunned to find the words, much less think of anything that would repay the saving of a life, and that's just as well because Tim wouldn't be comfortable taking anything from them.

This is probably the single most important fact about Tim Fischer at thirty: he is a hero. He doesn't know it; doesn't think about it; doesn't consciously attempt it. If you watched the world closely through his own eyes you might never see it. But there is something about him—something born into his nature that is like the grail knights who were his ancestors.

It is a fact that shapes and changes everything Tim Fischer does.

At midnight the plane climbed a few thousand extra feet, trying to avoid turbulence. And as it climbed, the cabin pressure shifted—

What woke Tim wasn't the droning thrum of jet turbines outside his window, and it wasn't the turbulence, and it wasn't the air that pressed on the inside of his ears like a pair of sharp sticks. The thing that sent him bolt upright out of his sleep was the infant back behind him in the plane, screaming in confusion and fear and pain at the pressure in her own tiny ears.

And that was the end of the only hour of peace Tim'd had since the lawyer called that morning. It didn't surprise him to have it end so suddenly; there's only so much peace to be had on an airplane bound for Omaha. In a seat so near the plane's engines. Half a dozen rows forward of a woman traveling with an infant who screamed shrill and phlegmy every time the cabin pressure rose or fell. There would have been no peace at all if the plane hadn't been so nearly empty; Tim had a window seat, and there was no one in either of the seats beside him.

He rubbed his eyes. Tried to wander back down toward sleep. Failed, and knew that hard as he might try he'd continue to fail.

It was too much. All of it. The lawyer. The trip uptown to Grandpa's house, and what he'd found once he'd got there. The letters Grandpa left for him. And most of all the tension in his gut and in the muscles that spread out from his upper spine. He wasn't ready—not even remotely ready, and he didn't know whether he ever would or could have been prepared to cope with the responsibility. Not with his heart, at least. But ready or not, able or not, he had to cope; it was a duty, and it wasn't in his nature to be able to refuse it.

Grandpa knew that, too, Tim thought. And as soon as he'd thought it he knew that the thought had been unworthy. Of *course* Grandpa knew that; Grandpa always knew that kind of thing. Just looking at you, Grandpa could see deeper into your heart than you could ever hope to see yourself.

Tim took the large manila envelope off his lap, where it'd dropped when he'd fallen sleep. Opened it. And began to read that letter for the tenth time, at least.

He read the one letter among the dozen that bothered him most of all. Like the others, it was scrawled longhand on yellow legal paper.

> *Dear Tim,*
>
> *There will be times when you ask yourself why the Cross must always be a secret. Lord knows I've asked myself often enough. There are times when the Stewardship is just too great a thing to bear all by my lonesome. And if the secret's been a less lonely thing since you were born, still, it's more than lonely enough.*
>
> *And what a blessing it'd be, for all of us, if man could see the Cross! If the world could only see what you and I have seen—see how dearly Jesus loves us, and see. . . . But it isn't His way, Tim. You know that. And so do I.*
>
> *Still. That's the least of it, and open to debate. The real problem is in the nature of the Cross itself. We've talked about this, haven't we? There are times when all the years seem to run together, when things I'd meant to say are hard to tell from those I've said. Age, I guess.*
>
> *But follow me, anyway. You've seen the Cross—many more times than once. You know what you've seen in it. And because of it. Have you seen the miracles that happen near it, sometimes? If you haven't seen them, you must have felt them. Miracles are always on the edge of happening all around it.*
>
> *Think about it for a moment. Think about the implications. What causes miracles like*

that? What makes them? God does, of course. Who else could make a miracle?

Miracles aren't a common thing in this age of our world. God has . . . well, stopped doing that. Mostly, at least. So: why are there miracles in the proximity of the Cross?

Because the essence of God is caught up inside that fragment of wood. *His passion and His agony. His love for all mankind. And more than that. A tiny part of God Himself is bound by His passion inside the Cross—made real and whole, touchable and tangible on earth.*

And if the wrong people set hands on it. . . .

It could be dire, Tim. The power of the Infinite lies inside that fragment of the Cross. In the wrong hands, it could lay waste to worlds.

And that's the reason that the Cross must be our secret. Because if the world knew of it, there'd be no way to keep it safe. Not forever. Maybe not even for long. And that could mean the end of all of us.

The letter went on from there for several more pages. Working through the ideas, the possibilities. They were frightening, but nowhere near so frightful as the possibilities Tim could see himself. Or as frightening as the fact of Grandpa's death. He turned toward the window beside him, to look out and away from the things that he didn't want to face. But there was nothing to see; stars covered the sky above and below the plane, made a darkness that was pure and complete.

He wanted to go home. Wanted to turn back at the Omaha airport, get himself a seat on a plane bound southeast, and say to hell with all of it. It was still possible, if he got his connections just right, to get back in time to be at work in the morning. He smiled, savoring the idea. The lure of it was strong enough, almost, to draw him. Even just a couple more days of peace and everyday life—what would it hurt? It was conceivable—just barely—that it'd make no difference at all. And it made a kind of sense, too. He needed time, didn't he, to put his affairs in order?

Right, he heard himself thinking. *Go ahead. Lie to yourself.*

And felt his cheeks flush with embarrassment, even though there was no way that anyone else could have heard what he'd been thinking. There wasn't time for stalling. Too much stood at stake; just as Grandpa'd said, the possibilities were too dire.

He thought of what he'd found at Grandpa's house, and felt a chill.

Or hadn't found, more to the point.

As soon as Tim had read that first letter from his grandfather, there in the lawyer's office, he'd known that things were desperately wrong. Dangerously wrong. He'd excused himself and gone running from that office with everything he'd had. Stood impatient and uneasy waiting for the elevator and then inside it as he rode down. Got to the ground floor and bolted out the door as the security man at the desk hollered after him, insisting that Tim had to sign out before he left. Tim ignored him; there wasn't time for details like that. Not now.

When he got to his car he climbed in and took off, driving as fast as the Honda's engine could take him— and to hell with whether or not it would get him a ticket. Grandpa's house was a good fifteen miles from Downtown, and there wasn't a car made by man that could get him there quickly enough to suit Tim.

Later he was amazed that he didn't manage to get himself pulled over. But he didn't, and because he drove as fast as he did and because it was Sunday morning and there was so little traffic on the highway, less than half an hour after he'd sat in the lawyer's office opening Grandpa's packet he was pulling into the driveway of the big old house.

Opened the door and climbed out. Reached back in and took the small envelope with the key off the passenger seat, where he'd tossed it. Looked up at the house—and realized that something else was wrong.

It was nothing he could point at, nothing visible

anywhere nearby. But Tim knew it, felt it, all the same.

Someone's here. Inside. He focused himself on the feeling down in his gut. *No—not inside. But very close, and watching.*

There wasn't any evidence; there were no cars in the driveway other than his own. None out on the street—not near enough to see, at least. There were the neighbors' cars—parked in their driveways. Tim couldn't imagine an intruder parking in one of those driveways. It'd be too conspicuous, too sure to get the attention of the owners of the house.

He walked to the front door. Took the key from its packet. Turned the bolt free and opened the door.

There was a powerful emptiness inside that house, as though Grandpa's passing had taken something vital away from it. But once he was inside Tim felt the sensation of being watched fade away, and he knew that no one else had got there before him.

Thank God.

He turned. Flipped on the lights. Closed and locked the door behind him. Best was to be quiet, to listen; even if his heart was certain that he was alone inside the house it wasn't wise to run around in such a hurry. There was enough angst in him to let him pass a burglar in the hall without noticing. Or pass the room he stood in. Tim took three careful steps toward the stair— and bolted when the hurry down inside him got to be too much. Ran. Up to the second floor. Down the hall. And up again.

All the doors on the third floor were closed, untouched. That gave him some small relief; he slowed a little to cross the last half-dozen paces, opened the door at the end of the hall.

The room where Grandpa kept the fragment of the Cross. The room where it had been every time Tim had seen it.

Opened the door, and found the room empty.

Utterly, totally, unquestionably empty.

Except for the sun that streamed in through the uncurtained windows.

No. Dear God, no.

He took in a deep breath. Tried to be calm.

Grandpa was traveling. He had it with him—he must have had it with him. Either that or he hid it away someplace, for safekeeping.

It was true. It had to be true. Why else would whoever it was out there be watching . . . instead of running away with it.

Almost on cue, Tim heard the sound of a window bursting downstairs. Whoever it was was trying to break in, to—

Tim turned again, ran to investigate. He couldn't let anyone inside here; if Grandpa'd hid the Cross inside the house. . . . He had to have. But where?

There wasn't time for that question. Not now. He was going down the first-floor stair, and there was glass all over the floor in the foyer. Tim set himself for a fight, which was maybe a silly thing considering that he was thin and gangly and not especially tall—

And wasn't necessary, either. What he found on the first floor was a broken window, not far from the door. With a hole about the size of a man's fist. The floor, covered with tiny shards of broken glass.

And halfway across the room, a rock. Lying on the floor where it had fallen after it had broken the window.

And the rock was covered with blood.

Tim went out of the house, to find whoever it was who'd thrown the rock. But by then there was no one in sight, and no longer any feeling of presence. After a few moments he gave up, went back inside, and started searching for the fragment of the Cross. He searched for it all afternoon—looked in every crack and crevice he could find or imagine in that big old house—but hard as he looked he didn't find a trace of it.

Toward evening he'd given up. Called information, got the lawyer's home number. Called the lawyer and asked him seven questions. Called a travel agent. And got himself a ticket to Omaha, which was only a hundred miles from the stretch of road where Grandpa'd died.

• • •

Tim tucked the papers back into their envelope, closed it, folded home the metal clasp. Slipped the packet into his travel bag, which lay on the seat beside him. There was a movie showing on the screen at the front of the cabin, but it didn't look like his sort of thing and anyway it was hard to see from this far back. So he turned and stared mindlessly out his dark-dark window. He didn't sleep—he was still too tense to sleep—but he wasn't really and truly awake, not anymore. It was like a trance, almost, brought on by tiredness and the wear that the day's events had put on his heart.

Toward the end of the flight, about when the seat-belt lights went on, he finally did fade down into something that was like sleep. Or might have been.

In that peculiar state, Tim had a dream.

A strange and frightening dream, that might not have been a dream at all. Because it might have been a vision.

In the dream he saw the Christ again, as he had so many years ago on that Saturday morning. But where then He had hung from His Cross, nailed, bleeding, agonized, and dying, now He lay tied to it, prone as the Cross rested on the ground. He was well, still. Unhurt. His face quiet and determined, full of love. Ever so slightly—so slight that Tim was uncertain that he saw it—there was fear in His eyes.

Tim tried to wake himself. Whatever this dream was, whatever it was about, he didn't want to see it. There wasn't room left in his heart for another dream like this. It wasn't any use; when he tried to open his eyes they were only the eyes of his dream, and already open.

A man approached from behind Tim, and passed before Tim could see his face.

He could see the man's hands, though. Even from behind Tim could see what that man held in his hands. In his right hand he held a crude-looking hammer.

In his left he held two nails.

Thick, heavy nails. Like railroad ties, but smaller.

Tim recognized those nails. How could he help but recognize them?

He'd seen them before. Many times—first on a Saturday morning when he was five.

"*No!*" Tim said. Shouted it, in fact. "No—no—*no!* Stop it, damn you!"

But no one heard. He was a witness to the vision, not a part of it.

As he watched, the man knelt. Set his knee on the Lord's hand. And pounded the first of the nails through the Lord's wrist.

Jesus groaned, quietly. But He didn't cry out.

There was a lot of blood. All over the man's hammer. On his hands. Welling and rising to cover the Lord's arm and the wood below it.

The man stood, stepped over Christ's torso. Knelt, and began to drive in the second nail.

And something went wrong.

Instead of sliding cleanly through, as the first nail had, this one slipped sideways—and something burst as it went through to the wood. A vein, maybe. Or an artery. And where the blood from the first wrist had welled, this gushed and spurted in every direction. Like a fountain, a fountain of blood.

But especially it gushed into the face of the man pounding home the nail.

And the man screamed, and he turned away, dropping his hammer. Losing hold of the nail. And Tim saw his face covered with Christ's blood, in his eyes, his beard, everywhere—

And the man screamed and screamed and screamed as he tried to wipe the blood from his eyes, but there was too much of it—

Which was when the plane touched ground with a jolt, waking Tim all covered with warm thick sweat that for the longest moment he *knew* was blood.

God's blood.

The sensation of *presence* came back to Tim in the Omaha airport. Somewhere between the landing gate and the car-rental desk it came to him that he was being followed; a moment later he recognized the feel of it. It was the same sensation that had come over him yesterday afternoon. The watching, outside Grandpa's house.

Oh, it wasn't exactly the same. Not precisely. If the feeling had been a flavor in his mouth, he could have distinguished it from that other—but the two would have shared a tang so distinct as to overshadow all else in their nature.

Tim looked back. Scanned the long, windowed corridor. He *was* being followed, of course. There were at least two dozen people in the hall behind him. Most of them headed the same way he was, since they were fresh off the same plane Tim had just departed. He scanned their faces; looked for some clue of the identity of his shadow. The businessman, there, with his plane-rumpled suit and his tie pulled loose? The young woman in the blue knit dress? The middle-aged couple, there—the ones carrying the child whose crying had woken Tim during the flight? One of the others?

No. None of them. If there was any way to recognize the *presence* in that hall, Tim couldn't find it. It was as elusive as it had been outside Grandpa's house; knowable but unfindable. Watching and unseen.

Then he was at the rent-a-car desk, getting in a line that was already half a dozen people deep. All the while he stood there he looked around that wide, broad room—more furtively than he'd have liked to admit—but still he saw nothing. Saw no one whose eyes held the presence he felt.

If Grandpa were here, Tim thought, it wouldn't be a problem. Grandpa always knew these things. When Grandpa's gut told him something, he never had any trouble digging out the root of it. Tim had the same things in his gut that Grandpa had—or had, at least, when he was alive—but Tim didn't understand them. Not like that. He didn't have the years and years of learning to know. Maybe the day would come when he did, but Tim didn't see it anywhere on his horizon.

Grandpa *had* died too soon, damn it. Tim was

supposed to be ready for this. And he wasn't anywhere near ready.

The whole situation scared Tim.

And just a moment after he admitted that fear, he began to grow angry.

Grandpa wouldn't approve of that anger, Tim thought. It wasn't like Grandpa hadn't ever got mad. But he was real careful about it. He might rail about something for half a day, but Tim never saw him act out of anger. He'd act *on* the things he was mad about, sure. But not until he'd got himself calmed down and sensible about matters.

Tim wished that he could say the same about himself. More than once as he was growing up he'd got himself into fistfights over things people said. Or did. A couple of times because they'd just looked at him kind of nasty.

Whoever it was was closer, now. Tim felt the presence almost as though it were someone standing behind him, looking over his shoulder.

And much as he tried to calm himself, much as Tim tried to be the kind of man his Grandpa had raised him to be, all he could think was how someone had murdered his Grandpa. And much as he tried to deny it, Tim wanted his pound of flesh. He wanted to find the murderers. And he wanted to kill them.

I need some sleep. I need to calm down. To forget— for a while, at least.

The problem wasn't being mad. Not by itself. The problem was being mad and rushing off half-cocked. Acting out of spite. He needed to get himself a hotel room, get himself some sleep. Wash the bloodshot from his eyes before he went out to see after what remained of Grandpa. *That* was the essence of what Grandpa always said about anger: a body had to cool himself down before he saw to important business, else he'd end up doing things he regretted.

The trouble was, Tim didn't ever see himself getting easy about it. These people *murdered* Grandpa, damn it—!

Breath, on his neck. Before he realized what he'd done, Tim had whirled around, thrown a punch—

—into dead air. No one stood behind him.

It was nine thirty before Tim got into the hotel room; filling out paperwork for the car, finding the hotel, checking in had taken more than an hour and a half. By the time he sloughed off his jacket and loosened his tie he was a nervous, overtired wreck.

He let himself fall onto the bed. He didn't bother with the blankets.

The sensation of being watched had faded away after he'd made a fool of himself at the car-rental counter. But the anxiety had stayed with him.

As it was with him now, pressing and pulling at his gut. He rolled onto his side, trying to find a more comfortable position, but it didn't give him any ease.

I'm too tired, he thought. *That's all it is.*

The thing to do was to lie still. Relax as much as he could. If he didn't worry about whether or not he slept, didn't think about comfort or discomfort, he'd drift off eventually.

That's what he told himself, anyway. Even then he didn't believe it.

As he shouldn't have: Tim rested fitful, sleepless, for most of seven hours. And finally it was five in the afternoon, and he knew that there wasn't any sense trying any longer. And he got up, showered, dressed.

By the time Tim checked out of the hotel, he was even more ill at ease than he had been in the airport lobby.

Tim got to Running Board at eight thirty in the evening. It was a small town, even as Nebraska farm towns go. A hundred forty miles from Omaha—all but due west along SR 39, where it meets the Platte River in Polk County.

The watching in the air came back only an instant

after Tim passed the sign that read WELCOME TO RUNNING BOARD—POPULATION 718 AND GROWING EVERY DAY!

He slowed the car, pulled over onto the shoulder of the road. Reached into the glove box and checked the directions that he'd taken from the local sheriff yesterday afternoon. Which said that the sheriff's station for this part of the county was up ahead on the right, just before the river.

Watching.

Tim looked around, trying to find the eyes he knew had focused on him. But there was no one anywhere in sight. No more than there'd been at the airport who looked as though he was watching.

The only motion anywhere around him was deep in the wheat—there, flitting in and out of sight. A dog? A wolf? No, it was too slight, too small. Wolves were larger creatures.

Coyote. That's what it is, a coyote. It could be, he thought. He'd never seen a coyote in the flesh. If there were any of them in the parts of Florida where Tim grew up, they hid too well to see. But the beast was too feral, too hungry looking to be anyone's pet. And too skittish to be a wolf.

Watching. Someone was watching, and it wasn't any damned coyote.

Or was there anyone out there?

Am I going out of my mind? Or maybe he wasn't going crazy so much as getting addled from stress and lack of sleep. He thought about killing the engine, trying to nap here in the car before he drove the last quarter mile into town. Decided it was a bad idea. Put the transmission into gear, checked the highway for traffic—there wasn't any—and headed off.

Five minutes later he was opening the door of the sheriff's office. Or deputy's office, more accurately. This place was a substation. The Sheriff himself was over in the county seat, miles away. It had taken Tim three phone calls and most of half an hour yesterday afternoon to get it straight.

Opening the door set off a bell that seemed to startle

the deputy behind the counter; he looked up at Tim from his paperwork more than a little unsettled.

And wary. And ever-so-slightly hostile.

"Can I help you?" His tone was unfriendly, too.

"I'm Tim Fischer," he said. "I spoke to you yesterday. . . ? Or someone here. About my grandfather."

Tim looked close to read the name on the white-on-black tag just above the deputy's badge. JOEL KIMBALL, it said.

The hostility in the man's eyes was clearer, now. Just shy of blatant.

"Yes. That was me."

He reached under the counter, lifted out a wide, thick key ring. "You'll have to . . . identify the body. You're aware of that, aren't you?"

Tim closed his eyes for a moment. Tried to clear his head. He wasn't ready for the sight of his Grandpa's corpse. Didn't think he'd ever be ready.

"Yes. Is it here, did you say, or—?"

"No. The coroner's office. Over toward the county seat. I'll take you there."

It had confused Tim, yesterday. Still confused him now. Why on earth had the man sent him out to this tiny office in the middle of nowhere? The phone number that the lawyer had given him was for the main office of the county sheriff. He called that number, and as soon as they figured out what exactly it was he was asking after, they'd started shunting him from pillar to post. And finally, an hour after he'd made the first call, this man had called him back, and given him directions that had sounded suspect.

"I can follow you," Tim said. "I won't mind the drive."

The man shook his head. "No. Policy. We have . . . problems sometimes. People often aren't up to driving after an identification."

"And if I insist?"

"We'll wait here," he told Tim, "until you change your mind. One death's enough, here and now."

It was suspicious. Too suspicious. It had *been* suspicious, right from the first moment he'd called the sheriff's department. There was a big part of him that regretted getting on that plane. Regretted before he'd made the reservation. And wanted now to turn tail and leave this place without ever looking back.

Not that he could. He had to see to Grandpa's remains. Had to make arrangements. Had to claim his effects.

The only reassurance in the whole business was the fact that this place really did seem to be a sheriff's office. It wasn't much reassurance.

"Are we going, or not? Don't just stand there."

The drive was only twenty minutes in the twilight over the flat, dry land. There was something about that land that seemed unreal and frightening to Tim. There were no more hills in Florida—where he'd grown up— than there were here. But in Florida the things that covered the land, the pines and the palmettos and the swamps, the things that covered the land were full of texture and difference. Everything here was flat, rolling grass. What trees there were provided a powerful relief.

"Strange accident your grandad died in," the deputy said. "Real strange."

Tim let that hang in the air for a long moment. It was a peculiar remark. Contradictory. Yesterday, when he'd called here, a woman in the sheriff's office had given him a brief description of the wreck. The details hadn't sounded strange at all. Grandpa's car, she said, had wandered off the road in the middle of the night, and struck a telephone pole at high speed. Her best guess was that he'd fallen asleep at the wheel. It happened often enough.

Nothing strange about it. Nothing that could support Tim's absolute certainty that Grandpa's death was a murder. Not that it had shaken Tim's conviction. There were a lot of people in the world who were likely to make claims about their future or the future of events, but Grandpa wasn't like that. Hadn't been like that. If he said he knew how he'd die, if he wrote Tim a letter about it, telling him in detail, then by damn he had cause to know.

Grandpa was the Steward of the Cross. All he had to do to know a thing like that was look at it.

Had been the Steward of the Cross.

And if something had derailed the train that carried Grandpa from his past toward his future, that something wasn't any accident. It had to be a something with a powerful lot of manna behind it. Something with *purpose*.

"Strange?" Tim asked. "How's that?"

The deputy shrugged. "Didn't strike me as the kind of man likely to have that accident."

Something clicked.

"You knew him?"

No answer.

They slowed, pulled into a badly paved drive beside a weathered plastic sign. POLK COUNTY CORONER'S OFFICE At the far end of the drive was a small, one-storey concrete building.

No other cars in the parking lot. If there was anyone else inside that place, they'd come by foot. Or been left here, to wait for them.

They parked. The deputy took the keys from the ignition, hesitated a moment. "Are you ready for this?"

Tim braced himself. Nodded. And followed the man into the building. Through a short, dark hall that ended at a steel door that could just as easily have been the door to a meat locker.

"You're certain you're prepared for this?"

Tim nodded before he could actually think about the question.

And the deputy unlocked the cold steel door covered with dew sweat. Pulled it open.

Inside were three tables shaped like stretchers. Shaped like the tables in a doctor's office, the tables that you lie on during an examination.

One of the tables was occupied.

By a misshapen body, covered with a sheet.

The deputy crossed the cold room to the unvacant table. Tim followed numb and mindless.

Pulled aside the sheet to show Grandpa's face. And his neck that lay at a *wrong* angle. And just a hint below that, the topmost edge of the impression that the steering wheel had gouged when it crushed his chest.

And the numbness turned to rage.

And for that long moment there in the tiny morgue, standing above his Grandpa's already-rancid corpse—for that long moment Tim wanted with all his heart to see the murderer burning, suffering in Hell.

Tim was the one who found the old tom.

It was a week before Easter-time, and Mom and Dad and Tim had all gone over to Grandpa's for the day. All the grown-ups were in the parlor talking grown-up talk. Presidents and countries and things like that.

This was the year right after the Christmas that Tim had first seen the Cross.

After lunch the four of them—Mom, Dad, Tim, Grandpa—had all gone to the parlor. That was when Dad asked Grandpa about who he was going to vote for in the primary election next month. And Grandpa told him, and Mom scowled and said what she thought about that man, and inside of a minute they were so wrapped up in talking politics that none of them even noticed when Tim got up and headed for Grandpa's library.

Tim really loved that old room. It was full of the air of books and papers, and souvenirs and trophies from a thousand different times and places. But mostly why he went there that afternoon was to find the old tomcat. The old tom—his name was Ben Franklin—always slept in the library, right dead center on top of Grandpa's desk. And usually when you didn't see Ben Franklin prowling around the house, it meant that he was asleep on the desk in the library.

Only this time when Tim got to the library Ben Franklin was nowhere in sight. Not all *that* strange—like as not it meant that he was out in the back yard hunting squirrel. So Tim sat down in the chair behind the big oak desk. And scanned the room, looking for something to explore. It only took him a moment to spot the atlas.

The atlas was this huge old leather-bound book that Grandpa kept on one of his highest shelves. It wasn't much like the atlas in the public library—except for the size. The one at the public library was full of printed maps that made the world look just like a brand-new globe. But this atlas here—it was something special. Old-old, with strange heavy paper like all of Grandpa's oldest books. And where the maps in the public library atlas were printed, the maps in Grandpa's oldest atlas had been drawn by hand. Tim had seen them, once, looking over Grandpa's shoulder while he checked the big old book so he could write it in a letter to somebody on the other side of the world. Tim had asked Grandpa then why the book looked so different from all the maps he'd ever seen. But Grandpa only said, "Time," as he closed the book and put it back up on his highest shelf, and that wasn't any answer. Right then he'd wanted to ask Grandpa to get it down for him so Tim could give it a good look over. But Grandpa had been distracted, caught up in something or other because of that letter. And even then Tim had known about Grandpa when he was distracted. Just wasn't any sense trying to talk to him; if he wasn't going to say more than two words to you at a time, then that was all he was going to say. So Tim had promised himself that he'd climb up there and get it down to read later. And then he'd gone and forgotten about it for all these months.

But now he remembered. And he was going to go up there and get that book.

Getting up to the highest shelf wasn't as tough as it could have been, since Grandpa kept a ladder in the library. A special ladder made of polished dark wood that matched the shelves. Tim pushed the ladder to the right part of the room, started to climb. . . .

He was halfway up when he noticed the scratch marks.

Marks from cat claws.

Which meant marks from the old tom, Ben Franklin.

Now that was strange for a couple of reasons, but most of all it was strange because Ben Franklin was a considerate cat, where furniture was concerned. He didn't use the couches to sharpen his claws. He didn't spray, unless he was outdoors. And in all his life Tim had

never seen the cat leave a single scratch on anything he'd
climbed.

Something's wrong. I hope that cat is okay.

What he ought to do, Tim thought, was go get
Grandpa and show him the scratch marks. If the cat was
acting strange, then Grandpa ought to know about it.
Thought about that for a minute. Thought about how
Mom and Dad and Grandpa had fallen into that talk
about politics-stuff so fast it made his head spin. Thought
about how they got so caught up in it that none of them
even noticed when he left the parlor. And decided that
whatever was wrong with the cat would keep until they
had a chance to wear out the topic.

The last rung of the ladder, and there was the
leather-bound atlas. And now that he was near Tim could
see that cat up on top of it. Still as stone, lying on top of
the books. Sleeping, to judge by the look of him.

"Come on, kitty," Tim said. "Time to wake up. I've
got to get that book."

Ben Franklin didn't move a muscle. Well, Tim
thought, if he was going to be stubborn, then Tim could
be stubborn, too. Just reach up and take that book out
from under him. He'd move then, all right.

Only when Tim reached up with both hands—
balancing with his knees on the ladder, since he needed
both arms to pick up a book that big—when Tim took the
atlas from the shelf, something went very wrong. Instead
of getting up and moving, the way any sensible cat does
when it's disturbed, when Tim grabbed the book Ben
Franklin came tumbling down from on top of it—falling
like a sack of rocks, right into Tim's face. And Tim was
still balanced by his knees on the top rung of the ladder,
and the weight of the cat and the force of the fall were
just enough between them—

—to sway him back. And his knees lost contact with
the rung, and he tried to press up with his feet or throw
himself forward but he already had the atlas up in the air
and its mass and momentum turned the push from his
legs out toward the air behind him.

After that came the falling panic mixed with vertigo
that went on for a moment that lasted hours in the wind

between the high shelf and the floor. Tim tried to cry out for help or in fear, but his voice stuck in his throat; and anyway there wasn't time for screaming no matter how long the moment lasted in his heart. Then he landed on his back and his butt a pounding thud that forced every iota of breath from him in a loud low grunt, and it didn't matter if there was time or if his voice was stuck; there was nothing in him left to scream.

In all that moment of the fall and landing there was only one consolation, and that was the way that the atlas came down three feet from him where it couldn't do any harm. It was a luckier happenstance than he had any right to expect. If the book so big so heavy had landed on top of him it would have broken bones, no matter that his bones were soft and elastic the way the skeleton is in a boy who's not quite yet six. As it was the fall bruised and bent but did not break him.

He was less lucky with the cat. The cat landed just a moment after Tim did, and it landed soft fur and too-hard flesh in the crook between his shoulder and his neck, and right away Tim could smell and feel exactly what was wrong.

Knew that the cat was dead.

Dead for a long while.

Tim had never seen a death before, nor even the remains of one. But no one had to teach him the smell of a body dead for days. He knew that smell instinctively, just as he knew with his marrow the stiff caress of rigor mortis against the skin of his neck.

Not that knowing was accepting. Tim put his hands on the cat, lifted him gently as a mother lifts an infant.

"Ben Franklin. . . ? Are you okay?"

There was still pain in Tim's back and in his rear. But it was as far away as the moon; all of Tim there was to give was caught in concern for the cat.

"Be okay, Ben Franklin," he said. "Be okay, huh?"

Sat up. Set the cat down gentle on the carpet not far from the great book. It was cool and stiff and heavy in his hands, just as though it were an old roast. Once it was on the floor it looked quiet and serene, and Tim almost began to believe—really believe—that the cat was only sleeping.

He sat up, still not feeling the pain in his back. Stared at the cat, trying to come to terms with what he knew and didn't want to know. Reached out, stretched forward, petted the soft, cool fur. He said "Kitty-kitty-kitty," because he thought that maybe if he tried to call the cat back from the dead, just maybe it'd come. But it didn't wake from that last sleep; didn't even stir.

"Tim?" Grandpa's voice, right out of nowhere, scaring Tim, giving him a serious start. Grandpa always seemed to turn up out of nowhere at moments like this.

"Hi Grandpa," he said. But Tim didn't look up to see him; he was too busy watching the cat, trying to call it back with his love from wherever it had gone.

"Darn it, Tim," Grandpa said, "I should have been paying more attention. I had a feeling something like this was up today." He sighed.

Out in the parlor, Mom and Dad were still arguing. Louder, now—loud enough that if Tim had wanted to pay attention he could have listened in from here.

"And then I went and got myself caught in that same silly debate. Politics. . . ! What was I thinking of?"

Tim· wasn't paying a whole lot of attention to Grandpa, either. Or he didn't pay any attention until Grandpa knelt down beside the cat and set his big hand on Ben Franklin's small, soft head.

"You've got to let go of him, Tim." Grandpa frowned. "Each of us has his time."

Something clenched down in Tim's gut when Grandpa said that. Part of that something was denial; part of it was sad. But most of all it was anger—pure clean fury built of outrage and violation.

And what he was angry at wasn't the cat who'd died, and it wasn't the God who'd allowed that death.

What Tim was angry at was Grandpa.

Tim was almost six years old, and in all his life he'd never once been mad at Grandpa. Not even once. If it had been in his heart to consider such things, the whole idea would have seemed incredible to Tim.

Not that there was room in his heart for consideration. Tim was consumed with the cat and the rage and a fire in his heart that almost began to feel like he hated Grandpa. And as he raged, the inspiration came to him.

The Cross.

The image of Christ suffering on His Cross came back to Tim, fresh and clear as though he'd seen it only a moment before, instead of four months in the past. The image was beautiful, and it was full of God's love for Tim and Grandpa and every other thing that ever had or ever would live on the face of the earth—

And remembering, Tim was absolutely certain that Christ loved Ben Franklin the cat enough to give him back his life. And before Grandpa could so much as blink, Tim had gathered up the cat and headed out the library door at a dead run. Through the downstairs hall and the foyer; halfway up the first flight of stairs before he heard Grandpa running behind him, calling after him.

Mom and Dad were still in the parlor, shouting at each other. Oblivious to anything outside that room.

"*No*, Tim!" Grandpa shouted. Tim could hear him starting up the stairs, but it didn't matter; Tim was already at the end of the second-floor hall, turning, starting to climb again—"Stop *now*, darn you."

Tim didn't stop. He *ran*. Up the stairs and through the hall toward the door that Grandpa always kept locked, but he didn't let that stop him, he ran full tilt into the thing and the catch popped free and the door opened—

—to show an empty room. Utterly, totally empty. The spot in the center of the floor, the spot where the fragment of the Cross always rested—that spot was bare.

Grandpa was cresting the second stairway.

Tim's stomach was a twisting mass of need and desperation, and fear, too; he whirled around looking back at Grandpa, coming toward him in the hall, looked everywhere desperately trying to find the—

There. Just where it always was. Lying in a pool of sun that flooded through the curtainless south window. In the center of the floor. Battered and worn and faded and brilliant all at once.

The Cross.

Seeing it, Tim knew, was a gift from God.

And because he could see it, he knew that it wasn't important anymore whether Grandpa caught up with him or not. He stepped forward, into the center of the room—

And everything changed again. The sunlit room went dark as night lit with torches far away, and Christ hung before him bleeding, suffering on the Cross, and as Tim watched mouth agape with fear and joy and love, He pulled Himself up, sucked air into His lungs, and blood oozed from His wrists.

"Jesus?"

He didn't answer, but Tim could see from His eyes that He'd heard.

"Jesus, my friend, my cat . . ." He held out the stiff, heavy feline corpse. "Can you help my cat, Jesus? He . . . he died, I guess. And I love him, and I miss him."

He was listening. But He wasn't telling Tim anything one way or the other.

Grandpa was in the room, now. But he wasn't doing anything to interfere.

And Tim waited, hoping . . .

"Jesus?"

It was like He was waiting for Tim to realize something that he already knew. What Grandpa had already told him? *No.* Even if he was Grandpa, he was just acting about that cat like he didn't care.

Then what. . . ?

Look into the cat. What do you see?

Tim wasn't sure if the words came from Jesus or from himself. They didn't *sound* like words that had come from God. Still, he opened his eyes wide as he could, opened them from all the way down into his heart.

And with his heart open to see, he looked.

And he saw that there wasn't any *cat* inside the cat that all of what had made Ben Franklin himself was gone.

Where has he gone?

Tim looked up into the Lord's eyes, trying to find the question there. But there was no sign of it.

And neither was it absent of him.

Turned, looked back at Grandpa. But it wasn't Grandpa's question, either; it was clear, looking into Grandpa's eyes, that he was only here to watch. Maybe, Tim thought, he'd try to catch Tim if he sank too deep into the moment and began to drown. And maybe not.

So Tim opened his heart again, wider, and he tried to see into the cat's past. Tried to see the moment of his death. And he *did* see, too; saw a moment wrapped in deep sleep, and something in the cat's breast like a visceral sigh, only more mysterious and final. And the *cat* inside Ben Franklin faded like a candle when the fire reaches the nub but not like that because instead of going out the light was going . . . elsewhere. To a place Tim couldn't see, exactly, but he could see the trail that took the cat from here to there like it was a thin, strong cord, and he knew that if he grabbed hold of that cord with his heart—knew that here in this room, with Jesus and miracle all around him, if he grabbed the cord with his heart he could pull the cat back from that place to this.

And that was what he'd come here for, wasn't it?

It was. Tim had come here to save the cat from the fate that waited for him. But. . . .

He bit his lip. Was it the cat that he wanted to save—or was it just that he didn't want to lose the cat for himself?

He didn't know.

Tim looked up into the Lord's eyes again.

"It isn't right, is it?" Tim asked. "This is just me being selfish."

Jesus didn't answer, no more than He'd answered any other question. But even so, Tim knew what was right. He stared up into those eyes so full of love, and he nodded and he turned back to Grandpa. As he did, the strangeness faded all around him, and the room was once again bright and sunny and bare.

"We have to bury him, don't we, Grandpa?"

"Yes, Tim. We do."

Tim sniffed. Felt as though something cold washed over him. Grandpa turned, opened the door that Tim hadn't noticed when it closed. And they left.

Downstairs, Mom and Dad were still arguing about congressmen.

And Tim and Grandpa went out to the back yard and buried Ben Franklin near the roots of a great old grapefruit tree whose highest branches extended nearly as far into the air as the roof of the house.

It should have been a final thing, a task that set old ghosts to rest. But all while they dug Tim was uncertain he did right by letting go of the cat's life. And that night when he slept he dreamt bad dreams that the cat was suffering in some hell reserved for simple souls. Long as he lived, Tim was never sure that what he did that day was right.

In the morning, when he woke, the bruises he'd got in the fall came home to roost. Mom had to take him to the doctor, but all he prescribed was liniment.

"Are you there? Did that old man turn you into a vegetable or something?"

Tim blinked; tried to clear away the memory. This wasn't the time or the place to be fading off into a daze.

"Huh? Give me a second."

He rubbed his eyes with the backs of his hands, opened them again—

What was he saying? A vegetable? What did this man know about Tim, or Grandpa, or. . . . And then he looked at the deputy, and something clicked. The airport. The presence outside Grandpa's house. On the road just outside Running Board.

Everywhere in the morgue was that same air of presence—or a presence that was nearly the same. Tim looked hard into the man, trying to find something in his heart or in his past. But the rage and the grief and the fear that filled his heart left his sight dim and uncertain; there wasn't any way to *know*. . . .

But it was obvious, once it occurred to him to ask

the question. Who else could it be? Why else all this curious nonsense?

"It's you, isn't it? You're the one who killed him."

The deputy laughed. "It took you long enough to ask. The old man didn't raise a bright one, did he?"

The rage was growing again. Growing all out of bounds. If Grandpa were talking to him, right now, right here—he'd tell Tim to turn the other cheek. For now, at least. Turn and walk away and act later, when he had better sense about him.

But Grandpa wasn't here. And Tim had already grown too angry for good sense.

"Not just stupid, but deaf and dumb, too, huh? Well, what is it if I killed him? Can you prove it? Do you think for a moment that the law here would come after me? It doesn't matter how he died, or who's responsible. So long as he's dead. Good riddance to him."

And Tim snapped.

It wasn't a smart thing to do; he was thin and not quite wiry where the deputy was heavyset and tall. But just then he wasn't running smart any more than he was sensible; he dove for the deputy's throat, caught the man off guard. In a moment they were on the floor, and Tim had him pinned to ground, knees digging into the man's biceps. And the man struggled to get Tim's hands away from his neck, and Tim pulled his hands away, and punched him backhand. Which felt so good that he pulled the other away, too, and he hit the man again and again and again—

And then he realized what he was doing, and for just half a moment Tim was ashamed of himself. But that half a moment, that fragment of a pause, it was enough.

"Do you really think," the man asked him, spraying blood and spittle, "do you really think you have the nerve to be a murderer?"

And the passion and the rage and the moment went cold as the ash that's left in a fire two days after it's burned.

And Tim knew that he didn't have the heart to kill the man—no matter what he'd done.

He sat up, pulled away. "You're right," he said. "I

don't have that kind of nerve." And he got to his feet, and he turned and began to walk away from the room and the deputy and his grandfather's corpse.

It was just about the stupidest thing he did that day, and he'd done a number of stupid things. Tim hadn't gone five steps before the deputy was off the floor, coming at him so quickly that he barely had a chance to realize what was happening before the man grabbed him by his belt and his collar, and threw him like he were an empty sack. Tim hit the far wall hard, and his head hardest of all, and after that it didn't matter whether or not he realized what was happening to him, because the whole world went black, and it was long hours before he saw the light of day again.

Part of the reason that Tim lay so long unconscious was the blow; the other part was exhaustion. He'd hardly slept to speak of since Grandpa's lawyer had called early Sunday morning, and by the time the deputy bludgeoned him it was late Monday night.

That exhaustion mixed with the cold in the morgue and the scent of corrupted human flesh, and the three together with the weight on Tim's heart colored Tim's dreams black and blood-red and terrifying.

He dreamed awhile of the daughter he'd only known well enough to love before she'd died, and the dream hurt him worse than anything Deputy Joel Kimball could ever have done to him. Just the dream, just the act of remembering—in its way that tiny bit hurt worse than the entire loss of Grandpa.

Then his dreams filled with images of the man he'd dreamed on the plane from Florida. The man who'd driven the fat-thick nails through Christ's wrists into the Cross.

Strange, unsettling, unpleasant; and in its nightmarish way a relief, because to see that fearful man banished all thought of his lost daughter.

So he dreamed of the Bleeding Man, and he was afraid, and glad, too.

That was how Tim thought of him: as the Bleeding

Man. And in every dream-glimpse Tim saw of him, he *was* bleeding. From his hands that had spilled the Saviour's blood. From his eyes where the geyser of that blood had struck him. And most of all that blood was in the Bleeding Man's spirit, and what it made his soul was wondrously strange and frightening. The touch of God was on him—there was no mistaking that. But that touch was tainted somehow by the violence of the act, and what should have been entirely glorious and mild . . . there was a cruelness about it. A twistedness of virtue bent back upon itself until its nature altered.

The air that came from the Bleeding Man was everywhere in those dreams. As though he stood so tall through two thousand years of time and half a world of distance that he could bend down to watch Tim sleeping from a near reach. Whenever he felt the Bleeding Man near him, Tim would run. But a dream run covers no real distance, and hard and fast as Tim ran the Bleeding Man was always close nearby. Once, he turned to confront the man. But that was useless, too; the moment that he turned to focus on it the presence dissipated like the ghost that it was.

That Tim thought it was, at least.

Toward the end of his nightmare, Tim realized why the air from the Bleeding Man was already familiar to him when the dream began.

When he recognized it.

From the airport.

From the field.

From the deputy.

And from long before that, too—from someplace so deep in his past that he couldn't know it anymore.

The sensation of *presence*.

Not an identical presence, no—but the air that came from the Bleeding Man was a thing so similar that it surprised Tim that he hadn't known it sooner.

And then it didn't matter whether he was afraid anymore; anger and the need to know were more important. In the dream he stopped running, and he held his ground. Waited where he was to confront his pursuer.

But the Bleeding Man came no closer than he already was. He stood somewhere just beyond Tim's sight in the fog that was the dream, watching with eyes that no mere fog could blind.

Eyes washed in the blood of the Lord.

Stood watching, felt and known but unseen.

After a long moment Tim grew impatient, and he started toward the dim possibility of a shadow he could make out through the mist. Not that it made any difference; before Tim reached him, the Bleeding Man had disappeared as thoroughly as though he'd never been there.

But before he did, the mist parted for an instant, and Tim caught a glimpse of his face.

A face wrinkled as though it were old as time.

And webbed with runnels of the blood that leaked steadily from his eyes.

It wasn't long after that before the cold and the smell and the hardness of the floor began to sift more literally into Tim's sleep. And once they did, it only took him a few more moments to realize that he was sleeping in a place where no one in his right mind ought to let himself lie. Still, it wasn't an easy thing to wake from; he was exhausted, and his head ached fierce from the impact with the wall, and worst of all was the cold that had wound itself down into his marrow. Cold was worst because it took away the will to move, made his muscles feel stiff as though they were dead as Grandpa's corpse on the table beside him. Tim had spent nearly all his life in Florida, and that cold in his bones was as alien to him as the far side of the moon—it frightened him, panicked him; and that was good because tired was so bad he might never have woken without fear to press him.

But he did wake, mostly by forcing his eyes open, and after that it was just a matter of grabbing hold of the table that held Grandpa's corpse, pulling himself to his feet. Standing, staring too long a moment at Grandpa— and then it was easier to force himself legs one after the other to stumble him across the room. Because if he didn't get out of there, out and away from the crushed hulk that used to be Grandpa—if he didn't get away he was going to scream. Yanking open the cold-cold iron handle of the locker door. Pushing himself out into the coroner's office, warm as the rest of the Nebraska summer, and then at least the physical part of the problem—the murder-deep cold ache in his bones—wasn't getting any worse.

Not that it was getting better. The cold was all the way down inside him, and there were hours left before the pain would ebb.

Tim stood braced against a counter, hurting for most of twenty minutes before it occurred to him to wonder how he was going to get away from this place. He wasn't in any condition to put out his thumb and hitchhike, much less walk a distance it'd taken most of half an hour to drive on fast country roads. Besides which he had damn little memory of the route they'd taken here from Running Board. It was possible he could find his way back by instinct and good sense—but it was just as likely that he'd end up thirty miles farther from the middle of nowhere than he already was.

He blinked; tried to focus. Were there windows in this room? There'd been a light in the cold locker, but there'd been nothing but dark since the locker's steel door had swung shut behind him. Over there, on his right—that could be the outline of a window, couldn't it? Yes, it *was* a window. The darkness there was fainter there than it was elsewhere in the room. Looked closer, and thought he saw stars—though it was hard to be sure of them with the throbbing in his head. All right, then: it was night, and he was stranded in a Coroner's office in the middle of nowhere. And the only familiar thing for two thousand miles in any direction was the chill corpse of his grandfather in the morgue behind him.

What he ought to do, he thought, was go into the morgue, take the opportunity to look over the remains while he could do it without suspicious people taking notes as to what he did and didn't observe. He bit his lip, trying not to think about the cold in his bones, the cold in that morgue. Knew in the time that it took to draw a breath that he didn't have the heart for the cold or for the sight.

I need to get out of here. It was more an admission of defeat than it was a realization. *I can't stand here forever.* It wouldn't be long, he knew, before he collapsed again. Sleeping in the cold had taken too much out of him. And if he was going to black out, he didn't want it to happen here; people would show up in the morning, and if they did there'd be questions he wouldn't want to cope with. He had to get out into the fields someplace where the wheat was tall enough to hide him. . . .

It took most of five minutes to get himself out the door. Most of that because it was too dark to see the door; some because his muscles had stiffened again in the time he'd stood braced against the counter. And there was at least that much trouble again getting the door open, once he'd found it—the damned thing was secured by three bolts, along with the lock in the door knob; finding and disengaging all three of them would have been trouble even in a well-lit room. Would have been trouble even if his head had been clear, instead of throbbing and full of muddled, half-formed thoughts.

But after a while he did get out, into the Nebraska summer night whose coolness felt near as cold as the morgue. It would have been trouble if someone hadn't parked Tim's rental car just outside the coroner's door.

Had they taken the keys from him? He patted his pockets as he moved toward the car. Empty, except for his change, his wallet, his comb. Opened the driver-side door, and there was light from the ceiling dome that hurt his eyes accustomed to the dark. And there were the keys in the ignition. He climbed into the seat, pulled closed the door to kill the light.

I should go, Tim thought. Back to Omaha, get a hotel room. Rest. Clean up. There was still business to take care of; he had to have the body shipped back home. Which meant papers to sign and checks to write.

But before he got even as far as turning the ignition, he'd blacked out again.

• • •

All through the night as he slumped blacked out in the car Tim heard the sound of howling, howling yipping at the moonless feral sky. It haunted his dreams. Drew a deep slick sweat out of his pores. And followed him into the dawn.

He woke half an hour after the sun came up, and the car was hot with trapped light that made him sweat even harder. In spite of the heat and the sweat, Tim was chilled and aching; soon, he thought, he'd be feverish. He was coming down with something vile. Which meant that if he had any sense he'd see a doctor and get himself some antibiotics before things got worse than they already were.

He put his hand on the ignition switch, went to start the car. Hesitated. Looked back at the still-open door to the coroner's office. *The body*. He really needed to go back and look it over carefully; something in his gut was dead certain that if he didn't do it now, by the time he had another moment to examine it by himself, it'd be too late. Something strange was going on, and there was no way he could trust these people.

He took the keys from the ignition. Got out of the car, went back into the office, back into the cold locker. Lifted the sheet that covered Grandpa, and even though it hurt him to see, he looked the body over careful as he could. Even thought to look for the pocket Bible that Grandpa always carried with him. Grandpa sometimes made notes to himself in the margins of its pages, and if Tim could find it he might find anything Grandpa'd known about the people who had killed him.

But the Bible wasn't in the breast pocket where Grandpa almost always kept it. Nor were there any readable clues in the condition of the corpse—only rancid flesh and the deep crater that the car's steering wheel had left in Grandpa's chest when it crushed the life from him. However they'd killed him—and Tim was certain that this was murder and no accident—however they'd killed him, there was no proof of the act in Grandpa's remains.

• • •

It was ten o'clock by the time Tim got done at the Omaha walk-in clinic and got himself checked into the hotel. Another twenty minutes to get to the room, undress, take the capsules that the doctor had given him, get into bed. But only another moment after that before he was asleep, sleeping the mercifully dreamless sleep of the damned.

And when he woke, not quite five hours later, he was well and rested, even if his muscles and bones still ached too much to call him fine. Still, less than fine was fine enough, or had to be. There was barely time left in the day for the business he had still to do, and Tim was certain that he didn't want to spend another day in this place.

Not if he could avoid it.

By three thirty he was showered, dressed, and on the road back out to Running Board.

Where a different deputy waited for him at the substation desk. This man was nowhere near so hostile as Joel Kimball had been, nor as tense. He was downright friendly, in fact, when he asked Tim his business.

"I'm Tim Fischer," he told the man. "I'm here to see after my grandfather's effects."

Which got him a raised eyebrow, and a curious look. "Can you wait here for a moment, Mr. Fischer?"

And before Tim could answer the deputy went into the substation's back room, and closed the door behind him. Where Tim heard him talking on the telephone. His voice only barely carried through the door; Tim could hear him, but not well enough to understand what he said. Less than a minute later he came back.

"Mr. Fischer, the sheriff wants to speak to you. Would you mind following me back to Osceola?"

Osceola was the Polk County seat. Where the main sheriff's office was. What was going on? First the strange deputy, the one who'd so obviously had something to do with Grandpa's murder—now this. . . .

"Of course. You mind my asking if there's some kind of a problem?"

"Best I let him discuss this with you himself. If you know what I mean."

Tim didn't know, of course. But he followed anyway—ill at ease, not quite afraid.

The sheriff's office was a big, imposing, modern-looking building cut into a wheat field at the north edge of Osceola. The deputy led Tim to a back lot full of green-and-white patrol cars, motioned Tim into a parking spot a hundred feet from the back door. Parked the patrol car a few spaces away. He got out without bothering to lock the doors. Which seemed a little odd to Tim, until it occurred to him that the whole idea of stealing a patrol car from outside a sheriff's office was a little unlikely.

Still, Tim locked the rental car and closed its windows—not so much because he was afraid of theft as out of long habit. When he got done he saw the deputy waiting for him on the sidewalk. He closed his door behind him, tried the handle to make certain that the lock was still engaged. Which it was.

"All set," he said. "Where do we go from here?"

"This way." Which was in through the back door, past a reception to an elevator, and to the third floor—the building's highest. Down a long hall until they reached an enormous corner office.

"Over there." The deputy nodded toward a plush chair on the near side of the desk. "Sheriff ought to be with you before too long."

And left, without saying another word. Without even waiting for Tim to take his chair. And Tim didn't sit—not for a while, anyway. Instead he took a long moment to look around the room. A spacious, comfortable office with waist-to-ceiling windows that filled up the south and west walls. North and east were paneled with oak. There were photos on those walls, here and there. A little-league football team. A man, a woman, three children standing in front of them—the sheriff's family? Most likely. A posed picture of a couple dozen men and women at a barbecue, and a parking lot full of cruisers in the background. There was a bookcase built into the north wall, and one shelf held three little-league trophies.

"Mr. Fischer?"

An imposing, authoritative voice. But not an unfriendly one.

Tim turned away from the bookcase, smiled.

"That's me."

"Sit down—please. This may take a while." He sounded distracted, unhappy. "Strange business, here. None of it pleasant."

The chair was even more comfortable than it looked. "How's that? What's strange and unpleasant?"

The sheriff looked up annoyed from the papers on his desk. "There's no need to be coy, Mr. Fischer. We've got a pretty fair idea of what's happened the last few days, even if we can't make sense of it. We may not be very well informed, but we aren't ignorant out here in Nebraska."

Tim frowned.

"What can I tell you?"

The sheriff nodded. "That," he said, "is a good question." Looked down at his desk, shuffled through papers. "You should know, first off, that you're not a suspect of any crime. Nearly as we can tell, there hasn't *been* any crime. But something peculiar has happened in this office, and it bears looking into."

"Yes," Tim said. He closed his eyes for a moment, tried to sort out the implications of the sheriff's statement. No crime? Certainly both Tim and the deputy— Joel Kimball? Yes, Tim thought, that was his name— certainly both of them were guilty of assault. Had they really left no sign of struggle in the coroner's office? It was possible they hadn't, but it didn't seem likely.

"I'm going to tell you the story the way we know it," the sheriff said, "and when I'm done, I want you to tell me what you have to add to it."

"Sure. If that's what you'd like."

The sheriff hesitated. Frowned. Looked Tim in the eye, as though he already had the idea that Tim was holding something out on him.

And Tim *was* holding out on him, of course. Never

mind the fight; if the man stared Tim in the eye and
asked him what had happened in the morgue, he
wouldn't hesitate that long to tell of it. But there were
things he could never tell the sheriff, no matter what—
things that concerned the Cross.

After a moment the sheriff dropped his stare back to
the papers on his desk, began his story.

"We know," he said, "that Deputy Kimball took a
very peculiar interest in your grandfather from the
moment he set eyes on him. Two days before your
grandfather died, Kimball spotted him while on a rou-
tine patrol with his partner. At Kimball's insistence, the
two spent the rest of that shift following your
grandfather—discreetly, to hear the partner tell it. I'm a
little skeptical about how discreet they could have been,
following the man all day in a marked cruiser."

All of this was strange news to Tim. Though it did
begin to make a bit more sense of the situation.

"None of this showed up on Kimball's report for that
afternoon—or on his partner's report. I learned of it only
this morning, when things became obvious, and I called
the partner—Deputy Darren—in for a chat. Kimball,
apparently, had persuaded Darren to cover for him.
Which isn't SOP around here, but up till that point—
hell, up till this morning—Kimball wasn't acting *that*
peculiar. And in a department this small the deputies
tend to know each other well, and when one or another
of them gets a wild hair we're mostly inclined to indulge
him."

The sheriff paused for a moment, shuffled through
papers.

"If Kimball had anything to do with you or your
grandfather in the two days after that, no one here knows
about it. It's possible Kimball was following him on his
own time—I don't have any way of knowing about that.
But when your grandfather had his accident, Kimball
and Darren were first on the scene. They were there
only a moment after the wreck, in fact. From what
Darren tells me, it could have been chance that put
them on that stretch of road just then. And just as likely
not; it was Kimball behind the wheel that day, and the

two of them were on patrol, and in retrospect the coincidence seems a little much.

"Coincidence or not, Kimball and Darren got to the wreck and found your grandfather dead behind the wheel. Darren went back to the cruiser and radioed in. While he was on the radio he saw Kimball search your grandfather's car. This was the point where Darren finally began to get suspicious. As soon as he finished reporting to the dispatcher, he confronted Kimball—but Kimball managed to calm him down in pretty short order. Not too surprising when you consider that the two of them worked together for years, and knew each other for years before that."

Another pause; more sorting through the material on his desk.

"Did Kimball find anything in Grandpa's car? Did he take anything from it?"

A raised eyebrow from the sheriff. A nod. "What do you think he was looking for?"

Tim looked away, stared out the window so that he wouldn't have to look the sheriff in the eye. There was no way he could tell the sheriff about the Cross; he knew better than to share a secret like that with a stranger. Besides, it wasn't something the man was likely to believe anyway.

"A . . . an heirloom. Something that's been in my family for a long time."

For the longest time the sheriff didn't say a word. And stared at Tim, waiting for him to be more specific.

He knows I'm holding something back from him. He's going to sit there staring at me until I tell.

The sheriff coughed.

I could lie. But for the life of him Tim couldn't think of a lie that sounded even half-credible.

"Did Kimball find anything in Grandpa's car?"

There was a long moment when Tim thought the sheriff would ignore the question all over again. Until finally he cleared his throat and said, "Darren didn't seem to think so. Told me that Kimball was cursing and frustrated, still sifting through the trunk, when he got off the radio and confronted him."

Tim nodded. "Good."

"Are you going to tell me about this damned relic of your grandfather's or not?"

Tim closed his eyes. Opened them. "It's something very . . . personal."

The sheriff sighed, pounded his frustration on the desk with his fist. Made a sharp *thudding* noise that startled Tim. "Damn it," he said, "something happened here. Kimball may even be responsible for your grandfather's death. There's no way I'm going to get to the bottom of this if you're not up-front with me."

Tim didn't say a word; there wasn't anything more he *could* say. After a while the sheriff gave up and went on.

"Kimball's behavior got a lot more suspicious after the death. Again, no one here really caught on to it. The man was a deputy, and a good one, and everyone in the department has known him for years. How can you get suspicious of a guy like that? I'll tell you: you can't. Not until it's already too damned late.

"He arranged with the dispatcher to field your call when it came in. Which is why you got the run-around when you first got in touch with us. I don't know for certain exactly what he instructed you to do when you got out here, but I can make a guess or two about it—"

"He had me meet him at that substation up in Running Board. When I got there, he took me to the coroner's office."

The sheriff nodded. "That's what I thought. The coroner's office was pretty obvious, what with the mess the two of you left behind. And when you turned up at the Running Board substation, it wasn't hard to figure that was where he'd had you meet him. Anyway. He took you up to the coroner's, the two of you had some kind of an altercation. And five a.m. the next morning Kimball shows up here and leaves a letter of resignation for me. And leaves town, real carefully—one of the boys here was coming back from vacation when he ran into Kimball at the Omaha airport this morning. But none of the airlines there has any record of selling a ticket to anybody name of Joel Kimball.

"Now you're here, seeing after business you ought to have been able to take care of yesterday. And you show up looking like—nothing personal, you know, but you really do look like hell. What the hell is going on here? What did Kimball say to you, there in the morgue with the two of you looking at your grandad's body? And why the hell haven't I heard from Mike Darren since early this morning?"

"I—He said—" Tim tried to think, tried to remember the deputy's exact words. "Kimball talked as though he'd killed Grandpa. He said things that were meant to provoke me. He was alone—when you mentioned Officer Darren a little while ago it was the first I'd ever heard of him."

The sheriff nodded. "Darren's out of town with Kimball, most likely. What did you do about it when Kimball provoked you?"

Tim hesitated. The fact was that he'd assaulted the man, and assault on an officer of the law isn't the sort of thing you ought to confess without a lawyer real handy.

"He went after my goat, and he got it."

"You want to be a little more specific?"

"I don't think I should."

The sheriff just sat there, staring at him. Waiting patiently for Tim to be a little more forthcoming. And after a while, Tim was.

"I dove for his throat. Knocked him over, pinned him down. And then I hit him. And kept hitting him."

The sheriff still watched him, poker-faced.

"When I saw what I was doing, I got sick with myself. I got up, and went to leave. Before I could get to the door he was all over me. Threw me against the wall, head first. Knocked me out. Left me in the morgue. Where the cold damned near killed me—if I hadn't woken when I did, I'd be in the hospital now. Or worse."

Still the unreadable expression. "About what I'd figured. I really ought to lock you up, you know. Laying hands on a deputy is a serious offense. Even if he is operating way out of bounds." He reached into a drawer, took out a tape recorder that was already running and set to RECORD. Hit the STOP button, and then ERASE. "Unfortunately, I neglected to record your confession. And we haven't been able to locate the only witness. Which lets you right off that hook."

What was he doing? And why? It didn't make any sense. "I don't . . . understand. Why do you want to protect me from that?"

The sheriff frowned. Snorted.

"I'll tell you, Tim Fischer. Something very strange is going on here. I had the coroner do an autopsy on your grandad this morning. Had him look careful as he knew how—and he's good at what he does, even if he does work out here in the middle of nowhere. And you know what he found? Not a damned thing, that's what. Your grandad died in that accident when his car hit that phone pole. Steering wheel killed him when it crushed his chest."

It wasn't news to Tim. He'd been certain that was the case since he'd checked Grandpa's body this morning.

"There isn't a court in this state that could look at the evidence I've got and say there was a murder. But I know damned well there wasn't any accident. I got a little twitch on the back of my neck that tells me that. Imagine you do too. Somebody killed that man, and if it wasn't Kimball then it was somebody working with him. You want to beat the crap out of him? Do it again, if you want. You've got my blessing. Just don't get caught at it."

Tim nodded. "Yes."

"You got anything you want to add to the story? You want to tell me what exactly it was Kimball wanted to find in your grandad's trunk?"

A rock hit bottom in Tim's stomach. "No. I can't."

Another hard, close stare from the sheriff. "It wouldn't've been anything illegal, would it? Your grandad likely to be carrying contraband? Drugs? Stolen property?"

Which made Tim laugh before he remembered that it wasn't really appropriate. "No, nothing like that. Just a family heirloom. Something so valuable that we make a point not letting people know that we have it. If they don't know it exists, they can't steal it, can they?"

The sheriff took a moment digesting that. He looked like he believed it—which was good, since it was mostly true. "Doesn't seem to me," he said, "that keeping it a secret did your grandad a whole lot of good."

Tim winced. "No," he said. "It didn't."

The sheriff gathered up the papers on his desk, tucked them into a manila folder. Set the folder in a filing tray. "Enough of this. It's getting dark, and you still have to go through your grandad's effects."

The sheriff had a deputy take Tim out to the wreck of Grandpa's car. Grandpa's suitcases were still there in the trunk, which struck Tim as being a little strange—didn't they have property rooms for things like that? But anyway it wasn't worth trying to chase down the why of it, and even if it had been Tim didn't have the heart. Going through the trunk and the glove box, carrying the luggage out to the rent-a-car—it was grim business. And even grimmer was looking through the inside of the car, misshapen from the wreck and bloodstains everywhere. It left him with too little spirit for asking unimportant questions. Not that there was any way to avoid it. Tim knew the moment he set eyes on the wreck that the Cross wasn't inside it, but all the same he had to check. And to be as absolutely certain as he possibly could be, because there was so much at stake.

He found nothing unusual—the car held little but what any car would hold when its driver traveled a great distance. Two suitcases full of clothes, some of them dirty, most of them clean. Two novels tucked in among the shirts. A small leather traveling case, full of toothbrush and razor and similar things. A glove box that held a dozen maps and two months' worth of gas station credit card receipts. In the trunk a spare tire and a few odd tools—enough to change a flat, but not a whole lot more than that. Tim searched it all, carefully and methodically as he could, but he found nothing.

When he was done—when he'd searched the wreck's last crevice and loaded the last of Grandpa's belongings into the rent-a-car—the deputy led him back into the sheriff's office, where he spent most of an hour filling out paperwork. Forms that attested he'd identified Grandpa's body; that he'd claimed his personal effects. A release to allow the corpse to be shipped to Florida for burial. Another to allow a scrap dealer to haul the wreck away in exchange for towing charges. Tim didn't think about any of them as he signed; if he had it might have begun to hurt.

It was half-past ten when he finished with the last of them, handed the pile to the clerk, and left. Outside the sun had finished setting, and the parking lot was dark as pitch in the moonless night. Which was strange—he thought he remembered seeing long high streetlight poles in among the parking spaces. Maybe someone had forgot to turn them on. It didn't really matter, he thought; after all that trekking back and forth with Grandpa's bags, he knew well enough where the rent-a-car was parked to find it in the dark.

He wasn't alone in the parking lot.

He didn't hear anyone else. Certainly didn't see anyone in the moonless dark so thick. But just as he'd known so many times in the last few days that someone watched him, he knew now that someone waited. It wasn't the same sensation as that had been. Wasn't much like it, in fact. Where those presences had been probing, unsettling, this was . . . menacing.

I should go back inside, he thought. *Wait them out. Whoever it is can't lurk in the dark forever.* He hesitated. He was a good forty feet from the building's back door, and the lot was pitch dark. If he got himself turned around it wouldn't be hard to lose his bearings. Glanced back. The door, at least, was plainly visible—as an outline where indoor light leaked around the edges of its frame. He started to turn around, nearly tripped over a stick or something similar that rested on the pavement. And heard himself shout with frustration so loud that it surprised him.

And knew that he couldn't go back inside, because his pride wouldn't let him. He was tired of being intimidated, and he was sick to death of being afraid, and the car was right over *there*, damn it, not sixty feet away, and to hell with lurking menace in the night.

And without another moment's pause Tim strode out toward the car—

And walked right into the men who waited for him. Literally; his face and his shoulder met with a tall man so heavy-set and so hard-muscled that he could just as well have been a wall. There was no way Tim could have seen him—nor his companions—with the night as dark as it was. But if he'd even moved a little more carefully, he'd have heard the sound of their breathing far enough away to have warning as to where they stood. It might have made some difference.

And just as well might not have. There were four of them, at least, and in that dark place where they could somehow see and he could not each was more than a match for Tim. Their punches landed purposefully, the way a punch lands when you know where you're hitting and the other guy doesn't see you coming. All Tim could do in that blind night was flail wildly. Once he felt his left fist swipe a face, and he reached for the eyes, trying to rip away whatever lenses allowed his attackers to see him. But there were no goggles, no glasses, and then someone dragged him down to the pavement from behind, and two others grabbed his arms. He kept struggling after that, but it wasn't a whole lot of use—all he could do was writhe on the blacktop.

Someone leaned close. Spoke softly only inches from his face.

"You've got the Cross," the voice said. A strange male voice, old as time. Steady. Frightening as creation. "Where did you put it?" But strange and frightening as the voice was, Tim could hear no evil in it. No, that wasn't right. A voice with nothing evil . . . would be different, somehow. This voice was anything but innocent, but neither was it the voice he wanted to imagine would come from the throat of a murderer.

And it was the voice of the man who'd killed his grandfather. Tim knew that just as sure as Grandpa had known months before Tim's birth that Tim would be his heir. And he knew it for the same reasons, and with the same chamber of his heart.

A droplet fell onto Tim's cheek. Was the murderer drooling onto him?

"You're out of your mind," Tim said. Another droplet, and it was running down toward his ear. He wanted to wipe whatever it was away with his sleeve, but two people still held his arms down against the blacktop, and there wasn't any way.

"Out of my mind? As may be." The faintest trace of an accent—Middle Eastern? "But whether I'm out of my mind or not, I assure you that you will tell me where you've put the Cross. I've a talent for extracting what I want from the unwary."

Tim felt his heart go cold. The man was threatening him, and the threat wasn't idle or unconsidered. And more than that, Tim knew that the man was capable of making good on that threat—and worse. (Which made him wonder, for an instant, exactly how he could have thought he heard no evil in the man's voice. No—it wasn't evil that the threat come from. What he heard in that voice was the fact that this man would do anything he had to—anything at all—to achieve his ends. And when Tim realized that, it frightened him more than the possibility of evil.)

"That isn't what I meant," Tim said. "I haven't *got* the Cross. I wouldn't be looking for it out here in the middle of nowhere if I did." Which was a lie—to a degree, at least. Even if the Cross had been waiting for him in Grandpa's upstairs room, he'd still have had to come out to Nebraska to see after Grandpa's remains.

The man grabbed a fistful of Tim's hair, yanked up and down again, pounding Tim's skull into the pavement. "Don't lie to me, damn you. You know who I am. You know I'm old enough to know a lie when I hear it. *Where is the Cross?*"

And Tim *did* know who the man was. And, knowing, he was terrified.

And the fear humiliated him.

And the humiliation shamed him.

And the shame made him furious—angrier even

than the certainty that this man had murdered Grandpa. Which was only that much more shame adding to the anger inside him.

Something snapped inside his gut.

"I don't *know* where the Cross is!" His voice was panicked and furious, out of control. Bellowing.

The man's voice was very quiet.

"You don't, do you? Damn me." He pulled up and away from Tim's face. Stood. "Then there isn't any point in this." A chuckle. "But you're awfully angry, aren't you? If I tell Bill and Anne to set you loose you'll be after us in a moment. And we'd have to hurt you. To make you stop. Better to get done with you now."

Tim barely had a moment to brace himself; he heard the wind from the kick just an instant before the man kicked him just below the ribs. Rearranging sweetbreads; forcing out his air—

"Leave him," the man said. "We'll be far away before he finds it in him to stand."

It was true, too. When the two let go of his arms Tim tried to get up and stagger after them. But the effort left him doubled over on his knees, whimpering alone on the tarmac.

Crawling the thirty feet to the rent-a-car took Tim most of twenty minutes. The pain in his abdomen had eased a little by then, but all the same it was sheer agony slipping up into the driver's seat and behind the wheel.

Inside, he saw his face in the rearview mirror. Saw the lines of dried blood that ran from his cheek toward his ear. They weren't any surprise; he'd known for a while to expect to see them, though nothing had broken the skin of his face. The blood had dripped down onto him from the face of the man who beat him. But it wasn't his blood—no more than it was Tim's.

The blood was the substance of the Lord, welling out from the eyes of the man who'd beat Tim—flowing just as it had flowed for two thousand years. For the man who'd attacked him was the Bleeding Man. Old Abraham, that was what Grandpa called him, back—back

when they'd talked about him, that one time. After the
baby and what happened to her, back while Jill was still
in the hospital.

"Old Abraham" or no, after the dream he was the
Bleeding Man in Tim's mind, and there was no way he
could be anything else.

A ghost from his dreams, ridden up through time
two thousand years to haunt him.

He shivered, rested his head against the steering
wheel for a moment, trying to clear it.

And blacked out.

A dog howled somewhere in the distance.

Tim woke slumped sideways against the car door.
How long had it been? An hour? Three? Longer—he
checked his watch and saw that it was twenty minutes
past midnight. He'd been out long enough that it was a
wonder that some deputy hadn't noticed him and
stopped to check. Maybe the dark was too thick for
anyone to notice him. Yes, that had to be it. Even now
with that sliver of moon risen overhead the darkness was
so complete that there was no way for him to tell
whether anyone sat in the car beside his. . . .

And as he thought that thought, as he turned to
focus on the world outside his car . . . he felt it again.

Presence.

Watching.

That same strange watching feeling; that same
peculiar . . . what?—It was like a personality hanging
in the air. Oh, this one wasn't the same as the one from
the airport, and that one wasn't identical to the lurker in
the fields yesterday afternoon, and none of them could
match the air of the Bleeding Man that had filled his
dream last night in the morgue. But there was a deep
and abiding commonality about them, a resemblance
like the resemblance between sisters.

Or between a father and his son.

This presence was new. Quieter; less menacing.
Though there was no mistaking its close relation to the

others, and feeling it Tim was certain that it did not mean him well.

If it meant him anything at all.

He opened the door, stepped out of the car.

Hesitated a moment waiting to feel the awful bruises from the Bleeding Man's kick—but pain was a twinge, only a twinge. His body had always been quick to heal, but this was something new. Something strange.

Time to think about it later.

Now he looked out into the dark.

Ghosts, he thought. *I'm chasing after ghosts*.

And realized that that was exactly what he was about to do—step out into the dark and chase the ghost that haunted him. He closed the door, stood for a moment staring blind at the night, waiting for his eyes to adjust to the absence of light.

"I know you're out there," he said. "Why are you watching me? Come out of the dark. Tell me what you want."

He was sure that any moment now a deputy was going to step out of the back door of the building, and see him shouting into the night like some lunatic, and he'd have to explain himself away.

Humiliating.

There isn't any need to shout. I can feel whoever it is—over there. Over there in the dark.

Out toward the far edge of the parking lot. East toward the rising crescent moon.

Tim stepped away from his car, stepped carefully out in the direction of the watcher. "I know where you are," he said. He spoke quietly, now, intimately, as though he were speaking to a lover. He could feel the watcher breathing, feel the tiny disturbances his movement stirred in the still night air.

Twenty feet; ten; and Tim thought he could see the silhouette standing close against a delivery van—as though the watcher thought himself hidden in the deeper shadow. But it was just the opposite; the pale darkness of the sky so near the moon gave silhouette to—

A woman. The lurker was a woman, not a man.

Again, howling in the distance.

Even in this darkness there was something about her that he recognized. Something personal beyond the aura she shared with all the other watchers.

"Who *are* you?" he asked, staring into her eye. "I know you, don't I? Where did I meet you?" Said it so intimately, so directly that it finally came through to her that Tim knew where she stood.

And she ran.

And what could Tim do? He ran after her. There were questions he had to ask, things he wanted to know. And she was going to tell him, by damn.

Ran through wide, empty, fallow fields of tall wild grass and stray wheat—ran in the dark where there was no time to focus on the uneven shadowed ground beneath the grass. Twice Tim's left ankle found its way into ruts, and both times he nearly went tumbling head-over-heels into the grass. But managed to recover; to stay on his feet and find his balance. The woman wasn't so lucky. After Tim's two near-falls, when he was far behind her in the darkness, she glanced back at him just long enough—

—just long enough that somehow, *somehow*, she didn't see the enormous rotted log that stretched across her path. A log large enough that Tim could see it clearly from all the way back here. She ran dead into it, and with all her momentum her legs went flying out from under her, and her head snapped down in reaction so hard so fast that Tim heard the impact from where he was—this despite the fact that she hit nothing harder than prairie grass.

Tim winced at the sight—had she hurt herself? Was she well, whole?—and he ran faster to help her. But before he got anywhere near she was on her feet and moving again. Staggering, now; now faster, faster. Moving at a dead run, as though she'd never fallen.

Moving forward and off toward the right, toward a long low hill topped by a thicket of pine trees. Forward and to the left Tim could see a baseball diamond, empty and lit by floodlights despite the hour. The hill obscured one edge of the fenced-in field, and looking at it from

here Tim suspected that the floodlights were brigh
enough to light the thicket—light it dimly, at least.

And she was heading into the thicket. Why. . . ?
He couldn't imagine a reason. He'd be able to see her
there, he thought. Didn't she realize that? Or did she
think that she could hide among the trees. . . ?

Maybe she could. Maybe the shade and the shad
ows would be deep enough to hide her.

More howling, and a long sharp series of yips.
Closer, now—close but the sound so warped by the
endless barely broken flatness of the grassy plain around
them that Tim couldn't tell what direction the sound
came from. Couldn't even begin to tell.

She was limping—even if she'd got right up after
her fall, she was hurt. And Tim was gaining ground on
her. If he just kept moving he'd catch up to her—he
looked ahead, guessing at timing and distance—he'd
catch up to her in the woods. Just a little while after they
reached it.

If he wasn't lucky she'd find a shadowed tree and
stand beside it quietly, and in the dim light mixed with
pitch he'd never find her.

He hurried, hoping to catch up to her sooner. But it
was no use. And less than none when he stumbled for
the third time, a dozen yards behind her as she entered
the wood.

He damn near broke his ankle that time. A miracle
he didn't, what with the speed he was moving at and the
way his foot caught in the gopher hole and *stuck* there.
But instead of holding onto his foot the way it could've
instead of breaking his ankle and sending the bulk of him
slam into the prairie dirt, the edges of the hole gave way
and before Tim could finish falling he was back in
motion, lurching forward and struggling to regain his
balance—

But she was gone by then. In the woods and hiding.

And there wasn't any call to hurry anymore. Better
to go slow, go careful. Look hard into the woods that
were just as he'd known they'd be, spattered light and
dark where shadows blocked distant light from the
ballfield. And because there was that faint light the dark

was all the harder to discern in contrast and on account
of the way his eyes narrowed in the light.

Growling—a dog growling somewhere here in the
wood.

And it finally occurred to him to wonder: *What's a
dog doing here, so far from any farm—from any home?*

Bad, bad business. The answer was obvious—there
wasn't any dog here. Because the creature growling was
a coyote.

And if there was one, wouldn't there be more?
Weren't coyotes pack animals?

*Lord in heaven—what has that woman wandered
into?*

A sinking down in his gut.

"You don't want to be here," Tim said. "The coyotes
have made this woods their den. It isn't safe."

No response. Only quiet thick as night pulled over
them.

"Do you hear me?"

And still nothing.

She was here, damn it. Tim knew she was; he could
feel her presence as though it were a shiver in his heart.
He stepped forward, careful, careful, following the
inkling of her he could feel. No, not there; that way,
that way; and then he turned again to follow because
the feeling moved, though he neither saw nor heard the
motion.

Close now, close to a clearing. A clearing in the
center of the woods, and didn't she know that he was
right behind her, not ten feet behind her, and he'd see
her clear as day the moment she stepped in there
because the ballpark light was clear to shine directly into
that place. No, no, no sense. She was walking right into
it, walking in as though she were a mouse about to spring
a trap—

And it occurred to Tim that maybe—more than
maybe as he thought of it, damn likely, in fact—the trap
wasn't set for her, but him. That made him hesitate just
long enough—

—just long enough to watch as she walked into the
clearing where the coyote stood angry guard.

She screamed the moment she saw it, and from the sound of that scream Tim knew that whatever she'd intended this wasn't it. She'd no intention of walking into the jaws of the beast that leaped at her as she pulled away the last of the brush and stepped out into the clearing. If she'd known, if she'd been ready, there was no way she would have stood there screaming mindlessly as bait—

O God O God—Tim was terrified, scared witless, and it wasn't himself he was scared for. Perhaps he should have been. But just as he'd been at the airport when he'd saved the toddler, his concern was only for the danger to the other.

This despite the fact that this woman was a stranger to him, and had given him every reason to believe she was his enemy.

Then he was in motion, moving even faster than the coyote.

Three long, hard, running strides, and he pushed the still-screaming woman aside, not gentle but not hurtful either. Pushed her out of the way of the beast still in midair and met the coyote face-on. And when in an instant it was close enough to touch he brought his fist up backhand into its neck, its jaw. Shoving it up, perpendicular to the ground, where its jaws snapped hard into the air where they'd meant to snap Tim's neck, and then it howled at the pain of the blow as it fell sprawling off balance into the underbrush.

It'll be back at me in a moment.

"Get up," he told the woman. "Get away from here before you're hurt."

And she looked up at him just an instant in the dark, and he thought that there was something like gratitude in her eyes, something like awe and reverence. And then she was gone, so fast, so silent that he hardly had a memory of her face. Later he understood that she was amazed that he'd let her go after pursuing her so hard, but in that time and place it wasn't even a concern for him: his only worry was for her safety.

Then the coyote had its legs back, and it was coming back at him again. And its brothers (sisters?), too—all but the one that hung back at the far edge of the clearing guarding—

Guarding their meal.

Which was the corpse of a man in a deputy sheriff's uniform.

And something snapped loose inside Tim when he knew that the animals that threatened him were man-killers. Something violent. He lunged at the largest of the three coyotes that faced him, lunged and grabbed it by the throat hard and faster than he knew he could move. And before the animal knew what was happening to it he'd turned it, pulled it, snapped its neck.

And it fell to the ground shuddering but already dead.

And now both the others were coming up at him, coming to kill him, not just defending against the alien but furious and angry to revenge themselves for the sibling's death. Tim ducked, spun away from the nearer on the left; but there was no avoiding the one on the right, which bounced and turned to lunge at him where he now stood. Tim batted him down with a fist against the side of his head, and when he was down kicked hard into the soft underside of the coyote's neck. And it screamed long and hard and on, and it quivered suffering in the grass, but it didn't get up to attack.

Not so the third coyote, now bounding up and around to attack again. Tim stepped aside it again, and this time grabbed the animal's rear flank as it hurled by, grabbed one leg and its tail and pulled, heaved it up and around—

And hurled it into the last coyote, the one that'd hung back to guard their communal meal.

It took both of them long moments to recover themselves, and when they did they weren't of a mind to fight any longer, but ran yipping-howling into the night.

Tim stood in the clearing panting for a long moment before he went to check the corpse. He didn't want to look at it; didn't want to stare into the grisliness of a mutilated body. But he knew he had to; after all, it was possible the man could still be alive. And if he was he needed help, and fast.

When he got to it, what he saw was a man hours-dead from a shotgun blast that had opened up his belly and the low part of his chest. Marks here and there to show how the coyotes made him carrion, but it was clear they hadn't killed him.

There was a badge above his shirt pocket, and it read DEPUTY MIKE DARREN.

Tim went directly to the sheriff's office to report what he'd found. At first it looked like he'd found his way into awful trouble with the law—at first it seemed as though he was the most obvious suspect in the deputy's murder.

Then, at three a.m., the coroner came into the interrogation room. And told Tim and the sheriff and three deputies who questioned him that there was no way Tim could've killed the man, because Mike Darren had died while Tim had sat in this very building, up in the sheriff's office.

TWO

T he plane back to Florida was even more miserable than the flight north had been, if that was possible. There was the deep, throbbing ache in Tim's side that seemed to find new ecstasies of pain with each change of thrust and cabin pressure. And his ears—the pills he'd got in the Omaha walk-in clinic didn't quite leave them clear enough for air travel; they caught the shift in pressure only just in time for landing, and held onto it for hours afterward.

In the airport, lumbering toward the taxi stand with his carry-on luggage, Tim found himself looking over his shoulder again and again. Looking for shadows. But there was no one; not even the sense of someone observing him. Nor was his cab followed as it drove him miles across town to his apartment.

It was strange, he thought. The Bleeding Man and his people had trailed him for so long that their absence gave him discomfort. How long had it been since he felt them nearby? . . . Outside the sheriff's office. The woods. The coyotes. When his head cleared from the violence, he'd been alone—and had been ever since.

Maybe, he thought, it was just that he was too tired to feel watched. Or maybe the medicines made him too dull to notice. No; that couldn't be. Tim *was* tired, and he *was* dull. But that peculiar air that hung around those people—there was no way Tim could miss that. There was no way he could ever miss it.

The taxi pulled into Tim's apartment complex, and Tim directed it in among the winding streets that led between the buildings. Had the driver stop near the entrance to Tim's apartment, paid him, got out, climbed the stairs, and opened his door.

There was nothing unusual inside. Nothing off, or alien; only an apartment left empty for days. He turned on the air-conditioning, left his bags on the living-room floor, and collapsed into his own bed. He was asleep less than three minutes later—deep, dreamless sleep that left him rested for the first time in days.

He woke sixteen hours later with the sun of the next day's dawn weighing on his eyelids through the half-open curtains of his bedroom window. The aches and the traces of flu from the events in Nebraska—they weren't gone, not quite. But they were smaller now. Small enough to ignore.

He went to his kitchen, put coffee on. Showered. Dressed, poured coffee—black—and sat down at his kitchen table.

He had to find the Cross.

Had to find it before the Bleeding Man set hands on it.

He bit his lip. There were assumptions here that he hadn't even examined. What would happen if the Bleeding Man found the Cross?

What would he do with it? What *could* he do with it? Why did he want it in the first place? Tim closed his eyes, tried to picture. . . .

Grandpa had panicked when Tim told him about Old Abraham. There wasn't any way to know for certain, but Tim was pretty sure that Old Abraham and the Bleeding Man were one in the same.—So Grandpa was afraid. Had been. Was that really sensible? It'd been years since that conversation about Old Abraham and all that time Grandpa had been quiet and secretive. But so far as Tim could tell nothing real had come of it; till Grandpa had died in the car wreck no harm had come to either of them, and any threat there was to them or the Cross was chiefly hypothetical.

Was it possible that Grandpa's death was nothing but untimely? Even after what he'd seen in Nebraska?

Tim wanted to think it was. There in the living room of his apartment, sipping coffee, relaxing—it was so appealing to pretend that there was nothing wrong. Nothing that he had to do but crawl back into his shell—

(—into the shell where he'd hidden since the week, the week in St. Petersburg in hell—)

—anything. He had to think about anything, anything at all but that.

The letter Grandpa had left for him.

The one he'd read on the plane to Omaha.

There were half a dozen letters like that one, in among the legal papers. A pang of guilt: there were two or three of those letters that he hadn't yet had the heart to read. Maybe more than that.

He ought to read them now. He glanced into the living room, toward the suitcase that still held those papers. He had to read them soon. No. Not now. Soon.

Right now he had to think about the letter he'd read. What was it that Grandpa said about the Cross? He'd said . . . he'd said that it was almost as though a part of God was trapped in the Cross. Because he'd suffered so near to it, so horribly. So long. The Cross was like a tiny bit of God, made whole and real and tangible on Earth.

And Grandpa'd said—he'd hinted that if you held it in your hands, you could *do* things to the world, just as God could, but wouldn't.

That made no sense at all. All Tim's life Grandpa had said that it wasn't possible to do things like that. Or—had he said that it was something you *shouldn't* do? It was hard to remember. Sometimes Tim thought, yes, maybe this was exactly right: that only Grandpa could do things like that with the Cross. Grandpa, and maybe Tim. Because they were the Stewards.

But if that was so, then why was it a problem if the Bleeding Man knew about the Cross? What was the problem if he stood next to it, even held it, if he wasn't Steward and couldn't do anything with it?

The Bleeding Man.

Tim pictured him as he'd seen him in his dreams; strangely brooding, unhuman, consumed with vision that made no sense to Tim. Thought of the voice he'd heard in the pitch-dark lot—and how, for half an instant when he heard it, he'd felt as though he might follow the Bleeding Man to the ends of the earth. Follow not because of any loss of heart or will or principle, but because hearing him Tim knew that he stood for something important.

There was something about that voice, Tim thought . . . Grandpa's voice. It was like Grandpa's voice: hearing him speak, you couldn't help but know that he was *right*.

But he *wasn't* right, damn it, and Tim was just as clear on that as he was on his own name. There was nothing right about murdering Grandpa. There was nothing right about waiting in the dark to attack a body who didn't know you were there. And there was something dead wrong about lusting after the Cross.

Anybody who wanted to have the Cross . . . it was the kind of thing that if you wanted it, you probably shouldn't have it.

Never mind if the Bleeding Man *could* take the Cross—What would he do if he set hands on it?

He'd take apart the world, Tim thought. *And put it back together the way he thought it ought to be.*

The idea made him feel cold and afraid inside, and he knew as soon as the words came through his mind that they were absolutely true. But the scariest thing— the scariest thing was the reason that he knew what the Bleeding Man would do.

He knew because he found the same desire in his own heart, hiding in his dreams.

The realization left Tim staring numb into his coffee. And he stayed that way for hours, his mind a total blank. On toward noon he blinked, looked out the window. *I should go away from here. Forget about the Cross, about Grandpa . . .*

He could, too. Get in his car, drive away from town. Never look back. Ought to: If his heart held the smallest desire to pretend to be God, then he was the last one in the world who ought to be the Steward of the Cross.

But if he did . . . the Bleeding Man would find it

soon enough. Not tomorrow, maybe. Maybe not the next day. But in a week or in a year, he'd find it, and—

What would the world be if the Bleeding Man had made it? Tim didn't want to think about it. Even more than that he didn't want to have to learn.

He swallowed a mouthful of cold coffee, shuddered. He had to find the Cross. Find it and bury it someplace so deep that no one would ever uncover it again—not even himself.

Which meant he had to look for it.

And the place to start looking was Grandpa's house.

Last time he'd driven out to Grandpa's Tim had been all full of panic and hurry and apprehension at the responsibility that'd fallen on him. This time the drive was anything but frantic. He didn't *want* to find the Cross. Knew that, when he found it, it would only be a thing that he ought not to have. Oh, seeing after the Cross was his obligation, and he'd follow it through. It'd been his obligation since the day he was born—Tim had known that for a long time now.

But whether it was an obligation or a curse or a thing that would make him a threat to the bedrock that underlay creation, Tim wasn't in any hurry to find the Cross. He didn't want it, and he didn't want to find it. So he drove slowly, taking back roads that made the fifteen-minute drive to the tall old house take most of an hour.

When he finally pulled into the driveway he stalled for a good five minutes—sitting in the car with the door half-open, trying to think of anything else he needed to do—before he finally went inside. Which was pointless: there wasn't any reason to delay. No more than there would have been a reason to hurry if he'd been inclined to rush.

The truth was, in fact, that Tim might just as well have turned around and driven away from his grandfather's house without ever looking into it. Because—as he saw when he finally left the car, walked to the front door, took out his keys, and unfastened the lock—the old house was empty of every stick of furniture, every book, every dish, towel, or rag—every discernible trace that Grandpa had ever lived inside it.

The house had been that way since Monday, when the movers the Bleeding Man hired had come and emptied it.

Tim opened the door, and he saw the emptiness where the effects of Grandpa's life ought to have been, and he felt his heart sink down through his gut and break. Right away he knew what had happened: while he'd been busy in Nebraska, the Bleeding Man's people had been here, loading everything into trucks.

And somewhere in the mass of what they'd taken was the Cross. Tim was certain of it.

He wandered through the house, hoping that he'd find something somewhere that they'd forgotten. But there was nothing; nothing but dust and bare walls and floors and here and there a tiny bloodstain droplet on the floorboards. Still, he checked everywhere. And did not find anything—not on the first floor, nor on the second. Carpets, drapes, everything—all of it was gone. Even the bulbs in the ceiling lights. When he got to the third floor he checked each room carefully, checked each closet, every corner. All of them were bare as they always were—Grandpa had never furnished any of those rooms, bar the room at the end of the hall. And that one had never held anything but the Cross. Tim went to the room at the end of the third-floor hall last of all, and until he opened its door he still held the least faint hope that the Cross would be there, sitting on the floor of the always-curtainless room, just as it had for as long as Tim had lived.

When he opened that door Tim saw only an empty room—the same empty room it'd been last Sunday, when Tim had rushed up here from the lawyer's office. He slumped against the wall, depressed and afraid and feeling as though he'd failed the only purpose his life had. After a time he let himself slide down toward the floor, where he sat with his back pressed hard against the wall until the depression deepened, and dragged him down to sleep.

Tim never noticed that sleep had overtaken him;

dreaming, he sat in his mind's eye still staring at the bare wood floor.

In the dream he heard footsteps on the stairs out in the hall. Footsteps coming toward him—steady, slow. There was nothing urgent in their pace, but rather something clock-steady inevitable about the sound of them.

They were Grandpa's footsteps. Tim recognized them. There was no way he could have failed to, knowing Grandpa so long, so well.

Grandpa crested the stairs, turned toward Tim, and started down the hall.

"Hello, Tim," he said. There was nothing strange nor unearthly about his voice—only disappointment, worry, a measure of concern. It wasn't the voice of a ghost. Nor was there anything spectral in his appearance; to Tim's eye and to his ear Grandpa was a visitation made of flesh and blood. It seemed to him that there was nothing strange about that—partly because he was caught up in the dream, and his dreams were always full of unlikely things seeming unexceptional. Partly because in the deep chambers of his heart he hadn't yet accepted that Grandpa was dead and gone.

"Hello, Grandpa." Tim reached into the numbness that was his mind, tried to find the question that he had to ask. Found it. "Are you going to tell me where you left the Cross?"

Grandpa frowned; for an instant he looked annoyed. "Where do you think I left it?" Biting, sarcastic. And then he sighed, and his expression became sad and disheartened. "No," he said, "this isn't the time for impatience. I'm sorry." He crouched down on the floor beside Tim. Stared out the window for the longest time. "I can't find the Cross for you, Timbo. You've got to find it for yourself."

It was quiet again for a long while after that. Tim knew that there was something else that he was supposed to ask or say or plead for, but for the life of him he was too depressed to think of it.

"Why are you here, then? Have you come back to stay?" And felt himself grow hopeful as he asked the question. If Grandpa were back and alive and here to take care of everything, Tim could leave it to him. Run away forever and let him find someone else to take the Cross when he passed on.

But Grandpa shook his head. "No, Tim. I'm not even here, much less to stay. You're dreaming."

Tim bit his lip. "Then why?"

"Because there's something else that I've got to show you. Something that I *can* show you. If things had gone the way they should have, I'd've given it to you a year or two from now. But they didn't, and you need the book, and even if it's too soon it's not so soon as to hurt you." He stood. "Come on," he said. "Follow me."

In the dream—and for all that Grandpa had said it was a dream, Tim still would have sworn that it wasn't—in the dream Tim followed his Grandpa down both flights of stairs, through the empty house. Past the foyer and the parlor; through the downstairs hall to Grandpa's study. Which was just as stark as it had been an hour before, when Tim was awake.

Grandpa went to the fireplace at the far end of the room, and he stood beside the mantle waiting until Tim reached him.

Tim looked at the bare mantle, into the empty-clean fireplace, looking for some small thing he'd failed to notice when he first searched this room. But there was nothing on the mantle but two days' accumulation of dust, nothing in the hearth but a trace of ash from last year's yule.

"You took me down here to show me an empty room, Grandpa? Please—don't try to talk to me in signs and portents. I'm confused enough as it is."

Grandpa smirked. "No, Tim. You're having a vision, all right—but it's a seeing you need to take literally." He stooped, pointed into the fireplace. "Look close. You see this brick? On the back wall of the hearth. In the right corner, three bricks from the base. Can you be sure to remember it?"

Tim nodded.

"Good. Because this won't work anywhere else. The rest of this fireplace is solid brick—you'd need a wrecking ball to take it apart. But right *here*—" he stood, stepped back, kicked the spot he'd pointed to "—if you kick this spot exactly, the mortar will collapse around these three bricks." Kicked again, and the brick fell out of the wall. The two above it sagged into the void it left.

As the bricks fell, Tim saw what it was Grandpa wanted to show him. Not the Cross, though Tim had hoped against hope that it would be. A book, tucked into a tiny niche hollowed out behind the bricks.

An ancient book with a heavy leather binding and thick pages made of something that wasn't paper. Grandpa reached into the cavity, brought out the book, handed it to Tim. Looked him in the eye serious as could be.

"It's your heritage, Tim. Things in there I should have told you years ago, but never did—even a long life can run too short, I guess. Read it. Think about what you read. And whatever you do, don't lose it—you owe that to the one who'll follow you."

And before Tim could say that he would, the book was gone and Grandpa was gone and there was this awful moment when Tim thought he'd lost that precious book already. But then he realized where he was, upstairs in the high room, and he realized that he was just waking up. And he didn't have the book because he wasn't in that dream anymore.

And realized that Grandpa had left—again—without giving Tim the chance to say good-bye. Well, if Grandpa didn't want to wait around long enough to say good-bye, then the heck with him; what did Tim need with him, anyway?

A long pause as Tim looked around the still-empty room. The truth was that Tim needed Grandpa more right now than he'd ever needed him. But that didn't matter: Grandpa was gone, and a phantom in a dream wasn't enough to take the weight of the moment from Tim's back. Tim sighed, stood, brushed the floor's dust from his trousers. And went down to Grandpa's vacant library. And looked carefully into the fireplace at the far end of the room.

Brick for brick, it was just as it had been in his dream.

Tim kicked the masonry, just as the dream-Grandpa had showed him. All he got for the effort was a bruised foot; Tim's soft running shoes didn't give him the kind of protection Grandpa got from his steel-toed work boots.

There had to be something, somewhere in the house, didn't there? An old pipe—anything that would do service as a hammer. Sure—Grandpa's old tool chest, down in the basement—but the thieves had left the cellar as empty as they'd left the rest of the house. So he kicked the fireplace again and again, kicked until he'd lost all feeling in the toes of his right foot. And looked down at the brickwork. And saw no difference at all.

No, that wasn't true: there were scuff marks on the brick where it'd worn away the sole of his shoe—barely visible, but Tim saw them when he looked close. He looked down at his foot, and thought that he could almost see it beginning to swell up inside his shoe. *I might as well be trying to kick my way through solid rock.* And felt a sinking weight in his stomach when it occurred to him that a brick wall *was* more or less solid rock. And if the wall was acting like it was solid, then odds were that it was. And if it was solid, then Tim's dream about Grandpa and the book wasn't anything but a dream.

If that dream wasn't anything but a dream, then he was stuck again—alone, afraid, and without a single tool to face his circumstances.

No.

Tim closed his eyes. There was hope in that dream—he wasn't going to let go of it unless he had to. If Grandpa had hidden something in behind the brick and mortar of the fireplace, then by damn Tim was going to find it. Or lay the whole damn wall to waste making certain that it wasn't there. Even if that meant getting a crane with a wrecking ball in here to take the damn thing apart.

He stood, hobbled toward the door. He had a hammer back at the apartment, didn't he? Better yet, he'd stop by the hardware store, pick up a sledge.

That was when he finally remembered the tire-iron in the trunk of his car. As soon as he thought of it he began to feel stupid; he'd damn near broken his foot for no reason at all. No—it was worse than that. Whether there were tools in the car or not it was stupid to hurt himself that way—not if it wasn't absolutely necessary. He needed to think before he ran headlong into things. Even if there'd been no one else to see it, Tim felt like an idiot. Felt humiliated.

Late afternoon in Grandpa's front yard. Cicadas, thrumming and screeching their steady, unpretty music. It was still too early for them, but there they were anyway, loud and ugly and comforting all at once because they were familiar. Tim looked around, trying to spot the bugs that made the sound, but as always they were invisible.

He did see one thing when he looked around: the neighbors' houses. They weren't that obvious—the houses here were far apart, and the trees and shrubs were so old and tall that they shielded most of the view. Shielded or not, they were neighbors, and there was no way Tim could imagine that anyone could pull anything as big and bright-painted as a moving van into Grandpa's yard without the neighbors noticing.

I'll bet they saw it. And if they did, at least a few of them will remember the name of the company that sent it. And if I can find out which company did the job, I can find out where they took it.

And he knew—knew with an absolute, irrational, gut-level certainty—that if he could find out where the Bleeding Man's people had taken Grandpa's belongings—if he could find that out, everything else would begin to fall together.

In his excitement Tim nearly forgot about the tire iron. The fireplace. The book he'd seen secreted inside it in his dream.

One thing at a time. I've got to stop running off half-cocked.

Opened the trunk, fished the tire-iron up out of the wheel-well. Carried it into the big old house, into the room that had been Grandpa's study but now was just an empty room with an enormous hearth. And he went to the brick that he'd seen in his dream, the brick that had all but broken his foot. And he pounded on it with the tire iron's blunt end until he saw it begin to come lose from the mortar that held it. And instead of beating it harder to force it in—the way Grandpa had in the dream—Tim forced himself to be quiet and methodical, and he used the iron's toothlike blade to pry the brick out.

Once it was free, the two above it all but collapsed of their own weight. It only took Tim a moment to clear them away. And behind them, just as in the dream, was the two-thousand-year-old book.

Carefully, carefully he lifted it out of the niche. When he held it mystery and awe consumed him—opened its cover, turned the thick-smooth vellum pages one by one, looked at the words written by the hands of his forebears in languages so ancient that few living men could read them.

Reminded himself that there was business at hand that needed seeing to. Closed the book, carried it out to his car, wrapped it in the jacket he kept in his back seat, and locked it away in the trunk so that no one else would see it.

Tim promised himself that he'd get back to it as soon as he'd finished speaking to the neighbors. But the way things turned out, it was a long time after that before he even thought of the book again.

Tim was ten when he asked his Grandpa about Hell and dying.

It was a Sunday, and that day he'd got up early—before his Mom and Dad—to watch cartoons. Only when he turned on the TV it wasn't on a cartoon channel.

Instead of cartoons what waited for Tim was a TV evangelist with great fiery eyes and a dire countenance and a voice so deep and unnerving that it haunted him for years.

Tim meant to turn the channel. He really did. But the voice and the words and the fire mesmerized him, and after a moment his hand fell away from the TV tuner.

Fell slack onto the floor beside him.

Repent, the evangelist said. *Repent now, you sinners. Repent now, because the fires of Hell await you.*

Tim blinked. Confused. Off balance. He'd heard of Hell. Heard about it in church. But until this moment it'd been an abstraction to him.

You'll burn in Hell, the evangelist said. *And though your body chars, utterly and totally engrossed with flame, yet it shall not be consumed. When you burn, burn you will forever. You will thirst until your lips and tongue split wide in the dry heat, and yet you will not drink while water burbles just beyond your reach. You will know desire and stand forever just beyond its fulfillment.*

The words frightened Tim. They made him feel alone and small and isolated and frightened the way only a small child can when there is no one around to protect him.

Be sure your sin will find you out. Don't let yourself believe for a moment that God doesn't know what you've done. All of it. No wrong, no matter how small nor great, no matter how dire nor dear—no wrong will go unpunished. Your deepest secrets are no secret to Him, nor will they ever be! Confess your sins and repent them!

And the audience answered, Repent!

Repent!

Repent!

And Tim got up from the floor, and ran from the television. Didn't even take the time to turn it off—headed upstairs to his room, where he hid under the covers until long after the sun came up and chased away the fear that finds children in the dark part of morning.

Mom was up when he got out of bed again. And the TV was still on the same channel, only now the program was a nature show about water buffaloes making friends in India. He could hear both of them downstairs, Mom and the TV, as he pulled on his tennis shoes and his T-shirt and his dungarees.

"Morning, Timmy," Mom said when she saw him on

the stairway. "You're looking awfully purposeful today."

"Uh-huh." He *was* feeling purposeful, too. Tim had had a mission in mind from the moment he'd lifted the covers off his head that second time. There was only one thing to do when something like this happened to you: you had to go talk to Grandpa.

Mom stopped. Looked him up and down kind of careful. "What *are* you up to?"

Tim shrugged. "Gonna go see Grandpa."

Mom sighed. Grandpa was Dad's grandfather, and Mom wasn't real comfortable with the way him and Tim spent so much time together. Not that she ever really tried to put a stop to it. And too she didn't care much at all for Tim riding his bike clear up to Lutz—but he'd been an independent child almost from his birth; and she'd never fought him on it.

"Get yourself some breakfast, first. The new box of cereal is in the cupboard."

"Grandpa'll give me something."

He was out the door and on his bike before Mom really had a chance to respond to that one. Forty minutes later he'd reached the big old house where Grandpa lived. He let his bike fall to the ground a few feet from Grandpa's holly, and went in without knocking. Mom was always telling him he ought to knock first, but Grandpa always looked at him kind of funny when he did.

"Grandpa. . . ? You awake?"

"In the kitchen, Tim. What do you mean, am I awake? Have you ever seen me sleeping this late in the day? Say what you will about me, but don't call me a layabout."

"I won't, Grandpa."

Grandpa was in the middle of making breakfast—Tim smelled ham and eggs before he got two rooms away.

"Hungry?" As Tim came through the kitchen door.

"Mmmm-hmmm." And Grandpa tossed another serving into the pan where the ham was sizzling. Broke two eggs and scrambled them with the others.

He sat at the kitchen table. Waited quiet without

saying a word while Grandpa cooked. It wasn't long before he was done, and then they both ate ham and scrambled eggs and thick slices of buttery toast. Grandpa had a way with food. A real way; he was twice the cook that Mom was. Tim was grown up enough that he hadn't made a point of saying that to either one of them. Both of them knew it, anyway. It wasn't the kind of thing that anybody could fail to notice.

All while they ate, Grandpa waited patient for Tim to speak his piece. Which he didn't. If Grandpa had asked him, point-blank, why that was, he couldn't have given an honest answer. Or not a complete one, anyway. A little it was because he didn't know which question to ask. And a little because he didn't know where to start. And a little because he was afraid to think about that fire-eyed man again. But there were other things that held his tongue, too, and Tim didn't begin to understand them.

It was Grandpa who finally broke the quiet.

Just like it usually was.

"Why don't you start at the beginning, Tim? Why don't you tell me how it started?"

Tim started to open his mouth to speak. But before he could utter a word he found another of the things that held his tongue: embarrassment. It'd been four years since that Christmas when he'd first seen the suffering of Christ. He was nine, now, and nine-year-old boys weren't supposed to get all scared because of something they'd seen on television. And when they did get scared, their pride got in the way and made it hard for them to talk about it.

Grandpa sat there, watching patiently. Waiting for Tim to come to terms with himself and get on with life.

And Tim let out a long breath, and let the stubborn part of pride out with it.

"On TV this morning," he said. "There was this minister. Talking all about Hell."

A pause. Tim let it go on for a bit, hoping that Grandpa would step in to fill the silence.

He didn't, of course.

"And he was talking about how everybody in Hell

was on fire and hurting and burning and suffering. Saying how God was going to make everybody suffer because of everything they'd done. It was scary, Grandpa. He looked out through that TV just as though he could see me, see everything I'd ever done. Like he hated me on account of it. And he made it sound like God felt exactly the same way, and I went upstairs to hide before either one of them could see me doing anything I wasn't sure about."

Grandpa was beginning to look angry. Tim wasn't too sure whether that meant he was angry at him or at the minister or at God or what.

"Is God like that, Grandpa? Did he really make a Hell to get us back for everything we've done?" Tim stretched himself, trying to find the exact words for the question he needed to ask. "Is there a Hell, Grandpa?"

Grandpa *was* angry. Positively furious. He pushed his chair away from the table, stood.

"We need to go upstairs, Tim. There's no way I can explain this to you here."

Upstairs. Upstairs didn't mean the second floor, where Grandpa's room was. It meant the third floor.

Up in the highest part of the house.

Where the Cross was.

Tim bit his lip. Nodded.

"I have to . . . I have to calm myself before I go up, Tim. I need a moment alone. You go ahead up there, wait for me by the door. You don't have to go inside without me, but you can if you want."

Tim didn't say anything. He wasn't comfortable with the prospect of climbing that stairway by himself again. But he was too proud to say so out loud, and anyway he knew that there wasn't anything up there he really had to be afraid of.

"Don't let it scare you, kiddo. Nothing's going to bite you." A pat on the back. "Go ahead."

And then he was halfway up the stairs, and just realizing that he'd gone.

The climb was a lot less unnerving now than it had been back when he was five. And faster, too—way back then it'd been an eternity of dread. Not that it was pleasant now. Not really. But he was older, and if he wasn't braver he was more full of bravado; in three minutes that didn't seem like much more than five Tim had covered both halls and both flights of stairs. And he stood by the door that was nothing but a door to an empty room.

And he waited.

No strange sounds cam through the door. No impossibly bright light shone under the jamb.

But something was going to happen. He was here and he was alone and this was the room where the Cross was and something strange had to happen just as naturally as one breath had to follow another.

And after a moment, it did.

Without making a sound, the door slid open of its own accord.

It wasn't any accident. Wasn't any coincidence. Grandpa kept that door closed firm. He was very careful about it.

Inside was nothing but an empty room with curtainless windows.

Empty, that was, except for the ancient shard of bloodstained wood that lay in the center of the floor.

Tim's heart began to slow. Nothing strange was going to happen. Nothing but a door that swung open on its own. He really wasn't up to anything strange right now. Not alone, and after the scare this morning. And with all the strange that could happen in this place, the door didn't count as much at all.

"Tim?"

So sudden, so out of nowhere that he nearly jumped clear out of his skin.

But it was Grandpa's voice. It wasn't anything to be afraid of.

"Yeah, Grandpa. Scared me."

Grandpa frowned. Shook his head ruefully.

"Of all the places in the world, Tim," he said, "this is the last one to be afraid of."

"I know, Grandpa." He *did* know, too. But it didn't stop him from being uneasy about this place where things *happened* that couldn't happen anywhere else.

"Come on in, Tim. Sit with me on the floor. By the Cross."

As he entered the room, the door closed behind him just as quiet as it'd opened. Tim did his best not to pay any attention as he sat down cross-legged, facing Grandpa.

And then, for the longest time, the two of them just sat there. Watching the Cross.

"What's the biggest part of your question, Tim? What bothers you the most?"

Tim looked away, out the window. Tried hard to think. Pressed with his mind against the things that scared him most of all. It took him most of five minutes to distill it into a question.

"I guess what I want to know, Grandpa, is: Is there a Hell? How could God make a place like that to put people in? I thought He loved us."

As he spoke, something else began to happen that frightened Tim—the image of Christ began to appear above the fragment of the Cross. Fainter this time than it'd been back when he was five. Like a ghost, maybe, or . . . or like the pale reflection you sometimes see on a pane of glass.

"'Is there Hell?' Tim?" Grandpa frowned. He looked troubled. "I don't know. I honestly don't know."

"How come, Grandpa? I read about Hell in the Bible. I did. And that preacher talked about it. And wasn't the Bible written by God?"

Grandpa winced.

"Tim . . . Look at Him, Tim." He gestured toward the vision that hung over the fragment of the Cross. "What do you see? What do you see when you look at His face, look into His eyes?"

Tim looked directly at the Christ for as long as his heart could bear. Which wasn't long.

"He *hurts*, Grandpa."

Grandpa nodded. "What else do you see?"

Tim didn't look again; he couldn't bear to. And anyway the image was still vivid in his mind. "He loves us . . . very, very much."

Grandpa smiled. But his face was still troubled. "Do

you see anything vengeful when you look at Him?
Anything vindictive?"

Tim had to take another glance, just to be certain.
"No, Grandpa."

"Tim . . . there are lots of angry things inside that
Bible. And when I look into His face over there. . . .
Well, it's hard to believe in those angry things. The only
thing we really know for sure is that He died on the
Cross, and that He did it because He loves us. And when
you get right down to it, you and I are the only ones who
really know that."

Tim was getting confused. "Then the Bible isn't
really the word of God? Is that what you mean?"

The old man shrugged. "Sometimes I think that
maybe there were some parts of the Bible that were
taken down by mistake. But there are parts of it . . . I
read them and I know, honestly *know* that they're true.
Unquestionable."

"And there isn't a Hell?"

"I have trouble believing that God could have so
little mercy that He'd send a man to Hell. Maybe it's
necessary to set some folk apart. But how can a merciful
Lord condemn anyone to suffer—let alone so many? And
so long?"

Grandpa said those words, all right. But as he spoke
his face was troubled, and looking at him Tim thought
that maybe his grandfather was as uncertain about it all
as Tim was himself.

Grandpa sighed. Looked at the vision over the
Cross, and Tim could see that his face was very sad, as
though he felt he was about to betray something he
loved dearly. "Maybe there is a Hell, Tim. But if there
is, then shame on God for causing so much suffering.
And if saying that means I'm going to Hell, then shame
on Him anyway. I love my God, but damn me if I'll sing
the praises of a thing I think is wrong."

The Johnson house was closest to Grandpa's. Tim had
known old Mr. and Mrs. Johnson all his life, though he'd
never known either of them well. Well enough to wave

hello when he saw Mr. Johnson mowing his lawn (bare-shirted, thick grey hair on his chest glistening sweat in the Florida sun) on a Saturday. Only barely well enough to recognize the couple the day three years ago when he ran into them coming out of the Theater Sixplex in the Eastgate Mall. (Tim winced, embarrassed, remembering that day; he always had an awful time recognizing people out of context. And the only context he had for the Johnsons was their home.)

Mrs. Johnson answered her door only an instant after Tim rang, so quickly that she must have seen him coming. Had to've stood behind the door waiting for him to ring.

"Tim Fischer!" she said. Her voice was friendly and full of counterfeit surprise. "Imagine seeing you here."

"How's that, Mrs. Johnson? It hasn't been that long since the last time I saw you, has it?"

"No, no—not that long. You were here with your grandfather and the carolers from church, weren't you?"

Tim couldn't remember ever seeing Grandpa get up for church on a Sunday morning, but every year Grandpa would organize the caroling. He'd only missed it once that Tim knew of: the Christmas after the house fire that killed Tim's Mom and Dad. Tim had been twenty-two, in his senior year at USF, and he and Jill Robbins had shared an apartment a few blocks from the one he lived in now. The blaze flared up in the early morning hours two days before Christmas. So hot, so fast, so sudden that it only took a few minutes to leave the house a char.

Dad died fast and quiet in his sleep, partly from the smoke and partly from the heat. But Mom was still half-alive when the firemen found her. She spent three days comatose, fading, before she finally passed away.

She never woke.

New Year's had come and gone before it occurred to Tim that he'd neglected Christmas. If Grandpa celebrated the holiday—even in the smallest way—Tim never saw it.

"That was me, all right. I was there."

"I thought so! No, it isn't you that's surprising. Tim

Fischer is familiar enough, all right. I guess I assumed that you'd moved away when your grandad did."

She *had* seen the movers.

"Grandpa didn't move away, Mrs. Johnson. He died Sunday."

Mrs. Johnson's face went pale and slack with shock. Tim thought he saw a touch of fear in her eyes—the same fear he always sensed when people seemed to see the shadow of their own passing in the death of another.

"I'm sorry," she said, "sorry for your loss." Her voice was very quiet. "Ben? Did you hear?"

Tim saw Mr. Johnson lumber into the foyer behind his wife. "Yes, Anne, I heard. My condolences, son. Is there anything we can do to help?" His face was sad and grim, but where his wife's eyes held dread the old man's were resigned.

Tim paused for a moment, trying to think of anything the Johnsons could do to help. Thought of nothing. "No, Mr. Johnson—I think I can cope. But there was something I wanted to ask you about. Something kind of strange."

"What's that?"

"Those movers you saw? What was it, Monday, I guess?"

"Tuesday." Mrs. Johnson smiled.

"I don't know who they were. I didn't hire them. So far as I know Grandpa didn't hire them before he died. While I was out of town, seeing after Grandpa's business, they came here and cleared out everything he owned."

The old man's expression became serious. "You're certain?"

"As sure as I can be. Did you get a good look at the moving van? Do you remember which company did the job?"

The old man nodded. "Trans-Continental. Trans-Continental Moving Lines."

"Ben? Are you positive? I thought—"

"Yes, Anne. I'm positive. Big red-and-yellow truck. Garish. Hard to forget."

Tim nodded. "Thanks, Mr. Johnson. That ought to get me started finding where they took it all."

"Don't think about it, Tim. And if you need it later on—if you end up going to the police—I got a good look at the fellow who seemed to be supervising the movers. Tall fellow, grey hair, deep tan. Leathery skin. Must've had a wicked cut on one of his eyes, or maybe the bridge of his nose. Blood seeping under the frames; had to keep wiping it away with his handkerchief. Damn thing was an awful bright-red mess by the time they left."

The Bleeding Man.

Mr. Johnson frowned. "You know this man? You look like you just saw a ghost."

Tim nodded.

"Who the hell is he?"

Tim bit his lip, lied. "I don't know," he said. "But he frightens me."

Something shifted in Mr. Johnson's eyes, and Tim thought that he'd seen the lie but didn't want to press it. "I'm sure you'll tell me," he said, "when you know."

Tim told him that he would, and said good-bye—hurrying away before he had to tell another lie.

Tim went home directly from the Johnsons', and when he got in the first thing he did was open the phone book. Find the number for Trans-Continental Moving Lines' local affiliate. And dial.

"West Tampa Trans-Continental—please hold." The woman on the other end didn't wait to hear him respond; she hit some switch or another and suddenly Tim was listening to Muzak.

Really *awful* Muzak.

And more of it, tedious and fluffy and annoying. And somehow it kept getting worse and worse, until finally after ten minutes (or maybe it was twenty) the woman took him off hold.

"West Tampa Trans-Continental—how can we help you today?"

"I need to speak to your manager," Tim told her.

"Manager?" A pause. "Who exactly would you like

to speak to, sir? I need a name to put you through. Unless you'd like to speak to a sales representative."

"Who is your boss? Who runs your office? That's the person I want to talk to."

"I need a name, sir. I can't put you through without a name."

Tim groaned, frustrated. "Look," he said, "two days ago one of your vans pulled up to a house that now belongs to me. And your people went in, and they carried away everything inside it. I didn't authorize your people to move anything. I didn't even know they'd been there until today, when I went to the house and found it empty. Do you want to connect me to someone who can tell me where it's gone, or do you want me to call the police?"

"Thank you." Friendly, cheerful—as though they'd just finished a pleasant exchange, instead of a shouting match. "One moment, please."

It took more than a moment, of course. More like twenty minutes, all of them filled with the same gratingly insipid Muzak Tim'd had to listen to during the first wait. After a while he set the phone on his shoulder (where the saccharine melodies were only barely audible, faint and distant) extracted his subscription copy of *Newsweek* from the pile on the kitchen table (where it lay buried in among the rest of the week's mail), and began to read. By the time the manager finally got back to him, Tim was so involved in his reading that she had to say hello five times before he realized she wanted his attention.

"Sorry," he said, lifting the receiver to his ear, "distracted. Got caught up reading while you had me on hold. You're the manager down there? You can tell me where you've sent Grandpa's furniture?"

"I can tell you where you'll find it," she said. Which was only half an answer to his question, but she only paused half an instant (the sound of shuffling papers) before she gave him the address, and then he was too busy taking down the information to think to challenge her. "The load you're looking for went to Summit County, Tennessee—up in the Smokies, a couple hundred miles east of Knoxville. The address is in a village called Still Ridge, but that won't help you much, since none of our maps list anything—town, ridge, or whereabouts—by that name: Hines Plantation, Tennessee State Highway 63, Still Ridge, Tennessee. There's a note in the papers, addressed to the moving crew; it says that the plantation is on the state road between Green Hill and Tylerville."

"Anything else? Which side of the road? What the place looks like? Landmarks?"

"Not in my papers. Now, if you'll excuse me. . . ?"

"Sure," Tim said. And then the line clicked and went quiet, and it suddenly seemed to him that there was something else he had to ask, something important, only he couldn't think exactly what it was. And anyway it was too late because the woman was gone.

Tennessee—Tennessee in the middle of nowhere. How in God's name am I supposed to get there?

There was only one way, of course. He had to drive. Oh, sure, there were a couple other ways to get to the middle of Nowhere, Tennessee. Bus lines go most everywhere, but taking the bus would leave him stranded in the boondocks without a car, and it was a sure thing he'd need a car once he got there.

Not five feet from him on the kitchen floor were his bags from the trip to Nebraska, still packed, still closed. For half a moment he imagined himself packing them up, hauling them back out to the car, taking off. It was a silly idea, of course; the clothes in those suitcases were dirty laundry. He'd have to go to his dresser, find fresh ones—

No. I'm getting crazy again. I need to lie down, think this through. It's already dark—starting a cross-country drive without getting a good night's sleep will only make things worse than they already are.

Tim put the phone into its cradle, sat down at the kitchen table. What did he need to do before he left town? All he could think was *laundry* and *sleep*. There was his job, down at the realty brokerage. It was almost a job, anyway. He had his realtor's license, and he went in to the office most days. Some months he even brought in money, and when he did it was awfully good money. Enough to live on, even when he only sold a house one month out of three. But mostly the realty office just felt like a way to mark time. A real job, Tim thought—*real* work—that was something that gave purpose to your life. There wasn't anything about the brokerage that made Tim feel that way.

No one there would miss him especially if he didn't show up for a few more days. Even so, he ought to call in, let someone know he wouldn't be in; it was possible—just barely possible—that one or another of the agents in the office would notice his absence. And if one of them did, there was a chance it'd cause some worry.

What else? Who else was there who'd notice if he wasn't around? What unfinished business?

There were the guys down at the bar he went to two or three nights a week, more for the company than for the two or three flat beers he'd drink over the course of an evening. Nothing to worry over there; he was a regular at the bar, but not that steady a customer. Chances were he could be gone a month before his friends noticed that he hadn't been around.

Grandpa's lawyer. Yes; he had to get back to that man. Tim'd left behind unfinished business when he'd hurried away from the lawyer's office Sunday morning. At the very least he had to call before he left town.

The mortuary. Tim didn't want to think about the mortuary. Didn't want to have to deal with it. But Grandpa needed burying. Or cremation. Or whatever was appropriate; in his letter Grandpa said he'd have made his own arrangements a month or two before his time, said that Tim didn't have to worry about anything but signing a few papers. But Grandpa hadn't died the way he'd talked about in the letter—ten years from now, quiet and painless in his sleep—and Tim had to figure out what Grandpa would have wanted. Figure out quickly, too; corpses don't keep well above ground. (Or so Tim assumed. The fact was that he'd never had to deal with a corpse before in his life—Grandpa had taken care of things with Mom and Dad.)

He bit his lip. He had to get the arrangements started before he left. Ought to do it now, if it were possible. Looked at his watch: eight o'clock. The funeral director was at home with his kids, watching television, if he had any sense. Tim'd have to call first thing in the morning.

But what should he tell the man to do?

Which was when it finally occurred to Tim where he had to look to find out what Grandpa had planned for himself. In the sheaf of papers he'd got from the lawyer Sunday morning. And Tim knew what he'd find there, if he looked hard enough. Not instructions; Grandpa had honestly expected to have taken care of that himself.

A deed to a grave.

And Tim knew that grave would be one of a pair. The empty grave would be Grandpa's; in the dirt beside it would be his wife. Tim's great-great-grandmother.

Tim had never seen her grave, but he knew that she was buried in the county someplace. Grandpa didn't talk about her—hadn't talked about her. Not on purpose, anyway. And those few times Tim had seen him wander onto the subject, Grandpa's eyes had got sad and kind of lonely; not mourning her, exactly. Missing her.

Yes. That was where Grandpa would want to be.

He glanced at the suitcases again. Which was the one he'd put the papers in? That one. He leaned over, pulled the zipper. Found the manila envelope sitting at the very top.

It took a while to find the deed he was looking for; the envelope was full of deeds and documents and certificates. The deed for Grandpa's house. A passbook for a Swiss bank account, the account's balance listed on its ultimate page—a balance so high that it surprised Tim, made him uncomfortable in a whole new way. More deeds: property all over the country, and in Europe, too. Most of it seemed to be undeveloped land, but not all of it. A statement from a stockbroker that went on for several pages detailing the year's performance of Grandpa's holdings. Extensive holdings.

None of that was news to Tim. Grandpa didn't live like he was rich, and neither had Tim's folks. But there was money in the family, money enough that none of them ever had to worry about working at a job that didn't suit him. Oh, the amounts were a surprise. The papers seemed to say that Grandpa was worth so much . . . so much that the numbers became abstract. More papers: legal-looking, notarized documents that Tim couldn't easily identify. Things that were too dry to read. He moved them to the back of the folder.

There. A handwritten letter on white legal paper, brittle and dingy with age. What was that doing there? The letters from Grandpa were all together, at the front of the pile. And this one was so much older than the others—the paper looked old as though Grandpa'd written it while Tim was still a small boy. Tim pulled it from the stack, began to read.

> *Dear Tim,*
>   *There is a man, Tim, who frightens me. All of my life I have known this man. Or known of him, more to the point: I have never met him, never seen him. Nor has he seen me, praise God; if he had my life would not be worth a whit. But from a distance I have watched him, or watched his works and their effects.*
>   *He is not a bad man—not entirely, and perhaps not at all. But neither is he entirely good; he will stop at nothing to achieve his ends. Good or bad, he has no heart at all. I have seen dead men and women strewn in a trail he has left behind him. I have seen him cripple children and leave them to their own devices. Famines, plagues, wars, worse things—these are tools he uses freely. If he has regrets, I see no sign of it.*
>   *And still I can't condemn him without reservation. His works, his goals—they are worthy things. At worst they try to be. His hand, like yours, mine, and those of our forebears, is long through time. Longer: he is older far than I am. The legacy of his years is full of great works and accomplishments; like me, like*

*our predecessors, he has used his time on earth
to steer our world toward better things. More
than once I have seen him pressing events in
the same direction that I press them myself.
But don't mistake me: we aren't the same. His
means are ruthless. I take great care of the
tools I use. His ends are often . . . I find
them ill-conceived. Perhaps he sees longer than
I can, and works to lead the world to Paradise
through Hell. But that's no path I'll suffer to
abide if I can do otherwise.*

*What other plans would one expect from a
man who would guide the world but has no
soul?*

*None of this is the reason that he frightens
me.*

*He frightens me because whatever his
sins, whatever evil he may stoop to commit, he
is one of us. More: ultimate father of all of us,
for he was the First Steward of the Cross.*

*Some who wrote in the book of our fore-
bears call him Old Abraham; and some call him
the Bleeding Man. Know him by his bleeding
eyes; if you ever see him pray he has not seen
you. If he has it's certain you will die, and
likely that the Cross is lost to him. (Pray God
he never gets it. If he does, everything—
everything—is forfeit.) The hour that you see
him, take the Cross and run. Leave your life
and all you know behind, and never look back
toward it. Move quickly, and run far.*

The letter stopped just there, two-thirds the way
down its second page. In the middle of a sentence, in the
middle of a line. Why had Grandpa stopped? For all the
letter told Tim, it left more unexplained—First Steward
of the Cross? How? Why? It meant the Bleeding Man
was Tim's ancestor. Didn't it?

And besides, the Bleeding Man who was Old
Abraham wasn't *that* dangerous. Tim had seen him twice
now, maybe more than that, in Kansas and here in

Tampa probably and back when he was still in his young teens. . . . Of all those times, it was only the most recent, up in Kansas, that Tim had felt afraid.

And why *hadn't* Grandpa finished the letter? It almost looked as though he'd reconsidered it, as though he'd left it deliberately unfinished and intended to discard the letter.

And if the Bleeding Man was as murderous as Grandpa said, why was Tim still alive?

(*He killed Grandpa. He'd've killed me too if he thought it'd get him the Cross. Worse than that: I'm alive because he thinks I might lead him to it.*)

Tim lifted the letter off the stack, set it on the kitchen table. Maybe the rest of it was somewhere out of place among the rest of these—

There. What he'd set out to find in the first place; a sheet of white vellum made yellow by time.

GRAVE RIGHT

And another, all but identical, just behind it. A careful diagram of a hillside cemetery, somewhere up in . . . he looked carefully at the map just below the diagram. Yes, that was Lutz these days. The roads had changed, but three of them still ran nearly the same course, and one still bore the name it had—Tim scanned the document, looking for a date—in 1885.

1885. Had Grandpa's wife been dead that long? Tim looked for mention of a burial date, and found none. These were only deeds to a pair of adjoining cemetery plots, not death certificates. Grandpa could have bought them anytime at all before she'd died, or even a little while after.

Tim set the grave rights on the table, beside the letter. Went back to searching through the stack. He looked at each sheet carefully, scanning both sides of every one for Grandpa's handwriting. But thorough as he was, he found nothing that could have been the rest of that letter. When he'd looked over the last of the papers, he put them back into their envelope, clipped it shut, went to his office, and put the bundle into the top drawer of his desk.

When he got back to the kitchen, he noticed the suitcases again and realized that he had to do laundry tonight if he was going to have clean clothes for the trip tomorrow. Sighed, got up. Carried the bags into his bedroom, emptied them onto the bed. Sorted out the dirty laundry. Stuffed it into the half-full hamper in the bedroom closet, and began to haul the hamper out to his car. When he got to the front door he hesitated; he had a nagging sense that there was something else he needed to do before he left the apartment. But it was only a sense, nothing clearer. He stopped a moment, tried to root out the source (standing by the door, fumbling with his keys for most of a minute and a half) but hard as he tried to root it out, Tim couldn't. And finally he gave up, and locked the door, and carried the bulging plastic hamper out to the car.

But even if he gave up on the feeling, it didn't give him up. It stayed with him all the way to the laundromat, shadowed him as a tiny dread—an irrational certainty that he'd made some awful mistake whose effect waited for him, foregone, only a moment in his future.

And kept with him for long hours after that. All through washing and drying his clothes, and while he folded them. But nothing happened—nothing untoward. Not even anything striking or remarkable.

But something else came on as he loaded the last of the clean clothes into the trunk of his car—another feeling. This one much more familiar than blind dread. Very familiar, since it had haunted him all through his trip to Nebraska: the sensation that there was someone watching. The first hint of that feeling triggered something in him.

Tim snapped. And in a moment he was shouting.

Perhaps he snapped because of the tension he'd built up in hours of waiting for his dread to become real—or perhaps it was pent anger at the lurking and the beating and the wolves and the murder of his Grandpa and every other horrible thing that'd happened in the

Midwest. And maybe it didn't matter; maybe it was just time to stop trying to hold it all in.

Maybe it was time for rage.

Whatever the reason.

As soon Tim felt the eyes somewhere pressing on him, he looked around and tried to spot them. And when he saw nothing, he started screaming.

"Who are you, damn it? Why are you out there, sneaking around in the dark? Why don't you come out here, where I can see you, and ask me what I'm doing? Come on. I'll tell you, all right. There's more than one damn thing I'd like to tell you!"

There wasn't any answer, of course. Though he got a nervous glance from an older woman filling her laundry cart from a car at the far end of the parking lot. And the look on the face of the laundromat manager—that was much worse. (Standing staring on the far side of the plate-glass window, left hand perched indignant on his hip. The right was on his forehead, pushing back his hair, showing his eyes bulge with fear and anger and incredulity. Looking at him, Tim was unsure whether he was about to run and call the police, run for his life, bolt the front door, or maybe even step outside and try to wring Tim's neck. To look at him—tall, heavyset, broadchested—Tim thought it was likely he could do it.)

Most days Tim would have seen people look at him like that and want to crawl under a rock somewhere and hide and never come out. But just then he was too angry, too tired of being haunted and intimidated to care what anyone else thought about him. He looked around again, trying to figure out where he'd be if he were spying on a man about to leave a laundromat. . . .

There was the laundromat itself. Well lit, and kind of obvious—which almost made it an elegant hiding place: who ever thinks to look in the obvious place? No, not there. The only people inside were the manager, the older woman who'd just hurried through the door, laundry cart in tow, and the dark-skinned man (Arabic? Pakistani? Indian?) with the three small children. Tim looked at each of them carefully, and knew seeing them that none were spying on him.

There were woods on the left, and there was the empty lot to the right. Beyond the lot a warehouse with neither doors nor windows on the side that faced him. Across the street an abandoned diner with a chained-off parking lot.

The lot and the diner were empty. The warehouse was a useless place for spies. The woods—the woods might well be a wonderful place from which to hide and watch, but they'd be useless the moment Tim left; there was no way to get a car out of them quickly.

And Tim was about to leave. The watching had started only a moment before he'd been ready to go.

The street.

The street was lined with parked cars. All of them empty, by the look of them. . . .

But all you have to do to make a car look empty is lie down on the front seat.

Tim closed the trunk, headed out toward the street.

Started on the far left on the near side of the street, with the polished white late-model Buick. Something was wrong with the car's grille; it looked as though the driver had recently had a run-in with a telephone pole. (No—not a telephone pole. The damage to the grille was deep, but it went no deeper than the grille. It was the sort of wreck you'd expect from hitting something much softer than a telephone pole, and at high speed. A small animal, perhaps. Or a child.)

Tim looked carefully into the windows of the Buick—half-convinced by the scar on its front that he'd found his lurker—but the car was empty. And for all that there was something plainly evil about that grille, the interior was innocent enough.

What am I going to do if I find someone?

And surprised himself when the answer came quicker and harder than he expected:

I'm going to reach into the window—break the damn thing if I have to—and drag the bastard out by the scruff of his neck. And then I'll teach him whose business he ought to be minding.

Next was an old Dodge, battered and shabby looking, its pale-blue paint chalky with oxidation from years in the Florida sun.

This isn't him, Tim thought. He was sure that the Bleeding Man's pawn would be better equipped than that.

But he was wrong.

Even as he walked toward it, someone in the old Dodge was sitting up in the front seat. Cranking the engine, turning on the headlights. It took Tim a long instant to realize what was going on, and in that time the driver already had the car in motion, back and forth, easing it out of its parallel parking slot.

No, damn it. You're not getting away that easy.

And took three long running strides and launched himself at the car, as though it were a game beast and he some primeval hunter. He landed on it hard because a car is not an animal, because its flanks are made of steel instead of flesh. Knees bashing hard on the trunk; chest on the rear window so hard it amazed him that the glass didn't shatter. The knees and the chest hurt, but not near so bad as his face where his upper front teeth and his nose smashed hard into the place where the back windshield met the roof.

The car was out of its parking spot now, and beginning to gain speed as it moved into the street. Tim reached up, grabbed the left edge of the roof, and held on for dear life.

"*Stop*, damn you! Stop this damn thing, get out of it, and look me in the eye!"

The driver didn't stop. Didn't slow down. Just the opposite, in fact; the car was still gaining speed.

Tim pounded on the rear window with his free right fist, hoping to break it. It did no good. The glass didn't feel as though it were likely to give at all.

We've got to end up at a traffic light sooner or later. Then the driver'll have to stop. And what was he going to do then? It wasn't as though he'd be any more able to break in than he was now—not if the windows were made of something stronger than ordinary glass.

Up over the top. If I can get a good view through the windshield, if I can get a look at the driver—it's better than nothing. Probably all I can get, if there's no way to drag him out of there. Better yet: if he could get in front of the windshield, he could block the driver's sight of the road—he'd have to stop to get rid of Tim.

Hell—I don't even have to wait till he stops. I can crawl over this damn thing right now. It was true—or felt true, anyway. The ride on the outside of the car seemed a lot more stable than he'd have imagined.

Tim pressed against the trunk with the soles of his shoes, used the forward press to ease up onto the roof.

Farther, farther—and he was up on top of the car, and his perch still felt amazingly secure. Or did until he made the mistake of looking off to the side at the city rushing by, and suddenly there was vertigo right down to the center of his deepest bones, and the wind felt like a hurricane that made him nothing but a flag snapping in the breeze.

Calm down, damn it. Panic now and you'll get yourself killed.

Closed his eyes. Drew a deep, deep breath.

Keep going. Forward. Then you can worry about getting off this thing.

He didn't bother opening his eyes this time. He didn't need the scenery draining away his nerve. And besides, the wind up at the front was so intense it would have dried them till they burned.

Forward. A little further. He gripped the roof with both arms now, one hand gripping each edge, his arms bent into a wide hug as much as the curve of the roof allowed. Inching up now one arm at a time, farther, farther—his forehead was cresting the windshield—

Cursing from inside the car, and the car was slowing. Just a little at first, and then more and more— the driver had his foot on the brake. Tim opened his eyes—

Just in time to hear the sound of the brakes locking, tires screeching.

Just in time to lose his purchase on the car as the force of deceleration became so great that it threw him off the roof. Out over the windshield of the pale-blue Dodge, and into the street.

He almost managed to get a look at the driver before he sailed out into oblivion (dark glasses green onyx in the dim glow from the dash lights, and the hood of a windbreaker pulled up over the hair looking so much like the cowl of the Angel of Death)—and then he hit the pavement, headfirst, and everything went black.

Unconscious on the roadside as cars roar by, Tim dreams a dream. In his dream he sees three figures, living figures cut from some luminescent stone shining bright against the formless night that encompasses his vision.

All three of them are archetypal—very nearly they are statues of character than they are persons with character. So truly is each of them the model of his type that there is no room in any for the small changes and gridwork of fine inconsequential flaws that give personality.

Seeing them, Tim thinks: This, these people. People? Whatever; these are the ones that the first men dreamt when they made their minor gods.

First of these figures is one Tim calls the Wise Man Who Loves. Seeing him, Tim knows him intimately. (This is the nature of archetypes: to see them is to know them.) He is deep-hearted and warm, and his eyes see the most amazing things—when he sees a fallen leaf he knows the tree that dropped it, and when, and why. Things that you or I might learn, if we had time enough and tools enough to learn from careful study of the evidence. But this man needs no tools, and he knows as quickly as he sees—and where you and I are prone to error when we comb for evidence, this man is never wrong.

This man is so like Grandpa that Tim cannot help but know the connection between them. Not that he looks much at all like Tim's grandfather—rather he bears the physical form that is the true face of William Fischer's soul.

Beside the first figure, standing close, is a second, brighter figure.

This figure is mirror image of the first. Is he (she?

Tim isn't certain) the Blind Keeper of the Grail? Yes, that name will do. It is not foul by nature where the other is fair, but blind and broad and soft where the first is sharp and deep. And for that it has no weakness, but rather enormous strength—its softness is the softness of sand, which yields easily but cannot break. It blindness is the blindness of the sea, which has and needs no visions; its broadness is like unto air that covers all the world.

Tim has never seen this archetype in all his days, but he knows that it, like the first, is a possibility for him. Both of these archetypes have modeled for Stewards of the Cross.

The third encompasses all virtues of the first two—but it is utterly without a soul. This is the Bleeding Man. Look at his face, which is no face but rather blood-bright piercing eyes set into an otherwise featureless skull. Look deep to see his heart, which is no heart at all but rather the desire to consume one.

Look at his mind, which is entirely calculation without mercy or consideration.

Look for his soul and find nothing.

He came to sometime later—Tim was never certain how much later—bruised and battered and all but broken, lying in the hard, rough red clay at the side of the road.

There were lights in his eyes.

"He's got his eyes open," someone said. A man's voice, deep and mature but not yet old. Just enough of a north-Florida accent that Tim heard no accent at all. There was no way to know anything more than that; the light in Tim's eyes made it impossible to see anything else. "Are you okay, son? What's happened to you?"

Disorientation—the same out-of-phase he always woke with, but much, much worse. Where was he? When? This wasn't any bed, and that was a clue, and so was the fact that he lay out of doors. This was a roadside, wasn't it? Had to be. Red clay like this (Tim knew it by the chalky-gritty touch beneath the fingers of his left hand) meant Georgia, Alabama—maybe Tennessee. And Tim was pretty sure he wasn't in any of those places. But home in Florida they'd truck the stuff in, lay it in the roadbed before they put down tar because the sandy Florida dirt was useless stuff to build a road on top of.

Lying blacked out and bruised on the side of a road, deep in the night and a flashlight in my eyes. . . .

And then it began to come back to him. The laundry; the lurking; jumping onto the trunk of the car as it tried to get away from him. And he groaned.

"Can you hear me, son? I said, 'Are you all right?' "

Tim tried to sit up. Failed. "Uh—" partly a tic; partly another groan "—don't know. Where am I? What's going on?"

"He's fine." Another voice this time, and suddenly the light wasn't in his eyes anymore.

Night. Streetlights off in the distance; warehouses across the street. The thrum of I-275 not far away. Somewhere on Nebraska Avenue, it looked like— somewhere up above Fletcher, where it turned to a potholed two-lane ruin.

"Nebraska Avenue—about a quarter mile south of Skipper Road. What are you doing here, not knowing where you are and looking like you tried to French-kiss a semi-trailer? You feel like you need a doctor? Call you an ambulance if you want."

"I'll be up in a minute." Police—these men were police officers. No, not police; this was north of the city line. They had to be Hillsborough County sheriff's deputies. He should have realized it sooner. Anybody could buy industrial-size flashlights like those, but they were standard-issue for the sheriff's department, and almost always when you saw one it was a deputy who was carrying it.

Things were enough of a mess already and the last thing Tim needed was to get the police caught up in them. He forced himself to sit up, in spite of the way it made his head swim, in spite of the wrenching in the thin muscles that webbed his ribs.

"You going to tell us how the hell you got here or what?" The second deputy's voice, impatient, just shy of demanding. If Tim didn't tell him something soon he'd get nasty. He thought fast, lied badly.

"I was with a few friends, last I remember," he said. "I was lying on the trunk of one guy's car, talking with the rest of the guys. Must've dozed off. Not sure how the hell I got here—maybe it was his idea of a joke to take off down the road with me sleeping that way. Maybe he just didn't see me there. I don't know. Either way, he must not've known I fell off here—Jim ain't so bad a guy as to leave me for dead."

The second deputy looked skeptical; the first one wore no expression at all.

"Jim, huh? What did you say this guy's last name was?"

Tim blinked. He was going to get caught in this lie if he didn't watch himself.

"I don't believe I did say, sir. Him taking off with me on top of the trunk like that—that'd be illegal, wouldn't it?" The first deputy nodded. "I thought it was. And I can't see getting my friend into that kind of grief. If you know what I mean."

The first deputy rolled his eyes, turned away. The second shook his head.

"You don't really expect us to believe a story like that, do you? Be serious."

Tim shrugged. "I don't see as it matters, sir. I don't have any reason to lie to you—so far as I know there isn't any law against lying banged-up on the side of Nebraska Avenue."

The deputy looked away, after his partner. Who was already back in the patrol car.

"Have it your way, then." And he turned and left. In a moment he was getting into the passenger seat of the cruiser; a moment after that the car was roaring away into the night, and Tim was standing alone in the dark in the middle of nowhere, a hell of a long way from his car.

And the only way to get back to it at that hour of the night was to walk.

And walk.

Could've offered me a ride back to my car, if they'd had any common courtesy. But when he put himself in their position, with Tim so obviously lying to them, he could kind of see why they hadn't. And thought about it

some more, and decided that it was just as well they
hadn't, since taking him back to the laundromat would
have made the holes in his story stand out even more
starkly.

Well, the walk wasn't as bad as it could have been.
Tim consoled himself with that. After the first quarter
mile he managed to forget all about the aches and pains
and bruises.

After the second the walk almost became a pleasure;
south of Fletcher Nebraska Avenue was mostly im-
proved, wide smooth lanes and broad white-concrete
sidewalks on both sides of the road. By the time he'd
gone a mile (halfway, now, between Fletcher and
Fowler—and halfway to the laundromat) Tim knew that
the long walk really was for the best, so far as his body
was concerned. It was working out the tightness from
the beatings and batterings he kept walking into these
last few days.

Another half hour and he was crossing the empty lot
beside the laundromat—half a mile south of Busch
Boulevard, two or three blocks shy of the Hillsborough
River.

The laundromat was still open. Came as a surprise
to Tim, but it shouldn't have—the words OPEN 24 HOURS
were in big letters up there on the marquee, just below
the even-larger LAUNDERAMADAMA.

The laundromat was open, and it was empty except
for the manager. The same barrel-chested man who'd
looked at Tim like he was a lunatic when he'd started
shouting. He stood by the glass front door, watching Tim
as he approached. He had a look about him that said he
wanted to know what in God's name was going on, and
Tim couldn't blame him for that.

But he couldn't cope with it, either; in his mind's
eye Tim saw the scene with the two deputies replaying
itself.

Damn. Damn damn damn. And suddenly he was
feeling the bruises and the battering again. And feeling
dog-tired from a walk too long when he wasn't fit for it.
And he wanted to go home and crawl into bed and pull
the world in over him like it was some great quilt.

But hiding from the world wasn't a great idea. Wasn't even an option, when you got right down to it. So he looked the man in the eye from halfway across the empty lot, and he called out to him.

"Evening," he said. "You having a good one?"

The manager nodded. "Fair enough," he answered. Wary, but not threatening. Not entirely unfriendly, either.

Tim nodded at the man, headed toward his car casual as though he'd just come out of the laundromat. He almost got away with it—got the car unlocked, got the door open, even started to slide in behind the wheel. But then he felt the manager's hand grip his upper arm. Not holding so hard that it hurt, but firm enough to make it real clear that Tim wasn't going anyplace without seeing after his accounts.

"You want to tell me about it?" He said it like it was a question, but it was clear from the man's tone that there was only one answer he was going to take.

Tim frowned. "No," he said. "There's nothing I can say."

"I could call the police. They might be interested to hear. . . ."

Tim shook his head. "Yeah, you could. So? You think they ain't got enough to do already? You think they've got time for me?"

There was no answer.

It wasn't until he pulled out of Launderamadama's parking lot that Tim realized he wasn't going directly home. It wasn't a conscious thing by a long stretch—but it wasn't exactly involuntary, either. He did his three-point turn, got the car facing out toward Nebraska Avenue—and then he turned right where he should have turned left if he was heading toward his apartment. And suddenly he was driving north, toward Busch Boulevard, and damned if he knew why.

He took his foot off the gas pedal, let the car slow: it was just a mistake. He needed to turn around and go home. Then it occurred to him that it wasn't like a

mistake at all, that it felt purposeful and necessary, even
if it made no sense at all. So he put his foot back on the
gas, and he let his self recede into the dusty corners of
his mind. And he drove—or, more exactly, he let the
preconscious roots of his mind guide the car toward what
destination it thought it needed.

So Tim watched from his far grey perch as he drove
the car up Nebraska Avenue, out of the city—retracing
the ground he'd just spent an hour and a half covering on
foot. It only took five minutes to reach the spot where
he'd started—and when he got there, Tim surprised
himself. Instead of pulling over, stopping the car, looking around as he'd expected he would, he just drove on.
Past Skipper, on up to Bearss Avenue, and then round
and about through miles and miles of circuitous back-
road highway. Mostly east, and sometimes south, but
most all of that time Tim had no idea what direction he
was going. He didn't know these roads. He'd never
driven them. But the part of him that guided the car was
always certain of its turns. It never hesitated at a stop
sign an instant longer than the law required. Never
doubled back; never found itself chasing down a dead
end.

And then, a thousand forevers later, Tim realized
that he was on 56th Street, just south of Fletcher.

*Where am I going—out to the bar to have a couple
beers?*

There wasn't any answer.

Up ahead, just south of Whiteway on 56th in
Temple Terrace was the beer bar where Tim hung out
with his friends. A mile or two ahead, anyway. He'd be
there in two minutes if he caught the light at 56th and
Fowler.

He was still detached, watching passively as some
distant part of him drove the car—but now he was
curious and watching more intently. Surely, it seemed to
him, if his unconscious mind needed a beer and the
company of friends—weren't there easier ways to do it?
More direct, more ordinary ways: a craving for beer, a
lonely twitch, a yen for familiar things? And why the ride

all through hell and creation in the north reaches of the
city?

I need to get things settled quickly, he thought. *If
my back-brain has got to go through all this to put a beer
into me, I must be falling apart at the seams.*

Sure enough, Tim found himself turning right onto
Whiteway. Left twenty yards later—through the back lot
of the Temple Terrace Dairy Queen. Along the back
access to the little shopping center, until he reached its
remotest corner. And pulled into a parking slot, and
killed the engine.

Had the old blue Dodge come here—were the people
who'd been watching him expecting Tim to come here
tonight? Still in the half-trance, he scanned the parking lot.
Was he looking for the Dodge? He didn't see it. No, not
the Dodge. He was walking toward a late-model Toyota.
Looking carefully at the license plate—a Georgia tag,
which didn't mean anything to Tim one way or the
other. Looking carefully at the exterior, looking for
scratches, dents? There weren't any. Only polished, new-
looking, navy-blue paint. Looking in through the
windows—it didn't matter here that it was night. This lot
was lit with close-spaced streetlights—not bright as day,
exactly, but close enough.

There was nothing inside the car at all—nothing but
the seats, the dash, the steering wheel. Not even so
much as a speck of dirt on the carpet.

And then Tim looked up, and suddenly the trance
was over, and he was in the parking lot behind the
Nine-to-Five Bar, standing hunched over a car that
wasn't his own. Feeling, for the instant that it took him
to back away from the window, like a car thief.

What the hell was all of that about? Tim waited
three long beats for some kind of response from down
inside him, but there wasn't any answer. He shrugged.
Long as I'm here, I might as well get myself a drink.

Crossed the bright-lit lot, went in through the back
door. Tim almost always used the back door, since there
was hardly any parking to speak of in the front.

Inside the bar was mostly empty. The only one
there from Tim's usual crowd was Donny James—sitting

at the bar with a full mug of beer and a half-empty pitcher in front of him. When he saw Tim he patted the bar stool on his right.

"Tim," he said, "how do? Have a seat. Have a beer." He reached over the bar, grabbed a clean mug from the far side of it.

Tim sat down, but he wasn't for drinking any of Donny's beer. Donny did construction work, and that paid well enough, but he didn't like to work any more than was necessary. A week here, a week there; enough to pay the rent and keep him in folding money, but no more than that. When he drank (which was often), he drank what was cheap. Tim wasn't especially fond of cheap beer. Wasn't that fond of beer at all, for that matter—what he liked was sipping good whiskey, long and slow. But the Nine-to-Five had a license for beer and wine, and that was all; and anyhow even if Tim could've gotten a whiskey here, and even if he could've gotten one that was good (not likely, since it wasn't the kind of place that sold expensive things), it wouldn't have been appropriate. It was the kind of place where drinking whiskey warm and undiluted from a glass would have been macho and showy. That was the last thing Tim wanted.

Tim got the waitress's attention, ordered a Budweiser—for as Tim was concerned Bud was all right. Not that it was anything he'd order if there was something better to be had.

The waitress brought his beer, and Tim slipped two bills onto the counter; when she brought his change he left it for her on the counter.

Donny was watching the big television set above the bar. Which looked as though it were tuned to MTV—hard to be sure, since the music that came from the jukebox had nothing to do with the picture at all.

Sometimes Tim wondered why he spent so many evenings at the Nine-to-Five. The bar didn't really suit his taste, and there were things about it that he found honestly unpleasant. Noise. Thin beer. (Bud was the best they carried, bar Michelob, and Tim had never found the difference between the two to be worth an extra penny.) The awful music from the jukebox. The only things about the place he liked without reservation were the hot deli-style sandwiches and the salty-fresh potato chips that they served from the big Charles Chips tin—and even if he liked them, he wasn't generally hungry when he got here, and he didn't order them often.

Why did he end up here—what was it, two, three nights a week?—More sometimes? There was something about it that was home, he guessed. If he thought about it too long it made no sense at all, but all the same Tim knew that it was so.

"Where you been?" Donny asked. Tim glanced up, saw that there was a Coke commercial on the television. "Haven't seen you around all week."

"Out of town," Tim said. "Family business." He liked Donny well enough, but he wasn't up to telling him about Grandpa's death, and there wasn't much of the rest of it that he could tell.

Donny nodded sympathetically—family business was something Donny could understand. Donny's own family was always leaning on him in the worst way, and Donny, like a fool, always sat still for it. His brother Jessie was always in trouble with the law, constantly calling Donny at odd hours of the morning to bail him out of the county lockup. Jessie lived on Donny's couch more than anywhere else, and he ate Donny's food, and ran the AC full blast. Sometimes he'd even take money from his brother's wallet. Donny's folks abused his good nature, too. The man was twenty-eight years old, and they still had him over every weekend doing yard work till dusk, Saturday and Sunday both—this from folks who "just couldn't see spending the money to send a boy like Donny to college." Tim had been there to hear Donny's old man say those words, at a barbecue back of Donny's apartment complex two summers back. He still got angry when he thought about it.

But Donny didn't. He'd just shook his head and rolled his eyes and smiled ruefully. Later when he'd talked to Tim he'd said his dad didn't really mean it the way it sounded. Because it wasn't polite to argue about a thing like that, Tim had kept his mouth shut. But he couldn't think of anything Donny's father might have meant that wasn't something vile.

Donny nudged him. "Who's that?" Tim looked away from the wall he was staring at. Saw Donny refilling his beer mug, saw him nodding at a woman at the far end of the bar.

Something familiar about that woman, Tim thought. But he was damned if he could put his finger on it. "Can't place her," Tim said. "But I feel like I ought to be able to. You recognize her?"

Donny shook his head. "Wish I did."

She was a pretty woman, and more than pretty. Not striking, exactly—quiet-pretty, with ordinary features that set *just so* against each other . . . amber-brown eyes, short, straight black hair just coarse enough that it had a powder cast where straight-haired people usually had a sheen. Slight, fine-boned arms and shoulders. Olive-tone Mediterranean complexion—but the lines of her face weren't Mediterranean at all; they were the soft rounded lines you expect on an Irish face, or Scots, or Dutch. Tied to all of that was the something else that Tim couldn't place, the something familiar that—

She looked up from her drink—red wine—into Tim's eyes, and suddenly Tim realized he was staring at her. And something about that woman who wasn't striking struck Tim in the most crucial way. Like—like something he'd touched had touched deep deep inside him, only infinitely more pleasant. As though . . . as though he'd just met the woman he was born to love and knew her even though he'd never set eyes on her before—never in all his life.

He blushed, looked away. The whole thought was absurd. What was he, an animal in rut to leer all carnal urges at a woman he'd never ever seen before?

If she'd been close enough to hear he would have apologized.

Had he seen her before? Why *did* she seem so damned familiar?

He glanced up at her again, trying to place her—

And saw that the woman was staring at him now,

wearing an amused smirk that made it seem as though she'd read his mind and thought that he was awfully silly.

Distracting. Very distracting. He *was* flirting, damn it, and that was the last thing he wanted. There was an itch at the base of his skull that wanted to know what it was about this woman, and how was he supposed to figure out what she meant to him if he got caught up in flirting?

If I look away long enough, she'll forget about me and look the other way. Then I can steal another glance, try to figure out. . . .

"What's going on with you?" Donny nudged him, brought Tim up out of the funk that had him staring intently at the empty aluminum beer keg that sat on the floor behind the bar. (Studying the darned thing, intent as though it were the secret key to the hidden meaning of life.) "You sure you don't know that woman? Sure acting like you do. And she's got a look on her face like she knows you awful well."

"Huh? No, nothing going on. I was looking at her, trying to figure out what made her look familiar, and she caught me staring. Pretty embarrassing."

Donny looked skeptical. "If you say so."

"Don't look at me like that. It is embarrassing. I'm not some damned masher."

"How's that? What's wrong with staring at a woman? I do it all the time."

That was true, all right. Donny was blatant about the things that were on his mind. It didn't wear that badly on him, though—mostly because he was casual about it. As though it didn't even occur to him to keep a lid on things. More than once Tim'd seen him proposition a woman before he'd said another word to her. Most women ignored him with disarmed endurance. A few would look angrily away. And every once in a long while there was a woman who was charmed by Donny's frank, easy advances. It'd mystified Tim every time he'd seen one walk away with Donny.

Donny belched, nudged Tim with his elbow again. "So? You going to tell me what's wrong with staring at a woman or not?"

Tim sighed, looked up toward the ceiling, and shook his head. "I know, Donny, I know. I've seen you do that. Nothing *wrong* with it when you do it." And that, it seemed to Tim, was exactly true. "But it just doesn't feel right to me."

Donny set his beer down on the counter. Another belch—louder, this time. "You're one peculiar man, Tim Fischer."

"I guess you'd know."

Donny took that as the mock insult it was intended to be, gave Tim a shove with the heel of his hand. "Go on, boy. Don't you give me any of that."

Tim was still trying to think of something sharp to say when he felt the tap on his other shoulder. He turned, expecting to see Rick Mitchell or Frankie Munsen or John Taylor or one or another of the boys—

And there she was.

The woman from the far end of the bar.

What? What's she doing here?

It wasn't an especially politic thing to think, but at least he hadn't said it.

"Hi," she said. "Is this seat taken? Can I buy you a drink?"

What? "No—yes." Tim was blushing, head to toe; he could feel it. What was this about? This wasn't the kind of bar where a guy went to meet anybody at all—and it sure wasn't a pickup place. More like a red-neck bar, only a little different since it was full of young people from the suburbs. "I mean: sure. Sit down if you'd like. And I'll buy *you* a drink."

But all he could think was, *What on God's earth am I doing?*

It was a Sunday morning—early-early on a Sunday morning—when Tim found out about sex. It was the summer after he turned twelve, and he was old enough that somebody should have thought to tell him about it already, and maybe they had thought about it but just hadn't gotten around to it yet. That was his dad's thinking on the issue, at least: The boy was only twelve, after all; there was time enough before his body gave him the lecture itself, wasn't there?

Well, the truth was that there wasn't.

Grandpa got caught by surprise, just like he always seemed to get caught by surprise when Tim hit a milestone—only Tim suspected that maybe Grandpa wasn't surprised at all, but only hanging back, watching as Tim discovered things for himself. Standing in the distance, watching to be certain nothing got out of hand.

Oh, it wasn't like Tim knew nothing at all. Not quite. There were things he heard from the kids at school, but they sounded awful silly. People didn't really do things like *that*, did they? It all sounded so . . . undignified. And kind of unsanitary. Maybe even painful. And there was that book he read, back when he was six—the one about Where Babies Come From. It had this picture of two frogs in it, one of them on top of the other, doing something but it was hard to tell what from that profile. But people weren't frogs, were they?

They sure weren't.

When Tim thought back about it later, he was pretty sure that that was how it was. After all, none of it would have happened like it did if Grandpa hadn't slept in that Sunday morning when Tim got up so early.

Mom and Dad were on vacation, taking their "second honeymoon" (only to Tim's count it had to be at least their fifth or sixth), and Tim was staying with Grandpa for the weeks that they'd be out of town. Nothing strange about that; as time went on Mom seemed to resign herself to Grandpa and the way he got on with Tim, and lately Tim'd been spending a lot of time over at Grandpa's big old house.

Tim woke all at once, clearheaded and ready for the day, just the way he always did. It was early—earlier even than he usually woke up, so early that it was still dark outside, and in Florida in June that's very early indeed. Tim got out of bed, shucked his pajamas, put on shorts, a T-shirt, tennis shoes. Opened the door to his bedroom at Grandpa's (two doors down from Grandpa's own room) and headed for the stairs.

When he passed Grandpa's room, Tim saw the old

man splayed out in his wide four-poster bed with the
enormous crucifix over the headboard. Snoring.

"Grandpa?"

So hard asleep he might as well have been dead to
the world.

Almost always when Tim got up Grandpa was
already downstairs cooking breakfast—Tim might be an
early riser, but Grandpa was almost always up before
him. Not this time: the kitchen was empty, quiet, dark
because no one was up yet to turn the lights on. Tim took
care of that quick enough himself: turned on the overhead lamp. Hauled the stepladder out of the cupboard
closet, climbed up into the cereal cabinet, and got down
the raisin bran. And a bowl from the cabinet beside it.
Milk out of the fridge, and he was in business. Who said
Grandpa needed to be up for Tim to get breakfast? Not
Tim, no sir.

Trouble was that it only took him five minutes to eat
his breakfast once he'd made it. And then there was
nothing to do.

Tim sighed. Got up and cleaned up after himself—
put the cereal back up into the high cabinet, put the milk
back into the cooler. Set his bowl in the sink and ran
water into it so as to make it easier to clean.

Usually when he was staying here he'd get done
with breakfast and then he and Grandpa would talk, and
then maybe they'd figure out what to do with the day, or
Grandpa would have business that needed seeing after
and he'd ask Tim what he wanted to do, or Tim would
have to go to school or something and Grandpa would
take him there.

But Grandpa wasn't here—he wasn't awake—and
none of that could happen till he was.

What it meant was that Tim had to figure out
something to amuse himself with in the meantime.

Well, he could cope with that. When he was home
he always had to, since Mom and Dad never got up
when Tim did, unless it was a serious emergency. That
was the place to start: what would he do if he was home?
Watch TV, maybe—Sometimes there were cartoons on
Sunday mornings. Nah—not cartoons. He didn't feel like

cartoons today. He could go outside—Tim backed away from the sink (where cool sulfury water from the tap still ran through his cereal bowl) so that he could glance out the kitchen window. And saw that there was dawn creeping into the night-morning sky.

He shrugged, closed the tap: this was as good a time to get started as any time would be. He didn't know what he'd do once he got outside, but he wasn't going to find out standing here in front of the sink.

A moment later Tim was stepping out onto Grandpa's back stoop, closing the kitchen door behind him. There was morning fog everywhere, turning the start of the day into something eerie and magical and maybe even miraculous, since it somehow made him think of the room at the end of the third-floor hall, and What and Who was inside it. Maybe there was something magical about that mist, in fact; it was the kind of mist you expect to see every November morning in central Florida. But this was June, and morning fog was unlikely—if it wasn't completely unheard of.

But whether it was a sorcerous mist or just a fog brought on by high humidity and an unseasonably cool dawn, it wasn't the only thing that waited for Tim in Grandpa's back yard that morning.

No.

Fate waited for him in the back yard two doors over.

Her name was Erica Skolner.

Tim had known Erica Skolner for at least two years, and maybe he'd even seen her before that, but if he had it wasn't something he remembered. Erica was from Long Island, up by New York City, but she spent her summers with her grandparents. He'd met her the summer she was seven (Tim was ten that year), more because he couldn't avoid her than anything else. Met her when Tim and Donny James and Rick Mitchell were building a tree fort out in the deep woods back of Grandpa's place, and then Walt Fulton showed up with Erica in tow because she was a second- or third-hand cousin of his or some such, and he'd gotten stuck with seeing after her that morning. (This was June when Walt brought Erica to the tree fort, a good six weeks before

Walt died in that car wreck on the highway. Or maybe didn't die. A year later Walt showed up again at his school, and all kinds of strange stuff happened, and though it had been a good while since then Tim still wasn't clear on any of the details.)

Anyway, Tim and Donny and the boys had all done what they could to tolerate Erica that day, seeing as she was Walt Fulton's third-hand cousin and all. (Or maybe she was the daughter of a friend of his mom's? Tim couldn't remember.) It hadn't been easy to cope with, but they'd managed. And after that they hadn't had a whole lot of truck with her. Not that they'd gone out of their various ways to be mean or rude to her or anything like that. But after all, she was a girl, and who had time for girls when they were eight or nine or ten years old?—None of Tim's friends, anyhow. Still, even if he ignored her mostly, Tim had this vague, sort-of-peripheral awareness of Erica Skolner and summers at Grandpa's house.

And that day when he stepped out into the dawn on Grandpa's back stoop his awareness of her turned into another sort of thing altogether.

"Tim? You're Tim Fischer, aren't you? I know you." Surprised Tim, that was a sure thing. A voice right out of nowhere in the half-lit fog. Girl's voice, with a funny accent. Nobody attached to it that he could see, and at a time of not-yet-day when Tim hadn't expected to find anybody awake or about, nor anything to do but carve his name into the trunks of trees with one of those rusty nails from the can Grandpa kept in his shed.

"Who's there?" Tim called. "What do you want?" There was a little tremor in his voice that would have embarrassed Tim if he hadn't been too scared to hear it.

"It's Erica Skolner. Over here in Granny's garden." And Tim looked hard through the fog toward the Skolners' yard (just past the Johnsons', and back then you could see that far since Old Man Johnson's trees were still only saplings), and sure enough, there was Erica Skolner. Looking kind of alien the way all northerners did, and especially the ones from New York. Her accent was strange almost exactly the same way, Tim thought.

Like she was a Martian trying to talk Earth-language through her nose or something. "What are you looking so scared for? Something wrong?"

And now Tim *was* embarrassed. Bad enough he had to go and get scared of a nine-year-old *girl*; getting caught at it was humiliating. He decided right then and there that he was going to get as far from her as he could as fast as he could without making a big show of it. And then he was going to find someplace to bury his head in the sand so he wouldn't have to look anybody in the eye for a while.

"Nah. Nothing wrong. You just gave me a start is all."

Erica was coming toward him now, moving through the waist-high fog and he couldn't see her legs so she kind of did look like a ghost, all floaty-like. "A start, huh? You want to start something with me?" and then she smiled at him real funny, kind of like he'd never actually seen anybody smile in person, but he'd seen it on TV. If he'd been old enough to know the word, he would have thought it was a catty smile. But he wasn't old enough to know, and to Tim that smile was just one more alien thing, just as alien as everything else about Erica Skolner.

"What do you mean, start something with you? I don't fight with girls. Ain't right."

Erica sighed a sigh as unrecognizable as her smile. "You know what I mean," she said. Tim was about to protest that he didn't have the first idea, but there wasn't any chance, because Erica was still talking. "Never mind that. What're you going to do this morning? I never see you out this early. You doing something special?"

Tim shrugged. "Nah. Me and Grandpa always get up early—but Grandpa's sleeping in. I'm on my own till he wakes up." Tim bent down, fished a chip of concrete out of the sand at the base of Grandpa's stoop. Stood up again, hauled back, and threw the chip as far and as hard into the woods as he could. Damned if he knew why he did it, but it seemed important at the time. "Probably—ah, I don't know. Probably going to go play in the tree fort or something. How about you?"

Erica was looking off at the horizon with that same unknowable something in her eyes. "I'll come along, if you don't mind."

This is about when Tim began to smell a rat.

Well, not a rat, exactly, since whatever it was didn't seem quite that nasty. Not necessarily. But all the same his gut was telling him that there was something going on that wasn't at its root exactly what it seemed on the surface. And being as he still didn't have the first idea what it was this girl was leading him into, instinct should have kicked in and made him leery.

But instinct failed him. Or failed to function, anyway.

Oh, heck, Tim thought, *she's only a girl. And she's only nine. What could she do to me?*

"Suit yourself," Tim said. "You want to come up to the fort, I guess you're welcome. Heck, you helped to build it, didn't you?"

"You know I did."

Tim stepped off the stoop, started out across the yard. After a moment he realized that Erica wasn't following; paused, turned back, looked at her. "You going with me or what?"

She didn't answer right away. "Didn't you hear me say I was?"

Tim nodded. "What are you waiting for?"

She didn't answer. But she did start walking toward him.

Definitely. Definitely there was something going on with this girl that nobody'd taken the time to tell Tim about. He thought about that picture with the two frogs, shook his head. It was all, Tim decided, one of those mysteries that God didn't tell you about till He was good and ready. Which is to say probably never.

The fort was up in four close-together pines a hundred yards beyond the edge of Grandpa's yard—out where the pinewoods gave way to that big, open field of palmetto bushes with their saw-blade stems. Three storeys, each one a little higher above the one below than a boy could stand—but the first one was way up in the air, a good twelve, fifteen feet off the ground. Tim and Donny had had to shimmy up both pairs of trees in tandem (each of them one-handed, on account of holding hammer and nails and one end of the board under their arms) to get it up that high, and they'd had to be real careful nailing the darned things in, or they'd've ended up knocking each other off balance. But they'd managed to do it, and once those boards were up the rest of the fort had been easy, relatively speaking.

There wasn't any need to shimmy all the way up there now, of course. One of the last things they'd done when they built that fort was nail slats into the trunk of the biggest tree to use as ladder-steps. (Soon as he'd finished putting the last one up, Tim knew that it was stupid to wait that long to do it. Would have been real useful when they were building; saved all that wear and pine sap on his best pair of shorts. Not to mention on his thighs. And Donny's. And Frankie's. And Walt's.)

When Tim got to the ladder tree he went right up it, taking the steps two at a time. Didn't bother looking back to make sure Erica was going to be able to get up—at least partly because he was a little annoyed with her for acting so darned strange. Not that it mattered; by the time he was halfway up he could hear her right behind him, climbing more careful-like than he was, but darned near just as fast.

Tim got to the top step, swung himself around the broad trunk of the tree, onto the floor of the tree fort. The first storey didn't have any walls—just two-by-fours nailed waist-high for guardrails. And that one side that Tim'd swung in on didn't even have that.

Erica was at the top of the ladder now, eying the distance between the top step and the floor. Were her arms long enough to let her swing around the trunk the way Tim had. . . ? It looked as though they were, but it wasn't something you'd want to be wrong about, being as the drop was pretty severe. And even if Tim was annoyed at her, he didn't especially want to see her break her neck.

"You need a hand there?"

She glared at him, and Tim got the idea that he'd somehow hurt her pride.

"No," she said, "I'm fine." And she hugged the tree trunk with her right arm, gripped the topmost slat-step with her left hand to push, swing her legs forward, onto the floor of the fort—

Tim saw it all in slow motion. Saw how the arc of her swing wasn't quite enough to carry her up onto the platform that was the first floor of the fort. Only barely not enough, with the soles of her shoes scraping the edge, sliding back and away, and then her legs were arcing back again, and dragging her down. So much unexpected weight that her arms weren't strong enough or ready enough to hold her—

And he didn't think. Didn't think even for an instant how lunging forward to save her was going to get them both killed, instead of just Erica by herself. He just jumped, not to grab her near right arm because Erica was already falling and there wasn't time, but straight at the tree arms open like a swan dive that turned into a flying tackle pressing Erica into the pine bark, pasting her into the spot where she was falling and *bam!* Tim's head smacked like a hollow nut on the trunk. Hugged the tree and held for all he was worth and then some, Erica pressed inside his arms so hard it didn't matter what she had hold of or didn't—

This is where Tim learned that a body ought never to try to tackle a pine tree. Doesn't budge the tree an inch, and it leaves you bruised something fierce.

Still, still, once things stopped moving and ringing everything was mostly pretty all right. Tim's grip on the tree was hard enough and firm enough to hold both of them—miracle of miracles!—and if they were just careful how they got themselves disentangled they were going to get out of this in one piece.

"Grab the step by your left hand," Tim said, "and when you've got it pull yourself over—slow!, or I'll lose hold—over onto the ladder. That's it, climb up ahead of me. I can get to the ladder once you're clear."

Tim was on the ladder just a couple feet below her when he saw Erica reach the top. And hesitate, and a tremor ran through her left leg just above Tim's face.

"Wait," he said. If she was scared the odds were

even worse against her making it across than they'd been the first time she'd tried. "Hold tight—I'm going to climb up behind you and go first. Then I'll help you across."

She didn't protest this time. Didn't even say a word. She hadn't spoken at all since she'd first tried to jump from the ladder to the platform.

"You okay?"

Erica nodded, a little uncertainly.

"You want to forget this, go back down?"

"No," she said, and then there was this little pause in the air about her, like maybe she was going to say something else. But she didn't.

Tim shook his head, confused, and started to climb. Carefully, reaching around Erica to grip each slat in turn tight as he could. Pressing against her hard as he'd hugged the tree a moment before. And as he climbed, something happened—something that confused him just as much as Erica's inviting smile and her coy remarks.

Only this time it wasn't Erica that the strangeness came from.

This time it was Tim.

As he pressed himself against her, clinching hard to hold on for dear life, his body—was doing something. Feeling something warm and delicious and new and wonderful, and he wanted to pull away confused and scared but he didn't dare because if he did he'd die, so he kept going, kept pushing, climbing because he had to get it over with, damn it, or he'd never get away.

He was right behind her, now—up at the top, feet on the same step where Erica stood. She made a small noise that Tim didn't understand, like maybe she was afraid she was going to fall or something, only not that exactly.

"It's okay," Tim said. "Almost there now." It wasn't the right thing to say, and Tim kind of knew it when he heard himself say the words. But he was damned if he knew what was right.

He stretched his right leg out toward the platform, getting a feel for the distance and the angle he'd be coming in at—different just a little because of the way he was standing with Erica between him and the tree. And different too because he couldn't just hug the tree and swing the way he usually did, not without crushing Erica's face into the tree trunk with the lurch and press of it on his arms wrapped around her around the tree.

Sidle—he'd have to sidle over to his right. Hold on with his arms till he was tiptoe with his left foot only on the slat. Stretch his right leg forward onto the platform, use it and his arms to pull him over slow and measured.

There. Managed to plant the right foot and hook it in behind the tree. Easy, easy, and now he could feel that the center of his weight was up over the platform, and that meant he could relax since he had it all but done—

And his arm slipped, the left arm back there wrapped over Erica's shoulder, slipped as the fabric of her blouse slid against her skin, and suddenly Tim was falling dear God—

Over backward, he was going to tumble head over heels backward off the other edge of the platform—

And *whump!* his back hit the two-by-four rail on that side of the platform, and thank God for it or Tim'd be a crumpled mass at the base of the tree.

"I'm okay," Tim said, right arm catching the rail on the rebound, saving himself another *whump*. "I'm okay." He was answering something, wasn't he? Only Erica hadn't said anything he had to answer, hadn't said anything at all. But she was staring at him, all bug-eyed with terror like she was about to see him putrefy right while she was watching.

He got to his feet, stretched his back a little to make sure he hadn't hurt it bad or anything—ached a little, but not like he ought to worry about it.

Erica was still wide-eyed afraid. "Don't be scared," Tim said. So scared that the sight of her made him ache with sympathy. He stepped forward, leaned against the tree to brace himself. "Give me your arm," he said. "Stretch your foot up onto the floor and I'll pull you up. That's it—don't get nervous. I've got you."

And then she was up on the platform, standing beside him. Trembling a little. Without even thinking

about it he reached over to her and hugged her and held
her that way almost like a baby, because if he felt like the
look in her eyes that's what he'd want. "Don't cry," he
said. "Don't cry." But she started crying anyway. Not so
it made a whole lot of noise, but really crying anyway,
soft sobs and hard spasms of her chest that rocked them
both. Heavy wet tears on Tim's T-shirt, and he could feel
them soak right in through the cotton onto his chest.

He kept holding her till the crying stopped, and
then for a long while after that. Then he took her to the
tree in the far corner of the fort, one of the corners
where there were rails on both sides, and he sat her
down with her back leaning against the trunk. And went
and sat down against the tree not far away.

Both of them sat there that way for a good long
while. Not talking or anything; just letting the fear and
the apprehension sift out of their blood. After a while
Tim began to come back to himself, but Erica just sat
against her tree, wide, vacant eyes looking off into the
distance at nothing at all. He sat still waiting for her to
come back to her senses till he began to get bored and
antsy—and then he decided that they might as well do
something, because if he didn't he was going to start
fidgeting in a serious way.

And what was there to do, alone, without anything
but the fort here, without even the rusty nail he was
going to bring for carving stuff into the tree trunks? Not
a whole lot. He could climb up to the top of the fort,
maybe, and look out at things from high up. Why not?
There were all kinds of things you could pretend to be
when you were that high up. Tim got to his feet, climbed
the ladder (this one was, more sensibly, on the inside of
the fort) to the second floor (all walled in, like a proper
tree house) and on up to the third (which was really just
a roof for the second floor railed in to make a widow's
walk).

The view was there, all right. West was the palmetto grove, and way out beyond that the big muddy
pasture where the Conrads grazed their cattle. None of
the cows or bulls were out there this morning, and Tim
wasn't quite sure where they could have gotten to. The
Conrads didn't have a whole lot of land that you couldn't

see from here. But half the time when he looked out over their fields the cattle were there, and the other half they weren't. Did cows sleep in barns or something, maybe? Didn't seem to Tim as that was really necessary, but he guessed that it could be so anyway.

South the woods extended to the interstate highway. If you could cross over that highway (instead of walking all the way around it to the overpass) and walk through a whole bunch more woods, eventually you'd come to Donny James's neighborhood—same neighborhood where the Fultons lived. Where Walt used to live, back before . . . before whatever happened to him. (Tim asked Grandpa about Walt, last year after all the commotion. Asked him what had happened and exactly what it all meant. Grandpa just shook his head and said he didn't know. Said he didn't know because he didn't want to know, because there were some things that it's better not to think about too much. Tim had looked at Grandpa kind of funny, since Grandpa wasn't a man who minded his own business when there was somebody who might need his help. And he'd said that to Grandpa, more or less. Grandpa said that he'd been watching pretty carefully from his distance, and if there'd been anything he should have done or could have done, he would have. But in his opinion it was a matter Walt had to see through on his own, and if Grandpa'd gotten himself involved, it only would have made matters worse for the poor boy. Tim asked Grandpa why Walt was a poor boy, but Grandpa just ignored that question.)

North were these woods, and more of them all the way up to some old road. Tim had hiked up there once, with Donny and Frankie Munsen, but they hadn't stayed long—the road went on in both directions as far as any of them could see, and there was nothing anywhere to see but trees, trees, and more trees. And why bother with trees on the side of a road when there were whole woods full of trees?

Noise down below. Which had to be Erica, coming out of her daze. It sounded as though she was climbing up toward him. That was good, Tim guessed.

East about two hundred yards was Grandpa's house, close to that the other houses on his street.

Erica was standing on the steps from the second floor, looking up at him. Just staring, nothing else. Most of the scared was gone from her eyes, but she still looked a little rattled. Was she going to say something, do something? Tim kept waiting for her to drop the other shoe. And waiting. Erica just stared.

"Do you want to come up here? I can help you up here, if that's what you need."

She shook her head.

"What do you want, then? How come you keep looking at me like that?"

She shrugged. "I want you to come down here. I guess. I think I like it better where I don't have to see how high we are."

"Suit yourself," Tim said, and crawled toward the ladder. Just as well, he decided. He was running out of directions, and he didn't know what else there was to think about.

Erica moved off the steps, into the walled-in part of the tree fort to let Tim get by. When Tim got down onto that floor he saw that she was sitting against the far wall. He started to sit against the wall opposite, but she stopped him.

"Sit here," she said. She patted the floor beside her.

Too damn close for Tim's taste—sometimes he'd see grown-ups sitting that close when they didn't have to, but he was darned if he could understand why—but he could see how the girl was still a little shook up, and it seemed to him a pretty small thing to humor her under the circumstances.

And he sat down beside her. . . .

It wasn't any big thing at first. Sitting next to her—and as soon as he'd sat she'd scooted close to press against him—had a little of that strange warmth he'd felt when he'd had to crawl over her on the ladder. Only a little; part of that feeling, Tim was sure, had come from being scared half out of his wits and certain he was going to die.

After they'd sat there that way for a while she rested

her head on his shoulder and took his arm and—well, held it kind of funny. Partly like she was hugging it, partly like she was cradling it. Would have sounded real cumbersome to Tim if you'd tried to explain it to him just a moment before, but in practice it wasn't uncomfortable at all.

"You ever seen a naked girl, Tim Fischer?"

Even with all the peculiar things that had happened in the last hour, the question was so alien, so unexpected that at first Tim didn't even understand it. *Seen a what-what?* And what did that have to do with the rising price of M&Ms down at the 7-Eleven? And then he finally put it into focus without getting the subtext at all.

"I saw the girl on that box of soap," he said. "Least I think she's naked. Can't really tell for sure, what with all the bubbles and the way the tub kind of blocks the view. What's that brand of soap?"

"That's not what I mean. I mean up close, and without anything hidden, so you can really see."

Tim thought for a moment. There was the day Walt's sister Anne lost her bathing suit down at the pool in Rick Mitchell's back yard. After a big dive that made this awful splash. But that didn't really count for what Erica wanted to know, since she'd gotten on it again when she was still deep underwater, and besides Tim hadn't been close enough to see.

"Can't say that I have." The admission troubled him a little for no reason he could name.

"I've seen boys. Lots of times. Real close."

"Lots of times?" She might just as well have told Tim that she liked to swim across the Atlantic to London on Tuesday mornings. What would a girl want to do that for, looking at boys who hadn't got dressed yet? It wasn't . . . well, it wasn't dignified. Or something like that. Tim tried to imagine himself naked and standing in front of her and he felt silly. Embarrassed, even. "What for?"

"Oh, stuff. Maybe not lots of times. But more than once."

"Why?" Tim heard himself, heard his voice sounding almost frantic. There was something about this subject that wasn't just confusing—something unsettling. Which only added to the confusion. "Why would you want to do something like that even once?"

Erica shrugged. "Mama said I shouldn't so I had to try it. And it's fun."

Tim thought that over. There was a certain logic to her reasoning—a logic he could understand, even though he never paid much attention one way or the other to what his mom said he couldn't do. (Grandpa he had to listen to—more because Grandpa was Grandpa than because he was boss. And Dad too, because Dad *was* boss. But Dad never had a whole lot to say, except those times when he was mad for no good reason at all. And when Grandpa told him something Tim listened, and if he didn't he always ended up wishing that he had. Grandpa had this really awful way of being right almost all the time. It wasn't a good idea to ignore him.)

"What's so fun about it?"

Erica started to speak, stopped herself. For a moment she looked thoughtful. "I don't know—it just *is*. You want me to show you?"

Tim didn't—he didn't know what to say. Part of him was about to say *Sure, go ahead*, because part of what was in Erica's voice was a dare, and he wasn't one to back away from a dare. But something else made him hesitate, something that told him he was getting in over his head without even realizing it. But whatever it was, he couldn't quite put his finger on it, and when it came to a dare his pride was at stake, and he was twelve and he valued his pride infinitely more than he was cautious. So he looked away for a moment, and he pursed his lips, and then he nodded without saying a word because he didn't want his voice to betray his unease.

"Okay," she said, "start by taking off your shirt."

And suddenly it came over Tim why he was so ill at ease: this could just as easily be a setup that'd leave him chasing after her bare-ass naked through the woods as she ran away with his clothes.

As it happened, he was wrong. Erica wasn't up to any prank, and what she was leading Tim toward was a thing infinitely more disturbing than any practical joke.

But Tim didn't know that at the time.

"Are you going to take yours off, too?"

"Of course I am," she said. "It wouldn't be much fun if I didn't."

And when she began to unbutton her dress, it put Tim's fears to rest. It shouldn't have, but he'd guessed wrong, and it did.

He reached down with one hand to grab the tail of his T-shirt, raised the other up over his head. Pulled the shirt up and off. Once he was free of it he looked for a stray nail to hang it on, but there was none. After a while he let it fall to the floor.

Erica was looking at him. Strangely, strange as before, but where then the light in her eyes had confused him now it seemed *right*. She reached out to him, touched the center of his smooth chest with one finger. Let the finger slide inches down. . . . Her dress was unbuttoned to the naval, hanging open but not wide. He was looking, trying to look inside past the flaps that wavered as she moved, but he couldn't see much, and now she drew his attention away with her finger drawing across his stomach, describing the lines of his torso—and the finger pulled away from him, and Erica shrugged off her dress, not even bothering with the final half-dozen buttons, just letting it fall off her shoulders, past her waist, to her ankles, stepping out of the cloth circle at her feet—

Her breasts were flat and spare, like a boy's breasts. His eyes paused to see them only for a moment, and he looked down, looked down to see—

She wasn't wearing panties. Below her waist, between her legs, Tim could see a net of fine dark hairs that didn't quite obscure the skin beneath them. Hairs like the hair of a man's beard. Like the hair that had begun to grow around Tim's own groin early last year—but more of it.

"Take off your pants," she said.

Tim didn't hear at first. He was too busy looking to hear. Fascinated, marveling at the sight of her, and still not understanding why. . . .

"Tim? You there?"

Embarrassment. "Oh—sorry." He almost tripped getting them off.

"I thought you had hair," she said. "You looked like you did."

That observation made Tim feel violated, though if Erica had asked him why that was he couldn't have told her. "Hair. . . ?" It was a question, but he already knew the answer.

Erica pointed at the thin dark fluff that bristled from the skin above his pubic bone. Tim blushed.

"Yeah," he said, "that."

She touched him again: this time it was her fingers, not just one but all of them sifting through that hair like a comb, nails scratching that made an icy-fiery chill spread through him, and his knees nearly buckling in surprise, and his hand reached down for hers half expecting to find her hand webbed with electric wires but there were none and she took his hand, lifted it away from between his legs—

Half a moment of focus, half a moment to almost get himself on balance while she still held his hand but that was all the touch between them, until he realized that she wasn't just holding his hand, but leading it, and now he was touching her, pressing her with the pressure of her hand on his. Feeling the soft, intricate, almost-damp folds of flesh nestled at the apex of her thighs, and Erica made a small noise like a sigh but made from breath drawn in.

"Yes," she said, "that's it."

Tim was damned if he knew what he'd done, but he wasn't about to say so.

She let go of his hand, reached for his groin. Lifted his penis.

And that, right there—that was the revelation. Everything that had come before, everything strange and wonderful and exciting and unknowable, all of it was pale in comparison. The sensation that spread through his groin and all back into the whole of him demanded every iota of his attention, his heart, his *self*. Now his knees did buckle from beneath him, and Tim would have fallen to the rough-wood floor of the fort if it hadn't been for Erica, tucking herself in underneath him, pressing her shoulder in under his arm to brace and hold. . . .

"What . . . are you doing?"

"Just touching you. Nothing else."

Amazing. Incredible. How could a touch be so much infinitely more than a touch? "I didn't know. . . ."

Erica smiled. "I know you didn't." A small half-laugh, or maybe it was a giggle; it sounded like mischief. "You want to try something else?"

Tim hesitated, wondering what it was she had in mind. Thought of the two frogs riding piggyback absurd, and thought how he really didn't want to be a frog, no matter how good it felt—

It was just as well that he hesitated that moment. Because that was when he heard the footsteps.

Heavy, grown-up footsteps; slow and steady. Moving directly toward them. Not in any hurry.

Someone was going to see them, see them all naked and doing . . . *things*.

He looked at Erica and saw that there was panic in her eyes.

And even if Tim didn't know enough about sex to give it a name, he didn't want anyone walking into the middle of anything that felt like this.

Then he recognized the footsteps, and he knew who it was and he knew why and he knew that from the very first moment of the morning he hadn't really been alone with Erica or alone in any way at all. Knew that he'd stumbled into something that was planned or if it wasn't planned entirely foreseen.

It was Grandpa down below.

And Grandpa knew every last thing that had happened in the last two hours, else he wouldn't be here in the first place.

Tim yanked on his shorts, his T-shirt—found to his amazement that he still had his tennis shoes on.

"You wait here," he whispered. "I know who it is—and he's here because of me. I'll go down—you wait here till we're gone."

Erica nodded. She looked afraid all over again. "Who is it? Who'd know to look for you here? And now?"

"Grandpa." Tim could feel his skin getting red again, partly with the blush of embarrassment, partly with the angry flush of annoyance.

"What is he, a mind reader? You didn't tell him where you were going, did you?"

"Sometimes I think he is. And no, I didn't tell him anything. Did you?"

Erica took just a moment too long to answer.

"No."

And suddenly Tim felt as though there were eyes everywhere, watching him, waiting to see—

But there wasn't time for that kind of worry. "Get dressed," he said. He was pulling on his shorts; he already had the T-shirt on. "Don't just stare at me—do it."

And he turned and started down from the tree fort without saying another word nor waiting to hear one. When he got to the place where he had to hug the tree and *swing* to reach the steps, it occurred to him to wonder how Erica was going to get past that gap without help. But only for an instant; there wasn't time for that worry any more than there was time for the others.

Grandpa waited for him at the base of the tree when he got to the bottom.

Tim looked up at the old man. Looked him in the eye. And for the longest time the two of them just stood there that way, staring at each other.

Tim was mad.

And as he stood there staring quiet into Grandpa's eye, all he got was madder.

Mad, the fact of mad all by itself—it was a surprise. Tim could count on one hand the number of times he'd been mad at Grandpa, and every last one of those times he'd felt like a fool for being angry. Felt a fool from the instant he realized he was aggravated. But this time he didn't feel even remotely foolish.

He felt tricked. Tricked and humiliated.

"You did this," Tim said. His voice sounded as angry as he felt. "You planned it all, every bit of it. Didn't you?"

Grandpa shook his head. "No." He looked out toward the highway. "I only felt it happening."

That threw Tim off his track a little, but not entirely; the eyes-watching feeling was still there.

"Then why are you here?"

Grandpa looked up at the tree fort. There was no way to tell from the look of it that Erica was inside, but they both knew that she was.

"We need to have this conversation privately, Timbo. Come with me."

For half a moment Tim thought about protesting—and then he realized that he didn't want Erica listening to this any more than he wanted Grandpa looking in on the other thing. And he nodded, and when Grandpa began to wander off toward the highway, he followed.

After a while they got to the rusty three-strand barbed-wire fence that looked over the interstate. Grandpa leaned on one of the wood posts that held the fence, stood staring off at the traffic.

He hadn't said anything since they'd walked away from the tree fort. He still said nothing.

Eventually Tim got tired of waiting for him, sat down on the dirt a few yards away, and leaned against the fence post there.

When Grandpa finally figured out what he wanted to say, his voice was very quiet—barely loud enough to hear from where Tim sat.

"You're older than I thought you were, Tim. Parts of you are." A silence longer than a pause, not quite long enough to invite response. "I didn't think you'd react this way."

"What did you expect?" Just faintly sarcastic.

Grandpa frowned, hesitated; it looked to Tim as though he'd asked a question Grandpa didn't want to answer. But couldn't avoid.

"I expected you to act embarrassed. To act as though you'd been—caught with your pants down, as it were." He sighed. "But you were on to me—you knew what I was up to the minute you heard me coming, didn't you?"

Tim scowled. "You know I did."

"I thought it, but I didn't know it. I don't know what I know just now."

"Why, Grandpa? Why'd you have to go and show up in the woods?"

Grandpa shook his head, but he didn't say a word.

And then the both of them were silent for a good long while, and Grandpa watched the cars go by and Tim stared down into the dirt by his tennis shoes. When they'd been that way a while Tim realized that he'd lost his heart for being mad. He didn't say anything about it, but he got the feeling Grandpa knew it anyway.

"Something like this was going to happen to you sometime soon. Tomorrow, maybe. Or next week, or next month, or next year. And before you knew what was happening to you, you'd be in over your head, and there'd be no undoing what was already done."

All Tim could think was how it'd felt, back in the tree fort. How intense, how incredible, how—*good*. And how could anything that good be a thing Grandpa needed to save you from?

"That doesn't sound right, Grandpa. What was wrong with . . . *that*?"

A long, hard breath. "Nothing wrong with it, Timbo. But it isn't anything you should take lightly, either. Sex is a thing God made to bond men and women together. Something important. And because it's as powerful a tool as it is, you can use it for things the Good Lord never intended. But you ought to give it a little thought before you do."

There was another long while with Tim waiting for Grandpa to go on and Grandpa just standing there staring out at the highway. There was a strange, alien look on Grandpa's face, partly made of reminiscence, partly something else.

Took Tim a minute to recognize that other something, and when he did it surprised him.

Because it was guilt.

Imagine that, Tim thought: Grandpa looking guilty.

"I wish that I could tell you," Grandpa said, "that I haven't been with a woman since your Grandma died. I can't. The body's got needs, Tim, and sooner or later you end up giving in to them—one way or another. But don't get me wrong; carrying on like sex was idle conversation isn't anything I'd recommend. Sex is . . . I don't know. God put something special into sex, something that binds a man and a woman together. And if you treat that binding stuff like it was something cheap, it gets to *be* cheap. Meaningless as noontime chatter. And that's a loss. As big and powerful a loss as I can think of."

None of that sounded especially sensible to Tim. But he listened to it anyway, and he thought about it. And when he ran into Erica again, two days later, he didn't try to pick up where they'd left off, even though she seemed amenable.

And when he'd thought about what Grandpa said long enough, when he watched the world and the way people acted, the things Grandpa said began to make a kind of sense.

So he held off, and he bided his time, and the next time he was with a woman it was because he was certain it was right and that she accounted for something important in his life.

That was the year he turned fifteen. And he spent the next six years with Anne Fulton, and he would have spent longer but as they got older they grew to be different kinds of people, and wandered away from each other so gradually that neither one of them saw it happen till the gulf between them grew so wide that there was only a thing like nostalgia to bring them together.

And that was okay.

Twice since then he'd lived with women: Jill, his senior year in college—only for a few months, because her heart was stormier than he'd realized. And Betty for five years in his middle twenties; she'd gotten a wild hair one day and left him, which maybe was his fault. There were days even now when he still missed her.

They were sitting in the bar, and Tim was trying his darnedest not to have to look the strange woman in the eye.

"What are you drinking?" he asked her. He turned

slightly toward her as he said it, so that she'd hear him through the barroom din, but as he did he looked toward the barmaid, hoping to get her attention. Would the barmaid know this woman? When she saw Tim sitting beside her, would there be recognition in her eyes, something to show that at least somebody knew who she was? Even now, unsettled as he was, Tim thought it was a silly thing to wonder about. But it seemed important anyway, for no reason he could name.

"Red wine and soda."

The woman sounded positively amused.

Donny nudged him; Tim turned in time to see him wink. "I got to run, Tim," he said. And stage-whispered: "Looks as though you could use some privacy anyhow."

Tim felt panic surging in his gut. And knew it was irrational. He wasn't in danger alone any more than he was in Donny's company. He *knew* how to fend off the attentions of a woman on the make. It wasn't a skill that was often necessary, but half a dozen times in his life he'd had to do it, and it wasn't hard.

"Hold up," he said. "Don't leave on my account."

But Donny was already on his feet, leaving money on the bar to cover his tab. Ready to head for the door.

"I'm not," he said. "I got work tomorrow, bright and early. I'll have enough of a hangover as it is. If I don't get out of here I'll never be able to drag-ass out of bed."

The barmaid appeared, leaned out over the counter to gather up Donny's money. And looked at Tim as she did.

"You wanted something, Tim?"

He flushed again. And nodded toward the strange woman. "A drink for the lady." Watched the barmaid carefully as he said it, looking for some sign of recognition or its absence or any reaction at all. And of course there was none. "Red wine and soda."

And the barmaid looked at the woman beside him, and Tim watched as she did—

Donny's hand on his shoulder, distracting him at just the wrong moment.

"Tim," he said, "I meant to tell you: Walt Fulton's in town. He's looking for you. Gave him your phone number." And he shrugged, and he looked toward the ceiling as if to say he didn't understand it either, and before Tim could respond or press him for details he'd turned and left and was out the door already and there Tim was alone with the woman because the barmaid was already getting the wine spritzer. He had this vague sense that some kind of an exchange had taken place between the two women while he'd been speaking to Donny, but there was no way to be sure and no way to know its substance regardless.

And what in the name of God did Walt Fulton have to do with any of this? Walt who'd died in that car wreck and then wasn't dead and then was so completely gone from the face of the earth that no one had heard from him since? (There was a connection here, too—a strange one. That weird business with Walt Fulton was the one thing Grandpa had refused to explain to Tim, right up till the week he'd died. And if Walt was tied into this mess somehow, there were things going on that Tim couldn't begin to understand.)

Something is wrong here. If things don't quit getting stranger I'm going to lose my grip. I swear it.

The woman beside him was speaking. "Thanks," she said. And Tim turned and saw her sipping on the wine spritzer he'd ordered for her.

"Sure," he said, "my pleasure." Which was a lie, of course. It wasn't any pleasure. Tim was downright uncomfortable. *Why don't I just get up and leave?* He could make some excuse or other. (Thought of that silly commercial he'd heard on the radio, with a comedian pretending to be a man who sold excuses for a living. What was the excuse he was trying to sell? *I need to organize my sock drawer*—that was it. Just tell her he needed to tidy up his drawers and take off; the woman would have to understand.)

He looked at his watch, started to speak. But she beat him to the punch:

"I didn't catch your name," she said. She held out her hand. "I'm Gail Benjamin."

And what could Tim do? He shook her hand. "Tim Fischer," he said. "Do you come here often?"

"No," she said, "never been here before tonight."
She looked around. "Seems pleasant enough."

It was pretty much the answer Tim had expected.
He nodded.

"You're a regular, I take it?"

Tim didn't really think of himself as a regular, but he
drank here often enough that it wasn't a thing he could
honestly deny. "Sure—you could say that." He glanced
at his watch again. Excuse. He needed a good excuse,
and all he kept drawing were blanks.

Looked up just in time to see her watching, taking
in the fact that he was looking for a reason to get away—

—realized that there was something, something not
just about her, but about the way he felt about her. As
though he'd known her all his life, and felt for her, felt
something important that he didn't understand but
recognized, recognized but couldn't place in context—

—déjà vu, that's what it was, the sense that he'd
been here with her before, been here with her in this
room at this bar on this bar stool all his life just waiting
to realize where he was—

And that was when the television blew.

Spectacularly.

The big, bright, full-color picture tube exploding in
a cascade of high-voltage sparks and glass shrapnel and
bits and pieces of the case and tiny bright-edged bits of
electronic television guts, and in half a moment there
was fire.

Hot fire that spread quickly into the dusty smoke-
grimed drop ceiling, and the wood paneling of the
nearby wall and everyone in the tight-packed too-dense-
for-any-sensible-weeknight crowd was lurching, pressing against each other trying to get out in one big
stampede that wasn't possible because the doors were
too narrow and at such opposite ends of the bar that
there were people in the middle fighting against each
other to go in opposite directions.

"Oh shit," Tim said. This was a place to die in, if that
fire kept spreading so fast and the people didn't calm
down and move orderly out of the place.

Someone screamed, up near the front, and the big

plate-glass window shattered. Tim saw the glass falling outward, and for half an instant he thought that it'd be a way to relieve the pressure of the crowd—until he noticed that the big neon signs that had covered the window were shattering too, and there were more sparks flying and even if that wasn't another fire about to start (which it probably was) somebody was going to get himself electrocuted for a sure thing.

And it was still too packed here by their bar stools to stand, let alone to get up and run.

People were screaming everywhere.

The fire in the ceiling was spreading, more slowly now but hotter, deeper, more intense. Weren't ceilings like that supposed to be fireproof? And weren't there supposed to be sprinklers? There were sprinklers— there, there, and there. They weren't working. Lord knew why the ceiling was so flammable; dust, maybe, up in the rafters. And maybe that grit from years of cigarette smoke was flammable, too—it seemed reasonable that it would be.

Somebody's got to calm these people down, Tim thought, *or they're all going to die.* And as soon as it occurred to him, he knew he had to do it, or to try to do it. But how was he going to calm them down and get them to act orderly from here in the middle of the bar? The trouble was at the doors, where people were too busy shoving to be first to clear the way, and just outside where those who'd already escaped stood gaping too close.

He got up, stood on top of his chair. Shouted: *"Calm down, damn it! One at a time. Stop pushing. Wait your turn, step through, and once you're clear keep going— get as far from the door as you can."*

And then something groaned in the ceiling up above him. And before Tim could look up to see what the sound meant, the rafter fell—struck him squarely on the head. The rafter was large, and moving quickly, but it wasn't large enough or fast enough that it should have been able to knock Tim unconscious. And it wouldn't have, if it hadn't struck the large swollen lump on the side of Tim's head—a lump he'd got not four hours earlier, when the old Dodge braked too quickly and threw him headfirst into the dirt.

Till the rafter hit, the knot had ached little enough that Tim hadn't even noticed it. But it was pain more than injury that blacked Tim out; the rafter glanced off the swollen knot on his skull (pressing the blood that caused the swelling out into the rest of his scalp, pushing skin away from bone) and the pressure added to the bone-bruise that made the lump, and brought him to an ecstasy of pain too intense for any conscious mind to feel.

He was unconscious even before the rafter struck his shoulder, pushing him off the chair and to the ground.

He came halfway back to his senses (disoriented, dazed, unsure of where or why he was) less than five minutes later. The scene had changed, dramatically: the crowd was gone, and the walls were all made of flickering, lapping fire.

And someone had hold of his collar. Someone was dragging him out.

He glanced back, over his shoulder, and saw that the one who was saving his life was the same strange woman who'd sat beside him in the bar. He wanted to say *It's okay, I'm awake now, you can let go and I can walk out of here on my own.* But his body was too dazed; when he tried to speak all that came from his throat was a low moan. He tried to get up, but the effort turned out to be even more useless than the attempt to speak.

Who is this woman? Why is she doing this? And as soon as he heard the questions in his mind he felt small and petty: he owed this woman his life, and all he could think of were ulterior motives.

Where was the fire department? Shouldn't they be here by now, helping her?

And then an explosion, so close, so intense that it must have been right beside them. And the woman who'd tried to save Tim's life was thrown unconscious on top of him.

And the fire was all around them, warm dry burning hotness that smelled like car tires ablaze.

Fire close enough to touch.

And Tim knew he was going to die. Knew that both of them were going to die.

For his own part, right then and there death would have been a mercy; he was ready to admit that life had defeated him.

But he wasn't the only one there. There was the woman who'd tried to save him.

He had to save her now.

Had to.

Even if she hadn't put her life at stake on his account he would have felt the same compelling need to keep her from dying in the fire; it wasn't in him to let others suffer if there was anything he could do about it. As it was he owed her all the more.

Tim forced himself to move, forced himself to ease out from under her and up onto his knees.

And saw that the fire was everywhere around them like a wall made of light. Just above his head was smoke so thick it made him think of a ceiling, a low ceiling since if he were standing it would only come to his waist.

The door was that way—there in front of him. He couldn't see it through the fire, but he knew the direction anyway.

How the hell was he going to get them out of here? He looked again at the flames that surrounded them. The only way out was straight through it. He bent, lifted the unconscious woman up onto his shoulder. Duck-walked (keeping low, keeping the his head out of the smoke) the half-dozen paces to the forward wall of fire. Closed his eyes to keep from burning them, and ran into the fire, running toward the spot where he thought the door was. Praying he was right about the direction, praying that there was nothing on the floor between here and there to trip him or even worse to stop him dead in his tracks.

Once he stumbled on something that could have been the leg of a chair turned to white hot embers. Whatever it was, it didn't trip him up; the thing shattered when his right foot kicked into it, and an instant later he felt something fiery and substantial searing the skin on the back of his left ankle.

Then he felt the surface underneath his feet change, and the heat was so much less that he thought he must be clear, and he opened his eyes in time to see the barmaid scream at the sight of him.

A fireman shouted at him: "You're on fire—get down on the ground and *roll*," and Tim if hadn't been so busy setting the woman down and doing as he was told he would have felt stupid for not realizing he'd turned himself into a torch.

When he finally came to a stop there was a man standing above him, looking at him. It took Tim a moment to realize that the man was a medical tech—an attendant from one of the ambulances over there on the shoulder of 56th Street. "Get a stretcher over here!" the man was shouting. He knelt, looked down into Tim's eyes. "You're awake, aren't you?"

Tim blinked; the man wasn't really looking for an answer, and Tim didn't feel much like answering. He lifted Tim's head, shown a light into his scalp. It only took him a moment to find the lump. "I thought so. Your eyes look like you took a blow to the head."

I should say something. If I don't say something they're going to haul me off to the hospital.

He didn't have time for a stay at the hospital—once you got yourself checked into a hospital it was days before you could get them to let you out again. Tim had seen it happen often enough; a couple of times he'd got stuck in hospitals himself. And tomorrow—early tomorrow—he had to set out for Tennessee.

"I'm fine," he said. "Go on and take care of the people who really need help. I'll be on my feet in a couple minutes."

The medic chuckled. "Yeah, you'll be okay. After they get a few stitches into that gash on your head. But you ought to quit worrying about the rest of the world— most everyone in that bar came out without a scratch. You now—you're a mess."

Tim tried to make his eyes focus a little better. "I really don't want to go to the hospital."

The medic shook his head. "I can't force you. But you're going to be sorry if you don't get someone to clean and stitch that scalp wound. And if you've got any sense you'll get your head x-rayed too—blow like that one could have caused a fracture. Better than even odds you've got a concussion."

A couple of times in his teens Tim had knocked his head and the family doctor had told him he'd gotten a concussion; far as he could tell a concussion wasn't anything but a bad knot that made you a little dizzy when you moved too quick.

"I'll cope."

The medic ignored him. He eased Tim's head back down onto the pavement, let the flashlight beam move down to scan the rest of Tim's body. "You're lucky," he said. "The fire did a real number on your clothes, but darned little of it got through them. You feel well enough to turn over?"

Tim didn't answer, but he did roll over. (Maybe he did have a concussion. The world swam around him as he turned.)

"Damn," the medic said. "That is a serious burn. On your left ankle, a little above your heel."

"I know about it."

The medic sighed. "Look," he said, "you can play macho if you want. If you want to sit here and tell me you don't want to go in to the emergency room, I can't make you. But you need stitches up on your scalp, and the burn on your ankle is so deep that I can see your Achilles tendon. You want to be tough, you can walk away from here. It'll hurt, but you can do it." He frowned, shone the flashlight into Tim's eyes. "Not sure how bad that concussion is. Maybe you'll black out a few times, maybe you won't. It won't be safe to drive either way. But the real problem is infection—if you don't get the gash and the burn cleaned and bandaged up, if you don't get yourself some antibiotics, you're going to pick up the kind of infection that can kill you."

I'm already on *antibiotics. The doctor back in*

Nebraska gave them to me for the bug I picked up in Grandpa's morgue. Tim thought they were antibiotics, anyway—he hadn't recognized the name on the prescription label, but the instructions were the kind you got for antibiotics. After meals three times a day for ten days or some such.

Trouble was, of course, that he hadn't taken them since the night he'd left the Midwest. Last night, wasn't it? Or the night before? It was hard to remember.

"I can clean them myself," he said. "I don't have time for a hospital stay."

"Suit yourself, then." The medic stood. "If you start getting blackouts, get yourself to a hospital."

And then he was gone.

Tim sat up. Tried to sit up; the motion stirred up vertigo inside his skull. *I do need to get to a doctor.* But the last thing he wanted was to have the ambulance haul him up to the hospital. All the ambulances in this part of town took people up to University-Community, where the emergency room was known for long waits, punctilious attention to insurance forms, and mediocre medical care. But there was an emergency walk-in clinic up on 30th Street (or Bruce B. Downs Highway, or whatever they were calling that stretch of road these days), and they were reliable enough. And the clinic didn't have hospital beds handy, which meant that it didn't have any special incentive to put people in them for days on end.

Tried to sit up again. Bracing himself for the vertigo this time, bracing himself against the wave of nausea that followed a moment behind it. And when the vertigo and the need to puke didn't go away, he set his teeth and ignored them. And looked around.

A circus. The bar burning wild and out of control. Fire engines all over the place—how could they get so many of them into a parking lot that was barely big enough for parking cars? They had somehow. Someone was going to have a murderous time getting them out of there. Flames shooting high up out of the bar, into the air. A woman wailing; two men shouting hysterically at each other. Over there, leaning against the fire engine, was the barmaid. She stared slack-jawed at the blaze; her eyes were wide with shock.

"Hard to believe, isn't it?"

Tim blinked. Who? He turned his head slowly, careful not to make the vertigo any worse than it already was.

The strange woman—the woman who'd been next to him when the chaos started. The one who'd tried to save his life, and who he'd ended up carrying out through the fire.

"I'm not sure yet," Tim said. "I'm still too busy coping to know how bad things are."

She nodded.

Tim was thinking, looking back over the chain of events. And it was a bizarre chain: just to begin with, he'd never in his life seen a television explode. Once, back in college, he'd seen an ancient black-and-white that had died in a shower of sparks—seen the wreckage a couple days after the event. But that old thing hadn't started any fire, and it wasn't the picture tube that had exploded but a handful of its primitive vacuum tubes. Weren't picture tubes designed to die quietly instead of blowing up?

Then there were the sprinklers that had failed completely. Tim didn't know the first thing about automatic sprinkler systems, but he'd always thought that the fire department had to come in and check such things every now and then. And wouldn't they have noticed if the sprinklers were useless?

And the way the fire had spread—that was strange, too. Modern buildings were supposed to be made of things that didn't burn—not that quickly, anyway. The bar couldn't have been more than a dozen years old (they'd put it up the year he'd gone to college, hadn't they?) and the whole damned place had gone up like kindling.

One improbable thing on top of another—it was almost, Tim thought, as though someone had rigged things to happen the way they did.

"Yeah," Tim said, "I guess you're right. It's strange, all right."

The woman raised an eyebrow. "Pardon? Right about what?—Oh. Yes. You took so long to answer I forgot I'd asked the question."

Tim nodded. "Sorry. Guess I did."

He looked up at her, more carefully this time. She was an awful mess of singed hair, charred clothes, and smeared ash, but that was all on the surface. He didn't see any blood, and she held herself as though she'd come through in one piece.

"You're okay?" he asked her.

"Yes. I got a little smoke, I think—it had me dizzy before the drop-ceiling fell on us. I think I would have blacked out in a few seconds even without help from the ceiling." A pause. "I guess I owe you my life, don't I?"

Tim frowned. "You don't owe me anything. The only reason you were still in there was because you were trying to drag me out."

She shrugged. "Somebody had to do it. And the rest of them were too busy getting themselves out to notice you. Funny when you consider that you were the only reason everyone else got out of that bar."

"Huh?"

"It's true. Until you started shouting they were all bunched up at the door, fighting to be first. Enough of them listened to you to stop the panic."

"That's good, I guess."

Tim was never sure how he was supposed to feel about things like that. A part of him wanted to be proud, because it made him a hero somehow. Another, larger part of him was embarrassed; all his life he'd been sticking his neck out when people looked like they were in trouble, and more than once he'd jumped into situations where he wasn't needed or welcome. Mostly, though, moments like this one confused Tim—he didn't know what compelled him, didn't understand it, and didn't even control it. He risked his life for other people because he had to, and not for any other reason.

She was scribbling onto a piece of paper. When she was done, she handed it to him.

Gail Benjamin—555-0321. Tim read it, and for a long moment it made no sense at all.

"My phone number," she said. "Call me when you get a chance. I like you—I want to stay in touch."

He should feel flattered, he thought. But he didn't. When he reached down into himself to find what he did feel all he found was vague confusion and a large flat thing that was no emotion at all. There was something under the two of these—something so big it frightened him. But he was only dimly aware of that part of his heart, and the fear he felt was almost as vague as his confusion.

"Sure," he said. And that was a lie, because he knew he'd never call her. He started to stand—

And halfway up, as he tried to press the vertigo of motion away from him, he blacked out. Not entirely, not for long—only for an instant large enough to send him falling into her.

She managed to catch him, to save him from falling face-first into the pavement, and Tim heard himself grunt involuntarily. She moved her hands under his arms, helped him to his feet.

"You need to get to a hospital," she said. "Your hair is matted with blood."

He'd heard that about the hospital somewhere before, Tim had. It didn't appeal to him much more now than it had then.

"Too much to do," he said. "I'm going out of town tomorrow. No time for the hospital."

She frowned, and said, "I know," and her face was so full of honest concern that it didn't occur to him to wonder how she could know he was going out of town.

"I'm going to the walk-in clinic—the one up on 30th. I can get there. I'll be fine."

She bit her lip. "Let me help you," she said. There was something in her face that said she was about to go against her better judgment. "Let me drive you there. My car is right here in front."

"Mine's in the back. Don't worry—I'm well enough to drive." And he turned a little to move out of her arms and head off to his car—

He never got there. Never got three steps, in fact; about the time he took the second, vertigo rushed up to claim him once and for all. He was off in some deep dark place long instants before he finished crumbling to the pavement.

Tim surfaced briefly on the way to the clinic. They were on Fowler, somewhere on the long dark stretch where the road ran past USF, and he was in the front passenger seat of an old car he thought he should have recognized. Lying there, more than sitting—in a strange position that could only have happened if someone had set him in the front seat and he'd fallen onto his side. His legs were down in the well by the glove box where legs are supposed to go when you sit in the front passenger seat, but the rest of him lay on his side, his head rested on the seat by the gearshift.

And the strange woman's right hand gently stroked his matted hair the way you stroke the head of an infant to calm him, and she cooed to him in soft reassuring nonsense syllables.

And then he faded away again.

He was only half-aware of the clinic, but even through that dim comprehension he knew that their appearance caused a stir. No waiting here, no sir—and Dr. Stout, his regular doctor when he came here, Dr. Stout was here, and when she saw him she started shouting orders in a tone just this side of hysteria. Why was everyone so upset? He was fine, or fine enough at least. There wasn't any call for hysteria. He just needed to get his wounds cleaned up, that was all. Maybe a new prescription for antibiotics. Nothing to get all het up about.

He tried to sit up from the stretcher they'd wheeled him in on (Stretcher? How the hell had he ended up on a stretcher? Tim hadn't even known they *had* stretchers here. This was the kind of place where you'd bring a kid because he had a bee sting. Stretchers were for the hospital, up 30th, just past Fletcher.) Tim tried to sit up in his stretcher and tell everybody to calm down—Dr. Stout included—but the fact of trying to sit up set off the

TILT alarm in the pinball machine that was his brain, and he went down again just like an aborted pinball game. Pffft. Black. Nothing.

Not that it mattered a whole lot. Just like before, he was back again three minutes later. And this time he was more or less in the same place when he came to. Kind of. That was a sign that he was recovering, wasn't it? It better be: he was going to be on that road tomorrow, caved-in skull or no.

More or less in the same place meant that he was still in the clinic—though now he was back in the back, and Dr. Stout was there, only instead of sewing him back together she was talking on the telephone.

Very irresponsible. But what did you expect from a woman? That was a sexist thought, and Tim knew it, but he'd spent a lifetime noticing how women never seemed to be able to get off the telephone. And if observing the fact of the business made him a sexist pig, then he was a sexist pig.

"Get an ambulance down here right away, would you?" she said. "I've got a patient here in the clinic with a serious concussion. I need to get him into the hospital for a few days, just for observation."

Took Tim a moment to realize just exactly what it was she was saying, but once he deciphered the words he hit the roof. Or tried to, anyway.

"Oh no you don't," he said. "You aren't putting me into any hospital."

The doctor cradled the phone against her breast. "Stop shouting, Tim Fischer. This isn't a barroom."

She wasn't exactly quiet herself. But Tim lowered his tone anyway, on account of the fact that he had a great deal of respect for Dr. Stout. He took a moment to focus his thoughts, so that he could speak calmly and sensibly.

"I really don't want to go to the hospital, Dr. Stout. I can't afford the time."

She sighed, raised the handset back up to her ear. "Hold off on that ambulance, would you, Bill? The patient's awake and arguing with me." Half a moment later she turned to hang up the phone. When she turned back to Tim she didn't look happy. Looked downright fierce, in fact. "Tim Fischer," she said, and she scowled again. "You've got a concussion. Have you got any idea exactly what a concussion is?"

Tim'd had concussions before, and they hadn't caused him any real grief. But the fact was that he *didn't* know what the hell a concussion was.

"No." He didn't say anything more than that for fear of wedging his foot deeper into his mouth.

"A concussion is a brain injury. Sometimes a minor injury; sometimes a very severe injury. Most often when someone knocks his head, all he gets is a bruised skull. But if you hit your head hard enough, it jars the brain.

"That's a concussion. You've got one, and the concussion you've got—it isn't minor. I can't say how bad it is yet. Bad enough for you to black out more than once. Not as bad as it could be, or you wouldn't be awake right now to argue with me. But either way, it isn't something to take lightly. If you aren't careful, it'll kill you."

Tim closed his eyes. He didn't want to cope with this. He was too damn tired, and even lying still he could feel the vertigo that had blacked him out three, four times already. But he had to cope: doctors were always way overcautious about these things—even sensible doctors like Dr. Stout. To Tim's way of thinking, there *were* times when a body needed to get himself locked into a hospital. Even a hospital like that one. When something inside you was crushed or broken, for instance. But this wasn't one of those times, and Tim was gut-certain about it.

"What do you want to do," Tim asked, "that I need to be in a hospital for you to do it?"

Dr. Stout rolled her eyes toward the heavens.

"I want you in for observation, Tim. I want to keep an eye on you for the next few days."

"What exactly do you want to watch for that I can't look out for myself?"

Another sigh. "With a concussion like this one, there's an outside chance—just a chance—that your brain could swell. Think of it as a bruise in your brain. That isn't exactly what it is, but it's close enough for now.

Every now and then, a bruise swells. Not often, but often enough. When swelling like that happens to your brain, there's nowhere for the tissue to go, because the skull encloses it so completely."

"And how are you going to know if it's swelling? And what are you going to do if it does—saw off the top of my head to give my brain a little breathing room?"

The doctor laughed. "No—there's no chance you'll be going in for brain surgery. There are drugs we can use to stop the swelling. Drugs too powerful for me to prescribe." She looked thoughtful for a moment. "We'll know that there's trouble if you keep blacking out like this. Shouldn't take more than a day or two to be certain."

Tim thought about it for a moment. A day or two—could he afford that much time? A wince, down in his gut. No, he couldn't. He was sure of that—dead certain. Not that he understood the hurry; if the doctor pressed him for an explanation he was damned if he knew what he'd tell her.

"I really can't spare two days, Dr. Stout. Not now. Be honest with me: this really isn't very likely, is it? This swelling business?"

She didn't answer right away. When she did she seemed to speak reluctantly. "No, Tim, it's not. But ignoring a concussion is too much like Russian roulette for my taste. If you want to refuse treatment, there's nothing I can do about it. But don't think you have my blessing." She turned away for a moment; when she turned back toward him she held a surgical tray. "Let's get this over with. Turn over so I can clean and stitch that gash on your scalp."

He'd almost forgotten about how the world kept swimming all around him. Rolling over brought it back to him.

It only took five minutes for her to clean away the dried blood, shave a patch of his scalp, stitch and tidy up the wound. Her cleaning and bandaging the burn on his leg took another ten, mostly because she spent so much time swearing at the ugliness of the wound. She didn't use an anesthetic—local, general, or in-between—on either of the wounds. When Tim complained about the pain (not all that bad, but the feel of surgical thread sewing him together made his skin crawl) she said she didn't want anything complicating his concussion. Said it with just a touch of sadism in her tone that made him suspect that she was making him pay for being such a pain in her neck.

"You're going to need as much sleep as you can get these next few days," she said when she was done. "I don't want you getting out of bed to do anything but eat and take this medication. Do you understand me, Tim Fischer?"

He rolled back onto his side—slow, slow, keeping vertigo at bay—so that he could look her in the eye as he spoke. "I won't." He was lying, and he had a feeling she knew it. If she did she didn't say anything about it.

Then she wrote out two prescriptions. The first for a powerful antibiotic, the second—*Hold on*, he thought. He didn't recognize the name of the drug she'd prescribed. But there was a glint in her eye when she handed him that slip of paper, and the name looked . . . intimidating. *She's slipping me a Mickey.* That was her way of making sure he got some sleep—prescribing something that'd give him no other choice.

"Darlene can fill these for you up at the front," she said. "Take the first three times a day, an hour or two after you eat. Twice a day for the second. And don't even think about driving for the next few days."

It was a Mickey, all right. He wasn't going to argue with her about it, but he wasn't about to take those pills, either. He slipped the prescriptions into his shirt pocket—didn't slip them in, exactly; slipping papers into a shirt pocket sounds more graceful and fluid than what he actually did. And there was no way Tim could be anything remotely like graceful or fluid lying on his side off kilter trying to put something in a pocket that wasn't meant to hold things sideways.

How the hell was he going to get out of here without blacking out all over again? If he did she'd have him in that hospital for a sure thing. He wasn't about to let that happen.

Very carefully.

Which, of course, was the only way to go about it. He did his best to look casual sitting up so gently it might have been a scene from a slow-motion film (so gently because he knew that if the sense of movement got to his head he'd be lost) but hard as he tried he knew he didn't come off looking casual at all. Well, fuck casual, then; he had to get out of here. That was the important thing.

Sitting up, now. And vertigo was still at bay. Legs over the side of the couch. (It wasn't a couch, exactly. One of those padded nauga-leather things that doctors have in their offices that aren't quite couches and aren't quite tables and aren't quite beds. If there was a word for the thing Tim didn't know it.) Now: feet to the floor and stand up real easy and he had the worst part of the battle done.

Damn that foot! Damn the leg! Or wasn't it the ankle? The left one, the one with the burn. When he put his weight on it the pain was suddenly so intense that his whole body tensed up, and he almost stumbled. This was ridiculous. What was he doing to himself? Was it really that important that he stay out of the hospital? He knew it was—knew it was even *this* important—but it was a lot easier to be sure about it when he was lying on his side than it was trying to walk out of the clinic in a dignified fashion.

Gripped himself hard, managed not to stumble. Managed not to do a whole lot more than wince. The doctor saw that, even still. He could tell from the vaguely fish-eyed look she was giving him.

Easy, now. One step at a time. No sudden movement. Careful of the leg; careful of the head.

He was out of the room with the table/couch/bed, in the hall. Feeling a sense of triumph. This was the best he'd done since he'd hauled himself and Gail Benjamin out of the fire, wasn't it? It was.

The door there by the reception desk—step, step, stop; open the door; step through and let the door swing shut behind him. Progress. He was so proud of himself.

Had to settle up the bill and pick up his prescriptions. The place to do both of these things was on this

side of the counter—when the Eckerd's up at Varsity
Plaza had stopped being a twenty-four-hour operation
the clinic here had started stocking most of the stuff that
the doctors prescribed regularly. They overcharged for
it, but at three a.m. with the nearest all-night drugstore
out in Carrolwood it was hard to mind the price.

He reached into his pocket awkwardly, took out the
two prescription slips Dr. Stout had given him. Handed
them to the young man at the desk—and looking at the
man he had a sudden picture of how he must look,
shambling awkward clumsy like Boris Karloff in the
Frankenstein movies. He would have blushed or
laughed but it would have taken too much out of him.

There was his reflection, there in the sliding window beside the desk. Didn't look like the Frankenstein
Monster, exactly, but he was a wreck all right. The
doctor had gotten most all of the blood from his hair
when she'd cleaned him just before the stitches, but
there were still smudgy traces of it on his neck. His
clothes were worse; the fire had done them in considerably. Big scorched swatches all over the place. Gaps in
his shirt in two places where the fire had burned
through; another one, bigger, on the right thigh of his
jeans. His hair was the worst, though—singed hair-ends
frayed out in every direction looking like they'd crumble
if he touched them. Even without the spot she'd shaved
bald his hair was shorter on one side than it was on the
other. Trouble was that the place she'd shaved was on
the long side, and now it was all hopelessly off balance.

The guy at the desk had his pills ready. Had the bill
for him, too. Tim reached into his back pocket, fished
out his wallet. Found the credit cards tucked inside it.
Pulled them out and just stared at them for a while,
trying to figure out which one it was he still had credit
on. (Tim'd never had real money problems. But he had
an awful problem remembering to pay bills.) After a
while he thought he remembered clearing off the Visa
card earlier this month, and he leaned over the counter
and handed that card to the man at the desk and hoped
for the best.

There were a couple of fuzzy moments after that

(leaning over the desk hadn't been a good idea) while the
man ran his card through the high-pitched-*beep* machine
that checks out credit, made up his credit-card slip,
fiddled with a few anonymous-looking papers. Handed
Tim the slip and a white-paper bag with his prescriptions. Tim signed the slip, took the bag, and there was
Gail Benjamin beside him all of a sudden (he'd all but
forgotten about her, what with having it out with Dr.
Stout, but there she was—she must have been waiting
for him there in the waiting room beyond the counter)
and they were free to get themselves out of that place.
Thank God.

Or almost free, the way it happened. Because when
they were two steps from the door Dr. Stout came
marching out of the back of the clinic with a paper cup of
water in her hand. And she was calling Tim's name.

"Tim Fischer!" she said. "I thought I'd catch you out
here before you left. I want to see you take the medication I prescribed. Go ahead—take it out of the bag. I've
brought water for you to wash it down with."

Jesus, Mary, and Joseph. The parish priest used to
say that, back when Tim was growing up. When he got
bad news during an unguarded moment. Anybody else
said it, and he'd accuse them of blasphemy—but Father
Magee used to say things like that quite a bit himself.

He opened the bag, read the labels on the pill
bottles. Two of these, one of the horse pills. The horse
pills were the ones meant to knock him out. Well, he
decided, that's easy enough: I put all three of them in my
mouth, and put the big one under my tongue so I don't
have to swallow it.

He took the water from Dr. Stout, put the pills in
his mouth—and something went wrong with the pill-
under-the-tongue trick. Darned thing didn't go under
the tongue like it was supposed to—went a little too far
back, toward the side, toward the back, half under and
half rubbing up against one of his molars. Which happened to be one of the gag-reflex spots in Tim's mouth.
And the next thing Tim knew, what with involuntary
reactions and all, the big fat pill was back on the nether
part of his tongue near his tonsils and there was no

getting it back without sticking a finger halfway down his throat—unless he gagged a little harder on the damned thing and puked it out which he was about to do if he didn't drink that water.

So what the hell, he drank the water.

And he looked at Dr. Stout and said, "Satisfied?" but what he was thinking was *Oh fuck*.

Dr. Stout sighed. Again. (Tim was a real trial on her patience, and he knew it.) "Yes," she said. "I'm satisfied. You take care of yourself, Tim. One of these days you're going to do yourself some real harm this way. Serious harm."

Tim started to nod, then thought better of it. "I will, Dr. Stout."

Then Tim was walking out the door again, still carefully but more relaxed about it now. He wondered how far the fire had spread before they'd finally put it out, and if they'd even gotten it out yet, and if it had spread far enough to damage his car, and what the hell he was going to do if it had. "Can I get you to drop me off at my car? It's in the back, behind the bar. Behind what used to be the bar, I guess. If we're lucky the fire engines will be gone and you won't have any trouble getting at it."

They were standing by her car, and she gave him a look, one of those *Oh?* looks, and Tim wasn't sure exactly what she meant by it. Like maybe she had other plans which Tim wasn't up to physically or emotionally, and besides he was pretty hesitant about that sort of thing anyway. Or maybe it was just a look that meant *Of course that's where I'm taking you—what did you expect?* Whatever the look meant, she said "Sure," and she opened door of her car, got in, reached over to unlock the one on his side.

Tim sat in beside her, pulled his door shut. Settled into the seat aching and exhausted. Rested his head against the head rest—which was a mistake, since it met the back of his head right where it was a bloody aching stitched-up mess. He eased forward, away from the pain. And wondered how long he had before that pill kicked in and knocked him out. Well, he decided, if he started to feel sleepy on the way home he'd pull over and rest in the car until he felt awake enough to drive.

And then Gail hit the speed bump at the far edge of the clinic's parking lot. Hit it a little too fast and a little too hard, and Tim's head jolted into the headrest. And he blacked out again. And how he was going to get himself home became irrelevant, because by the time he would have come to the sedative had kicked in, and there was no way he could swim up from the depths inside him.

There was a grey moment, sometime close to dawn. Tim was in a strange room, and he knew it was a strange room because the half-light of the not-quite-dawn was leaking in around the window drapes, and he could almost see furniture and walls he'd never known.

Gail Benjamin lay beside him, curled against him sleeping like a lover. He tried to wonder how he'd got here and why and where he was and what he'd done he had no memory of. But in the thickness of the drug-fog that surrounded him there was no way Tim could worry about those things. Life was all that mattered; life and breath and the warm dry touch of her naked breasts pressed against his skin.

And it was good.

When he woke—really woke—it was late afternoon and he was alone and Tim felt like a hangover from hell. He was alone in a strange room in a strange bed and he was very nearly naked, and his head ached from the concussion but it ached more, he thought, from whatever it was Dr. Stout had made him take before he'd left the clinic. It was hangover that his head felt like, not concussion. Not just concussion, anyway.

He was sitting halfway up in bed before he remembered that he had to be careful about moving or it'd black him out. But he wasn't blacking out—the world was rocking like an earthquake, and his ears were roaring, and the stitched knot at the back of his skull throbbed like to make him groan. But he was still there.

Still awake. Still alive. It had to mean he was recovering, didn't it? He'd be fine for the drive to Tennessee, so long as he was careful about it.

He looked around the room: this was Gail Benjamin's apartment. Or if it wasn't Tim couldn't begin to think where he'd ended up. He half remembered lying here in the early morning, Gail beside him, holding him. And the room certainly looked like a woman's bedroom. Silk flowers on the nightstand. Cosmetics scattered on the dresser. And that telephone—a peculiar, round-edged pale-blue thing, too pretty to imagine in the home of a man.

He pulled the sheets off, let his legs slide off the bed. He still had on his underwear. And his socks. (What was left of them. The left one was a mess from the embers that burned through it. And from the way Dr. Stout had cut through the thing to clean and bandage the burn.) He tried to imagine Gail Benjamin undressing him—she had to have done it, didn't she? Unless his clothes had vaporized while he was unconscious.

The whole subject made Tim even more uncomfortable than he would have imagined. He decided not to think about it.

Up. Push up, off the bed. Stand—and the dull raw ache in his left ankle was suddenly an explosion of agony as the weight shifted onto it, and Tim collapsed back onto the bed before he knew what was happening to him. Air grunting out of his lungs, and an involuntary noise that was mostly throat, not from the vocal cords at all.

I can walk on it. I'm sure I can walk on it. I did last night, didn't I? Just got to take it a little easier, that's all.

He tried standing again, more gingerly this time. Shifted a little weight onto the left leg, and then a little more. That position, right there—that was what he needed to avoid. As long as he avoided it, the pain from walking wouldn't be much worse than it was when he sat down.

"I tried to wash your clothes"—Gail Benjamin's voice, coming from another room—"but they didn't make it. Fell apart in the washer, would you believe it? I've never seen anything like it before."

She appeared in the doorway, dressed in jeans and a white blouse. Her thick black hair was shorter than he remembered it. Had she gotten a haircut while he was asleep? There'd been time for it, Tim guessed; the clock on the nightstand said it was four thirty-three, and the light outside the window meant it had to be late afternoon. Then he remembered the sight of his own hair, last night. Reflected in the glass by the clinic's front desk. He'd be needing a haircut himself today, and for exactly the same reasons.

"I managed to salvage the tags, anyway. Which had your sizes on them. So I picked up a shirt and slacks for you while I was out. Got a friend to drive your car here for you, too, so you wouldn't feel stranded."

Tim blinked. *What?* Something was going on, and he didn't get it. "Thanks," he said. Which felt as awkward and uncomfortable as everything else about this woman did. "You didn't really have to." Which was worse, since it made him feel like an ingrate. "Even falling-apart clothes would have been enough to get me home."

But Gail Benjamin was smiling all pretty-eyed at him. "I didn't mind," she said. "I didn't spend a fortune on them."

Tim didn't know what to say to that. "What do I owe you? You shouldn't have to pay—"

"No. I wanted to." A smile. "Shower's over here, just off the hall. I'll get the clothes for you."

She was gone before he had a chance to respond.

It was just like last night: something was going on, and Tim just wasn't getting it. Women didn't act the way Gail Benjamin was acting. Just didn't. There was a degree of familiarity here that he'd never asked for. Didn't really want. More than that: you got familiar with someone by knowing her for a long time, and the only thing he knew about Gail Benjamin was her name. Even his grip on that was a little loose.

Then Tim had a thought that set off an alarm

somewhere in the back of his head: she could have known him longer than he'd known her.

There was something there, and he didn't want to think about it. He *liked* Gail Benjamin. How could he not like her? She'd tried to save his life, and nearly gotten herself killed trying. And if that wasn't enough she'd spent most of the time since then looking after him—and much as· he wanted to think otherwise Tim knew he hadn't been able to see after himself these last dozen or so hours. He owed her, and in a large way; he didn't want to have to think about strange behavior and bells going off in the back of his head.

He shook his head (gently, and still there was the sound of wind rushing in his ears) and headed toward the shower. Where more discomfort waited for him: the tiny room with its fluffy-pink curtains and the matching throw rug and toilet-seat cover; the bathroom counter with the scattered containers of women's-brand deodorant and feminine hygiene products; pale-blue towels embroidered with sunny flowers . . . all of it was so distinctly and intimately hers that Tim felt like an invader. Or maybe felt as though he was trying on borrowed underwear. Well there wasn't any way around it; he *needed* that shower. He let the water run till it was hot, took off his drawers and his tattered socks, turned the middle knob so that the water came from the shower head. Climbed in and let hot water (stinging hot, but real hot showers always sting until you get used to them) and let the hot water knead his skin.

Did that for a long time. Let the water run hard as he shifted slowly under it, letting it work away the dirt and ash and the bits of crusted blood on his neck and in his hair.

Soap. Shampoo. More discomfort: soap and shampoo were even more intimate than the bathroom was. He did like Gail Benjamin, he really did. But he didn't know her well enough for this kind of intimacy.

Not that there was any real alternative.

He stooped over to soap up his legs, and saw the bandage Dr. Stout had set on his ankle so carefully last night. Waterlogged now, damn it. He'd have to replace it—if he was lucky Gail would have something he could use to replace it. He pulled it away from the skin of his ankle slow and easy, careful in case scab had cemented it in place. Which it hadn't. When it was free he leaned out of the shower and tossed it into the wastebasket on the far side of the commode.

Finished washing, let the steamy water clean away the soap. God, but it felt nice to be clean.

He was still rinsing the shampoo out of his hair when Gail knocked on the bathroom door.

She didn't wait for an answer before she walked right on in. Tim guessed she had a right to do that, since it was her bathroom, but it gave him an awful start all the same. Right in the middle of saying "Yes," in answer to her knock, and all of a sudden the door was opening and the shower curtain didn't feel opaque enough to give him any privacy.

"I've got your clothes," she said. "Took longer than I expected—all those pins in the shirt collar. And cardboard, too. They do package men's shirts thoroughly, don't they? I'll leave them here on the bathroom counter." The sound of a cabinet opening and closing. "A towel for you right beside them."

"Uh," he said. "Thanks." He thought he was grateful, anyway. All he knew for sure just then was that he wanted a little more privacy.

And then the sound of the door opening and closing, and Tim was alone and he let out a sigh of relief he hadn't realized he was holding in. Why was all of this making him so damn tense? It was strange and uncomfortable, sure, but he'd known last night and he knew it now: he wasn't going to do anything he didn't want to do. Still, he was uneasy; as his sigh finished it turned into a shudder.

Relax. I've got to relax. I feel pent-up and crazy. There's no reason for it.

That was the moment Gail decided to show him that she hadn't really left the room after all. By poking her head in around the edge of the shower curtain and scaring the wits half out of him.

Tim let out a loud, harsh sound that was part scream

and part howl and partly some word he couldn't even understand himself while Gail was in the middle of asking, "Mind if I join you in there?" But she didn't finish asking it because she was too busy laughing at the sight of a grown man scared by nothing at all.

"Sorry," she said. "Are you okay? I didn't mean to scare you. I thought you knew I was still here."

"I'll get over it. Heart'll slow down eventually." Tim felt awful stupid. Too dumb to worry about being embarrassed naked as she looked in at him, staring at his privates.

"You will. I'm sure." And then she climbed right into the shower without even giving him time to make up an excuse as to why he wanted to finish up alone.

She was naked, of course. And pretty, too. In spite of himself Tim was getting aroused, and naturally that was patently obvious.

Gail Benjamin was smiling.

"Do my back, please? The nice thing about having somebody around is getting my back scrubbed." She turned away from him.

What am I doing? Washing her back, that's what he was doing. He had the soap in his hand and he was washing her back. He had to get himself out of this gracefully and quietly and without making a scene, but back-washing was one of those basic human needs that you couldn't deny somebody when they needed it. Tim really felt that way, since there'd been lots of times when he'd pined to get someone else to scratch that unreachable spot in the center of his back.

"Like that—harder. Use your fingernails."

He had a raging hard-on—so hard that the damned thing hurt. He had to back away from her to keep it from brushing up against her ass.

He wanted her something fierce. He really did. She wanted him too, else she wouldn't be here. But he knew that if he let himself do it there'd be a bond between them that neither one of them had earned yet. And that whatever perspective he still had would be lost and irretrievable.

And the skin of her back, firm flesh all glisteny and slick from the soap.

And the sweat-smell of her hair.

And the sound of her voice groaning in her throat as her knees buckled a little and she braced herself against the wall.

God he wanted her. It took everything he had to hold himself back, but he managed to do it all the same.

"You're good," she said. "My but you're good." And she sniffed, and she shook her head to clear it. "Your turn," she said, turning back toward him.

And then she saw his hard-on.

She smiled hungrily.

And reached out to take it.

There was an echo of déjà vu somewhere down inside the rushing in his ears: she touched him, took his penis in her hand. And powerful and incredible and wonderful as it was, he reached out to take her wrist and gently move her hand away.

He tried to explain—at first all he could do was groan. Whether that was from pleasure or denial or the steamy air he wasn't sure. "I like you, Gail. I do. But let me get to know you better first, okay?"

He was sure she was going to take it badly. Positive. And at first she seemed to—the look in her eyes was hurt and embarrassed and maybe insulted.

There was accusation written all over her face: *You want it. I know damn well you do.* She was looking at his penis.

And he thought: *I know damn well I do. But I'm not going to do anything about it.* Maybe that was written on his face; maybe it wasn't.

And then she looked him in the eye and saw how cross-eyed he was with desire but holding himself back—

And she started to laugh. Giggling like a schoolgirl.

After a moment he was laughing too, giggling first then belly-laughing as pent tension boiled out of him. Both of them were leaning back-flat against the bathroom wall because it was the only way to keep from sliding to a fall. Facing toward the shower curtain, and after a while not laughing quite so much anymore. And then not laughing at all.

"You're sure?" she asked him. She looked like she honestly didn't believe it.

"Yeah." The more Tim thought about it, the stupider he felt. But it was the right thing to do. Or not do. Or whatever. Whatever it was, he was sure about it.

"Well," she said, "if that's what you want. Switch places with me, will you? I need to rinse the soap that's in my eye."

Which meant this off balance business with Tim sliding against the wall toward the back of the shower and Gail easing forward facing him, and they were touching again and that was intense. Maybe not quite as bad as it'd been just a little bit ago, but intense all the same.

They got through it, switched places in the too-narrow shower that was really a tub with a shower nozzle and curtain added as an afterthought. This was about when Tim realized that he was done with his shower. He'd been nearly done when Gail decided she wanted to join him, and what with the hot water beating on him all the while since he'd gotten himself pretty well rinsed. It was time to get out—the only reason to stay was to enjoy the fine sight of Gail Benjamin's rear end, and he'd seen quite enough of that already, thank you very much.

So he slipped out real quietly, without making any big point about it. Toweled dry and started dressing; by the time Gail stepped out of the shower Tim was tucking in his shirt.

"I've got to get going," he said. "Going out of town today." His wallet, change, comb, keys were on the counter next to where the clothes had been. He stuffed them into his pockets

"I know." She smiled. "You mentioned it last night."

"I'll be in touch after I get back."

"I know you will." And then she leaned over and kissed him, not forceful but lightly on the lips and very sensual.

She was something, he thought. Really something. He could get to like her an awful lot.

"How long do you think you'll be?"

He frowned. "Not long. Less than a week, most likely."

"I'll see you then. Call me. Call me the moment you're back."

"I will."

She walked him to the door, still naked and carrying her towel. And kissed him again before he left.

The only other important thing that happened before he left town was in the parking lot as Tim was leaving: he saw the old blue Dodge.

The car whose driver had shadowed him last night. The car he jumped on as it left the laundromat.

Parked a dozen spaces from Gail Benjamin's apartment.

He walked up to it, looked in through the window, and saw no one inside. Not that he'd expected anyone; he'd already gotten used to knowing when someone was watching him. There was no sense of lurking in that parking lot.

He went home, packed, stopped at the mall long enough to get a haircut (flattop: it was the only style that the barber could make of him after the shave he'd gotten from Dr. Stout); and then to B. Dalton to pick up a road atlas and plan his route. By dusk Tim was on I-75 heading north. His head didn't feel anywhere near so bad as he'd expected. But his left leg—his left leg nagged him something fierce. There was no way to get it comfortable in the foot well of the driver's seat. Tim counted his blessings. If it had been his right leg, driving cross-country would have been—well, not impossible. But close to it.

After a while he forgot about the discomfort. Forgot about everything, damned near; the drive was simple, long, and steady, straight up I-75 past Ocala; Gainsville; Valdosta, Georgia. On for hours after midnight past a thousand small towns in south Georgia, and then Macon, where he had to wake up enough to change lanes, or he'd have gotten onto I-16 and ended up in Savannah.

Seventy miles past Macon came Atlanta. Atlanta was a mare's nest, at least as far as the interstate system is concerned. Even at four a.m. it was congested and confusing—and just when Tim thought he'd gotten himself clear of it he noticed a sign overhead telling him that he was on I-85 just outside Chamblee, Georgia.

And cursed.

And got off near Chamblee, and looped around to get back on the highway heading in the opposite direction.

Five miles later he damned near missed the sign pointing him toward 75 north, too. Had to veer across two empty lanes of traffic to make that turn.

At five a.m., an hour outside Atlanta, it suddenly dawned on Tim that he was beginning to blank out. (In point of fact, he'd been nodding off behind the wheel for most of thirty miles. He was only now noticing.) He'd planned to drive straight through—but it wasn't a plan worth getting himself killed over. If he needed to get off the road for an hour or two and nod off in the car, he had the time. Something up in Tennessee was pressing, but it wasn't *that* pressing.

Up ahead on the right was a truck stop. An enormous one; it was still two or three miles off, and clearly visible from that distance. Big orange 76 globe—must have been the size of a house to look that big from here. Motel 6 sign below that—nowhere near as big, but big enough that he could read it.

He thought of Tom Bodette singing Motel 6 on AM radio—fiiive-oh-five, six nine one, *six*-one *six*-one. How that man could make a cheesy truck-stop hotel chain sound so homey and appealing was a mystery to Tim. But he certainly did it—did it well enough that the thought of a warm bed in a "clean, comfortable room" had an almost irresistible pull. Well, why not? He could take a room, get a few hours' sleep. A shower and a change of clothes and he could get back on the road by noon. He would do it. He was pulling off the interstate, and from here he could see that the vacancy sign was on.

Truck-stop hotel and the way truckers keep strange hours, they probably wouldn't even be surprised to see him checking in at five in the morning.

It took him a moment to find a parking spot—the near section of the parking lot was marked off for full semi rigs, and there were NO CARS signs posted in three places. Just as well, he decided when he finally did find the right part of the lot; the car parking was nearer the motel's front desk.

Ten minutes more and he was registered. Five minutes after that he was asleep in his "clean, comfortable room," and even if it wasn't as homey as Tom Bodette made it sound the bed was soft as heaven.

And sleep was bliss.

Such bliss, in fact, that Tim overindulged. He slept well on past noon. Past early evening, too, though he did wake enough to read the bedside clock at seven. At ten he opened his eyes again, and saw the time and saw that it was dark. And panicked. That woke him up, all right. What was he doing, sleeping seventeen hours at a stretch? It had to be his head. Maybe the concussion was worse than he kept trying to pretend. Had to be, if he could sleep that long.

But he felt—not that bad. Logy from sleep. But his head wasn't throbbing at all. Well, maybe that much sleep was just his body taking time to repair itself. He hoped so, anyway.

Out of bed. Into the shower. Dress. All in a daze—the same daze he almost always woke with. He needed his coffee, his newspaper.

The truck stop's restaurant would still be open. At a truck stop this big it'd be open all night.

Outside, the air was so much cooler and drier than the Florida nights he was used to that it woke him up a little. Two stops before he went to eat: first out to the car to get the atlas, then by the rack of newspaper machines out front of the diner. Reading the newspaper was important where waking up was concerned. Almost as important as coffee.

Moe's 6+76 I-75 Diner wasn't anywhere near as bad as it could have been. The coffee was so good, in fact, that it surprised him. Tim'd eaten in truck-stop diners before, and always regretted it. He had trouble believing that restaurants as unsavory as those could stay in business—truckers, after all, were likely to be repeat customers, and why would anyone eat twice in a place where coffee was greasy greyish sludge and eggs were sulfury-putrid things littered with crunchy bits of shell? Maybe the truckers liked their food that way, or maybe it was just the fact that it was hard to find anywhere but a truck stop to park a semi rig. Tim didn't know; whatever the rules were that governed truck stops, they didn't seem to apply to Moe's. The fried eggs were perfect, fresh and cooked till the white was firm but not cooked so long that the yolk wasn't wet. Bacon done just the way he liked it—firm but not yet dry. Golden toast still hot enough to melt butter when it got to his table. Crisp tasty home fires with little bits of onion and red pepper. And the Atlanta paper he picked up from the vending rack outside was good reading, too—literate, intelligent. Not at all a bad way to start a day, even if the day was beginning just an hour shy of midnight.

Which was when he finally got around to opening the atlas: midnight. It wouldn't have taken that long just to eat (it was only ten thirty-five when he got into the diner), but the Atlanta paper was so much better than he expected that he ended up reading almost all of it.

Atlas. He took the paper off the counter, folded it up, set it on the stool next to him. Opened the atlas. Turned to the page with the map of Tennessee. The bottom edge of the map showed the northmost counties of Georgia—he looked closely, following the line that was I-75. Right there, that was where he was. Summerville, just before I-75 and the state of Georgia fell off the page and into oblivion. He traced I-75 back up out of Georgia, into Tennessee. Through Chattanooga; on up toward Knoxville. He'd have to take 75 past Knoxville most of the way to the Kentucky. He looked closely again; the names of the feeder roads and the small towns were in fine, fine print. There, that was the road he needed. State Highway 65. It met 75 at a little town called . . . Pioneer. He'd have to take 65 five miles past US 27. That was Tylerville. Another five miles beyond that was Green Hill. Somewhere between was a place called Still Ridge that wasn't on this map—nor on the thick desk atlas Tim had at home. He had a feeling that it wasn't on any map, and that no matter how hard he tried to find a map that showed it he'd find nothing.

It didn't matter. He'd find the place, with or without a map. He had to.

He looked back down toward Summerville, Georgia. How far between where he was and where he thought he needed to be? Three hundred miles, at least. Three-fifty easily; as much as four hundred if the roads did more winding than they seemed to on the map.

Tim closed the road atlas, picked up the meal check that had been sitting on the counter through the last three refillings of his coffee cup. (There'd been two before that. Tim didn't generally need to drink six cups of coffee to wake up, but the coffee he made at home was very strong. This coffee was good, but it was American-style coffee and a little thin.) He left money to cover the cost of the meal and a generous tip, and then he left a couple more dollars to cover the fact that he'd taken his spot at the counter for so long. And then he left.

Back to the room where he gathered up his clothes; up to the front desk to check out. Out to the car and back on the road.

Road signs going by, all through the night: Dalton, Tunnel Hill, and Fort Oglethorpe in Georgia. Up into Tennessee where Chattanooga waited for him. And then northeast past Cleveland and Athens and Philadelphia (yes, all of these in Tennessee, and not Ohio or Greece or Pennsylvania) and at least fifty less-memorable towns. He hit Knoxville a little after four a.m., and 75 swung northwest. Another hour along 75 and he was pulling off just outside Pioneer, Tennessee.

Pioneer was a tiny place—five houses, a laundromat, and a 7-Eleven. Amazing that they'd marked it on the map.

How small was Still Ridge, if it had been left off? This was going to be a problem. Tim had a bad feeling about it.

The sun was coming up somewhere just beyond the slope-shouldered mountains on the eastern horizon. It was a good thing, too, because Highway 63 wasn't quite as easy to figure as I-75. It was marked in the atlas as a scenic route. Which meant that it curled around soft hills and low ridges an extra mile for every two it went forward, and its two thin lanes were no larger or more prominent than any of the country roads that fed into it. Twice the road forked (where the map had shown no forks at all) and Tim nearly turned off the highway without realizing it.

Then, finally, the junction with US 127, and after that 63 straightened out considerably. He was in Tylerville before he realized it.

Tylerville, Tennessee was a quiet place at six a.m. At the edge of town Tim saw two pickup trucks (complete with gun racks and drivers who looked like farmhands) speeding in the opposite direction. A cruiser farther in, toward the center of things (if you could call one TG&Y and two supermarkets a town center). Inside the cruiser were two sheriff's deputies drinking coffee, talking animatedly. One of them was smoking a cigar. Tim doubted that either one had looked up long enough to notice the speeding trucks.

Highway 63 did a goofy bit of business in Tylerville: Four blocks past the TG&Y there was a small sign, a sign no bigger than a parking sign, pointing left. So small he didn't see it till it was whizzing past and it was already too late to turn onto the road it pointed toward.

**TENNESSEE
HIGHWAY
63**

←

And just like that Tim was on the wrong road.
Damn.

He slowed, looked for a place to pull in and turn around. And the first place he saw was the veterinary office on the right. A tiny little place with wood siding that looked as though it might have been a convenience store in another incarnation. Tim turned in, saw two cars in its parking lot. (He noticed the license plates. One of them—the white Lincoln—was an unmarked sheriff's cruiser. The number, and a six-point star, and below that the word SHERIFF. And wondered what was going on inside the veterinarian's office. And wondered why it was that law-enforcement types would go to all the trouble to use unmarked cars and then make their license plates so obvious.)

He started to turn the around. Looked up at the front door of the veterinarian's. Put his foot on the brake, and paused—

There was something about that building. Something important that he ought to know.

Something he should have known for a while.

But how could he have known anything about it? He'd never been to Tylerville, Tennessee, before in his life.

Maybe he ought to park the car, go in and ask.

Looked at his watch. Six twenty. Did he have time? Probably—there was no way to be sure. He was here a day later than he'd hoped to be. No way to know if another few minutes would make a difference—though it didn't seem likely that it would.

Shifted into park, cut the ignition. Unbuckled his seat belt, opened his door—and hesitated again.

No. It wasn't time to go in there yet. Not now, but soon.

He didn't know where the thought had come from, but there was something in it that he trusted. Something that made him sure.

Sure even if he didn't understand.

Closed the door, belted in, started the engine, and left.

Right to get back onto the highway.

Here it was a straightaway, straight as a city street, ignoring the rolling contour of the hills it passed over. As though the highway had some mission in mind and wanted to get on with it as directly as was possible, and never mind the cost of running roads straight up.

Was it trying to take him directly to his destination?

No. Of course it wasn't. A road is a lifeless thing, made of tar and bits of rock. Tim knew that. Roads didn't have intentions, nor motivations nor any such thing. Someone drew this road deliberately straight and spent a fortune paving it. God knew why he'd done it, but that was years ago, not now. The road had nothing to do with Tim.

He watched the sides of the road carefully, looking for some hint of a tiny town called Still Ridge.

He saw nothing. Nothing but woods and tall weeds and more of both. And more still—five miles of nothing but arboreal abundance.

Then off to the right there were burned, desolate trees—an enormous swath of forest burned . . . not recently. A year ago. Maybe more.

Tim pulled his car over onto the shoulder of the road so that he could take a better look. Got out, stretched. Scanned the charred woods.

Did the burning have something to do with Still Ridge? There was nothing in the desolation you could call a town. Or ever could have called; the ruin here was the charred-tree-stump ruin of a forest, not the ruin of a town. No hulks of ruined houses crouching in among the stumps of trees. No sign of roads, paved or otherwise. Besides, whatever was happening with Grandpa's death and the missing fragment of the Cross was happening *now*. The destruction in the woods was something from the not-too-recent past.

No—there was nothing here. Nothing that bore directly on his problem. He got back in the car, started the engine, pulled back onto the highway.

A long steep hill lead away from the desolation. When he crested it Tim saw a town. His heart surged— was this Still Ridge, so plain and obvious after he'd spent so much effort looking for obscure things off the highway?

No. As he drew close he saw a small, boarded-up roadside café. The sign above it was still readable, even if it was in bad repair.

GREEN HILL CAFÉ

He'd overshot. The woman at the shipping company had been clear on that: Still Ridge was on Highway 63 between Tylerville and Green Hill.

Had she sent him on a goose chase? Tim groaned at the idea. And felt a little panic, too: this was the only lead he had.

(Or was it? Something nagged at the back of his brain. Something. And then it came back to him. The book. The book he'd found after the dream with Grandpa. It was still in the trunk of the car where he'd put it that afternoon—two, three days ago? Time was such a blur that it was hard to be certain. He had to sit down and read that book, and soon.)

What he needed were directions. If there was a small town—or something less than a town—between here and Tylerville, the locals would know about it, wouldn't they? There was a boy over there, sitting in the grass near the dead café's parking lot. Tim turned in to the lot, parked, rolled down his window.

And called to the boy. "Excuse me. Son?" He didn't feel old enough to be calling anybody *son*, but he didn't know what other word to use. "Can you tell me where I'd find a town called Still Ridge?"

The boy didn't even look up.

Rude little cuss.

Or maybe he was deaf.

Maybe he didn't even know Tim was trying to talk to him. Tim got out of the car, let the door hang open. (And that annoying *thing* inside his dash said, "The door is ajar," in that grating voice that made it sound like *The door is a jar*. Tim swore he was going to find a mechanic who could get that thing permanently disengaged. But he'd sworn the same thing at least a hundred times.)

Tim crossed the dusty-dry red-clay parking lot, crossed the weedy lot beyond it. Stooped in front of the boy. If he was deaf, he'd probably be able to read lips, wouldn't he? Tim hoped he would.

"Son?"

The boy was staring at the weeds off to Tim's left.

Tim reached out, touched his shoulder, trying to get his attention.

"Son?"

But it didn't seem to make any difference. The boy didn't respond to his touch. Didn't even seem aware of it.

Dear God, the poor boy is autistic.

What was an autistic child doing alone here in the field? Someone should be here to watch after him. Something was very wrong. It wasn't right—it wasn't safe for this boy to be so close to the road and unattended, was it?

This is all I need. I don't have time to find this boy's folks and get him back to them. Not that he had any real choice. He couldn't just leave the boy here to wander out into the highway and get himself run over. It wasn't in Tim to be that unconcerned.

He reached down, took the boy's hand from where it lay not quite limp on the grass—

And the boy looked up at him.

And Tim saw why the child was here alone and unattended.

Saw it in his eyes.

Like Grandpa's eyes, dead Grandpa in the morgue, but the emptiness here was deeper and more infinite than the eyes of a corpse could ever be.

softer stiller than the breath of an unborn child never born but dead, dead now in its womb

How could it be otherwise?—The boy was alive, and breathing, and Tim suspected that he'd flinch reflexively if something hit him. But every human thing inside him was gone, drained away somehow.

As though, Tim thought, some powerful force had sucked away his soul.

No—the soul is in there. Far, far down inside. And dormant, somehow—seeing the traces of it made Tim think of a moth wrapped in its chrysalis, hibernating. Recovering from something so awful that it had to hide from the memory.

What could do that to the heart of a child? Suddenly

Tim was angry—very, very angry. What foul *thing,* what unspeakable act?

the heart of his child

He wanted to scream.

And then he *did* scream, in rage and horror and grief for the boy dead and alive both at once. He never meant that scream—rather it took him from some deep-inside place he didn't know recognize or control.

Off in the distance someone shouted in reply.

Something happening right here, right now. Something happening to the boy.

Something small, at first.

A blink.

Another.

And then the miracle of miracles bloomed before Tim's eyes: the child's eyes went wide with life and terror, and he cried out in fear and pain.

And lived.

As Tim watched he could see something inside the boy opening out to flower and live and breathe, and the sensation of the boy's spirit bursting its cocoon made hair stand on end electrically all across Tim's arms.

Like an infant crying out in terror at the sight of the world.

Tim almost broke down and started crying himself: it made him think of a time and a place and a love he didn't dare remember.

He picked the boy up and held him in his arms and hugged him. "It's okay," he said. "Don't you worry. It's okay now."

The sound of the boy's crying *was* the sound of his infant crying as it had never breathed to cry, gentler now that Tim held him but still full of simple natural fear of the size and color of the world. "Don't worry, baby. You'll be all right." He heard what he was saying, and heard what it meant when he said it. And pulled away for fear he'd lose his grip on the world around him. "I'll find your mom."

Tim didn't have the first idea how he was going to do it, but he knew that he had to. He sure couldn't leave the boy here—not now. Not after this.

Then he heard the sound, and he remembered that he'd heard someone shouting from far away. It was a tiny sound, the kind a person makes by breathing, or stepping on loose gravel. It meant someone stood a few feet behind Tim, watching him very closely.

Tim looked around, quickly, half-afraid that some awful thing had crept up behind him while he was caught up with the boy. But no; it was another boy, just another boy maybe two years older than the first.

The two were brothers; Tim could see it plainly in their features.

"Who *are* you, mister?" the older boy asked him. He stared at Tim as though he were some strange, inhuman thing. Or perhaps his eyes were full of disbelief. "What did you do to Sean?"

"I—" *I didn't do anything*, Tim was going to say. But it wasn't true, and there wasn't any reason to lie. What had he done? Tim frowned; he felt his brow knit up with confusion. He wasn't sure what it was he'd done, but he knew that it was something important, even vital.

The older boy stepped closer, took his brother from Tim's arms. Tim watched him staring at the younger boy as he took him, saw his face as he recognized the new light in his brother's eyes. And when he turned back to face Tim, the older boy was gaping.

"Who *are* you?"

"My name is Tim Fischer."

The older boy shook his head. "That isn't what I meant," the boy said. There was something about this boy . . . Tim wasn't sure what. But it almost made him nervous. It felt—as though the boy knew him. Because there was some link between them? Tim blinked, surprised: there *was* a connection from him to this boy. Not just because Tim had been here to watch his brother wake. No, this was something terrible, frightening. Something linked—not the Cross itself. Not Grandpa, either. The Bleeding Man? A lurch in Tim's stomach: not exactly that. But it was very nearly so. "And you know it damn well."

"Who do you think I am?"

The boy's eyes were wide, staring hard. "I don't

know who you are," he said. It looked to Tim as though he were lying. "But you're someone special. And you did something for Sean that was—needful. I owe you for that."

Tim coughed, looked away. He hadn't done anything—or nothing he'd understood. There wasn't any debt. But he didn't think the boy would take that for an answer, and it wasn't a thing he wanted to argue about.

"I think your brother needs some rest," he said. "Let me help you get him home to bed."

The boy seemed to be weighing Tim again. "My name is Thomas Brady," he said. "My brother's name is Sean." He shifted his still-crying brother to his feet so that he could hold him up with his left arm. Held his right hand out to Tim. "Your help would be appreciated."

Tim took his hand, shook it. "Good," he said. "How far away do you live? Might be best if we took my car."

Thomas Brady nodded. "I reckon that it would."

"Here," Tim said. "I'll take him." And Tim lifted the younger boy, carried him to the car. "Open the door for me, would you?" But it wasn't really necessary to ask; Thomas Brady was already there, opening up the car, moving away the newspaper Tim'd tossed into the back when he'd left the hotel last night. When he was done Tim eased Sean into the seat, where the boy curled himself like an infant into the upholstery. "Do you think you ought to ride back there with him? In case he starts to . . . I don't know. There isn't even room, the way I've set him in there. And I suspect you'd have an awful time getting him to move."

Thomas shook his head. "I think he'll be just fine. It isn't like we're going far. Home is just down the road and up around the hill a ways; won't take more than a couple minutes."

"I guess." Tim closed the back door, reached over to open the front passenger door for Thomas. Walked around the car, slid in behind the steering wheel. "Don't just stand there waiting for an invitation. You going to show me where we're going or not?"

"Right." Thomas got into the car, closed the door behind him.

In a moment Tim had the car turned around and pointed out of the parking lot. Thomas directed him left onto the highway, and left again a hundred yards later. Another quarter mile down a badly paved feeder road. And then to a sudden stop in front of a house that looked as though it were at least a hundred years old. The place was three stories tall, made of weathered wood—its pale-green paint looked as though it had begun to blister at least half a generation ago.

Thomas Brady was staring at him. Watching Tim as he looked at the rotting old house. He was being obvious, wasn't he? He was wondering why the house had gone to seed, why no one had bothered to paint it in so many years. Why that shutter there on the second floor—third window from the left—why did it hang askew? And there, on the overgrown lawn—weren't those shingles fallen from the roof? What was wrong, here?—were the Bradys blind and impervious to the weather leaking into their home? All those questions and a dozen others were written on Tim's face. And Thomas Brady had seen them there. Tim turned to face him, to look him in the eye. "What's happened here? Is there something you need to tell me before I carry your brother inside?"

The boy sighed. Turned and looked away into the pinewoods run riot beside his home. "If I told you," he said, "you'd think I was touched. Maybe I *am* touched, come to think on it. But I'm still not going to let my mouth go flapping like a fool's. Huh. I could show you, I guess, but there isn't anything left for me to show."

Tim shook his head. "I don't think that there's anything you could say that'd make me call you a fool."

Thomas turned back to face Tim. Looked him in the eye dead-serious and so long it made him want to ease away uncomfortably. Shrugged.

"I don't know," he said. "I don't know what you need to hear. We're touched, is all. All of us. Me and Sean and Mom and Dad and everyone here in town—all of us are touched."

"Touched? Touched how? By what? What do you mean?"

Thomas shook his head.

"I said enough already. Come on—help me get Sean into the house. None of us going to hurt you. Nothing going to do you any harm because of what I didn't say."

He was already out of the car, opening the rear passenger-side door. Easing his brother up and out of the back seat.

Enough. The boy meant him no harm—that was plain enough. If there was trouble waiting for him inside that house, then Tim would cope when he found it. "Wait—don't try to carry him by yourself. He's a heavy kid; you'll break your back." Tim got out of his seat, hurried around the back of the car to take Sean from his brother's arms. "Oof—even heavier than I remembered. How did he get out to that field, anyway? You didn't carry him all the way out there, did you?"

Thomas shook his head again. "No. The way he was—he'd follow you, once you got him on his feet. Got him started walking. Sometimes he'd stop, but he'd always be there waiting when you went back for him. Now and then I take him out with me just to get him in the sun."

"Ah. I see. Door's over there, isn't it? Where're you going?"

" 'Round back to the kitchen door. The front goes right in to the parlor. We don't use it much. Used to, back when folks'd come for dinner—no call for that now. Not since last summer." He cleared his throat. "This way—you're walking right past the door."

It was true, too. How had he missed it there?

Sean was crying again, quieter than before but still crying. Maybe that'd distracted Tim.

And maybe he hadn't seen the door because he hadn't wanted to see it. Decrepit. Spongy-rotten wood that hung askew on rusting hinges. Stains in what was left of the blistered white paint—they looked like bloodstains. Old, old bloodstains.

"You okay?" Thomas asked him.

It wasn't till then that Tim realized he'd stopped dead in his tracks.

"What? Oh. I'm fine." Too much. Bloodstains. Something was wrong here. So wrong that he was a fool to ignore it. "Those stains on your door. They're from blood."

He'd seen movies just like this, Tim had. The *Texas Chainsaw Massacre*. Other films, too—the kind of movies they showed in seedy Ybor City theaters when the police arrested them for playing pornographic films.

Maybe Thomas hadn't seen those movies. If he had, wouldn't he understand why Tim had to ask the question? He didn't, though. His eyes were wide with self-righteous anger. And surprise and alarm—and dread.

"You aren't going to call the police, are you? Please don't do that to us. Not again. Haven't we been through enough already? Haven't we suffered enough yet?"

What?

"Stop it, Thomas. You're scaring me. I didn't say anything about calling the police—but I do want to know where that blood came from. Do you live in a slaughterhouse?"

Anger.

"No." The boy looked mad enough to kill. "We aren't any butchers. We couldn't see that stain—not till last year. Same way we couldn't see the house falling out from under us. And now . . . Sean's sick, Mom and Dad are so sick with themselves that they don't hardly leave their room. It's only me to do these things. And what can *I* do? Hard enough to make sure everybody eats. I got no time to fix this place. Even less for cleaning."

Tim blinked. He was beginning to get a picture of the events that'd made this town what it was. And already wishing it away.

"Are you going to carry my brother into his room or not? Give him to me if you haven't got the nerve."

"I'll take him." It was a stupid thing to do, and Tim knew it. Leatherface waited for him just beyond that bloodstained door.

Tim *knew* it.

He went in anyway, following close behind the boy.

Into the kitchen that smelled of rotten wood and spoiled food—smelled of stagnant water left to soak in dirty pots till the filth and the water and the pot-metal itself all began to ferment. . . .

Snap.

The sound of something breaking loud and not too far away out of sight out of the room somewhere in the rest of the house and who the hell and what the hell and Tim knew he was going to die die die—

And he screamed.

And screamed again.

And nearly dropped poor Sean, who'd started crying again, afraid because of the noise and the tension and the feel in the air of something about to pounce.

"What are you doing? Trying to scare my brother out of his wits? What's *wrong* with you?" Thomas turned, called out to the dark, empty-looking hall. "Mom? Dad? Is that you?"

Footsteps. And then a voice: "Yes, Thomas, it's me." A woman's voice, quiet and tired and worn by time. "I hear crying, Thomas. I hear a child crying. Is that you? Have you brought a friend? Is he hurt?"

"No, Mom. Somebody's with me, and he's making a racket. But it's Sean who's crying, not Mr. Fischer."

"That isn't funny, Thomas." Impatient. The woman sounded as though she were on the verge of hysteria.

"I'm not kidding you, Mom. Sean's changed again. Mr. Fischer woke him up somehow."

The footsteps started again. More quickly now. Moving toward the mouth of the impenetrably dark hall. (Light—light. Didn't these people have electric lights? Yes, they did; there was a dead bulb mounted in the ceiling above them. Didn't they believe in using them? And how could this house be so dark when it was broad daylight out—had they lowered the blinds and sealed them shut?

(That was when it occurred to Tim that it wasn't *The Texas Chainsaw Massacre* he'd stepped into, but *Dracula*.)

Then Thomas's mother was in the kitchen with

them, out in the half-light that leaked through the kitchen window, and it was obvious that she couldn't be a vampire because she wasn't turning to dust, and in the movies Dracula always crumbled apart when he saw the sun.

Not only was she not a vampire, but the moment Tim saw her he knew he was a fool. She was just a woman, just a poor woman beaten by the circumstances of her life. Resigned; defeated. Grey-haired and weathered looking, despite the fact that she hadn't quite yet reached her forties. There was no menace in her. Her home was dark because she didn't have the heart to face the light of day.

Tim knew all those things just by looking in her eye. (It didn't occur to him to wonder how he knew so much. He was too busy feeling like an ass.)

"His room's over here, Mr. Fischer. We put him here off the kitchen because it's so hard to get him up the stairs. Set him on his bed so Mom can see."

Tim blinked, confused. Took a moment realizing that "Mr. Fischer" was him. The boy had called him that twice now; Tim didn't think he'd know the name if he used it a hundred times. Dad was Mr. Fischer, or maybe Grandpa was; Tim sure wasn't.

"Don't just stand there. Nothing in this room going to bite you, either."

Tim blushed. He followed the boy through a narrow doorway off the left side of the kitchen, into a room that was nearly as dark as the hall that the woman had come from. The bed Thomas directed him toward was near the window—thank God!—and even with the blinds drawn tight it let through a little light. Enough to keep Tim from stumbling as he set Sean on the bed. (Sheets, grey in the spare light: they were anything but fresh. Not as filthy as Tim'd been sure they would be, but stale enough that he could smell old sweat as he eased the boy into the linen. . . .)

"Sweet Jesus," the woman said. She was looking at her younger son now—as soon as Tim had set Sean down she'd eased in, pressed Tim away to look close at the boy. Put one hand on Sean's forehead to test for fever; took his right wrist with the other and held it as though she were making certain that he had a pulse. (But of course he had a pulse. He was crying, breathing, wasn't he? Tim's imagination was running away from him. But things *were* wrong here—all the little things, all of them were wrong.)

"Sean? Can you hear me, Sean?" She stared down into the boy's eyes, studying carefully, as though they weren't eyes but pools of deep, murky water.

"I don't think he can answer you, Mom. I tried to talk to him too. It's like—it's like he's a baby all over again. Can you imagine that? Can you imagine Sean a baby again, only all growed up this time?"

His mother only frowned and shook her head (ever so slightly—a motion so small so gentle Tim almost didn't see it). She didn't look away from Sean.

The sound of floorboards creaking in the kitchen, or maybe in the hall beyond it. Tim caught Thomas's eye, glanced out toward the kitchen and back again.

"Your father?"

Thomas nodded.

"I need to leave, I guess," Tim said. "I need to get back on the road."

"Yes."

Tim hesitated, reaching for the something else that nagged him from his stomach. That was it—there. *Still Ridge*.

"I need directions, if you know them. I need to find a place called Still Ridge."

A blank look on Thomas's face; the woman shook her head again, more vigorously this time. "I've never heard of any such place," she told him.

"I was told—someone told me that it was between here and Tylerville. But all I saw was woods. Not even so much as a shanty."

The woman sighed, impatient. She needed to see to her infant son, and the stranger chattering in her ear was nothing but a distraction. "Someone gave you bad directions. Hope you didn't come too far to follow them."

But Thomas—Thomas's expression was anything but distracted.

Thomas was alarmed.

Thomas looked scared half out of his wits.

He signaled Tim for silence, pointed him toward the door. Held up a finger as though to say *One minute*.

What now. . . ? It'd been one long chain of *wrong-ness* since he'd first stopped in this town. Tim was getting tired of it, tired of the way it unsettled and distracted him. The only consolation was that it'd be over soon.

He shrugged, stood up. Thomas was going to meet him outside the kitchen door? Maybe he shouldn't wait. Maybe he ought to get himself the hell *out* of here—

The kitchen. He was in the fetid kitchen, walking toward the door, and someone stood invisible in the shadows *watching* him.

Thomas's father.

Tim hurried toward the door. Opened it, stepped out into the so-bright-oh-thank-God-so-bright sun. He let the screen door swing shut behind him, glanced back—Thomas. He had to give Thomas at least a moment, had to wait for him at least that long or it'd be obvious that he'd run away. . . .

Then it was too late, because Thomas was bounding out of the house, pushing open the screen door with such force that it hit Tim's shoulder and rebounded—

"*Uhnn*—"

"Sorry, didn't meant to—and I was in a hurry to catch you before you left—"

Which meant that the boy knew what Tim'd planned, didn't it? Tim thought it did. Most likely because Tim'd been obvious, because he'd left it written all over his face.

"Slow down. I'm here. Wasn't going anyplace without you." That was a lie, but it was certainly more comfortable than the truth.

Thomas glanced over his shoulder, through the screen door into the dark kitchen. His eyes were anxious.

"I know a place," he said. His voice was quieter than a whisper. "But we shouldn't talk here. We'll frighten Mom and Dad."

Tim raised an eyebrow, hesitated. Resigned himself and shrugged.

Thomas led him out to the front yard, past it—he stopped by Tim's car and rested his back against it.

"There isn't any town between here and Tylerville," he said. "But there's a place. And I think—I think it might be the place you mean."

He stopped, waited as though he expected Tim to respond.

"Go on."

"The Stone—it wouldn't let us go anywhere near this place. Most of us didn't even know about it. I knew because of the day I got lost when it wouldn't pay any attention to me. And when it found out where I'd been it ripped me up and down. . . !"

"Stone? I don't understand. What stone? And why would a rock care where you'd been?"

Thomas looked puzzled. "You don't know? You really don't know? You've come all this way full of secrets to be here, and you don't know about the Stone?"

Tim shook his head.

Thomas took a moment; he looked as though he were searching for words. "The Stone was inside us, all of us at once, like it was a part of our hearts. Or maybe like it was our heads. But it wasn't just something you felt; it was real and black and big as day and hard as rock, so even though it wasn't rock exactly we called it Stone. It could only be you when you were little, so when you got old enough it'd made you forget you'd ever known what you knew. It did that to all of us, to everybody who'd ever lived in this town for as long as anyone remembers.

"It made us do horrible things. Made us? Helped us? *I* did things. Everyone did. It wasn't just the Stone using my hands. It found the part of me that wanted to do *hurt*, and made it grow. But it was me who did those things, not Stone. I know that. I remember.

"Stone is gone a year, and we all remember now. And most of the people in this town are so weighed down with the guilt of what they did—so sick with themselves that they can't face the world."

Tim closed his eyes, trying to make sense of the

fragmented story. Digesting what sense he had of it. There was a connection here—some connection to his own quest.

"What about you, Thomas? Why aren't you as shaken as your folks?"

Thomas looked away. "I got free before the rest of them. On my own. And I had a chance to start making amends."

"What was the Stone? How did it . . . touch you? And why?"

Thomas scowled. "How do you expect me to know things like that? I don't. Do you want to find the place you're looking for or not?"

"Huh? Of course I do." A pause—the boy kept throwing Tim off balance. "What brought that on?"

Thomas sighed impatiently. "Nothing brought it on. We need to take your car. Where we're going is farther than you want to walk."

Tim walked around to his side, got into the car. Reached over to unlock the passenger-side door.

"Get in, then."

And in a moment they were on the rutted feeder road, moving toward the highway just a little faster than was safe.

"Left here." Which was the direction Tim had come from.

Onto the highway anyway, and Tim floored the gas pedal—he didn't drive like this, not usually. Except when he was agitated. Which he was. Quite disturbed, in fact. For obvious reasons and for others that he didn't understand.

Faster, faster now—

"Not so fast," Thomas said. "You'll miss the turn."

What turn? Tim had been this way not long before. There weren't any turns. Just woods, woods, and more woods.

"Hmm?"

Already they'd covered a mile since the feeder road.

"Slow down! The place you got to go is so hard to see you could walk past it even if you knew where you were. This fast we'll drive right by—*Stop!* Now—yeah, now. You're going to have to back up. Ten yards back, there on the left—"

Tim finished bringing the car to a stop. Eased it into reverse. Back, back—there. Just as Thomas said. A split-rail fence, hiding in among the pines—and woven through by kudzu vine; even if Tim had known to look deep into the woods he wouldn't have seen it. The kudzu was too dense, too overwhelming.

That was a sign, wasn't it? A wooden placard mounted on the fence. Impossible to read from here, with the leaves and vine stems crowding out the carved-in words.

When he looked close as he could Tim saw a path beside the placard, a place that could once have been a fence gate.

And tire tracks. Right there, right down the center of the path—kudzu shredded as though a car had run it through just recently.

A car . . . or a moving van? Yes, a moving van stuffed to the gills with Grandpa's worldly life.

Tim pulled his car up onto the shoulder of the road; over it, into the kudzu and through it.

As he passed through the gate he drew close enough to read the sign through the leaves that covered it:

HINES PLANTATION
STILL RIDGE, TENNESSEE

ABRAHAM FISCHER,
PROPRIETOR

But it went by so quickly that he hardly noticed; Tim didn't grasp the connection for days and days and days.

"What is this place?" Tim asked. "Who lives here?"

"Old house—real old. Mansion from before the War Between the States. Nobody was there when I saw it, and I don't think they'd been there for a long, long time."

No one inside it? Something wrong about that.

"If there was no one inside it, why were you supposed to stay away?"

A low branch thwacked the windshield, scraped the roof of the car. Made a sound like fingernails through chalk.

"Because of the flowers."

Flowers? Tim waited for the boy to continue.

"Black flowers growing wild where all the gardens used to be. Glassy-black, hard as rock, strong like metal. Like that flower the Tompkins boy found when everything was flying to hell. Flowers that look like they was cut out of the Stone."

The Stone. That was the thing that had controlled their minds, Thomas had said.

"These flowers grow right out in the open? Out in the light of day?"

The boy looked puzzled. "'Course they did. You expect 'em to grow in a hole in the ground or something like they was mushrooms?"

Flowers made of black glass: Tim tried to picture them. And couldn't. In all his life Tim'd never seen anything like that growing in the earth.

It didn't matter whether he believed. In a moment he knew, he'd have a chance to see for himself.

"Been up here lately?"

"Nah." Thomas's eyes went tight for a moment as he stared hard out at the road. "Careful," he said. "The path splits up ahead. You need to bear to the left."

Path? That was the word for it, Tim guessed. But even *path* was an exaggeration; if there was a trail here the kudzu had obliterated it a generation ago. The vine covered the ground to a height of eighteen inches, and obscured the surface of the ground as thoroughly as tall grass. The only blessing was the fact that it was insubstantial—grass would have made for tougher going.

Something skittered through the vines. A squirrel or maybe an enormous rat—could even have been a small dog, but Tim didn't think so.

"I should warn you," Thomas said, "about those flowers."

"Huh?" Warn him about what? Tim felt dread wash

over him like a wave of tepid water. There was something waiting to happen, something to do with the boy
and his connection to the Bleeding Man—Tim had
expected it since . . . since back at the Brady house.
Or longer. He had. Whatever it was the boy was about
to say, Tim had known it all along.

"They make you see things. Or smell them, or hear
them. Like they get into your head, sort of. Like the
Stone used to do. But different, because they aren't all
bad the way the Stone was."

No—that wasn't it. That wasn't the other shoe he
kept expecting to hear. It was interesting, in fact.
Flowers that invade the mind? Tim thought of opium
poppies. No, not like that. The boy was too literal-
minded to describe opium poppies the way he'd described these flowers.

Flowers: there had to be a connection between the
flowers and the Bleeding Man. Had to be a connection to
this Stone the boy kept talking about too. *That* was the
shoe waiting to drop. That and one other thing, much
smaller.

"This house," Tim said, "do you know who built it?
You said it was built before the Civil War."

Thomas frowned. "Huh-uh. I just said that 'cause I
learned it in school: all of these big old-style mansion
houses were slave houses before the War Between the
States. I don't really know anything 'bout it at all, and I
never heard anybody talk about it in all my life. I just
found it one day, is all."

There was no reason for the boy to lie, was there?
No.

But there was something suspicious in the air.

The pinewoods were deeper, here, and there was
no kudzu. That didn't mean that the trail was any easier
to follow; it'd long since overgrown with seedling trees
and the odd green scrub you find on the floor of any
forest. If it weren't for the trail of broken vegetation
some other car had left behind, there'd have been
nothing to mark the trail away from the woods that
surrounded it.

Thomas gasped.

Tim looked up—

And saw the house.

And saw the garden run riot with black glass like volcano froth sand on some exotic beach—but where a beach ran out to meet the sea this ran up, up to form the crown of the hill where the haunted house stood threatening the sky.

Like Dorothy, Tim thought. *Like Dorothy in Oz when she comes over the hill and there are the poppies stretched out from here to kingdom come.* He remembered seeing that scene on television—the first time, back when he was six—and remembered awe just like the wonder he felt now; remembered watching dumbstruck and afraid as Dorothy set out to cross that sea of fearful blooming green.

He remembered seeing her fade to sleep, too, or nearly fade—

"*Hey!* Careful! That tree—you're going to drive right into it."

"Eh?—damn. Thanks."

Tim steered the car back onto the trail. It was harder to make it out here; obscured by decade-layers of pine straw and fallen branches. Rotted logs, too—more of those than Tim would have expected. What broke those trees?—At least two dozen of them littered the trail between here and where the woods gave way to the flower field that surrounded the mansion.

What did the flowers have to do with broken trees? And the mansion? And the Bleeding Man?

The mansion. When Thomas first used that word to describe the place, Tim had pictured some great antebellum structure—lines, lintels, columns after the fashion of ancient Greece; white-marble walls stretching up toward infinity.

This mansion was nothing like that.

It was like a castle, like a castle he'd expect to see in the deepest heart of mountain Europe, but uglier and meaner-looking than any castle meant to be. Craggy grey-stone walls so purposely uneven. Seven windows facing front, so deeply set to make the glass invisible inside them—from this far they looked like gullet holes

to seven caves. There, on the left, a turret stretched five
stories into the air, two flights up beyond the main body
of the structure.

The Bleeding Man had built that thing. No question
in Tim's mind. Who else would live in such a vile rock?
No one Tim could think of.

"You'd better stop the car," Thomas said. "The
flowers are stronger than you'd think. They'll slice right
through your tires if you try to drive on them."

Tim sighed; he wasn't ready to get out of the car yet.
He didn't want to be like Dorothy, losing his self-control,
collapsing amid the flowers. The car was his protection.
If he gave it up now there was no telling what else he'd
lose before he was done—

"All right," he said. And pulled off the trail, and
stopped between two rotted pines. Tim barely noticed
them—till he'd killed the ignition, opened the door, and
the near one caught in the corner of his eye. He blinked;
looked again and then away; and did a triple take. There
were mushrooms growing everywhere around those
trees, irregular layered fungal things ugly as rot growing
in a food cellar. On the ground here, too—all around
them on the ground pressing up through the pine straw
and mouldering debris.

What was this stuff? Besides disgusting? More
connections that Tim didn't want to make. Not that there
was any way to avoid it; there was a link between the
mushroom-stuff and the bizarre structure up above
them.

Probably, Tim thought, *the trees were dead already. Fungus, mold, rot—they're always on dead trees,
aren't they?*

Of course they were. Fungus was natural where
dead things were concerned.

It was absolutely true. Unquestionable. Tim felt
himself relax a little, reassured that the world wasn't
conspiring all around him, that the strange house up
ahead was nothing but a strange house; that the impossible black flowers that glittered in the sun were nothing
but lawn furniture for the home of a lunatic. . . .

And then he realized that he'd begged the question.

The question wasn't *Where did that fungus come from?*; it was *What on God's earth killed all these trees?*

And he looked around, looked carefully at the trees to be certain the impression in his gut was right, to be certain that the trees, all the trees here in the near distance, all of them every single one:

The trees were dead. So many dead trees, some decaying fungal where they stood—like these trees here—but most lay mouldering on the ground.

"These woods are dying," Tim said. "Something's killing them. Killed them? Was there a fire?"

"I don't know. It wasn't like this last time I was here."

Tim got out of his seat, stood leaning on the open car door. Looking at the rot, the gleaming black, the dark castle hoary against the bright-blue sky.

"It wasn't? What was different?"

"Outside, here. Back then—back when I was nine—the flowers were all up there by the mansion. And these trees weren't like this, neither. They were all big and sturdy, right up to about ten yards from the house. Wasn't hardly any of this mushroom stuff, just a little up near the last few trees."

The flowers were killing the trees? Or were they making the fungus grow?—If that was it, then the fungus likely was the thing that actually killed the trees.

It didn't matter. The real question was the flowers. They were the impossible thing; Tim was sure that they were right near the root of—

The root of what?

He had to go into the house. That was the only way he'd get the answer to that question.

"You wait here," Tim said. "I should be back in a few minutes."

"Huh?—I'm going with you. Sure ain't waiting here. It isn't safe."

What?

"Don't do this to me, Thomas. It isn't safe in there. You know that and so do I. Forget whatever's ready to jump out of the dark corners; that place is decrepit. The floorboards are likely so rotten as to crumble when you step on them. Get yourself killed if you want, but don't do it while I'm the only adult around."

Thomas hesitated before he shook his head. "To hell with that. We can go together, or I can follow a minute behind you. No way you're leaving me alone out here with all of these damned flowers."

A beat; another. And it finally sank through to Tim that he hadn't been listening. "Why are you afraid of the flowers?"

"*Because it* touched *me!*"

Tim didn't understand. He tried hard to listen.

"What touched you, Thomas?"

The boy didn't answer right away.

"The flower. The flower that I found outside the door that day." His voice was very, very quiet, and still wrapped up in crying. "It touched me down inside when the Stone wasn't looking, and it made me—*made* me—" He choked—on his own tongue? On nothing at all? "It made me look. That's all. It made me look at what I did. And I don't want to have to see that, not again. Not ever again."

And what was Tim supposed to do?

"Okay, then. Come on if you want. But be careful of yourself!"

"I'm not afraid of anything inside there."

Tim didn't know what he meant by that, and he didn't ask. He moved aside, locked, closed his door. And started up the hill.

Behind him, he could hear the boy hurrying out of his seat.

"Lock your door on your way out, Thomas?"

The boy grunted an answer that Tim couldn't quite make out.

The mushrooms gave out half a dozen yards uphill from the car. Beyond them a band of dead-dry ground—it wasn't more than a yard wide, but it wrapped around the hill as far as Tim's eye could follow. The ring of dirt was all but bare—nothing was alive inside it. No grass, no weeds, not so much as a seedling. Even the odd bits of debris caught up in the dirt (pine straw, desiccated grass; bits of twig and mummified fungus) seemed unnaturally wasted and withered. Beyond the ring the pine straw seemed like a thousand-thousand thin thin reddish twigs; here it was pale, whitish, and for a moment Tim mistook it for dried hay.

Inside the ring the ground was dense with those impossible black flowers. So dense that it was hard to walk without stepping on the things—and they weren't things to steps on, those flowers. All sharp edges and hard and strong, and so tough that the one Tim stepped on (when he was five yards uphill from where the ring began) like to pierce the sole of his tennis shoe. Like stepping on a pyramidal rock, or some such; a sharp point pressing up through his shoe and *damn* it hurt, and Tim looked down to see that it was just the creased petal of a roselike flower. So hard, sharp, rigid that it might just as well have been a knife.

Damn near slit the sole of his shoe, and the flower wasn't worse for it at all. Snapped right back up into place as soon as Tim took his weight off it.

He was more careful after that. Stepping gingerly onto the dry, dead ground (beneath the flowers the soil was as barren here as it was in the empty ring) putting caution into his footsteps to save his feet from immolation. Even being careful wasn't enough; twice Tim nearly tripped himself on the damnable things.

The sun was hot here. Incredibly hot. Did deserts feel like this?—deserts like the Sahara or the Gobi, real deserts where men died from heat and dehydration in the hot hot sun?—

Stop.

Back up.

What was he thinking? This wasn't any desert. And the heat—it *was* warmer here. Wasn't it? But the warmth Tim felt wasn't from the air or the sun, it was . . . what? All in his head? No. He was hot, damn it, hot and dripping sweaty. And this wasn't any desert: it was fifty yards of strange dead earth glittering with unnatural jewelry.

And the hot was hot like from a fever, hot coming from inside him—

Thomas had said something about that, hadn't he?

Something about the flowers, wasn't it? Flowers touching inside him. That was where this fever came from.

Tim stopped, turned carefully so as not to trip himself in the weird flowers. Looked back at Thomas picking his way through the glittery black a few yards behind.

"You feel it, Thomas? Do you feel the fever too?"

Thomas scowled.

"Of course I do. Don't think about it—you'll only make things worse."

Tim sighed. Tedious: the boy's cryptic curtness was beginning to get tedious. How in the hell was Tim supposed to stop thinking about a fever like this? How could he ignore it, once he'd recognized it for what it was?

Those damned flowers. They were the trouble. Tim was sure about that.

Well, if the flowers were pressing in on him, if the flowers were fevering him, well then Tim would do the same to them, he would—

He'd set them all afire, run back to the car and get a match from the glove box and set fire to the chaff that underlay the black leaves glittering with reflected sunlight—

And soon as Tim decided to destroy them, the black things lowered the boom on him.

Spectacularly: in a moment he was seeing visions, great vaporous things like the ghostly image of mountain made of opalescent stone, and he was on the mountain, on the mountain climbing climbing and the ground and the stone and the soil underneath his feet burst

erupted

went flying up all out from under him in a shower of shattering crystal

as the serpent exploded out from the bowels of the hill.

Serpent, yes, serpent, and that's how Tim knew he must be dreaming, because there were no serpents in his world, no garish monsters colored green and brown and grey flying out of the oval earth to devour him. Its long muscular tendonous neck snapping around as the vicious open-jawed head dove to swallow him whole—

"Go away," Tim said. "You aren't real."

And the serpent and the mountain and the massive biting fangs all were gone.

Thomas was staring at him like he was out of his mind.

"I thought—I thought—" Tim didn't know how to describe it. And maybe he didn't want to describe it at all.

"I told you not to think about it," Thomas said. "The flowers hear what you think, just the way the Stone used to. They don't do much about it. But you don't want to go thinking anything nasty about 'em. They don't like it. They catch you at it, they'll get you real good."

Tim blinked. "I know," he said. "Just found that out."

He was covered with sweat. Covered. His shirt, his slacks, even his socks were soaked through with perspiration.

"That's what they did to me, too," Thomas said. "Inside my head. I saw the mansion from downhill a ways, and I went up to see what it was. I got right up to it before I saw the flowers—back then there weren't so many of them. Only like a little garden up by the big front window. And another patch off to the side.

"Anyways, something came over me when I saw those flowers. I'm not sure what it was, exactly. Kind of like when the Stone decided he wanted to walk you puppet-wise, and not like that too, because the Stone wasn't watching me right then. I couldn't feel him, and I knew he wasn't anyplace near my head because if he had been I wouldn't have got anywhere near the mansion. Stone didn't like us going out this way.

"The Stone-in-my-head thing came over me when I saw the flowers, and before I knew what was going on I was trying to rip those things right out of the ground. Down on my knees, shouting and hollering, and one of them in each hand trying to tear roots and all from the dirt.

"First thing that occurred to me was how the

flowers all looked like they was made from the same glassy-black stuff as the Stone, and if that was so then maybe it was them that had hold of me. But why would they do a thing like that? Why would they want me to root them out? Well, they wouldn't, and that was plain right then, because I felt them seizing up on me. Out of nowhere, boom, like you just felt. Like the Stone—but different from it the way the twins were different from each other. I could feel how they were different, and I could feel how what made me want to kill the flowers wasn't the Stone, it was the little bit of Stone that lived in me or was me or I don't know.

"The flowers found me, just like they found you just now, and they strangled me from inside my head until it all went black. I woke up near dusk with a sunburn like you wouldn't believe—on account of lying face-up in the sun all day. I saw where I was, and I saw those weird flowers still hanging limp in my hands, and I took off running for all I was worth. I was halfway home before the Stone could see me again, and when it did it was *angry*—it like to do to me what the flowers had. Didn't, though—stopped a little short so's to make sure I got home."

Tim felt almost normal, now. Still a little warm, still sweaty—the air was too damp to dry his sweaty clothes—but the world was less distorted than it had been.

"Why?" he asked the boy. "I don't understand why. Why would you want to destroy the flowers if they'd done nothing to you?"

Thomas shrugged. "Stone hated them. So I hated them. Because they were like each other? The way sometimes brothers and sisters hate each other? I don't know. Just because."

Tim waited for the boy to go on, but he didn't. Maybe he had nothing more to say. Or maybe the flowers had gotten to him, the way they'd gotten to Tim a while before; Thomas sure looked pale.

"We need to get going," Tim said. "Are you up to it?"

Tim saw some expression flash on Thomas's face—

fear, maybe? Anger?—before he shook his head. "I'll be all right," he said. Which was just the opposite of a headshake. (Maybe he *was* afraid. God knew there was reason enough for that. And Tim could see the boy doing that, could see him say *yes* when his body knew the right answer was *no*.)

"You're sure? I can take you back to the car if you want. Or back to your home, if you aren't comfortable waiting here."

The boy shook a little, like to get hold of himself. "No," Thomas said. "I want to go in there. With you. I need to see."

See what?

"Well, then," Tim said, "let's go."

Grandpa took Tim and Donny James to Walt Disney World the Saturday after Labor Day. Early fall. And early fall in Florida that year was hot, muggy, and unpleasant as high summer. Sunlight blinding bright all along I-4—it made the pavement so intensely white that watching the road made Tim's eyes ache. He wondered how Grandpa managed to stare at the highway to drive, and thought about asking. But decided that light was one of those things that got easier to take as you got older—like raw onions, or cigarette smoke, or the taste of beer. And why ask a question with that answer? He'd heard it all already.

Not to say he couldn't handle looking outside. This was the year Tim turned twelve, and he was still all caught up in showing he was tough enough to take it. Whatever it was. Every now and then he'd look up from talking to Donny or Grandpa, and he'd see the road, and just to prove to himself how he was tough he'd stare long and hard at the road, and he'd keep staring till long after his eyes got teary and his head ached and his ears started to ring. Then he'd turn back to look at Grandpa or face Donny with a macho look in his eye. Neither one of them looked as though he understood, but that was okay. Tim knew about macho. It was a thing you had to make right with yourself, not something that was supposed to

impress others. Leastwise that was what he told himself
when nobody bothered to notice how tough he was.

Tim ended up consoling himself quite a bit that
morning drive. And more again as they drove in through
the Disney grounds, where Tim caught sight of an
enormous green dinosaur striking out to menace them,
and he didn't scream, didn't shout, just turned to face it,
to show it Tim Fischer was no one to be menaced—and
when he did he saw it was no living reptilian behemoth
but the sculpture of one, trimmed artfully from a series
of tall shrubs.

Not funny, damn it. But Tim didn't let it show how
his pride was wounded. Well, maybe it showed a little,
'cause right about then was when things in the car got a
little quiet and the air felt dense and tingly with
impending impatience.

Either Grandpa or Donny was about to ask him
what his problem was and why he was acting so anxious.
And he'd have to answer, and the minute he told them
why he was so mad he'd lose all his dignity, and he wasn't
about to let that happen.

So he sat quiet, staring out the passenger-side
window as they drove through endless parking lots with
names like Goofy and Dopey and Dumbo, drove in
seeming circles because the parking lot attendants kept
pointing them in new directions, till finally a man with a
bright-orange pointer steered them into a parking spot.
Spot five, Snow White aisle seven.

"Don't run off, boys," Grandpa said as Tim unlocked
his door, popped open the buckle of his seat belt. And of
course running off was exactly what Tim'd intended:
people were lining up at the end of the parking aisle, and
right now the tram was pulling up to get them. And if
they didn't hurry they'd get left behind, and Tim didn't
want to get left behind. Even if it meant leaving without
Grandpa or Donny.

If Tim'd stopped to think about it he'd probably
have felt different. Leaving Grandpa behind, after all,
was an intemperate thing. Grandpa had almost all their
money, after all. If Tim went on without him he had
maybe enough for his tickets and maybe enough for a

soda and a chocolate-dipped frozen banana in the theme park, but that wouldn't leave anything over for buying stuff in the too-cool Disney World novelty shop. And if he didn't have enough to shop there, what was the point of going to Disney World in the first place?—The novelty shop was the best part of the whole trip, if you didn't count Pirates of the Caribbean and the Country Bear Jamboree.

Besides, if he ran on without Grandpa and Donny, Grandpa would be real mad when he caught up with him. Maybe even mad enough to take Tim over his knee and swat him a good one. (Which Grandpa had done a couple times over the last year. The first time he did it Tim had been enraged and insulted. And almost as upset the second time. But after few weeks had passed Tim began to admit to himself that it was probably for the best the way it happened: both times Tim had gone running out into trouble despite the fact that Grandpa told him not to. And he knew now that there'd been nothing anyone could have done to make him listen to the fact that he was bound for trouble—nothing but clonk him over the head and pray Tim stayed dizzy long enough to sit still long enough to hear the facts.)

Anyhow, whatever the reason was he did it Tim hung back outside the door of Grandpa's new Toyota, waiting while Donny gawked at the sea of cars and Grandpa went to the trunk to get his travel bag. And sure enough, the tram pulled away just as they started off to meet it.

Grandpa sighed just before Tim was about to object. "Don't worry, Timbo. There'll be another one in just a moment."—And his timing was really something, because just as he spoke a tram pulled into sight around a corner far out in the lot, and it started toward them.

Tim wanted to say *But I wanted* that *one,* but there wasn't any use saying it. It was just another one of those things that'd make him feel stupid the moment it came out of his mouth.

It didn't help any that it took the tram fifteen minutes to get to them, what with the three stops it had to make and all the people it had to load on. And helped

less when it finally got to them and there were no three
seats together anywhere on the tram. They looked and
looked and finally gave up, and Grandpa took a seat four
or five rows back from the one that Tim and Donny
managed to squeeze into.

Which turned out to be real good luck: it left Tim
and Donny surrounded by girls.

Pretty girls, too. All of them sixteen, seventeen,
eighteen years old. All of them wearing bright blue
badges with white type too small to read from here.
Some kind of a tour group, Tim guessed.

He leaned close to Donny, whispered. "Girls, huh?
How about that."

And Donny looked around and smiled like he'd died
and gone to heaven and came back still remembering
what it was like. "Yeah."

It was a word that said volumes: these days Tim and
Donny spent lots of time up in the clubhouse talking
about girls. Tim knew exactly what he meant—but even
if they'd never said another word about the subject to
one another, he'd have known. Donny put a spin on that
word that no one who'd ever been a boy beginning to
notice girls could ever misunderstand.

For a moment Tim pictured him and Donny intro-
ducing themselves to two of the prettiest, talking a
moment or three and sneaking off to some hidden corner
of the theme park to . . . and then he remembered the
uncomfortable morning with Erica Skolner, and how he
still felt wrong about it, and still couldn't figure out how
to understand what was happening to his body and his
heart.

(Grandpa tried to explain it a couple months ago.
He said, "Tim, your body is changing the way a tadpole
changes into a frog. No, not so obvious on the outside as
the way a frog changes. But almost as dramatic on the
inside. You understand, don't you, how your body
sometimes pushes you to act one way or another? You
know how people get cranky when they're hungry, and
how some perfectly-fine folks have grouchy dispositions
that they have to work hard to keep in check?" And Tim
remembered pitching a fit at his mom about dinner just

the day before, and remembered how he'd felt all angry out of proportion, and felt bad remembering it. And he said *Of course I do, Grandpa*. "What's happening to you now, Tim, is that all the little tiny things your body pushes you to do every day—all of them are changing. Biology, plain and simple: when you're little your body wants you to work hard and take care of yourself and to grow. But as you get older your body pushes you to create and care for the next generation. It's a beautiful and wondrous change, but it's so large and confusing that it may be years before you understand it. The best thing you can do in the meanwhile is keep your eyes open and listen to the world and your body. And most of all try to relax. Remember that even if you do feel silly, every last one of us has had to live through the same embarrassment."

(Tim tried to keep Grandpa's words in mind. They made sense, and all by themselves that helped to calm him. But still sometimes he got flustered and confused. Days were when he was in an honest hurry for his body to metamorphose and get it over with.)

"Look," Donny said. "Isn't she pretty?" He pointed at a girl on the far end of the bench in front of theirs. She looked about seventeen.

When Tim looked at her he saw Erica.

It'd been what, two weeks since the last time he saw her? Three? Since she went home to her mom and dad on Long Island. But seeing her then was from a distance—he hadn't really talked to her or anything since that morning in the tree house when they'd found Grandpa downstairs waiting for them. That was two months ago, at least.

He thought about her a lot. More than he wanted to admit even to himself. He could've gone to her, he thought—any time since that morning in July he could've gone to her, talked to her, maybe . . . who knew what could've happened maybe. And Tim knew that she'd've been happy to see him. That all this time she'd been waiting for him to come back to her. Waiting for him to make the next move—that was the phrase people used, wasn't it?

He thought it was.

"She's awful pretty," Tim said. He was about a million miles away when he heard the words rise up out of his throat.

"Should I talk to her?"

Tim shrugged. "If you want."

He still wasn't quite sure why he hadn't talked to Erica again. He sure thought about it an awful lot, and once or twice he'd actually set out to do it. Oh, yeah, he'd talked to her that once, a couple days after what happened in the tree house. But that was just *hi* when she was with Anne Fulton and Tim was with Donny and they all ran into each other down to the 7-Eleven. Erica watched him all expectant-looking, but Tim had only smiled shyly and looked away at Donny talking to Anne.

He wasn't sure now whether or not he'd ever see her again. He wasn't sure whether or not that bothered him, or how much it bothered him, or whether all the botheredness he felt lately was a result of the growing-up things that Grandpa told him about.

But one thing was for damned sure: Tim was in a constant state of bother. He sure wished it'd go away.

The tram was pulling to a stop now, pulling up to the great wide plaza in front of the ticket gates. Not even stopped yet and already Donny was climbing over him to get out of their seat, putting himself into position to grab the attention of the pretty older girl ahead of them who looked just like Erica. Donny was a year older than Tim, and even so it was pretty silly to see someone as young as him going after a girl so old she was almost a woman.

He thought about looking away. It was embarrassing to watch his friend make such a fool of himself. But he couldn't bring himself to turn his head: he watched rapt by some morbid compulsion. There was something he wanted to see, something he had to know—the hopeful look in Donny's eyes? The confused, amused smile on the face of the girl when Donny stepped up to introduce himself? Neither of those, Tim thought. Maybe, maybe it was the way Donny stuttered three times before he finally got his name out, or the way she

said *that's nice* and smiled again and kept walking, not
waiting for him to go on.

But Tim didn't think so.

So he looked beyond Donny looking so disappointed, out into the plaza with its blazing-white concrete and its tropical plants withered in the sun. There
were people in Disney costumes, big bulky suits bulky
enough that each one of them could've held two large
men if they could've stood the heat. Even more inside
Goofy, there—he could hold two men and a thin girl,
too. If a girl was inside there she had to be sweltering.
Whoever was in there was sweltering. And inside
Mickey, and Minnie, and Pluto, and over there, one of
the seven dwarves. Was that one called Frumpy or
something? Tim had trouble remembering all the
names.

And scanning across the walking Disneys was how
Tim noticed the Easter Bunny.

Like the others it was man-tall and bulky as a
gorilla, and outside the bunny part of it there was a
gaudy-tacky costume. (Red vest and trousers; lots of gold
trim.) He was handing out beautiful-bright Easter eggs
way way out of season. Absolutely of a type, of the Disney
type—except maybe for the way it was handing out the
eggs, which was a pretty strange thing for a Disney to be
doing. And there was something . . . something about it
that when Tim saw the thing his stomach clenched and
alarms went off inside his ears and he wanted to run up to
the enormous rabbit and latch onto it and hold it still so he
could watch and watch and watch, and maybe after he'd
watched it long enough he'd understand—

—understand—

—understand—

And then it occurred to him what it was he saw. Part
of it, anyway.

That isn't any costume.

The Easter Bunny was real.

Maybe it was *the* Easter Bunny. But how could it
be? There wasn't any such thing as any old Easter
Bunny. No more than there was a Santa Claus. Tim
hadn't ever had any confusion on the subject; not Mom

nor Dad nor Grandpa had ever tried to tell him any of those "little white lies" about such things.

Wasn't any Easter Bunny any more than there was any such thing as an eight-foot rabbit walking around on its hind legs like a man. And still, here it was. Walking around the plaza real as you please, talking to the six-year-olds and giving out those eggs.

Tim nudged Donny, pointed at the giant rabbit. "Look," he said. And Donny looked, and after a moment his eyes bugged out and his mouth dropped open and it was pretty obvious he could see what Tim was pointing at.

"It's like—" Donny said "—it's like you can only tell when you know to look for it."

"Uh-huh." Tim nodded. Not that anyone had pointed it out to him, but he was different. Living around the Cross all these years made him . . . susceptible to seeing things. Donny didn't have that advantage, and neither did anyone else who was here to see the Easter Bunny. Except maybe Grandpa. It probably never occurred to any of the rest of them that the giant rabbit was anything but another of those walking talking Disneys.

"What should we do?" Donny asked. "Is it really some kind of a monster? Should we call a priest, or drive a stake through its heart, or . . . I don't know. Call the police, maybe?"

Tim scowled. "No, it isn't any monster. It isn't even bad. I'm going to go ask it what it is." He started off across the plaza without waiting for a response. Without even looking back to see where Donny or Grandpa stood.

There wasn't any call to look after Donny, of course. He followed not even half a step behind Tim all the way across the plaza. But Grandpa—he ought to have tried to figure out where Grandpa was. Things would've gone much better if he'd just taken the time to look over his shoulder.

But Tim didn't, and things happened just the way they did.

And the rabbit saw them coming. And after just a moment it saw that Tim and Donny had found it out—maybe by seeing the expression on their faces, maybe by the same weird magic that made him a rabbit too big to be real. And his wide shiny black eyes opened impossibly rounder. Which made Tim think of Donny's expression when he'd first looked at the bunny monster. Though Donny's eyes couldn't hold a twinkle to those great liquid orbs, no matter how bugged out they got.

Tim expected the rabbit to run. That was what rabbits did when they were scared, wasn't it? But no, the hulking thing was paralyzed, staring at them transfixed as the opossum that had trapped itself in Dad's headlights last year when they drove up to Tennessee for vacation. (The darn thing would've died, run over, if Dad hadn't been real quick with his brakes. Couldn't move for nothing, not till Dad stopped the car and leaned out his window and shouted at it. Even then it didn't move right away.)

The Easter Bunny stood watching them agape till Tim stepped up to him and asked his question. "Who are you?" Tim asked. "How. . . ?"

The Easter Bunny blinked nervously.

Tim grabbed its arm—and it was an arm, too, not a forepaw. Two or three times as thick around as a man's arm, but it was flesh and blood beneath the soft-thick white fur. Tim could feel a great wide artery pulsing underneath the tips of his fingers.

"Tell me," he said. "I have to know."

And he *did* have a burning need for the answer to his question. He didn't understand that need, couldn't have explained it if anyone had asked point blank, but he felt it nonetheless.

The enormous mouth opened, and Tim saw those great front teeth, the tongue the size of a cow tongue in the butcher's case. Working back and forth, stammering to find words. And finding none. There was a tiny green stain on the rabbit's right front incisor, as though it'd forgotten to brush its teeth after breakfasting on clover.

"Tell me," Tim said.

And then the rabbit smiled all warm and twinkly, and it straightened its red vest with the ornate gold trim, and it cleared its throat.

"Boys, boys, boys," the rabbit said. It had a deep, smooth voice, and the slightest trace of a lisp. "Wouldn't you really rather have an Easter egg? I have eggs that are rare indeed." It reached into the wicker basket that hung from its right arm. Drew forth a large round-ended egg that was nearly as big as the rabbit's oversize palm. "This is the egg of a rare grey ostrich. Painted carefully by an artist of unmatched talent. You see the graceful brushwork?—Yes, I see your expression. You're a perceptive lad; I thought you'd see." And it was a work of art painted on that great egg, even if it was just a portrait of Mickey Mouse. Mickey with a difference: The Mickey on that egg was a thing that could be as real, as flesh-and-blood as the rabbit here before them. "Yes, yes, you can have it if you like. Or give it to your friend if that makes you feel more at ease."

Which was exactly what Tim was thinking about doing when the Easter Bunny said those words. He took the egg, lifted it in both hands to pass it on to Donny, and when their eyes met he saw that the other boy was even more mystified and confused than Tim was himself.

Then Donny gasped, and Tim nearly dropped the egg as he turned to see—

Turned to see the rabbit was *gone*. Not just left, not walking away from them, but disappeared as though he'd never been there. And he wasn't hiding behind anything, either; here in the middle of the plaza there was nothing to hide behind for forty feet in any direction.

"Which way did he go?"

Donny shook his head. "He didn't. Go, I mean. He just—just vanished. Like he hadn't ever been there in the first place."

Tim frowned. "No, he was there, all right." A twinge in his gut—that way, there. Into the park. That was where the rabbit had gone. "It's just a trick. Like magicians play? He's in Disney World. All we have to do is find him again."

A throat cleared behind and above them, and Tim turned to see Grandpa looming over their shoulders. "Find who again, Tim?"

Donny was blanched-white. He looked embarrassed as though he'd been caught necking with a girl in the garden shed.

Tim thought about telling Grandpa the truth. He really did. It wasn't like Grandpa was somebody you couldn't trust. But there was a reason why Donny looked like he'd been caught in the middle of something really personal, and Tim felt it too. The rabbit was a thing they had to deal with themselves, and Grandpa didn't really belong in the middle of it.

"Oh, nobody special, Grandpa. We were talking to the guy in the Donald Duck costume, and Donny wanted to get his autograph, but he forgot. But I figure we can find him again over in the park by Main Street."

It was a real bold-face lie—ugly because it was built to be believable, and because Tim put a special spin on it for fooling Grandpa. And Grandpa was no easy fool. He looked a little suspicious as he listened to Tim, but when he'd finished listening he didn't challenge the lie. He just shrugged, and shook his head, and changed the subject.

"Well," Grandpa said, "the line isn't getting any shorter. Might as well get our tickets."

Then for at least two hours the visit to the Magic Kingdom was uneventful. They rode by monorail to the gates of the theme park; hiked up Main Street, through Frontierland to the Country Bear Jamboree; out and around to the Haunted House; way over to the 20,000 Leagues Under the Sea submarine ride.

All the while they hiked back and forth through Disney World Tim could feel the rabbit somewhere nearby. Now closer, now farther off; sometimes off to the right or left and once he'd have sworn the thing was due in front of them, or maybe following them or something. But when he looked up to confront the sentient beast it was never there—only some other Disney, like Mickey Mouse, or Donald Duck, or Roger Rabbit. (That last gave him an awful start before he realized he was staring at the wrong bunny.)

And then it was lunchtime.

Lunch was special: Grandpa had called ahead to get reservations in the fancy restaurant there inside Cinderella's Castle. They'd been there before: it was this nifty place that really did seem to be a tavern in an ancient castle. And the food was real good, too. Especially the soup: they served him cream of asparagus, and it had the strange and rich and subtle flavor that he wanted to concentrate on for hours just so he could understand it.

But it didn't go on forever, and hard as Tim tried to stretch out the experience it only took him ten minutes to finish. After he'd pushed the empty bowl away but before their waiter brought the salad Tim excused himself to use the rest room. Grandpa nodded, distracted; Donny didn't even look up from staring out the window at the Pink Teacup ride off in the distance. Well, to heck with them. If neither one of them cared whether or not Tim was with 'em for dinner, then Tim didn't care about them, either.

Out across the dining room. Up the three steps to the circular landing; down one flight of stairs to the men's room.

Coming out he passed a door ajar just before the short hall that led away from the john. Plain, unmarked door not more than half an inch open to darkness. The only noteworthy thing about it was the fact that it was all done up to match the castle, heavy dark wood planks bound together with iron—but here in this place a more conventional door would have been striking.

When Tim saw it little alarms started going off back behind his ears.

There there there he's in there go that way—the rabbit the rabbit go in there to find the rabbit.

He almost did. Almost went in right there, right then. Would have if he hadn't remembered Donny.

Donny was there before when he'd seen the Easter Bunny, and Tim was sure he had to be here now or something important would hang out of balance. (Not that Tim could've named or even pointed at that all-important balance. He just *knew* it, and knew to abide it.)

Up the stairs to the landing. Waving to Donny till he finally got the other boy's attention—waving so long that it was a miracle Grandpa didn't turn around and notice. Waving a couple more times to signal Donny to come here, to follow.

"What're you doing?" Donny asked him when he was close by. Their waiter stood not five feet away, staring at them.

"Never mind," Tim said. "Just come with me."

Donny held back a moment, as though he were going to argue. But then he sighed and started down the stairs after Tim.

When they got to the cracked-open door Tim looked both ways to make sure no one could see them—and so far as he could tell no one could. There wasn't anyone in sight, at least. But he'd heard stories about security cameras all around Disney World, and he knew there was no way to be sure there wasn't one of them watching them right this very moment. He hoped not. And why would they put a camera in this restaurant, much less on the entrance to the men's room?

Probably, he thought, they wouldn't. But he still felt real nervous as he slipped in through the heavy door (beneath the wooden planks it was just another institutional steel door, exactly the kind he'd seen in schools and hospitals and government buildings) into a tiny room lit only by the glowing-red EXIT sign above the door they entered through. At the far end of the room were two elevators, their doors barely visible in the dim red light. A pair of buttons, ▲ and ▼, between them.

Down down down take the elevator down he's down there.

"This way," Tim whispered. "Don't forget to ease the door shut behind you."

Crossed the room. Pressed the button marked ▼, which lit up, and after an instant Tim could hear machinery whirring somewhere down inside the door.

Donny leaned close to whisper. "Where are we going?"

"Downstairs. The rabbit is somewhere down there."

Something clunked, and the elevator door drew open, and the light from inside was so bright after darkness that for a moment it was blinding.

Stepped in. Scanned the buttons. *Which one?* The

twinge in his stomach that directed him only said *down*, not *down to B1* or *B2* or *B3*. He bit his lip and tried to guess. And chose the middle, and hoped he was right.

B2.

Down. Down for the longest time, as though *B2* were a place so deep in the ground that it took years and years to get there.

Or maybe it wasn't that far at all—maybe the trouble was just that the elevator was slow.

An indicator flashed on the strip above the door: *B1*. All this time and they'd only gotten down to the first basement. As he watched it blink on and then off something wrenched in his stomach, and he knew that they'd overshot—

No!

—the rabbit was somewhere on *B1*. And they'd already fallen past it.

"Darn it. I pushed the wrong button."

If their luck didn't hold out they'd be in awful trouble: every floor they stopped on was one more opportunity to get caught in here—

Thump!

—by someone waiting to get to another floor.

Stopped. And the door slid open.

No one. No one waiting in the dark alcove that led to *B2*. Praise God.

Pushed the button marked *B1*.

And waited the longest time for the door to close. So long that those faint footsteps in the distance had time to draw nearer, nearer—right to the door of the *B2* alcove—!

To open the door that led in toward them, and Tim ducked against the far wall out of sight, pressed Donny with him, clamped a hand over Donny's mouth to keep him from crying out like a fool in surprise—

And blessed be! the elevator doors began to close—

And the footsteps in the alcove broke into a run, trying to catch their elevator before it could leave without—

And Tim jammed his finger into the CLOSE DOOR button.

And he prayed.

The Lord must've listened to that prayer. How else could anyone explain how the door pushed closed gently, steadily, despite the fact that the woman's hand (red-painted fingernails, manicured so carefully) touched the safety bars, held the left one, tried to disengage it? Any ordinary elevator door would spring open the moment she touched it. Never mind the way Tim had his finger on the CLOSE DOOR button; with the door already closing that button was nothing but a place to put Tim's panic.

If everything in that elevator were working properly, it would've let the woman in. And Tim and Donny would've been in deep trouble, and they never would've found the Easter Bunny.

Then there was this awful moment where Tim was sure that the elevator was going to crush the woman's hand, close and close and close and close around it till flesh pulped and bone shattered, and then the elevator would take off still crushing the hand, and it'd shear off what was left of her wrist when it passed above the doorway—

—and it did, it did, the damnable thing clamped down on the bones of her hand—

—and the woman gave a start—

—and screamed the tiniest, quietest scream—

—as the elevator door came to a stop as it chomped down around her palm.

For a moment everything just stood there, with the door stopped dead by the bones of her hand, or maybe it still pressed-crushed against her—

—and then the woman grunted, and *pulled* away, and after a moment's resistance she managed to yank her hand free.

The elevator doors went *bang!*, hitting one another as they rushed to fill the gap her hand left behind.

And the elevator lurched into motion, and they were free.

Tim eased out of the corner, and as he did he saw Donny's eyes so wide with fear they made him think of saucers—yes, that's what they looked like, saucers when

Mom spilled a little of her coffee, and it collected in the bottom center to form a circular pool.

"It's okay," Tim said. "We're safe now. It's okay."

Donny looked like maybe he was going to believe that, like maybe he'd relax and stop being so scared—until the elevator banged to a stop, and the lights above them flickered, and then suddenly and loudly the doors rolled open.

Real scary. And even worse when Tim looked up and thought he saw two grown-ups there waiting for them angry.

But then he blinked to clear his eyes, and when Tim opened them again the grown-ups were gone and it was obvious they'd never been there.

It wasn't hard to lead Donny to the Easter Bunny after that. They had to stay at the edges of things, in among the fabulous pillars and machines' great whirring shafts that ran the theme park. There at the edges the machines cast deep shadows, so deep they hid the boys well enough to sneak them past the three or four maintenance people they passed. Then they came to the padlocked gate—the chain-link gate closed to a long dusty hall. Cement floor, sprayfoam ceiling, cinderblock walls that led out into a distance too far to see. Here and there on either wall an institutional-steel door.

And there in the thick-caked dust that littered the concrete floor—footprints. One set. Leading in, none out. The prints of something with very large unhuman feet.

The rabbit.

"Look," Donny said. He pressed his hand against the edge of the chain-link, where loops of metal bound the fence wire to a galvanized-steel post. And amazingly the links fell away, almost as though they'd been nothing but show. Or perhaps as though they'd been broken and then set back in place to divert attention.

Donny pushed the fence away like it was a curtain.

Tim nodded, ducked inside. Held the linkage while Donny stepped through. "Go carefully," he said. "If we go too fast we might miss where the tracks stop. If we follow carefully we can't help but find him."

Tim was absolutely right about that. When they got to the fifth door on the left, the lodestone in Tim's heart started screaming at him—and that was exactly where the tracks turned in. Before he even touched the doorknob (which hung slack and broken) he knew for certain that the rabbit was inside that room.

Which is why it came as such a shock when he opened the door and saw the old derelict lying propped against the far wall, bathed eerie and unnerving in the weird red light from the EXIT sign.

Not the Easter Bunny at all, but a miserable wretch of a derelict.

that's him that's him that's him

But of course it wasn't him at all. How could it be?

"You've found me, boys," the old man said. "I knew you would." He spoke with the strangest slightest trace of an accent Tim couldn't place.

Tim stood watching, too numb to reply.

"I knew no matter how I hid from you, you'd manage to track me down. There's something special about you." He looked at Tim as he said this. "And I can see that, just as you can see the specialness in me. It's just as well you find me now. My time is come, and because of the miracle that's trapped in me I know it. It is good I tell my tale this once before I pass."

That was when the miraculous thing happened: the old man who smelled of sweat and filth and cheap cheap wine metamorphosed. For a moment he sparkled all shimmery and weird, like a mirror-smooth leaf of tinfoil when you crumple it up. And then he was the Easter Bunny, and there was no awful smell, and the gloomy red light that had turned the drifter ghostly was a wondrous crimson radiance on the long white ears of the rabbit.

And that incredible creature was going to die. Or so it said, and how could anything so wonderful tell them an untruth?

"Who are you?"

"My name is Abraham," the rabbit said. "But it's

been years and years since anyone called me by that name."

"Why are you dying?"

"I'm old, young son. Surely you must know that. You've the eye to see my age."

And when Tim thought about it he realized that he could indeed feel vast age from the presence of the rabbit (or Abraham Whatsisname, or whoever he was). He'd felt that from the very first he'd seen him in the plaza—it was part of what had attracted Tim's eye to the rabbit in the first place. By itself it hadn't struck him hard enough to recognize—after all, Grandpa had the same strange aura about him.

It was Donny who asked the really obvious question.

"How come you're a rabbit? And how'd you change like that?"

The rabbit smiled. It was a very strange expression on his three-part mouth. "Yes," he said. "Yes indeed. Therein lies my tale."

"Huh?"

"He means that that's what he's waiting to tell us about before he dies."

Donny looked at him kind of funny, like he was asking *How'd you know a thing like that?*, but he didn't quite go so far as to give voice to the question.

"Precisely, lad. I knew you were a sharp one. What I'd give to hear your story!—But no, I know it's a thing you keep to yourself. Old Abraham has his own Eye, he does." He sighed. "My tale begins nearly seventy years ago, when I was the merest of lads. I was a ne'er-do-well in those days. Oh was I!" The Easter Bunny sighed wistfully; its great right ear trembled ever so slightly. "But that's not what I need to tell you, either. I need to tell you about that strange old house where I took that fateful nap."

The rabbit paused, gathering his thoughts.

And Tim thought: *House. . . ?*

Somewhere in the back of his mind things began falling into place—like a jigsaw miraculously solving itself. Before the rabbit could speak another word Tim knew what he would say.

"The year that I turned twenty I took a job as a carpenter's apprentice," the rabbit said. "It was a dull, slow year, and the truth is that I found the work unendingly dull. Whenever the opportunity presented itself I'd slip away and find myself a comfortable spot to nap. Old Max—the carpenter—was a kind old soul. The once or twice he caught me dozing he woke me gently and irelessly, tolerant of the fault of my youth. But it was rare that he caught me sleeping. Max was a man whose work absorbed him so fully that he had no opportunity to notice my comings and goings. Nor my absence. Max had no real need of an apprentice; he could easily have done without me. And in the end he did.

"This particular week we were working for a man named Fischer. William Fischer, if I recall correct. Adding bookshelves—four floor-to-ceiling walls of bookshelves to a room not too far off his parlor. Big, big house, and old for this part of Florida. Back then there was very little built up in this state, and his house was at least fifty years old already when I worked on it. For all I could tell it may well have been the oldest structure I saw up there, so far north of Tampa.

"Anyway, that morning I was especially groggy, as I hadn't slept to speak of the night before (I'd been out on the Spanish quarter, wishing farewell to three good friends), and Max and I had set out quite early to reach the great old house and still have time to complete our work before sundown. And long before Max was ready to break for our noon repast, I wandered away, looking for some obscure corner of the house in which to rest my head.

"Soon enough I found it. Or found what I thought was an unused, unfurnished room.

"But oh how I was wrong! Not that I knew it then. Or even later, when I found that sunny spot in the room's very center, and stretched myself out to sleep. . . .

"The strangeness came to me, first, as a dream. A quiet and quietly religious dream of sitting long long hours in the oldest church, sitting on a rough-wood pew waiting relaxed and patient for the Mass to begin. But no matter how I waited there was no beginning, and in due time it came to me that God and the Mass were not to come to me, but rather I was to go inward, into the tiny crude sanctum of that ancient church, and there in the quiet deep the Mass would come to me.

"Thinking back on it, the dream seems very strange to me, and perhaps even irreligious. But at that moment it seemed plain natural and reverent, and I knew that there was only one right thing to do.

"And I did it. Easy, quiet because sudden loud acts are disrespectful in a church, I stood and left the pew. And walked up to the Altar (bare wood finished only by two thousand years of touching hands) and into the Sanctum.

"I gasped as I pressed through the age-old curtains. For what I saw in that sanctuary changed every thing I thought I knew about myself and about the world: I saw Our Lord Jesus Christ, huddled and bloody still bleeding in one corner of the room, wrapped in white sheets like a shroud stained sanguine where the blood still welled gently from His wounds.

"I fell to my knees at once, for though I'd never been a religious man there was no way I could behold that vision of the Lord Our God in pain suffering so dear with the love for us.

" 'My Lord,' I said, 'Why have they abandoned you? Why have they left you here in the lonely place to die?'

"But the Lord only smiled sadly in my dream. He did not respond to me directly.

"I asked, 'Lord, Lord, how can I unburden you?' for though I was a sinner I saw his love and knew it. And knowing how could I but wish to help?

"Again He smiled His quiet enigmatic smile, and now He shook his head."

The rabbit wiped a tear from the corner of his impossibly large eye. "What was there for me to do? Nothing, nothing at all. So I clasped my hands in prayer and bathed in His Glory and the Agony of His unhealing wounds. In a moment it was too much for me, and I swooned, and closed my eyes. Just before I reopened them I felt a touch on my cheek that set my every hair on end—yes, son, in my dream I was touched my the hand of God.

"'Lord,' I said, 'O Lord tell me what I can do to further Your Mission on this Earth.'

"Now he frowned and shook his head. 'O MAN,' He said, 'YOU DO MY WILL WITH YOUR EVERY THOUGHT AND BREATH. TO SERVE ME LIVE WELL AND JOYOUSLY; AND SPREAD YOUR JOY OUT AMONG ALL PEOPLES OF THE WORLD.'

"And then I was awake, breathlessly gasping. There in that once-empty room in the twilight dim of early evening. Once empty because I no longer lay alone on that floor bare of all but dust and cobweb: William Fischer stood near the door, watching me patiently. He looked as though he'd stood waiting there for hours, watching till I woke.

"There was something hard and rough beside my head—it felt like a block of crumbling rough wood. But when I turned to examine it I saw nothing, despite the fact that I could feel it up against my cheek as I stared at nothing but the wall. And splinters—I could feel splinters in my cheek and on that side of my scalp. Later when I tried to find them with a mirror I could see nothing but the redness of my welted skin.

"William Fischer still stood by the door, watching me as though I were some dangerous wild animal. Ho! Ha! The only animal my heart resembled at that moment was a mouse, a shy embarrassed field mouse caught out in the light of day where he does not belong. His catching me at my nap, and now his watching—I felt humiliated. I wished with all my heart that I were indeed that tiny mouse, and could scuttle away into the shadows that. . . ."

As he spoke of the mouse he wished he were, the most miraculous thing began to happen: the old derelict who'd once been an Easter Bunny now transmogrified into an enormous field mouse. And as he spoke and as he changed, he began to grow smaller and smaller.

"And then," the field mouse said, "the most miraculous thing began to happen. As William Fischer watched too astonished to respond, I did indeed become the mouse I wished I were. And I scuttled off into the corners of things, never to return to the world of man."

The field mouse stopped shrinking, quite abruptly. Smiled a self-satisfied smile, and folded its hands on its lap.

It was just a little larger than Donny now; not quite as large as Tim.

"Is that all?" Donny asked. "What about the rest of the story? And why did you change like that, and how do you change, and . . . what do you do besides wander around Disney World handing out eggs?"

The field mouse sighed. "The Lord came to me in my dream," he said, "and He touched me. And the way He touched me infused me with the miraculous wonder of His being. Don't you see? He made me special, so I could spread His joy out to all the peoples of the world. His miracle lets me change however I need."

He fell asleep in Grandpa's room at the top of the stairs, Tim thought. *He fell asleep* on top of *the Cross, and he doesn't even realize it. It wasn't on account of any dream he got changed like that.* And Tim remembered the splinters, and the last bit of the puzzle fell together. *Tiny bits of the Cross still stuck inside him. No wonder all those miracles happen around him.*

Something was happening. The field mouse—it was changing again. Not turning *into* anything else this time, but . . . crumbling. Turning all dusty and rotted looking.

"But now, lads," the field mouse said, "my time is come, and I am to depart this mortal coil. You two have been so gracious as to unburden me of my history. I bless you for that! I thank you! But—"

And as the field mouse disintegrated, a great white-winged angel rose up from his ashes like a phoenix. And the angel spoke to them with the voice of the field mouse of the Easter Bunny of the derelict.

"—there is nothing more for me in this world! I go to my reward! Farewell!"

And rose up through the concrete ceiling as though it were a cloud.

Donny gasped, and spoke in a hoarse whisper. "He's dead, Tim."

Tim wanted to say, *Don't believe it for a minute, he's just playing another trick on us*, and he almost did. But then he knew better, and knew that he never should've brought Donny with him into the secret in the first place. And he held his tongue.

They got back up to the theme park by following three EMERGENCY EXIT signs on through the gated corridor and up a stairway to the surface. Dinner was already served by the time they got back to Grandpa, but he didn't ask them where they'd gone. Tim had a feeling that he knew it all anyhow.

THREE

T he hill was easier once they got moving again. Twenty, thirty yards—whatever it was, it felt longer—and though the flowers made the air feel warmer than it ought to've been, they did no more. As they drew near the castle the flowers thinned again, and the ground began to come back to life; frail bits of green grew where the reddish dirt met the castle's dark grey rock.

A ramp, half a dozen yards long, that led up to the castle door: it looked almost like a stone bridge. Had there been a moat here once? If there had, time had long since filled it with dust. Scrawny grass and weeds littered that dust-moat; off to the left the frail stem-cord of a wild muscadyne clung tenuously to the castle's granite wall.

"What are you waiting for?" Thomas asked him. He sounded sick, tremulous, as though the hike uphill had worn him to his limit.

"Nothing," Tim said, "nothing. I was looking the doorway over. Looking for—I don't know. Signs of trouble. Traps."

"Go on—can't be anything inside worse'n what's out here. Sure wasn't anything dangerous about the door the time I saw it. Wasn't locked, either."

Tim stepped forward cautiously, walked slowly toward the door. Massive door. Twelve feet tall, or taller. Four, five, maybe six feet wide. Rounded at the top to fit into the arched doorway. It looked as though it were made of a single slab of wood.

Tim hesitated; glanced over his shoulder to see

Thomas's eye. Started walking again, but now more carefully still. "You didn't say that before," Tim said. "You didn't say you'd been inside."

There wasn't any answer.

"What did you see inside there?"

Tim's hand was on the great iron ring, set to pull the door open. He stopped, waited, held still to wait the boy's answer.

"What did you see?"

"I didn't see nothing," Thomas said. "It was dark, almost dark, at least. And I woke up and I knew that the flowers were sleeping, just like I knew when the Stone was asleep. I woke up 'cause the Stone was in my head, and it was angry, and it wanted me home. But when I got up to run, Stone said no, not so fast. Go look inside. So I did. I went right up to the door and opened it and looked in. But it was too dark out, and I couldn't see a thing, so I closed the door and turned around and ran."

Tim blinked, frowned. "You're lying to me. Why are you lying? Why did you lie before? You're telling lies meant to get me to open this door without knowing what's behind it. Why—Is there a trap inside? Are you trying to kill me or—?"

Or what? God knew; Tim didn't. His gut was sure the boy meant no harm. But he was acting so— suspicious. Utterly untrustworthy.

"Be straight with me, Thomas. I'm not going to do a damn thing till you are."

Thomas looked rattled—red-faced and panicked. *He's going to cry,* Tim thought. *The poor boy's about to pitch a fit.*

"Aw, come *on,* Thomas. You can't expect—"

And that was when Thomas really *did* go over the edge.

"Let me *through,* damn you—!" And he slammed shoulder-first into Tim, and even though the boy was only, what, thirteen, and not that tall, the force was enough to throw Tim off balance. Tim fell against the open door grabbing at the air trying to find something to cling to, but that was useless; the only thing there was to grab was the door handle, and that was dead-center against Tim's spine. (Where it hurt pretty considerable, dragging up along the knotty little backbones.)

Thomas bulled on through into the mansion-castle. Tim (lying in the rough dirt beside the door) watched wide-eyed and amazed to see the boy cross over the threshold into the—

—into the—

Into nothing special at all.

The room beyond the door was just the dusty parlor of an antebellum home.

The fact must've surprised Thomas as much as it surprised Tim, because the boy stumbled as soon as he was inside. Stumbled and fell onto the filthy floor like he was expecting stairs up or down or maybe something solid to run into like a wall or something. There wasn't anything like that. Just plain wood floor and dust piled thick above it like a fog, and over on the far side of the room sitting-room furniture all ancient and decrepit from dry rot.

There was no way.

No way at all Grandpa's furniture was anywhere inside that place.

No way in hell.

Tim should have known it for a while, he realized—at least as long ago as the moment he'd seen the hill all covered with those impossible flowers. Nowhere in all that sparkling black mess were the tracks he'd expect movers to leave behind. And wouldn't the moving van itself have left behind a trail? Damned right it would.

This place was a trap. It *was* a trap, and Thomas knew about it, and that was why the boy was acting so peculiar. If Tim stepped across that threshold he'd be in some awful kind of trouble, and he knew it.

It was time to turn around and get out of here. Cut his losses: to hell with the wasted time.

That was what he ought to do.

He glanced back at the car.

And realized that whether it was sensible or not, he wasn't turning back.

To hell with it, he thought. *Whatever it is inside there, I'm not afraid of it.*

And he stepped into the mansion.

Nothing changed as he went in. Whatever the trap was its spring lay deeper inside.

"You need help?" Tim stood above Thomas, leaned over. Offered his hand. Thomas took it without saying a word. "What's the matter with you? What was the rush to get inside here?"

No answer.

"Where's the trap? I know it's here someplace. Someone sent me here on a ruse. That wasn't any accident."

Thomas scowled.

"There isn't any trap. Can't you tell that? No one's been inside this place in fifty years. Maybe longer. You think anybody could've left a trap that long ago, just for you?" He looked Tim up and down. "You weren't even born last time there was people in this place." He coughed, spit dust out onto the floor. "I don't know anything about whoever sent you here. Don't even know who it was—asked and you wouldn't tell me."

The door behind Tim slammed closed of its own accord; Thomas jumped, startled, made a noise like a scream cut off by fear—

"Don't be afraid," Tim said. "It only means to scare you." He shook his head. "Let's go. I want this over with."

Thomas followed.

Nowhere inside the mansion was anything like a castle. The walls, the floors, the appointments, all of them were wood and plaster. The only stone was the marble flooring in the big hall north off the parlor. A great spiral stairway, spiral like a conch shell, winding wider and wider around as it went up, led up from that room into the cobwebs and the shadows. . . .

That was where they needed to go. Later they could check the kitchen, the storerooms, the basement. If they didn't find what they'd come for up there in the dark—

Tim blinked. What was he thinking? Tim already knew—knew—that Grandpa's furniture wasn't here.

There wasn't anything here for him. Was there? He had
an intuition that told there was something here he had to
see. To do. But what? What was Tim here for, if it wasn't
Grandpa's furniture? Something—there. That was what
the twinge in his gut was about: it meant that all along
he'd known that Grandpa's things weren't here. He'd
known all along, deep inside where he hid things from
himself, and he'd come here anyway.

Yes. That was it.

Tim was here exactly because this place was a trap.

This is stupid. Why would he want to walk into a
trap? Weren't there simpler ways to kill himself?

The feeling wasn't going away. He tried for a
moment to pretend that it came from the flowers
outside. But he knew it didn't. The feeling came from
inside him. It *was* him. It was the deepest part of his gut
talking to him.

"Is something wrong?" Thomas asked him. The boy
looked afraid.

"No." Tim grimaced. "We need to go upstairs. You
didn't think to bring a candle, did you? Or a flashlight?"

Thomas frowned. "I did," he said. "I'm surprised
you knew to ask me." He reached into his pocket, took
out a penlight.

Tim shrugged. "I didn't know. But I thought you'd
have one. The electricity doesn't work in your house any
more, does it? It looked like the power was out when I
was there."

Thomas handed him the penlight. "No power at all
this month. Daddy said it was 'cause a line went down."
A sigh. "I don't think he was being truthful with me. I
think he didn't pay the bills again."

That feeling he always got when he saw something
he ought to fix that he didn't have any business fixing:
sad, resigned, even defeated. He'd spent a good six
months learning, back when he was twenty, that there
were some kinds of bad you had to back off from and let
people live through. This was the twentieth century, not
the tenth. When someone put himself in an awful mire,
you had to show respect and let him pull himself
free—or not.

And Thomas was someone Tim respected, even if he was just a boy.

"Is there anything I can do to help? Do you need money?"

Thomas shook his head. "No, there's money in the bank. Dad just doesn't have the heart to see to it."

Tim nodded. "All right, then. I'll give you my number before I leave you off. If you need my help just ask for it."

"I will."

Tim started up the spiral stair, walking carefully out of fear that the whole structure would collapse beneath him. Some steps creaked loudly when he stepped on them; one, half a dozen feet up, sagged fast and for a moment Tim thought it would give way beneath him. Then the wood caught in some underlying brace, and held long enough to let him shift his weight away. He stopped, looked back to Thomas. "Be careful of that step," he said. "I think it's going to collapse."

Thomas nodded. It was still light enough to see him here, what with the curtainless window down low in this room. Farther up . . . Tim couldn't tell from here how far the ceiling was. Thirty feet? Forty? It was too high in the dark to see at all.

It was quiet up here. More quiet with the both of them stopped for that moment, not speaking nor moving, hardly breathing. And with the two of them so quiet Tim heard the sound for the first time.

Not breathing, exactly, though that was what it made him think of. The sound was steadier than breath, like a whir, but not mechanical. A pulse, almost. A heartbeat married to a blur.

Thomas didn't hear it. He was looking at Tim like what was the problem, why was he just standing there, why didn't he *go*, and he said, "What—"

Tim raised his right hand, motioned for silence. Let the hand fall onto the boy's shoulder, then turned to follow the direction of the strange sound that had to be something still alive. . . .

There. High, high up and to the left.

The sound was there.

Tim pointed toward it. "Listen," he said. "Listen very closely. There's a sound—over there. That's where it comes from."

Recognition. That was recognition in the boy's eyes. "What is it, Thomas? What do you know?"

"No. No, you don't hear that." And for a moment Tim thought he meant that Tim's imagination had run away with itself. "You don't hear that with your ears. I remember the Stone—it was like that all the time. You could always hear it when you were close, even if you covered your ears with the palms of your hands."

"The Stone is up there? Or something like it?"

Thomas shrugged. "We'll know soon. Come on. Let's go."

Tim nodded. "Yeah." He turned, stepped over the rotten stair. And climbed.

Up past the second-floor landing, where darkness, dust, and cobwebs enfolded them. That was where Tim turned on the penlight—not that it did a whole lot of good. The feeble bright that came from its bulb wasn't enough to show the step in front of them, let alone show where they were headed.

They took each stair carefully then. Especially there just before the third-floor landing, where Tim noticed the eight-foot length of banister-rail that had rotted and fallen away from the staircase. He noticed it the hard way, too—by reaching for support as his left foot slid away from a thick swatch of dust. He reached for balance, and found nothing, and the fear of death had welled up in the dark to swallow him as he started to stumble out off into the air—

Till Thomas caught his trailing wrist, and pulled him back to equilibrium.

Tim's heart raced; he let out the breath he'd held in without knowing, and the sound wasn't exhalation but a gasp of pent fear. His knees were weak. His free hand—the hand that'd reached out into the void— trembled no matter how he tried to make it still.

Sit down. I've got to sit down and calm myself.

He groped down into the dusty dark reaching to find the nearest step. Found it (not before he'd covered his hand with dust and cobwebs that tickled like fine hair), patted to be certain that the step was whole and strong enough to hold his weight. Shifted around *careful careful careful*; sat.

"I'll be all right," he said. Thomas hadn't asked. "Don't worry."

The boy made a sound that could have been agreement and could have been skepticism.

"Just give me a minute."

Silence.

And then as Tim was getting to his feet, as Thomas stepped out ahead of him, came the creaking sound of old wood moving somewhere up above them. What? Was someone up there waiting for them? Up in the shadows by that sound?

A glimmer of motion in the darkness. Direct above them, moving toward them—

Something was falling toward them. Something massive—even in this dark Tim had a glimmer of its size like a plummeting couch.

Something falling to crush them.

And the only thing Tim thought was: Thomas. Just like that; it was a reflex thing. He was about to die because something heavy and enormous was about to crush him, and all he could think was that it was going to kill the boy here with him, and he had to do something to save him

And he did.

Tim leaped into the air—not thinking about the vanished railing that'd nearly killed him only a moment before. Caught Thomas in a flying tackle and the boy didn't understand, of course—he must've thought Tim was out of his mind, because he struggled against Tim trying to take him up and away from the path of the falling—

"Damn you!"

Down around them, only now they were on the landing, ducking onto the balcony to hide as the rafter he could barely see smashed against the spiral staircase, smashed and bashed and tumbled off the stairs down toward the marble floor below them.

(Tim paused a moment to look at that floor—it was farther down than he'd realized. They were only up two flights, weren't they? No, only one. Only one flight up. It looked farther than that somehow—much farther than they'd climbed. At least a hundred feet. Maybe more than that.)

"I'm sorry," Thomas said, "I didn't mean—"

"Don't worry about it." Tim patted his back. "Let's go."

Up again, and now the stairs swayed with the motion of their walking, and the wood creaked loudly with the sound of that sway, and Tim was sure the staircase would collapse before they reached the top of it. When they were still a few feet below the fourth floor something groaned high up above them, groaned and shuddered and shifted hard and fast, and thank God there was a rail here and thank God it was intact, or both of them would have fallen down and out into the black—

Thomas was off balance, clinging to the rail and making small sounds like he was scared out of his mind. "We've got to keep going," Tim told him. Thomas didn't respond at all. "This thing is going to collapse any moment. Come on—" And he still wasn't moving, Tim saw when he shone the light on him, so Tim reached out and lifted him up onto his shoulder—no small task; Thomas was anything but a small child—and carried him up the last dozen steps.

(Cobwebs in his face, in his dark-blind eyes as he stepped onto the fourth-floor landing. Not cobwebs—spiderwebs. And somewhere was a spider crawling through his broken net. Probably crawling on Tim, not crawling on his face because he'd feel that, but crawling on his shirt and in just a moment he'd feel its fine-fine sharp legs bite into his neck—)

He set Thomas on the floor where the landing opened into a hall that led deeper into the house. He brushed himself half-unconsciously. Startled without understanding why when his hand swept away something that might have been a bug.

"Thomas? You awake? You okay?" He shone the

light into Thomas's open eyes. The boy blinked, reflexively. "You awake?"

No answer.

Tim sighed. Looked away for a moment.

Right and left of them was a balcony that led onto several rooms—all of their doors closed but the door of the room where the noise was. Tim aimed the light at that room and saw the door broken, lying in dry-rotted shreds beside its frame.

Okay. That was where they were going. He could carry Thomas there if he had to.

"Thomas. . . ? Come on, kid. Don't clock out on me now." He ruffled the boy's hair, let his hand drift down across his face. Let his thumb rest beneath his nose long enough to make certain there was breath. Moved down to the neck to check the boy's pulse. No problem there; strong, steady beats, and the pace was calm.

Remembered what Thomas had said about the Stone, about how it would get inside him and push his self aside. How the flowers and the Stone and the house were all related.

And remembered how Thomas said that Tim made him think of the Stone.

He set his hands on the boy's head, and he imagined himself brushing away gauze, thick dense papery-white gauze that separated the boy from the world so thoroughly as to make him blind and deaf and dumb—

Imagined himself unwrapping and unwrapping, unwinding long sheets of the stuff that was tacky now that he was in past the initial layers. Sticking to his hands and hard to get it off

(but his hands were still here, here on the boy's head in the dark still strange but not fantastic dark, everything was as ordinary as a plain dull fall day in the suburbs, there was no gauze, no gauze nowhere but Tim's imagination)

getting the gauze off his hands. He was having trouble getting the gauze off his hands, so he said to hell with it, to hell with it and let it wear. Kept unwinding the stuff from Thomas's face and hair and eyes, only now

his hands were mittened by the white gauze like spiderweb this deep, and it numbed his touch so bad he could
scarcely tell what he was doing.

(He knew what he was doing, damn it—he was
letting his imagination run away with him. There wasn't
time for this. He was high, high up inside this place—
this was the fourth floor, but the ground floor below
them looked to be a dozen times farther than that—and
the stairs that'd led him up here were a bad bet for
getting him back down. And there was the boy, too; he
was responsible for this poor kid, and as long as he was
in this daze that was a large responsibility indeed. He
needed to keep his head clear, or he'd never get out of
here. The last thing he needed was to let himself indulge
in nonsense fantasies.)

The gauze on Thomas's head was thin, now—paper-
thin to see through, though that like as not meant there
were still a hundred layers of the crud left. The trouble
was Tim's hands: much thicker, much more restrictive
than any mitten now. Like plaster casts, almost.
Wrapped solid-stiff, so stiff they looked like the ghost-
white hands of a stuffed toy doll. All but useless; no
distinction left between his thumb and fingers; hardly
any between palm and digits. And of course he'd lost
hold of the peeling end of the stuff that covered the boy's
face, and of course there was no way to get hold of it with
his hands bound up so bad.

Time to clean it off

(it was hopeless—hopeless. he was completely lost
in the fantasy and there was nothing he could do to
extract himself from it. he'd tried, damn it, tried hard as
he could and even though Tim knew that he was still
kneeling on the landing in the dark-dark holding Thomas's head, even though he knew it there wasn't a damn
thing he could do about it because every bit of his self
was wrapped up in the idiot imagine of untwining gauze)

clean it off or he'd be stuck this way forever (he was
sure of it) and Thomas too, stuck just *this* far from the
world.

So Tim rubbed his hands against one another,
rubbed and rubbed to knead the junk up into a ball, and

it did ball up, all right, but it balled up with Tim's hands
still inside trapped like some misbegotten bug in a
spiderweb. Stuck hard, too—Tim tried with all he had to
yank his left hand *free* of it, back toward his shoulder and
nothing gave but he did feel like to rip the skin right off
of him, which was no damned fun no sir.

Tried twisting hands round and back and sideways,
too, like he was trying to get out of some Chinese finger
puzzle, but that wasn't any more help than brute force.
Less help, even, since it got him worse tangled up than
he was it the first place.

 no use no use no use

Calm down, he told himself. Calm down and think.
This goo isn't going nowhere just because you push and
pull it. No more than it yanked clean of Thomas's face all
at once. What I need to do is cut it off. Only how can I
cut it off with my hands all gummed together like they
are?

Well, I can't.

But I can do the next best thing: find something
sharp and saw myself free.

Something sharp was waiting for him, too, right
over there on the staircase. Lots of something: busted
wood. Mostly from the splintered handrails.

Tim stood, pulled away from Thomas. (And it was
like that, too, like pulling away. The distance between
them was a tangible thing that hurt him with every step
he took.)

Over to the stairs, and there thrust toward him
wedged into the balcony rail was a long jagged-
splintered shard of wood that'd once been a turn of
railing for the spiral staircase. Just the thing, just like
he'd thought it would be; the goo tore and bound itself to
wood harder faster than it'd ever bound to flesh. It
wasn't fast work (sawing back and forth, pulling and
straining and slicing the tacky mass) but it went fast
enough. Five minutes after he'd got to his feet Tim was
picking the last strands of gunk from his fingers.

He wiped his hands on his jeans to clean the sticky
feel (it didn't help) and started back toward Thomas.

Tried to, anyway.

But couldn't.

Because Thomas was gone.

(Was gone was gone was gone, really *was* gone, Tim was there in the real world outside the vision that had taken him, and Thomas was nowhere, Tim knelt on the balcony cradling nothing in his hands still as they'd been holding air. And try as he might Tim remembered nothing, nothing about how or why or when the boy had disappeared.)

He had to find him. Tim could hear his blood rushing in his ears, pressing against his skull so hard he knew that any moment now the arteries that fed his brain would burst. What had he done? What had he done? He'd lost track of a child not fit to see for himself in a house that might just as well have been the devil's.

Perhaps it *was* the devil's house.

Had to find the boy. Had to find him, wherever he'd gone. Gone? How could Thomas go anywhere, blind and deaf and dumb as he was? No, Tim decided. The boy hadn't gone anywhere. He'd been spirited away, somehow, by someone. Never mind that reason said they were alone here. Never mind that no one could've stepped within a dozen yards of Tim without setting off alarms inside his skull. The boy was kidnapped, and Tim knew it; to hell with reason.

But who had taken him? And where?

There was no way to know. All Tim could do was open his eyes and look.

He groped on the floor till he found the penlight (he'd let it drop back when he'd first taken Thomas's head in his hands); turned it on; let the beam wander over the floor of the balcony.

He saw no sign of struggle. Debris everywhere— the dust, of course; shattered wood from the staircase; sticky threads and bands of fluff from the mask that'd covered Thomas's eyes, but no sign of Thomas, no clue as to where or how he'd gone.

Wait. The dust. Dust everywhere, undisturbed forever in the mouldering house: the boy would leave a trail in it, wouldn't he?

And so would whoever had stolen him away.

Carefully, now—Tim shone the light slowly carefully across the floor, scanning for some sign. . . . There were his own tracks, back and forth between here and the landing till they weren't tracks so much as they were a trail. Nothing else was anywhere near so obvious as his own trail . . . there. What was that? In the dust not far from him (ten feet away?—no more than that), glistening with reflected light when the flash-beam touched it. A tiny jewel? A hint of red. Strange: The penlight was scarcely bright enough to show color at all. If the glint shone red, then it was red indeed. He crossed the distance to it carefully, looking for signs of passing in the dust—and saw none. And shined his light directly down onto the spot of brightness—

And saw that it was blood.

Red-deep-red opaque like only blood could be. Liquid. Wet red spreading at the edges. Gathering dust—tiny blood-wicking filaments clung to the slick surface.

Thomas. . . ? No, it couldn't be Thomas, Tim thought. Thomas wasn't bleeding. Hadn't been bleeding. Someone could've cut him, couldn't they? Or he could've cut himself.

How?

No. Not like that. It wasn't Thomas's blood.

(There was no sensible way Tim could've known that, much less been sure of it. Even in this unreal place halfway between the imagined and the observed. Still, he knew it; and the fact was that what he knew was right.)

All right: even if it made no sense. Whose blood was it?

He waited for the answer to come to him, just as it always did in dreams. But it would not. Where an answer should have been, just out beyond the tip of his tongue, was nothing.

Nearly nothing.

Except maybe for . . . it was like a flavor, Tim thought, imagining the answer that wasn't at the tip of his tongue. A strange, unnamable flavor made of salt and ferment and urea, and it was the essence of someone he knew but could not remember.

There was no other sign of passage in the dust. Only blood.

Tim let the beam shine forward over the dark balcony floor—and saw nothing on it but grey dust undisturbed for decades.

Except there. Ten feet up ahead? No, a little more. Gleaming in the shadows. Just as the first had.

A hint of red.

Tim knew it was blood long before he was close enough to see it clearly. What else *could* it be?

And it was, of course. And three yards beyond that was another, and beyond that another, and another.

They led to the door he'd been going toward in the first place.

The door to the room where the unknowable thing still whined—was that the word? No. Partly crying, crying quietly but intensely, like a small child in agony. And partly like a song. A melody he recognized but couldn't quite remember.

He hesitated there at the dark broken door to the singing room, waiting to be sure he was prepared to face—

To face his Maker, that's what Tim was thinking.

But it was wrong. He'd seen his Maker the first time years and years ago, seen the Christ way back when he was six, and in the time since he'd grown to know Him well, and to love Him not just as Lord and Saviour, but love Him as one loves those dear, precious, and familiar.

There was not a chance that the Lord stood beyond that door, waiting to talk to Tim. Something waited, all right, but it wasn't the Maker—it was something foul and murderous. *Listen to it*, Tim thought. *That song. I know that song.* He shuddered; there was something in the melody that chilled him to the bone. A smell, too: an odor in the air, mingling with dust and mold. He tried to place it, and very nearly managed to. He thought of matches, and putrefying eggs. Thought of the stink of Florida well water, full and rich in the air when sprinklers irrigate the lawns in high summer.

He didn't think of sulfur. And he should have, because of who he was and where he was and the fact that sulfur was the greatest part of all the smells that came to mind.

Stepped forward, into the doorway and through it. (The noise was louder, now—deafening where before it'd been almost too subtle to hear. He had no memory of any change in volume, as though it'd gone up gradually across time. But just a moment ago was when it'd been so quiet. . . .) Forward again, one more step. Another. Now there was a second sound mingling with the first, the sound of a child's panicked, tortured breathing no louder than it ought to've been with Thomas frightened for his life, and loud, too, so loud that it was clearly audible in mixture with the screaming thrum—

And Tim lifted the penlight to see—

Saw the boy bound gagged still blindfolded with unnatural white-white cloth—

Saw the room strange lost in time room with its ancient furniture dustless beautiful—

Saw the telephone anachronic on the vanity—

Saw the vase sitting on the vanity, the vase filled with pitch-black flowers—

Saw the Bleeding Man.

Holding a gun.

Aimed at Thomas, not two inches from his forehead.

And gasped.

Behind Tim the door slammed shut with a sound solid as old iron—despite the fact that only a moment before it'd been shards of rotten wood.

It shouldn't have surprised him to see the Bleeding Man standing above the boy, ready to murder, no more than it should have surprised him to hear Thomas whimper full with terror for his life. But it did. All this while as he'd fought his way here against strangeness and the dark Tim'd lost sight of the Bleeding Man's hand guiding events. Maybe because of the sorcery of this place;

maybe because he didn't have the heart to face the truth of it.

And here he was.

(And Tim opened his eyes, his *real* eyes, and saw the boy alone sitting uncomfortably on a high rough-wood bench, a bench that was no special thing, no strange or frightening relic of some bloody ritual. . . .)

"Put it down, damn you," Tim said. "What do you want with the boy?"

The Bleeding Man laughed. "I own this child. What do *you* desire of him?"

A lewd suggestion in his voice, wrapped around his emphasis; it made Tim furious to hear it. He wanted to tackle the man, tear him to a shred. Rip out his throat and feed it to him. And would have, too, but didn't because there was no way to be certain he could kill before the Bleeding Man pulled the trigger and pasted Thomas's brain to the wall and the—

Altar, altar, Thomas was bound to a bloodstained altar, and seeing it, *looking* at it, Tim knew that at least a thousand children had died bound there, tied just as Thomas lay tied—

"Let him go, damn it. What's he got to do with this?" Tim saw the gun wave away from Thomas. Saw the Bleeding Man aim it at him—but that was nothing. He didn't fear for himself. "Why have you lured me here? You have my grandfather's belongings. As far as I know the—" remembered Thomas, bound to the altar and looking as though he were aware of the events around him "—what we're both looking for is with them. Haven't you found it?" And if he had the Cross, what would he want with Tim? "What are you doing here?"

The Bleeding Man laughed and laughed and laughed. And raised his gun toward the ceiling—

And fired! *Bam!* The sound of a gun in close quarters, so loud, intense, unpleasant that it made him want to scream—

And the ceiling shattered in a spray of glass black-painted half a thousand times, and light was everywhere to blind them because their eyes were so adapted to the dark (Tim's ached, honestly ached with the strain of his irises squeezing out the light) and the boy was on the too-high bench that maybe was an altar (nothing like the one from Tim's dream, but maybe an altar still) and there beneath him on the unpainted wood those stains, probably they were stains from blood.

Light.

And the floor was bloodstained too.

And Thomas was tied to the altar, and gagged by rope. . . .

And the Bleeding Man was gone. Gone without leaving, as though he'd never been there. Certainly he left behind no trail.

Tim scanned the room and saw that even the blood spots he'd trailed to lead Tim here were gone.

Tim blinked, his eyes still adjusting to the light. Looked up at the ceiling—it'd been a skylight, once. Long ago, before ages of paint and grime and debris. That single bullet had destroyed it all: glass, paint, and the stuccolike shell of grime.

Why? Why had the Bleeding Man drawn him here? What was the purpose? What was the point? Was he trying to pull Tim off balance? It was the only reason Tim could imagine, and it was senseless.

Draw Tim off balance.

Then the telephone rang.

He knew damn well enough not to answer it; knew that his only hope there and then was to turn, and grab Thomas, and *run*. But answering telephones was reflex, and it didn't matter what he thought or meant to do. He crossed the room and answered before it could ring a third time.

"Hello?" Still blinking away the sun. Beads of sweat forming on the bridge of his nose. Thomas staring at him wide-eyed, looking scared out of his mind.

The sound of breathing on the far end of the line. Nothing else.

"Hello?—Answer, damn it."

"Tim." He knew the voice from that one syllable. "I'm sorry, Tim." A pause. "Will you ever forgive me?"

Gail Benjamin.

Calling him here, in the middle of nowhere three

states away from where he'd last seen her. Three states away from the only place he'd ever seen her. Calling him in a place where she shouldn't have been able to imagine him, much less telephone.

Gail Benjamin.

How. . . ?

It wasn't really Gail, was it? This was just one more thing he was imagining. Just the Bleeding Man, still trying to derail him.

Wasn't it?

It had to be.

(He focused himself to clear away the still-lingering gauze that was his imagination of this place. Listened carefully, carefully to be certain that he knew what he was seeing. The telephone; the ancient bloodstained room. Hearing the sound of Gail Benjamin breathing into the telephone receiver. It was real. Undeniable. And Tim wanted to deny it, too, wanted to deny it because a big piece of him loved Gail Benjamin (even though it hadn't told him; even though he hadn't known her long enough to learn to love her) and there was nothing in the rest of him that wanted to turn away from her and never look back.

(Which was what he had to do if she belonged to the Bleeding Man.

("Gail," he said, "is that you?"

(The sound of hesitation; quiet like the roar he'd hear listening inside a seashell.

("Yes, Tim, it's me. I—I'm—"

("No, Gail. Don't say it. There isn't any need." And then silence, again—but where before the quiet had been loud with things unsaid this was restful, or nearly so. Because now there was no need to say. . . .

(Then there was loud clattering interference on the line, as though someone had torn some cord clear from its socket, and a final click that made Tim think a phone had been set into its cradle. Until he heard the sound of laughter, thick raucous masculine laughter, and that was the Bleeding Man, come to mock him/mock them/mock everything that Tim held sacred—

(*"Damn you!"* Tim shouted. *"Damn you! Damn you*

and your children and their children after them—damn them all!"

(He blanched to hear himself make that curse—he'd never made a curse before that, let alone one so vile.

(But it only made the Bleeding Man laugh that much harder.)

He let the phone fall back into its cradle. His back sagged. He felt exhausted, demoralized.

Defeated.

Behind him, the door flew open, slammed closed— seven times in quick succession. Tim turned to look and saw that there was light outside there now, too—caught a glimpse up into the rafters where the shattered skylight was much larger than the tiny one in here.

No, he thought. *Not now. Not after all this.*

And the sound of evil laughter, sourceless, filled the air.

It was time to get out of here. Time to get out of here *right now.*

Right now.

Three steps and he was across the room, untying Thomas. Thirty seconds fumbling at the knots— agonizing seconds where he thought he'd never accomplish the obvious—and then finally he had the boy free.

Thomas pulled the gag away from his mouth as Tim opened the last knot. Sucked in a deep, desperate breath, and let it out.

"Are you going to be okay? Are you ready to run? It's time to get out of this place. And get out in a hurry."

Thomas looked for a moment as though he were about to say something—as though there were still some unfinished business that needed attention. But whatever it was, he didn't say it; instead he nodded, stood, set the rope on the altar, and started toward the door. "You're right," he said. "Let's go."

The door opened of its own accord as they grew close to it. Tim caught it, pushed it to the limit of its arc; held it there forcefully as he could. It was a prudent thing to do, and provident, too—as Thomas stepped near the threshold, the door jerked and pressed violently against Tim's arm—

"Out—get out—"

So hard, so powerful a force behind it that Tim knew that in a moment it'd throw him out of the way. Or his arm would break; he wasn't sure which would happen first. He kept tense against it as Thomas slipped by. Then let it force him out into the hall gradually, slow slow and holding fast for fear it'd swing press or pull to batter him.

It took him a full two minutes to get clear of the door that way. The time was necessary, what with the door yanking back and forth, straining to bludgeon him. Which was exactly what it tried to do the instant he let go of it. It would have gotten him if he'd spent an instant more getting out of its way.

The balcony looked different in the light. No less ancient, and more forbidding; it looked in danger of collapse at any moment. The wooden mezzanine looked so frail, so delicate against the endless smooth white plaster of the wall. As though at any moment it would lose its grasp on the mansion, and fall booming to the ballroom floor. And it wasn't just old wood, but wood that showed its age. Would it disintegrate before it fell? Certainly its finish had disintegrated, and long since— beneath the dust Tim could see powdery white haze that might once have been layers of shellac and linseed oil.

The doors—three of them lined against the wall between here and the stairway landing—bore that same whitish cast. How long, Tim wondered, did it take a finish to disintegrate that way?

Thomas stood over the rail (it too was wood bared to dust by time), staring down at—at what? Tim had never seen the view from here—not in the light. Not when you could see it. He stopped beside the boy, craned his neck forward to steal a glance.

"Look in the shadows," Thomas said. "There are people down there. People with guns."

Tim choked when he saw the height—they were a hundred, two hundred feet up. Easily; it could be more than that. The room below them was so great, so empty that it was almost impossible to put it in scale. . . . that was when it finally occurred to him the great room with the marble floor like a ballroom was a ballroom.

A ballroom? Tim didn't want to think what guests would come to a ball in this foul place.

He didn't want to think who would have built it. Nor who would live in it. But he knew both those things, because knowing them was more than anything else a question of admitting the answers to himself.

"Where?" Tim asked. "I don't see anyone."

Thomas pointed, and Tim saw a tall cloaked figure skulking in the shadows near the south wall. And saw the glint of a rifle barrel in the figure's arms.

Then Tim began to see more of them—there were so many of them that they saturated the shadows; every dark spot down below held a lurker with a gun.

Who were they? How had they gotten here, and when? Had they come while Tim and Thomas were inside the room with the altar? Or had they been here all along?

Ghosts. They're the ghosts of this place, like the image of the Bleeding Man, but not like that because they're tied here forever.

How were they going to get out of here without going past the ghosts? Surely the guns were more than ornamental. If they went out through the ballroom they'd be shot.

Wouldn't they?

Unless maybe—was it possible they'd been there when Tim and Thomas had first passed through that room? The shadows had been deeper then; darker. They could've passed right by the hooded ghosts without seeing . . . maybe. Tim wasn't sure; he thought his hackles would have stood on end to pass a ghost. (Or had they? Now that he thought of it, it seemed that his hackles had stood on end continuously since he'd first turned off the road in Tylerville.)

They had to try passing through the ballroom. Trying to find an alternate stairway would take more time than Tim wanted to waste; and anyway there were all but certainly lurkers there, too. They would be everywhere, Tim thought. Anywhere sheltered to block the direct sunlight.

"We'll have to ignore them," Tim said. "If there are that many they could have killed us both already." He nodded toward the stairway landing. "Come on."

A snap—like a shotgun clapping back in place after it's been loaded—and then the closed door second from them toward the landing flew open. A man stepped out of it. Perhaps a woman; the cloak the figure wore covered its face, and it was far too loose to show details of anatomy. Stepped out, and leveled a two-barrel shotgun.

And fired.

If Tim hadn't heard the loading *snap* the two of them might have died right there and then. But he did hear, and he'd seen the shotguns down below, and when he saw the door swing open he knew what was happening, and he was already rolling forward, grabbing Thomas as he made a swan dive into the dust-gritty balcony floor.

The blast shook the air just above Tim's back. Shook it and sent wind like warm breath into the collar of his shirt.

When he looked up the gunman was gone.

Two reactions in his stomach, tearing him in opposite directions: fight and flight. Should they duck back into the room they'd just escaped? Should he chase after the one who'd tried to shoot them? He spent a moment trying to decide, and before it was past Tim discovered he was already halfway down the hall toward the still-open second door, heading full into the face of fire—

Which wasn't fire at all, of course. When he got to the open door he found nothing but an empty room—it was shadowy, unlit, but plainly visible by reflected light from outside. Empty—utterly. No furniture; no closets. No doors. Precious little dust.

The gunman had gone toward the balcony, then. Tim stepped away from the open door, turned back to check on Thomas. Had a moment of fright as he realized that the last time he'd let the boy out of his sight in this place he'd nearly got him killed—but no, there he was, getting up off the floor. Filthy and spitting out dust.

"We're in trouble, kiddo. I think we'd better run for it."

Thomas was on his feet, still spitting. Nodding. "Yeah." As soon as he saw the boy take off, Tim started running himself. Five, ten seconds, they were on the landing. On the wide arc of the spiral stair taking the steps two and three at a time, and now in the light Tim could see how the rail was broken all through this part of the staircase, too, hanging loose in most places and in others it was gone. Poof. Gone. He could have slipped anywhere on the way up, and chances were he damned near did, and more than once. Worse, Thomas could have tumbled right off the edge, and there wouldn't have been a thing Tim could have done about it. Not a damn thing but scream.

They weren't going to slip now.

Tim was reasonably confident about that.

The stairs were all dusty, and maybe the dust made it easier to slip than Tim would have liked, but it wasn't anything Tim would call dangerous. After all, the staircase was wide—as wide across as the living room of Tim's apartment. As long as they kept clear of the edges stumbling wouldn't injure anything but their pride.

Ka-blam! Another thunderous shotgun blast, and the sensation of the staircase rocking underneath them—and for the longest moment Tim was sure that they'd been shot dead and hadn't had the time to realize it yet. No—Thomas was fine, still bounding down the arcing stair. What about himself? Was he hit? He kept waiting to collapse in his tracks and fade to meet the Lord once and for all; but it didn't happen. And finally it dawned on him that the gunfire was coming from below this time, not from above, and the staircase rocked because that was what had been hit. Hit on its underside. Right beneath the spot where they'd stood, to judge by the way it'd shaken them.

Ka-blam! Ka-blam-blam-blam! More shooting. And the stairs, the whole damned staircase, swayed, swung wider and wider and up above Tim could hear creaking from the struts that held it—

It's going to collapse.

The staircase groaned, shuddered.

They were still a good half-dozen yards above the third-floor landing.

Up above something gave way, and Tim heard it collapsing down toward them. Felt it collapsing, felt the groaning moving reverberating wood in his feet and in the calves of his legs. Felt himself suddenly standing at an odd angle to the ground, saw Thomas losing his balance to fall—

Not again, oh God not again—

But the boy was falling toward Tim, toward him and the direction of his fall would obviously carry him past and out into the air, and Tim stepped into the path of his descent to catch him—and did catch, though Thomas's inertial force was near enough to send both of them out over the edge that now seemed so close.

Up. Up. A moment ago they'd been up and across from the third-floor landing; now it seemed very nearly straight above them. Not that bad—it wasn't quite that bad yet, Tim told himself as he climbed. Carrying the boy. If it was that bad they'd have fallen off already. But it was nearly so.

Six, eight more steps before the landing. The staircase began to tear away from it. Boards splintering, splitting at right angles to their grain, and thrust up out of the staircase like malevolent grey-brown weeds. (The smell of fresh green wood impossible here, but he did, he smelled green wood brought out into the air by violence.) Breaking away, breaking away underneath Tim's feet that were flying out from under him as he lost footing because footing had ceased to exist, and there was nothing to do but heave Thomas up onto the landing and hope for the best.

And the back-push of thrusting Thomas away sent Tim reeling out into the void as the last underpinnings of the spiral staircase gave way, and Tim fell as the world came thundering down around his ears—

There.

Tim grabbed, grabbed hold of a plank so mangled-twisted that it looked like frayed wood, all splinters in a thousand directions. And he hugged it for all he was worth, and he prayed.

And it held.

And Tim thought: How is this board here, and how is it so green? It *was* green, too. Here so close he could see the faint green cast about the wood, so green as though it'd only been lumbered that afternoon. If he kissed that splinter there, he thought, he'd taste fresh sap.

He closed his eyes, tried to picture the floor upstairs.

Dust. Underneath that harder, grittier stuff—roach droppings; the desiccated stool of mice or some other small animal. Below that the silk-smooth powdery white residue of disintegrated wax.

And under that the wood.

Old, dry-hard greyish wood. When he'd stepped on it the echo had been brittle.

Opened his eyes, and looked at the board he still clung to.

There was no mistaking this one, either. This wood was fresh and new. Very nearly still alive.

There was one possibility, when he thought about it: wasn't it possible that this floor had been replaced just this week? Yesterday, more like it. Even wood in lumber yards wasn't this green.

But how. . . ?

He tried to imagine workmen coming in here, building floors and walls and stairs, rebuilding things, and leaving without disturbing so much as a grain of ancient dust. And almost laughed, despite the circumstances. It wasn't possible—not even remotely.

The wood here wasn't alive because it was new or freshly lumbered—it was alive because of something on the floor up above him.

Carefully Tim began to shimmy up the twisted wreck of the board. Once when he was only a few inches from the top something snapped loose somewhere, and for an instant Tim was falling again—and then it caught, stopped short. Two long heaves and he was pulling himself up over the edge, where he saw Thomas sitting

lazed on the floor staring at him as though he were a
ghost come back to haunt.

Which, of course, Tim wasn't.

Though he very nearly wished he were. If he were
a ghost he wouldn't have to worry about the jagged,
splintering mass here at the edge of the broken landing.
Like a bed of thorns. And slippery from the dust, which
meant that it'd be that much easier to impale himself.
Easier, hell; it was downright likely, with the spears so
sharp, so long and everywhere. . . .

"Don't just sit there, damn it. Give me a hand
getting over this nightmare."

Thomas blinked, blushed. "Sorry," he said, "wasn't
thinking, I guess." And he got up, started toward Tim.
Before he'd finished speaking Tim was regretting his
tone, and even regretting the request for help. It was too
dangerous here at the broken edge; he didn't want
Thomas getting any nearer to it than could be avoided.
And there wasn't any call to use that tone of voice
regardless.

But Thomas was here, and before Tim could protest
that he'd changed his mind the boy had him by the
shoulders, and together the two of them levered Tim up
and over the wicked mass of shattered wood.

"Thanks, Thomas." Tim frowned. " 'Pologize for
snapping at you."

The boy shrugged, nodded. "We shouldn't stand
here," he said. He pointed down into the ballroom.

Where three dozen robed ghosts stood watching
them, standing out in the open, shotguns aimed and
ready—

"Dear God," Tim said. It wasn't a curse but a prayer.
"They've been like that all this time? While I was
climbing back up here?"

"I don't know. I didn't see them till I stood up to
help you."

Tim set his arm on the boy's shoulder, eased both of
them back and away from the edge of the landing. He
half expected one of the ghosts to order him still—he was
sure they'd start shooting, and that he and Thomas
would have to dive out of the line of fire to save

themselves. And one of the brown-robed figures (monks, Tim thought, they look like monks) one of the brown-robed figures did lift his rifle silently to aim. But before he could fire they were out of sight, and then it didn't matter what the ghost intended.

(How could the ghosts stand direct sunlight now when before they'd so obviously avoided it? Was it growing dark already? No, too soon for that, Tim thought. But anyway he stole a glance at the sky above them as he and Thomas backed away. And saw not night approaching but impending storm; dark bright-edged thunderous clouds filled the narrow horizon he could see through the shattered skylight.)

"Rain," Thomas said. "We shouldn't be here when it hits. It won't be good if we are."

Tim turned to look at him—quizzically, wondering exactly what the boy meant.

"Rain was always trouble with the Stone. I don't want to see what happens when it hits those flowers."

There wasn't time for this. No time at all. There was barely time to cope with what was here waiting for them on the mansion's third floor, let alone things that waited in their future.

And how were they going to get down from here, anyway? Chances were that there was another stairway somewhere deep back inside somewhere. But Tim was sure that there'd be people in there, people hiding deep in the dark of an abandoned stairway waiting to find them shoot them kill them—

Hysterical. He was getting hysterical. He had to calm down; he had the boy to think of. He thought: *This ought to be a dream*, and then he shuddered as he realized that it wasn't a dream, and hadn't been for a long time, and he couldn't quite remember where the one had stopped and the other had started.

Calm. And forced himself, and after a moment he did calm a little. And he thought, *The situation?* And knew it was pretty bad. They were stuck up here, fifty feet sheer drop from the ground without a clue how they could get down. Everywhere that Tim could think of was full of people waiting to kill them. They had to get out and get away, and they had to do it soon. It was going to rain something fierce, to judge from those clouds. Any moment now. And if Thomas was right they'd be in trouble if they weren't clear of this hill before the rain started. Or—what? The flowers. Right. The flowers. Something strange would happen with the flowers. Tim didn't know what, and right then he didn't want to know; he wanted to be way the hell away from here before he had to find out.

How were they going to get out of here? The answer was a question: how *could* they get out of here?

They could look for back stairs. Of course.

They could jump here. Take their chances with the bizarre ghosts that waited down here for them, take their chances with the fall. Not a great alternative, but it was an alternative, anyway.

It took him a moment to think of the other possibility. Which was just as well, since it was a bizarre one: the windows. They could find a window on this floor, climb out of it. Try to find a way to ease themselves down to the ground. Might be possible; Tim remembered the exterior of this place being uneven stone, and weren't there vines? Ivy or something. Muscadyne? Yes, they were muscadynes clinging to the outside walls, dried, sun-scorched, but still alive vines clinging to the outside walls. Not that it was such a great idea, climbing out from this height. Better to check for a back stair first. If there was one, if it was safe, then that was best. If the stairs were dangerous then they'd have to take their chances with the outside walls.

"This way," Tim said. He pointed toward the hall that led into the center of the mansion. Thomas nodded, looking uneasy. He was afraid, and there was good call for that.

It didn't stop him. Didn't stop either of them. Neither one so much as paused before they both set off into the passageway.

As they moved away from the great open space above the ballroom the hall grew progressively darker. The landing, the balconies, both of them now were lit by the shattered skylight. But here in the hall there was only ambient reflected light.

Balconies, Tim thought, retracing his steps. There were balconies here, just as there'd been on the floor above. And the floors were just as dusty. He could feel that dust caking up around his feet, though he couldn't see it here in this dark part of the hall. This floor looked like a twin of the one above it—and yet there was something very different here. As different as the wooden floor he walked on. He listened to the sound of his footsteps, the sound of Thomas's. The tone *was* different. Softer, rounder. Was that the sound of a green plank? Tim thought it was, but he had no way to know for certain. He'd walked across new pine floors before, but he'd never seen wood as green as out on the broken landing—never seen it that green that wasn't still part of a tree.

Other things were different, too. Little things. Like the dust on the floor, just like everywhere else—but there wasn't grit underneath it the way there was on the other floors. And the finish on the wood—here it was still buff-dull wax, instead of the disintegrated powder like on the wood upstairs. Even the plaster walls seemed different somehow, though Tim was damned if he could describe the difference.

He wanted to stop, to test this place. To see if and what set it off from the floor above. Instinct told him that it was important to find out. If he didn't, he thought, his ignorance would cause him trouble. But there was another instinct, and stronger; a certainty that there wasn't time for any exploration but what was needed to get them out of there expeditiously as possible. Even then there wasn't time enough to be sure they could escape. Any of these doors they passed could be a stairwell. There sure wasn't time to check them all. Tim didn't think it'd be necessary; his sense of symmetry told him that the second stair would be in the back of the mansion, opposite the first. But that was only supposition. If he was wrong, or if there wasn't any other stairway, they could spend hours in here looking for it.

The corridor bent slightly to the left, and suddenly

there was light again. Light from a long series of windows that ran along the left wall of the passage.

The light was welcome, of course. And the windows would have been welcome even in pitch dark, since they were an alternate means of escape. The trouble was that if they were here, and this passage led along one wall of the mansion, then Tim's guesses about the floor plan of this place were meaningless.

Thomas looked powerfully disturbed. Tim thought: *That boy is like a weather vane. And we're in awful trouble.*

It was a fact. No denying it.

"Where are we?" Tim asked. He wasn't thinking as the words came out. It didn't occur to him before he spoke that the boy wasn't likely to know anything more about this place than he did.

That was just as well. Because Thomas did know, and he answered quite directly.

"The Stone told me about this place," he said, "that afternoon when it finally found me." They were near the first of the windows now, and as they stepped up beside it Thomas turned to look out. "Out there," he said, "it's different. If you went out through that window and tried to find your car, you'd never get there."

And that was patently true. Unquestionably so.

Because the window they stood before looked out on a different time.

Tim knew it did. He even recognized it.

It was the time of Our Lord Jesus Christ.

Tim had lived that time a thousand times before, in his dreams and in his visions. Outside the window was a narrow alley in ancient Jerusalem, crowded with watching thousands. Here and there people in the crowd jeered, threw rotten food, cursed the Lord carrying the Cross that would kill Him soon enough. And His Love showed through all violence, all hostility; every disrespect did nothing to the Lord Our God struggling and merciful in the hellish street. From where he stood Tim could only see the back of the Lord's head, the Cross and Crown of Thorns, but still he could feel the Love that encompassed everyone who saw Him. That Love wasn't just a thing in his heart, Tim thought; it was a thing that filled the air with joy.

Like the joy on Thomas's face right now. The joy not just of the Ecstasy of the Sight of the Lord, but the joy of discovery. As though he'd never seen the Lord, nor expected ever to find him.

"I thought you knew," Tim said. "You said you knew what waited here."

Thomas shook his head, ever so slightly. He whispered: "The Stone thought that this was the place where it was born. It knew that this window opened out to . . . someplace else. But it couldn't see inside.

"Stone was wrong. This isn't the place it told me. It didn't know this—it couldn't know a thing like Him. The Stone couldn't see anything that . . . *good*."

Tim didn't understand, and it seemed to him that he wouldn't ever be able to. He wasn't sure it mattered anyway.

They stood watching rapt for the longest time. Tim wondered *Where are the ghosts? Where are the guns?* when it finally occurred to him to wonder why they hadn't yet been followed. Half expected the thought to bring the ghosts down upon them—but it didn't. The hall was quiet, holy, and serene, and it stayed that way.

"He's beautiful," Thomas said. "He loves me."

Tim smiled. "He loves us all."

A pause; pursed lips. Thomas's expression showed him half afraid to say what was on his mind. And then he did. "This is your secret, isn't it?" He didn't wait for Tim to answer. "Why couldn't you share this with me? Why couldn't you share it with everybody?"

Tim winced; it was nearly true, what the boy said. And at the same time it wasn't true at all.

"No. God's Love isn't any secret. I'd've told you if you asked about it. And if I'd volunteered the fact, what would you have done? You'd have looked at me as though I were out of my mind, and wouldn't really have heard. Sure wouldn't have heard it the way you can see it here and now."

The boy ignored him. "I want to talk to Him," Thomas said. "I want to tell Him how I love Him too."

He didn't wait for Tim to respond. He grabbed hold of the window, raised it open (sticky; the smell of fresh sap), and before Tim could so much as tell him to wait he was halfway out the window, crawling out into the image of that time. . . .

Tim set his hand on the boy's back, told him, *No, no, it isn't what you think you see out there I know I know*—but Thomas didn't hear, or anyway he didn't listen. He moved away from Tim's hand on his back as though he'd never felt that touch.

Then there wasn't any choice. He had to follow; he couldn't leave the boy out there alone.

Squeezing through the window meant banging every ache and bruise he'd gathered over the last few days. Unpleasant. He was calmer here so plainly in the presence of the Lord, and as the adrenaline settled out of his blood he began to feel all sorts of things his body had forgotten. Like the ache in his head especially—up there the throbbing was dizzying, nauseating. How long had it been since he'd taken his antibiotics? Tim couldn't remember, and that meant that it'd been too long.

He finished climbing through the window and got back to his feet.

He walked out onto that alley in the ancient city of Jerusalem. And his fate was sealed.

He didn't know that. All he knew was that Thomas Brady was wandering loose inside a place that wasn't what it seemed.

"Thomas," he shouted, "wait." The boy was running ahead of him, running down the spare, brown-grassed hill that led away from—from what? Tim stole a glance behind him. A long, simple stucco structure—arched glassless windows spaced regularly along the wall that faced him. Nothing like the windows on the inside of the hall, but they were in the same places, and the size was more or less the same.

He hurried down the hill, away from his window, trying to catch up with Thomas. It was a losing cause; the boy was running full tilt. There was no way Tim could overtake him.

There was something wrong here. Something that *felt* wrong.

Unsettlingly wrong.

Till that feeling came on him, Tim had assumed that they'd walked into a vision from the Cross. A vision like all the others he'd grown up with. Maybe it came from the Cross itself; and maybe not. Tim didn't *think* the Cross was anywhere nearby, and he was certain that he'd know if it were.

But the vision here wasn't like those others. Not quite. Oh, that was the Lord, and this was the trail that led to his death. Tim had seen this place, this time more than once before. He knew them; could recognize them; could tell if they'd been faked or reproduced untruly.

What was different was the texture.

This rock, he thought, *this rock right here*. He kicked it with his toe. *This rock isn't true to its core*.

Yes—that was exactly it. True visions from the Cross were real, exactly true and knowable to their depths. This place wasn't a lie. But it was the truth projected onto a blank screen invisible on its own.

As he realized it, Tim saw half the vision fall away—saw beneath the scene before him a setting as dry and grey and barren as the surface of the moon.

And maybe it was the moon. It surely was no earthly place.

The boy was far inside the alley now, running in the gap inside the still-parted crowd. Running toward the Saviour still carrying-dragging His Cross—so-heavy Cross, and for the hundred thousandth time Tim found himself wondering how One so beaten and betrayed could carry a burden so great.

So awesome.

The crowd was thick around Tim. And blind to him, too; they only *seemed* to be here with him. Not even the Lord was here the way He seemed to be, though Jesus by His nature is always with us. Tim tried to press through, to slide between so many bodies, but it was useless; the crowd, trapped in time against him, stood barricade blocking his way.

Bad chance: it didn't block Thomas's way. Three

great strides and the boy was within a few feet of the
Lord, bulling between the Roman guards who prodded
Him, pushed Him—

No.

No-please-*no*.

The boy was trying to take the Saviour's burden
from His shoulders. Trying to take the weight of the
Cross upon himself—and how could he know that the
weight of every sin that Man had ever made was added
to its mass? He couldn't know, Tim thought. No matter
what he was, no matter what he'd been, he was too
young a child to know a thing like that.

Even in this echo out of time, even in this unreal
place, the weight would crush Thomas. Even the attempt to take it on could kill him.

Tim turned sideways, pushed himself *hard* into and
through the unyielding crowd. And past it, finally, into
the street. He broke into a run as soon as he could, but
that wasn't soon enough; by the time he ducked between
the two guards (so real to the touch, so solid like moving
stone and nothing Tim did moved or changed their acts
the least) Thomas was already there beside the Christ,
reaching over to tear the ropes that bound him to the
Cross—

"No, Thomas. If you manage that you'll only bring
the weight down on yourself. You aren't Him. You aren't
meant to take that weight."

Thomas turned to look at Tim as though he were out
of his mind.

"So? I'm not afraid. He loves me. He died for me.
This is what I can do to show I love Him too."

There was an answer to that. Tim knew there was an
answer to it. But whatever that answer was Tim didn't
know it, or couldn't think of it.

But he couldn't let the boy take that on himself. Or
could he? Thomas clearly knew what it was he meant to
do, and knew the consequences. Did Tim even have a
right to stop him?

There wasn't any answer for that question. But right
or wrong, Tim couldn't stand by and let Thomas kill
himself.

"Thomas," he said, "let me do it." It was a suicidal thing, to try to take the Cross. Even for Tim, born to be Steward. But there wasn't any other choice—there was barely time enough to preempt the boy. There was no chance to dissuade him.

And he stepped forward to press the boy gently out of the way. To ease himself forward and down beneath the free left arm of the Cross, and rise to take the burden on himself.

There, standing close and tall to try to take the weight, standing in this place that was and wasn't the time of Christ—His Cross was so *new*. Its wood so fresh, so green-new that Tim could smell the sap that oozed cloying through the grain. Could feel it pressed through his shirt into his skin by the weight he sought to shoulder. He heaved upward, pushed himself with all his might to take the burden from the God he loved—

It made no difference.

Of course it made no difference. How could he hope to change the past that was already done in this image of the Lord's time? Well, he couldn't. Maybe God could do it. Maybe Christ could reach back and redo His handiwork for change's own sake. But Tim found it hard to imagine that He ever would.

And how was Tim to hoist a weight that only God could carry?

There was no change whatever in the physical state of the Cross.

But the change in Tim—the change *on* Tim—was immediate and consuming. In the space of a moment it changed every fact about him: changed him because he was exactly right about the weight of our sins as they rest on the shoulders of the Lord.

No man nor woman could take His burden. There are those, like Tim, who have tried—and they've learned that the weight is so great that even the attempt to lift is self-destructive.

Tim didn't die: a happenstance to credit to the fact that he'd been born to lift the last extant fragment of the Cross in our time. But that fragment was as nothing even

the image of the Whole and True Living Cross; it was
s the fossil is to a living beast.

The fragmentary figmentary weight of Mankind's
Redemption did not kill Tim Fischer.

It crushed him.

Crushed him *inside*, where he lived; and left him
standing stock still in the spot where he'd tried to lift the
Cross up off the Lord's shoulder. After a long while he
fell to the ground, unconscious and dreaming.

He dreamed first that he sat waiting with Our Lord Jesus
Christ. In a place like a foyer, or like an office, maybe—
that was what the place *felt* like, though of course in its
details and appointments the place was like neither. It
wasn't even a room, in fact, for though it was a distinct
place apart from other places, no walls surrounded it.

He sat with the Lord quietly, neither of them
speaking as they waited. Hush moments, but not empty.
Tim felt them full with the presence of the Saviour,
presence simultaneously joyously Divine and human.
Knowable, almost sensual but not erotic in the intimate
male *man*ness of His worldly Self.

Tim sat beside Him, worshipful. Full with wonder
and awe.

He didn't know why they were there. Or maybe he
did know. It was hard to say. Whatever he knew or
didn't, though, was nothing he could explain. Not to
anyone—not even himself.

But he knew who they waited for.

They were waiting for God the Father.

Tim closed his eyes, tried to think. He could not
remember ever learning that they waited for the Father.
Could no more remember learning than recall how he'd
come to be in this unearthly place sitting in the presence
of our Lord and Saviour Jesus Christ. He was here, and
here was now, and now was a time that stretched on into
oblivion in every direction.

And the Lord loved him, and Tim knew, and it was
good.

Then suddenly there was a presence before them,

and it dwarfed everything, even the Christ—or nearl
so.

He was the Lord Our Father. For an instant
looking upon Him, Tim was reminded of the woodcu
face of Zeus he'd seen on the cover of his copy c
Bullfinch's *Mythology*. But that was only an instant—th
Lord Himself could in no wise be truly represented by
woodcut embossment on an aging book. No mortal han
could carve Him, not even if it knew exactly. And i
there were a hand to carve then there could neither b
wood to contain His Image nor ink to convey It, for th
Lord Our God is entirely outside the ability of the morta
world to comprehend or contain.

But the connection struck Tim nonetheless. Wh
did he think of the one thing, seeing the other? Ha
some ancient pagan set eyes on the Lord and added Hin
to an idolatrous pantheon? Was it possible?

It didn't matter. All that mattered was the Fathe
and the Son and the Holy Ghost everywhere surround
ing, encompassing.

There were no words among Them, but Tim fel
that there was debate—debate, he thought, like th
debate of his own heart pulling itself in three direction
simultaneously.

Part of that heart was God the Son, Jesus Christ
Who loved Tim so hard and deep and surrounding that i
made him ache to feel it. Jesus was arguing for Tim, an
God the Father was arguing against, only it wasn't really
against because the Father loved him too, loved him jus
as Jesus did, and more, maybe. Did they love differen
parts of him differently? Was that it? No, not that, no
quite—different in a way beyond Tim's ability to under
stand. Maybe it was like God the Father was looking
farther into Tim's future, as though He wanted what wa
best in the end, where Jesus knew his suffering and
thought the need to end it outweighed all else—or was i
like that? Tim wasn't certain of anything, not even here
in his dream. Except maybe that God the Father and
God the Son were both right.

And then Tim caught scent of what it was They were
actually arguing *about*, and it like to break his heart.

They were arguing about Grandpa.

About how bad Tim needed him. His help. His knowledge and experience.

"I love my Grandpa." Tim said it before he knew what he was doing. "Please let me have my Grandpa back. I love him. I miss him." And then he was crying, crying hard and there was no way he could stop because he'd held it in too long, and the loss had become unbearable. "I don't want to lose my Grandpa."

And saying it made him feel like he was four years old all over again.

And as he heard the words he knew that there was no choice and no chance; knew that he couldn't lose his Grandpa because he'd already lost him and there was no getting him back.

And suddenly context erupted into a *no* that wasn't any word and wasn't any one thing you could point at, and when Tim finished blinking he was on a green grassy hillside surrounded by a goldish skylike haze of unwhere or -when.

God the Father was gone. Well, not gone, maybe, because He's always with us, just as are Jesus and the Holy Ghost, and Tim knew that. But He wasn't right in that place where he could see Him, either.

Jesus stood beside him, holding Tim's hand. Waiting—was He waiting for Tim? To make a decision. To *know*—yes, to *know*, and then they were walking up the hill. Because that was what Tim knew: up the hill was where he had to go, up the hill and on into forever and ever.

And ever.

The Lord led him there wordlessly, neither pulling nor attempting to dissuade, and as they climbed and each successive step grew more onerous Jesus was a comfort to Tim, not just his God but a love that he held in his heart to bide him through adversity, and after a climb that seemed to stretch on for a year Tim caught sight of the great blinding light on the far side of the hill—

That was when it sank through to him just what he was doing.

It was the end of his life waiting for Tim on the far side of that crest.

Jesus brought Tim here in mercy, because the desire to withdraw was pleading in his heart. And as Tim stared out into that infinite bright he knew that that end was what he wanted more than anything else in the world.

But he also knew that there was no way he could let himself die, either.

He was responsible, and he had responsibility to see to. He was the Steward of the Cross, and there was no other to succeed him. If he died he'd leave the whole world akimbo, and leave the Cross to fall into the hands of the Bleeding Man, leave—

And Lord but the light was beautiful, and how the air was clear and thin and sweet when he breathed it in. And how the soil beneath his feet seethed richness that he could feel in his bones through the flesh of his heels.

He looked to Christ, looked at Christ, and for maybe the first time in his life he heard the Lord speak to him directly.

"EVEN WITHOUT YOU," the Lord said, *"THE WORLD WILL ABIDE."*

And Tim thought to speak, to say, *I know it will, I know it will, but this is my Grail and I must fulfill it.*

But before he could say the words he was awake and alive and gasping for air on the surface of the moon.

Thomas knelt above him, looking frantic.

"You weren't breathing," the boy said. "I thought you'd died."

Tim rubbed his eyes to clear them.

"I did, I think. But that's over now."

"I tried to make you start again—hit you, pressed on your chest to force the air in and out. But it didn't help. Nothing helped. You lay there stone dead, cold and getting colder. And now you open your eyes and talk to me like it didn't happen."

Tim was supposed to say something in response, but he was damned if he knew what it was.

"Please don't die like that again."

And Tim laughed, and for a moment Thomas looked insulted till he started laughing too, and then both of them were loud with roaring hysterical laughter not laughing because anything was or wasn't funny but laughing because it kept the world at bay—

Kept the moon at bay—

That's what it looked like now. Like Tim had seen hinted before, back when they'd first stepped out into this strange place.

The surface of the moon.

The Passion Play was gone, and every trace of it as well. In its place stood this empty world like a motion picture screen silvery and dead.

Void.

What *was* this place? What craft had Old Abraham the Bleeding Man to find or make it? Tim tried to imagine Grandpa accomplishing such a thing without aid of the Cross, and failed. What he saw was clearly impossible, and he saw it nonetheless.

"How long," Tim asked, "was I . . . ?"

Thomas shrugged. "Half an hour? I don't know. A long time, seemed to me."

Tim nodded. Sat staring out across the jagged lunar plain. He'd lost track of himself somehow. He knew— yes, he knew where he was. Knew how he'd gotten here. But where was he going?

There it was.

Right there, *that* memory, right there. He was trying to get away from this place, trying to find a back door to escape through. To get himself and the boy clear and away before the rain and the thunderstorm and then the fire—

Fire?

There was no memory of fire. He knew about it, knew it was coming. Damned if he knew how.

How much time did they have? However much it was, it wasn't enough. They had to get going, he had to get up—oh no. Not that fast. His whole body was one great seething ache. Every muscle in his body throbbed when he tried to move. He sucked in air, held it. Pushed himself steadily, carefully, quickly off the dusty silver-grey ground.

"What is this place?" Thomas asked. "Do you know?"

Tim shook his head. "I keep thinking that it looks like I'd expect the moon to be. But there's air here, so it can't be that."

"Like on the Apollo films they show in school? When that man said what he did about a little walking. It does kind of look like that, don't it?"

It took Tim a moment to realize what Thomas was talking about. "Yeah, like the tapes from when they went to the moon. That's what I'm talking about." He turned, started toward the now-sterile hill that had led them toward this place.

Up at the crest was the long-house with its line of windows—now they appeared as simple glass-and-wood frames, much as they had from inside. The long house itself was peculiar, geometric. Made of a sleek greyish substance like stucco, but smoother.

"Everything went plain like this right when you passed out," Thomas said. "I think that's why it all went away."

He was walking uphill, toward the window; Thomas was maybe a step or two behind him.

And in the window, in the first one, the same window they'd climbed through to get here, there stood a figure.

A vague, bulky figure. Ghostly. Dressed in a cowled robe.

"No, damn it. *No*."

And saw the glint of gun metal in the sourceless dim light.

And turned, whirled, pushed Thomas to the ground and the boy didn't see, he struggled, tried to keep his feet and his balance and there wasn't *time* for this kind of shit—Tim lifted him off his feet and *threw* him to the ground. And dove after only barely in time to keep from getting shot.

Ka-BLAM!

The sound of the rifle cocking, loading. They had

maybe a moment to move before there was another shot.
Maybe. Had to move, too; as it was they were in the
open, badly shielded from the line of fire.

There wasn't time to talk. He grabbed Thomas's
arm, dragged him to his feet as he got up from the
ground himself. And ran pulling the boy by the wrist.

"What are you doing, damn it?" The question was
belligerent, but Thomas was running, following now
under his own steam. There was no need to drag him.

"What do you think I'm doing? I'm getting us out of
the line of fire."

"But we can't just run out into the moon forever.
We've got to get back into the hall."

Tim was leading them down, away from the windows. To the right—there was a steep drop over there,
away from where they'd been before. Tim had a good
feeling about it. Something was there, something . . .
the mansion. If it was connected to this place up here,
wouldn't it be connected down below as well?

It had to be.

Thirty feet of flat ground, and then a drop so
sheer—

They should have stopped, gone around the thing.
It'd've been safer by far. But they were moving too fast,
and by the time Tim saw it the both of them were already
far over the edge and descending.

And then a drop so sheer that it was too damned
nearly a cliff—no, not a cliff.

More like the steepest face of a sand dune. Fluffy,
silvery-grey powder-dust fluff piled so near perpendicular that there was only barely slope enough to sink into
one leg at a time in great bounding strides, and if they'd
tried to stop they'd surely have gone tumbling head over
heels to the base—

Which Thomas did, anyway; three yards from the
foot of the cliff he hit a rock or lost his footing or lost
heart or something. And his legs flew backward and up
out from under him, and his torso in reaction snapped
down face-forward, *snap*, *snap* again, something in the
boy's back it sounded like, like his back breaking or his

neck cracking, and now he tumbled broken all limb, rag-doll limp to the force of momentum. . . .

The boy lay dead, spent, and broken at the base of the sand cliff.

And Tim had killed him.

No, he thought, *no no no there's got to be something I can do—*

He rushed to the spot where Thomas lay, where the hulk of Thomas lay. Lifted him into his arms and screamed at the sky.

"Damn it!" he shouted. "Damn damn damn damn *damn!*"

And Thomas opened his eyes and said "Damn what?"

Just like that. No miracles; no funny lights. Just the boy alive and asking questions because he'd never died.

"I thought—" Tim said. And stopped there as the train that carried his thought derailed itself, because he wasn't sure exactly what he *had* thought. "That noise, when you fell. Sounded like you broke your back."

A puzzled look—and then amusement. "Not my back. Jaw snapped shut when my face hit the ground. Happened twice. Maybe I broke a couple teeth, I don't know. Back's okay. Just a little banged up, that's all." A groan. "Hey, put me down, huh? Your arm is pressing right into a bruise or something."

He set the boy down. Noticed their surroundings, which were sand, nothing but sand stretching into a hazy distance. Or was this dust too fine for sand? Tim wasn't sure. He'd seen pictures of dunes in the Sahara, and in those photos the sand looked this fine. But this was different. In the Sahara the sand was beige, the dunes had texture from the wind. And the sky in those pictures was always the richest blue. Here . . . the color here was no color at all, as though it weren't a place but the image of a black-and-white photograph. Grey-white dusty sand, without even the first hint of sepia. The sky colored like a curtain lit only by a crescent moon. Soft, rolling, formless sand that went to the horizon.

Thomas rubbed his jaw. "I think I did break a tooth," he said. "Hurts like hell."

"Sorry. I should've been there to catch you. I wish—"

"I wish you'd let me take responsibility for my own trouble, damn it. I slipped. I could've broken my neck—didn't, but I could've—and if I had it would've been my own damn fault. I took that step too far, trying to keep up. It wasn't you that did it."

Tim blinked.

He didn't have an answer.

He knew good and well that Thomas was right, and he didn't really have any business to go taking people's troubles from them. Not without them asking him to. But it wasn't in him to do anywise but as he did. If he saw a body in trouble, he knew it was his responsibility to see it well, reason notwithstanding. If someone shouted *help* and he wasn't there in time to save the day there was a black cloud over Tim's soul. Despite the fact that he always knew and always did his best.

Maybe Thomas saw that pass across Tim's face. And maybe he just got impatient.

"Look," the boy said. "That way. Someone's walked this way before, and they left a trail."

Tim sputtered for a moment before he turned to see where the boy pointed.

Which was due away from them, toward a line of footsteps that bisected the horizon. A trail left by two sets of feet, Tim saw when he looked closely.

Someone had passed this way—recently? No way to be sure how far in the past. Since the last time the wind blew. But that could be forever, or only moments before they'd first climbed through the window. There was no wind at all here and now.

Who. . . ?

"It leads somewhere," Thomas said. "I think that's where we need to go."

Tim nodded. Of course it was.

Thomas was already moving, limping off to follow in the footsteps. . . .

To follow in the footsteps.

Casually, and for certain without intending to. Tim stood watching agape as each step Thomas took was a step into the footprints already set in the dust. The boy wasn't watching his feet. Even if he had been watching his limp was so bad that there was no way he could have matched the sand-tracks so exactly.

As he set off after the boy Tim knew without looking that he'd do the same. One set of tracks for Thomas; another one for Tim.

In all his life Tim had never felt anything doomed or preordained him—till that moment when he looked back to see the trail behind him just as he'd expected: the trail he'd left was the trail he'd known before he'd started.

How. . . ?

It was an article of faith to him—no, not faith, not faith but absolute knowledge—that his Lord had preordained nothing, and that no fate could save him from the responsibility of his acts. Responsibility for his circumstances. Grandpa had taught him so from his first days. And he knew it too from sitting so many hours as he had in the presence of the Cross which was the Essence of the Lord Still Corporeal and Tangible on Earth.

Yet here he was, walking seven paces behind a boy he'd never met before that day, and each of them walked a path writ down to its minutest junction.

Or was it?

Tim looked down into the dust, still walking. There—that dent there in the sand. That would be his next step, wouldn't it? Tim consciously forced his leg thirty degrees off to the left, into unmarked sand.

Stopped. Turned, looked back at the sand now behind him.

The first indentation—the one he'd avoided—was gone. The dust-light sand in that spot was smooth as though it were untouched in millennia.

Which, perhaps, it was.

There was a deep print where he had stepped.

It isn't destiny. It's advice.

After that Tim didn't pay any attention where his steps placed themselves, because it didn't matter whether Fate predicted him or not.

Thomas never even noticed. Never gave a sign of noticing, anyhow.

"What's holding you up?" Thomas asked when they were dead center in the middle of nowhere with the cliff just a scratch on the horizon behind them and whatever waited just a ray of hope in the other distance.

"I got behind," Tim said. "I'll be up with you soon enough."

"I bet you will."—Sarcasm that Tim didn't understand and hadn't expected. What was with the boy?

It didn't matter. What mattered was putting one foot in front of the other despite the fact that he was getting exhausted.

Exhausted.

Strange all by itself: only a few minutes ago, back at the base of the sand-cliff, he'd been fine. Or wide awake, at least; nothing was fine till they were far away from this place. Now each step he took seemed to increase his weight and the weight of this world upon him, till even the shirt on his back was an onerous burden.

Ahead of him Thomas stood stooped, trudging as though the mass of air above him would break his back in another moment.

"Thomas. . . ?"

The boy didn't answer.

"Are you okay?"

The boy coughed, stumbled. Tried to find his balance, failed; Tim saw him fall into a fitted mold in the sand.

Beyond where the boy lay the trail was but a single set of footprints.

I've got to carry him.

Tim stooped, lifted Thomas in his arms. So heavy! As though they both were made of lead instead of meat and bone. Could he walk and carry the both of them at once? It didn't matter whether he could or not. He had to, and that was that.

Tim was still telling himself that five minutes later, when the weight of the air and the boy and his own shoulders imploded on him, and he collapsed unconscious into the sand.

• • •

An instant later he opened his eyes, and as he did he was certain of the truth that had waited for him at least an hour now, and he'd lay blind to it all that while.

The truth of his own impending demise.

The instant Tim opened his eyes he knew what the scene before him meant:

The ruined stair fallen to the floor of the ballroom, its remains piled high around and above Tim; the flavor of dust as it gritted and steeped between his teeth; the shards of black-painted glass scattered out before him, obscuring the dust; his own blood easing out through his broken chest onto the ground; the sweat beads rolling through his hair toward his eyes in a wet trickle of salt-sting; they all meant that he'd imagined everything that had come to him in the last hour. They meant that he'd never made it up from the collapsing stair. That he'd never caught that breaking board, nor ever hauled himself up onto the third-floor landing where Thomas knelt confused and shaken to haul him to his feet.

They meant that everything he'd known since the stair had fallen from beneath him was a death dream, was a lie: something he'd imagined to stave away the pointlessness, misery, and despair that was his life.

despair

All his life, Tim thought. All his life he'd struggled and thrashed to thrive; to live; to grow as hard and fast as possibly he could. Struggled because it was instinct to live and grow; and how could he do anything else?

And now in the light of his doom he knew that there was no point. That life from birth condemned him to death.

"Repent your life," the Bleeding Man said. "Repent while there's still time for you."

The instant he heard that voice, high up above his shoulder, Tim knew that the Bleeding Man had stood with him all along.

"I—"

I do, that was what Tim was about to say. *I repent!* And in his heart he had repented life; for despair had overtaken him and held him in its grip. But a moment before the words could reach his lips, Tim heard them, echoing through time; and hearing knew the words were the ultimate and uttermost betrayal of his *self*.

His hair near to stood on end.

It isn't me, he thought. Despair held him; it engulfed and suffused him. But it was not his own.

The Bleeding Man stood above him, smiling wide and ravenously.

And knew that even when it hurt too much to abide, his life was precious beyond all possibility to measure.

Precious because it was the one true gift he knew he had from God, and more than any other thing it showed how dearly God loved him.

"No," Tim said. "I love my life. There's nothing to repent."

And the Bleeding Man screamed in fury and frustration.

And the false waking—for it was a false waking, and Tim still lay prone in the sand on a world that might just as well be the surface of the moon—the false vision of a waking shattered in an instant, and fell away.

He opened his eyes and saw the horizon away in the infinite distance of the luminescent desert. . . .

No. Not infinite. The horizon wasn't far at all, not more than another hundred yards from where they were. It only seemed so far because the ground dropped away there, just as it had at the cliff behind them.

He pushed himself up out of the sand; lost his balance twice as he got to his feet. So heavy! So tired! And the boy, lead-dense, massive, and limp—lifting him took all Tim's strength. He couldn't imagine how he'd carry Thomas even a single step, not till he managed that first one. And then—well, it got no easier. Harder and harder, both of them heavier and heavier every inch Tim moved forward. But the farther he went the farther Tim knew he could go, because he had faith that he had come here for a purpose. That he could triumph over the despair that set on him if he only persevered.

And suddenly the cliff was close before them.

Three more steps and Tim could see over its edge, look down into. . . . could they manage another cliff descent, this time with Tim carrying the weight of the both of them multiplied by five?

Look at the boy, he thought. Look at the skin of his face sagging unnaturally as an old woman's pulled by the impossible weight of flesh.

Was the drop as sheer as the last one was? If they were lucky Tim could just sit in the dirt and slide the both of them down, easy, easy—

Another step and he was there, there at the summit of the new drop.

It wasn't quite a cliff, this one. A slope, so sheer, so steep that there'd be no standing on it—nor even walking carefully—but if he sat carefully, rested the boy on his back beside him, they'd slide down easily enough. And there at the base was a pillowy pile of sand that'd break their slide gently.

Pile of sand.

Just beyond the pile of sand was a window that was no window at all, but a hole in the world, frameless, edgeless, impossible.

Was that where they were going?

It had to be. Where else was there?

Tim set the boy carefully on the sand. Sat beside him. Took a moment to peer down into that window before he pushed off into the slope.

There wasn't much to see. Warm brownish darkness; something coarse, gritty. Gravel? Dust? If that was a way back into the mansion, then most likely it was dust.

It had to be a way back into the mansion.

Had to be.

If it wasn't, they were in some awful kind of trouble. . . .

Halfway down the hill.

Which meant that there was no way they were getting back up again. Not with everything so heavy; not with this slope and the one before it so steep as they were.

If that doorway wasn't a way out of here, there might not be any way to get free at all.

Sliding faster, faster, faster till Tim began to think they'd gain so much momentum as to send them flying headlong through the window there below them. And faster now, and any moment they would take off and fly without the benefit of wings—

It didn't happen that way. They didn't fly. Instead they plowed down deep into the piled sand at the foot of the dune, came to a stop that jarred Tim's bones with its suddenness.

Thomas sat up, brushed the sand away from his face. Yawned.

The extra weight was gone, just as mysteriously as it'd fallen on them.

"Where are we?" Thomas asked. "I don't remember . . ." Blinking; spitting out sand. "You carried me here? How far have we come?"

Tim shrugged. "I'm not sure." He looked at his watch. Three thirty—how did it get to be so late? Last he'd checked the time was back in the car, early-early this morning. And knowing it was this late didn't tell him much, anyhow, since there was no telling how much of the time had passed since he'd followed Thomas out into this place. "Maybe a long way. Maybe not that far."

Thomas pulled his legs out of the sand, stood. Stared into the aperture. "What is it?" he asked. Before Tim could answer the boy had spoken again. "No. I know what it is. I mean, where is that place? What am I looking at?"

Tim had no idea, of course. All he'd seen was the shadowed image of a floor from high above—and for all he knew it was not a floor but some other thing completely that he'd seen.

"You tell me," Tim said. "It sounds as though you know more than I do." He got to his feet as he said this, of course; he might well ask such a question but he didn't expect Thomas Brady to answer it. Or, more to the point, no answer the boy could give would leave Tim without the need to see for himself.

"I couldn't tell you."

By the time Thomas said it Tim was already standing.

Seeing.

"I don't know how to say it."

Night sky, pitch and stormy; lightning flashed across it now and again, brightening the night only long enough to show hints of those great terrible clouds like mountains hung above them. Rain and wind; now that he stood Tim could feel spray bits of rain tickle his face like dust ice, driven by drifts of wind that invaded this alien place, made it stranger still. . . .

In the foreground was a narrow stone plateau surrounded by low walls.

The roof of the castle keep—the castle that the mansion was when you looked at it from outside. That was the place Tim saw. It had to be. Where else? Surely not a third world; it had to be the place he'd come from. And only the apex of the castle keep could look so high so—

And in the center of the plateau stood the Bleeding Man.

Even in this darkness he was plainly visible, recognizable. He seemed somehow to glow with some strange daemonic flame—Tim had never seen him so clearly before. Not while he was awake. Back in Kansas, when the Bleeding Man had beaten him, it'd been pitch dark. And then there'd been no daemon light about him.

How do I know him? How can I recognize him when I've never seen him before?

There was the blood, of course, leaking steadily from those strange eyes. And there were the dreams. Tim could remember some of those dreams clearly, though in them the Bleeding Man had been more a presence than a visible person.

But none of that was needful. Tim knew the Bleeding Man because he was the Steward on this Earth of the One True Cross, and like draws unto like even as a body knows his mortal foe before he's ever met him. The Bleeding Man was all of that, and Tim couldn't see him without wanting to attack—

No. There wasn't time for an attack, and there was

the boy, and most of all the fact was that Tim wasn't armed. And the Bleeding Man most assuredly was, for he stood there quite deliberately in the rain, poised, waiting for Tim as though he'd known for days that just this moment would come, in this place, in this *now*, and knew all else that would lead Tim here from long ago.

Screw him, Tim thought. *He can wait for me till the end of time. That doesn't mean I have to face him here and now.*

He was about to step around the doorway, continue looking for some other portal, when he saw that he couldn't: the doorway moved to follow him. To block his way.

How. . . ?

God knew how.

Tim didn't. He stepped to the other side, and was followed just the same.

He looked through the doorway. Looked at the Bleeding Man there, waiting for him. Smiling at him as he looked Tim in the eye.

And there, due behind the Bleeding Man, was another portal.

That was where they needed to be. That was the way out of here. The Bleeding Man stood where he did exactly to block the path.

Tim took the boy's arm, stepped out through the frameless door.

"What do you want from me?"

No answer. Not that Tim had expected any.

"Why are you here?"

Lightning flashed behind the Bleeding Man, transfiguring him to a grotesque and terrifying silhouette. When the bright faded Tim could see the Bleeding Man smile frightfully.

"Stand aside, damn you, and let us pass."

And the Bleeding Man laughed.

And he moved away.

Tim didn't stop to think to realize. Didn't realize that he was walking into a trap.

Which he was, of course. Oh, not anything obvious, like the Bleeding Man jumping them as they passed, or the floor caving in as they walked on it, or the world-door on the far side dissolving as they stepped through, cutting them apart in the distance between *here* and *there*.

Tim would have known any of those things; his sight, keyed by danger he knew surrounded him, would have warned him of any evil that lay in wait.

No. What lay in wait was no evil but a friend.

Across the stone roof of the keep, where the wind and rain grew violent and soaked them.

Past the Bleeding Man, who watched them smiling like a hungry cat.

Through the impossible door, where drops of water sizzled and sputtered as they fell against the rupture in reality.

Into a place more alien even than the silver surface of that moon.

A jungle. That's what this was. A jungle made of black-glass trees and flowers, and everywhere writhing crystalline vines—

Thomas gasped.

His eyes were wide with terror.

"What is this place, Thomas?" But Tim knew what it was, because the flowers that surrounded them were entirely familiar. They looked like sculptures cut from onyx, and Tim could feel them deep inside him, pressing at his heart.

"I didn't want to come here," Thomas said. "I swear to God I didn't." He was sweating, and his skin looked puffy red. "Stone was right when he told me that I never should."

This was the source of the flowers—and probably the source of the Stone that Thomas kept talking about.

"It's all right, Thomas. We'll be out of here in a moment." It wasn't a lie. Not even an exaggeration. Over there not twenty feet from them was another door. "Come on. This way."

Thomas didn't seem to hear. He didn't move a muscle—not even to breathe.

Tim grabbed him by the wrist, dragged him through

a bed of steel-hard flowers overhung with vines that twice spun down clumsily to grope them.

Thomas screamed and started to struggle to get away from Tim when that happened. But Tim held fast and pulled, and then they were pushing through the far aperture in space and time into a dark, dry room.

A familiar room.

Tim closed his eyes. Panted; tried to find the breath he'd lost to stress and fear and Thomas struggling against him. Opened them again.

No, this wasn't a room. It was a hall.

With the corner of his eye Tim saw the impossible door beside them fade from existence.

They stood in a narrow hall just off the ballroom that held the ruin that once had been the spiral stair.

Not the hall that had first led them to the ballroom, early that afternoon, but another hall that led away from it.

Tim stepped toward the ballroom. Stepped closer. The rain was still heavy. Still driving through the open shattered roof high above the ballroom. Turning the dusty floor to endless mud. Rinsing painted walls from decades of grime.

(*Bloodstains, there were bloodstains mingled with rainwater on the floor, and for an awful blackhearted moment Tim was certain that they were his own, that he could see the spot where he had/hadn't fallen from so high to die as the Bleeding Man looked on and coached him to despair. . . .*)

Up through the broken roof Tim could see the castle keep, and there atop it was the Bleeding Man. Looking down, watching. Was he still laughing? Tim thought he was, but there was no way to be sure from so far away.

Then suddenly the darkness parted, and Tim saw that it was not night but a blanket of storm clouds above them so intense so thick so dark that they occluded day entirely, and in a moment night was gone and day was on them and the Bleeding Man's scream was a thing that shook Tim's heart from here, not just loud but piercing, real as song—

And lightning struck.

Down, onto the keep, and then out from it in an arc—

Into the mansion. Into the ballroom.

Mud and staircase debris went off in every direction, breaking the walls, shattering windows painted by ages of filth, even here into the hall where they stood and Tim had to press himself and the boy against the left wall or that flying plank would have killed them surely—

When it was gone there was fire.

No, not some grand burning thundering inferno. But here and there a bit of burning board, a stair plank lapped with flame. All of them out in the broken ballroom, smothering in the rain.

The Bleeding Man still stood laughing high above them as now the clouds closed ranks again to block the sun.

No. Not that easily. He won't be shut of it that easily.

Tim stepped out into the driving rain that was the ballroom. Grabbed the burning plank nearest him. And brought it into the dry hall to let it burn. Set it in a dry corner, where the flame lapped slow but steady against the wall.

When he was done, Tim saw Thomas staring at him. Nodded when he caught Tim's eye.

"It's good," the boy said. Then nothing for a moment. "There's light this way. Sunlight, maybe. I think we can get out."

"We'd better be able to, or we'll burn soon." Glanced back at the corner and the lapping flame. Maybe not that soon; the fire wasn't going out, but it wasn't beginning to rage, either. "Lead the way if you think you know it."

A puzzled look, and Tim didn't understand why. But no questions; just a shrug, and a nod, and Thomas turned and led into the dark.

Which was light soon enough. Twenty feet and a short turn and there before them was an open door that faced west—the direction obvious because the sun, setting, was clearly visible on a horizon where the clouds had broke.

And they were free, and in a moment they'd be shut of this place. The idea took the weight of worlds off Tim's shoulders; he felt a relief so incredible that it made him want to cry.

Until something *snapped* in the darkness, and Tim realized that they weren't alone.

Ghosts. Ghosts with guns.

Tim had forgot about the ghosts.

Suddenly the shadows were thick with them, crowded with terrible dark figures not quite visible to see.

The boy. The boy was out in front of Tim, and someone was about to shoot him.

Tim reached forward, grabbed Thomas by the collar. Pulled him close. The boy started to protest—to resist—but stopped suddenly when Tim pointed into the menacing gloom.

Menace surrounded from every direction but straight ahead. And even there were shadows deep enough to hide—

—to hide the ghost who stepped out to confront them.

Stepped out, gun cocked, loaded, aimed, to block their path.

And waited.

Tim pushed the boy behind him to shield him, but he wasn't sure how much use that was; there were others back there and on both sides.

Above them in the dark for all Tim knew.

There was a way out of here. Tim knew there was. Had to be.

He was damned if he knew what it was.

And probably damned regardless.

"What do you want from us?" Tim asked. "Why are you here?"

No answer.

"We're leaving, damn you. Why don't you let us go in peace?"

Silence.

Tim screamed in frustration, in anger, and if he'd had one wit less self-control he'd have jumped straight into the gun sight, and damn the ghost if he fired, and rip the gun away if he didn't.

He couldn't do that with the boy so near, of course. Anything precipitous was out of the question.

He let his scream fade. Felt himself sag with defeat.

"Let us go," he said. His voice was very quiet. "Please let us go."

And the ghost pulled away his cowl.

And lost all ghostliness: in the light of day was solid, human.

And wasn't a he, but a she.

She was Gail Benjamin, and she had the gun aimed at him.

Gail Benjamin: the woman from the bar; from the fire; the woman who'd all but carried him to the doctor. Who'd nursed him in her home and then that morning come to him as he'd showered—

And she had a gun, and had it aimed at him. And she didn't hesitate to use it.

As she pulled the trigger to send him into oblivion Tim knew two things:

Knew that he loved her, no matter what, no matter how little time he'd known her.

Knew that his love was meant to be betrayed.

Before the blackness took him Tim thought he saw her crying.

Tim wasn't entirely himself the day he gave away the Cross. That morning in midwinter when he was fifteen his father banged on Tim's bedroom door and started shouting before Tim had even opened his eyes.

Things with Dad had gotten way out of hand these last few months. Seriously out of hand. Some of the fault was Tim's own; he'd been antsy and irritable for years now, ever since adolescence had first set in. He understood why he felt that way. Being twitchy and obnoxious was natural fallout from the way his body was changing itself.

He knew about that.

Knowing didn't make it go away, but it made it a whole lot easier to cope with himself.

But Dad . . . there was something seriously wrong between him and Dad, and it wasn't something Tim understood. It was tied into the fact that Tim was getting older, but it wasn't that exactly. Tim was sure of that—it felt . . .   *different.* Tim wasn't sure how different, and the one time he'd asked Grandpa about it Grandpa had got all quiet and sad and guilty-looking, and he'd said something quietly under his breath. Tim hadn't heard it too well. He'd been too amazed to see Grandpa looking guilty to listen carefully. Later, when he realized that he had no answer for his question, he'd thought about how Grandpa had looked depressed for two days afterward. It was too much; Tim didn't have the heart to bring up the subject again.

Which may explain why his father's fury so surprised Tim when the older man came pounding on his bedroom door.

And then again may not.

Slam! Slam! Slam!—A fist, three times on the bedroom door. Nearly hard enough to break it down.

"What the hell is this?" His father sounded mad enough to kill. "What've you done, you little bastard?"

Tim's first thought as he opened his eyes: *I'm not a bastard. What does he mean?* Because it was an absolute fact. He was his father's son, just as Dad was Grandpa's son's son. Not a thing he had to think twice about. And then the noise and the suddenness got to his blood, and the adrenaline was rushing around in the fog that only a moment ago had been deep sleep. And whether he wanted to be or not, Tim was almost as angry as his father.

"What do you want? You could try knocking like a civilized person, instead of pounding on the door like an ape."

That did it, all right. As Tim ought to've expected it to. Maybe he had expected it, in fact, somewhere in the back of his mind.

Fighting words. Well, he had a right to use fighting words, didn't he? Hadn't his father thrown the first blow by coming up here shouting and screaming at seven in the morning?

And one part of Tim thought *Damn right I do*. But the part of him that listened to the world—the part that saw consequences before they came down on him—that part thought *Yeah—so I'm right. So what? Do I really want this fight?*

But by then he'd already spoken, and Dad had already kicked open the door (look, there, look: the wooden frame hung in splinters where the latch burst through it), and he was stomping across the room, raging. His face bright red with the heat of his anger. The fat of his stomach shuddering each step the pace of his run. Tim sat up to face him, but there wasn't time enough; before he could finish Dad had a fist around the collar of his T-shirt, and he was shaking Tim, shaking him so hard that his ears rang.

"Stop that, damn it. What's the matter with you?" Tim heard the contempt in his own voice, but he was too angry to care about it. Not so his father; the disrespect turned the old man a much deeper shade of red than Tim had ever seen him before.

"What is the meaning of this?"

That was when Tim finally noticed what was dangling from Dad's left hand.

A condom.

An unforgettably bright pink condom.

Used.

He remembered that condom very well, and fondly, too; and remembered taking great pains to hide it deep at the bottom of the kitchen trash bag. How the hell his father had come across it Tim couldn't begin to imagine. More to the point, he didn't think he wanted to imagine.

"WHAT IS THE MEANING OF THIS?"

What did he *think* it meant, for God's sake?

"It's—" and he stopped, right there, right then, before any more hateful words could come out of his mouth. Which was a step in the right direction, but neither far enough nor adequately soon.

Because Dad was about to reach critical mass.

"It's what, you little turd? What? WHAT!? Is this something from your grandfather?" His lip curled up-

ward to form a sarcastic smile. "What, has the old man been diddling you all these years?"

Time slowed to an absolute halt.

An. Absolute. Halt.

Nothing Dad had done to that point hit Tim where he lived. None of it. Oh, it rankled him to have Dad come storming in here before he'd half woken up, and it didn't please him to be addressed as though he were a dog voiding its bowels on the living-room rug.

But it wasn't till Dad brought Grandpa into the conversation that Tim really lost control of his temper. Dad and Mom both resented Grandpa more and more as the years wore on. Mom pretty obviously because she felt the old man usurped her as a parent. And Dad— there was something very strange about Dad when he got anywhere close to the subject of Grandpa these days. Like now: accusing Grandpa of child molestation. Accusing Tim of incest! The kind of bizarre accusation you expect from someone who's done such things himself—

—but Dad had done no such thing to Tim, no more than Grandpa had—

—unless some horrible thing had happened between Dad and Grandpa, but that was just plain silly—

And Tim thought of the Cross. And thought: Why me? Why not Dad? Why not Dad's Dad, who was Grandpa's son?

It wasn't the first time it'd occurred to him to wonder. He'd even asked Grandpa before, back when he was much much younger. And Grandpa said *Tim, it's you, not him. He couldn't be the Steward; it plainly isn't in him. I knew that months before my son was born, knew it months before his son was born. Just as I knew you long before I saw you.*

Tim hadn't understood, but the talk about not-born babies made him seriously uncomfortable, so he hadn't asked for clarification.

Lots of times since he'd wished he had.

Especially since Dad hadn't ever seemed to know anything about the Cross or Grandpa. Oh, Dad had his vague suspicions. Sometimes Tim thought he could see dim realization on his father's face—as though he knew that there was something big and special that Tim and Grandpa shared that he couldn't begin to see.

But if he knew anything more than that it was a mystery to Tim.

"You're jealous," Tim said. "That's all this is. You're jealous of me because I'm the Steward's heir." Too angry for charity, sympathy, or patience. "Is it my fault you're a washup?"

And *oh!* how Tim regretted that question the moment it escaped his lips. So mean; so near the mark but wrong that it would surely haunt his father so long as the two of them should live. But it was gone beyond recalling, and anyhow there wasn't time to worry because suddenly Dad's eyes were bright, animated by a strange light that made Tim think of blood and death, and the older man's heavy-boned fist pummeled him again and again and again, pounded Tim's face till his nose bled free like a gentle spigot. And who had the heart for fighting back—?

"Stop it, Dad. You're hurting me." It wasn't that true, not yet. Tim's nose was a wreck and there'd be hell breathing through his mouth for a day or two, but so far all the greatest harm was to his pride, and with no one there to watch even pride held strong.

But sooner or later one of those punches would connect with something more breakable.

"*Stop!*"

Like his eye. *Bapp!* Fist in the right eye, and it sealed shut instantly.

Maybe it was burst. There was no way to tell without looking carefully in the mirror.

Something twisted in Tim's gut, and suddenly he wasn't man but animal tuned to the fight. No father, no Tim, no mother out in the hallway screaming for Dad to *Stop it Henry stop it stop it this very instant*. Only the animal reaching up to stop the next blow before it could land. And when new blows followed those it stopped, the animal reacted in reflex and without thinking: it attacked.

Tim had a very special sensitivity about him. An

ability to see down into the very heart of things; to see where they lived and where they stood vulnerable.

The animal part of him (as does the animal part in all of us) resided at the very heart of his sensitivity. It knew where to strike, and how, and knew which blows could cripple and which would only maim. Three, four, five hard fast blows to the most vulnerable points on his father's body and the older man lay sagged and gasping against Tim's bedroom wall.

Quiet. Dead-still quiet and his mother standing in the doorway with her eyes wide, her mouth open as though in a scream of horror running on but silent because the trauma was too much to let her breathe. The Tim part of Tim coming slowly back to focus disgusted with himself—disgusted but still angry. Still scared half out of its adolescent wits because of the loss of the eye.

His father must've seen that. Must've. Because the instant fear touched him his father grinned maliciously and rose to attack—

Tim didn't think. His gut surged at the possibility, and he spoke, and he didn't lie.

"Try it, Dad," he said, "and I'll break your neck."

Like a mask falling away. Maybe Tim had known all these years of his childhood that his father was no master to him. Maybe he hadn't. But surely surely his father had known no such thing. The light in Dad's eye went from anger to fear to supplication in the space of a moment.

Tim turned away from the sight of it. There was something very wrong to see his father lie afraid of him. Something that disquieted him very very badly.

And he knew even then that there was no cure for this disquiet, and that it would follow him the rest of his life. Mark his father, too, though less terribly, as children mark their parents infinitely less than is the reverse.

Tim excused himself as he walked out the door past his mother on his way to the bathroom mirror. Where he checked the eye and found no serious harm—only swelling and bruisage and vast quantities of spilt blood from his nose. He cleaned the damage carefully—

wincing twice when his damp tissue ran afoul of nerves—took a deep breath. Leaned against the wall. Where it dawned on him that the only thing to do was to pick it up and put it back together: if he wanted his life in one piece he needed to act as though it already were. Needed to take his shower, and go on to school, and treat the day as though it were any other.

It may be that this was a mistake. Certainly bad things happened on account of the track Tim took. But it may be that any other sequence of events would have made his life infinitely worse.

Into the shower and clean and out, back to his bedroom with a towel wrapped around his waist. His parents were gone now, and Mom must've straightened up because there was no sign that any untoward act had taken place.

Dressed. Gathered up his books and started down the stairs. Turned at the bottom toward the front door—

Dad waited for him in the parlor. Waited sitting in the big high-backed armchair where he liked to read most nights. He stopped Tim with a quiet gesture before he could reach the door.

Dad's face, still full with supplication.

"He tried to show me, once," Dad said.

Silence big as all the world. Tim said nothing. What could he possibly say to respond to that?

"When I was six he took me up to the room at the top of the stairs. And he waited and waited for me to react, waited for me to tell him what I saw. But there was nothing to see."

Listening to him it seemed to Tim that his father came to him for absolution—that he came asking for some unknowable mercy.

Came to him in supplication.

And he had to say something, because he couldn't just leave his father there in that terrible position. Didn't want to leave him waiting prone forever for forgiveness. So he said "Dad, I—" and stood in the middle of that sentence for a long long moment waiting to know the rest of it. But nothing came to him. His face and his pride still hurt too much for him to forgive his father, and anyway forgiveness was the least of it. What Dad really wanted was to be his father, to be master of his home for none to gainsay. And Tim wanted him to be Dad, too, because young men need folks to look up to and love. But there was no way Tim could give him that or take it for himself. Because it wasn't a thing he'd taken, nor that his father had lost: it was dust drifting in the wind, decayed to nonexistence.

He looked away and said, "I love you, Dad." And ran from the house without looking back.

Later that day was when he gave away the Cross. Tim, all twitchy and unbalanced, sat in study hall talking with his friends because their monitor was out in the hall someplace.

They were talking about religion. Talking about God.

"I know about Him," Donny said. "Them whasis, them Jewish people—they're the ones who sold Him out. Someone gave 'em gold or something and now just like those atheists say, God is dead. I heard about this in church. I remember."

Somebody hooted loud enough for their monitor to hear out in the hall. Anne Fulton—vanished Walt Fulton's sister; she was Tim's girlfriend ever since September, and Tim liked her a lot—Anne rolled her eyes toward the ceiling as if to say *What kind of a rock did you crawl out from under?* And Donny's brother Jessie shook his head in amazement.

Tim didn't really think before he started talking. "You got it all wrong, Donny. Jesus died to save us all from our sins, but He's alive again now. Only up in heaven mostly. And it wasn't any killed Him so much as He decided that He had to die to save us all—because He loved us so much. He could've saved Himself instead if He'd wanted to, but He loved us so much that He went to Hell instead. Don't go blaming anybody just because he's Jewish."

Quiet. Big thick quiet hung over all of them, as though no one agreed but none of them wanted to argue.

Hung over all of them but Donny, that was. "Shit," Donny said, "what do you know, Tim Fischer? You some kind of a preacher or something?"

Tim almost did it, right then, right there, right in front of everybody. He almost said, *No I ain't no preacher. But I seen Jesus, and I talked to Him, and I know about Him like you know about me. No way anybody could see Him and* not *know.* But even as shook up as he was from that morning with Dad, Tim had more sense and self-control than that. He said, "No, I ain't no preacher. I just know is all."

And he let it go at that.

Or tried to.

But Donny, Donny didn't let go of it for a minute. All that day he needled Tim when they ran into each other. Called him Preacher-boy, and asked him about his flock, and he kept complaining about the Sunday sermon.

Got on Tim's already-frazzled nerves in pretty short order, Donny did.

And at three thirty in the afternoon, when the two of them were hiking up 56th Street, walking home from school—at three thirty in the afternoon Tim snapped.

"So you going to tell us about the Last Supper this Sunday, Preacher Tim? You going to tell us what Jesus thinks about a good potluck dinner?"

At that moment they were on the bridge where 56th Street goes over the Hillsborough River, just before it crosses into Temple Terrace. Tim grabbed hold of his friend's shoulder, and one-handed he pushed Donny into the bridge rail, and held him that way with his head hanging backward over the water way way below.

"I had enough," Tim said. "I don't want to hear no more about this preacher stuff, you hear?"

Donny snorted. (You had to hand that to Donny: he could still act tough he when he was hanging thirty feet out over the gross-out Hillsborough River.) "It wasn't me who made you start talking like you talk to God every Tuesday night at the church supper."

And Tim spoke without thinking first, which was really really stupid. "I *have* talked to Him, damn it."

Boom.

The words were out there, hanging in the air over the fetid river.

Just like Donny.

Damn. Damn damn damn damn!

A chopped-short laugh from Donny; and then another. Tim wanted to haul off and finish shoving him over the edge of the rail. But he still had a little restraint left, and anyway Donny's laugh was loud and silly and infectious, and how could Tim hit the guy when he was laughing too?

Well, he couldn't've, not even if he'd wanted to.

Then for the longest time the two of them stood there on the sidewalk, leaning over the Hillsborough, laughing laughing laughing at the mosquitoes and the hyacinths and the blue-gill panfish down below them. Till they both got kind of quiet and Donny slapped Tim on the back, and they started back north across the river.

They were on Sunnyside, halfway to the Bullard Parkway, when Donny stopped dead in his tracks and asked the question.

"You didn't really, did you?"

For a moment Tim almost told the truth, because that was what came naturally to him. Then he realized what he was doing, and he said no, no, not like that I was just making that up because I got tired of you teasing me.

And Donny looked at him kind of agape. And kept looking at him.

"You're lying to me," he said. "It isn't possible, but I'd swear it."

And Tim said what you mean lying to you? Lying to you about what?

Donny said, "Tim Fischer, I known you almost all my life, and you lie worse'n almost anyone I know. I don't know why you never learned how to do it, but you haven't done it yet. You don't lie like no rug."

Tim turned away and started walking again. Watching the cars whiz by up ahead on the Bullard Parkway. Trying not to think about what kind of shit he'd gotten himself into.

"Tim, where you going? Wait up, damn it. What the hell is this stuff you're talking? What did you see? Tim, Tim whatever this is you got to show me, Tim. You got to."

Tim didn't respond. He didn't wait for Donny. Didn't even slow down—fact was he tried to hurry on ahead of him. Not that it worked.

"Tim—you don't tell me what this is all about I'm going to start shouting. *HEY EVERYBODY—TIM FISCHER SAW GOD HE SAW HIM I KNOW IT AND HE WO—*"

That was about as far as he got before Tim jumped on him and started trying to shove a fist down his throat.

Literally.

"Whoa! I'll shut up! All you got to do is show me God." By half when Donny said that there was a snicker in his voice. But the other half was dead serious, as though Donny somehow realized that he'd stumbled into something very very big.

Which he had. It was a plain fact, was all.

"You can show me," Donny said. "I won't tell nobody."

Like hell you won't, Tim thought. But he knew he was up against it. What choice did he have? "We got to get our bikes," he said. "Got to ride out to Grandpa's."

Donny lived here in Temple Terrace now; two years ago his dad had hit it good with his insurance sales, and they'd all moved into this old ranch-style house in the live oaks up off the golf course. Grandpa's place was a good long way from there. Bicycle distance—next year, Tim thought, next year he'd be sixteen and he could drive on his own and Grandpa's place would be a heck of a lot closer.

Donny considered. About the bikes. Going after their bikes meant that they had to split up—go each of them home and meet again. Tim had some half-formed idea that maybe he'd go hide someplace instead of taking Donny to the Cross—and from Donny's expression it was real real clear he was only half a step behind him.

Then after a while Donny nodded carefully and said, "If you try to trick me you'll be sorry. You will, I promise. I'll go talk to my preacher, and *he*'ll find out. He sure will, just you mind me."

Preacher. Oh, Lord, Grandpa was going to have a cat when he heard about this. Tim didn't want to face that—not today, not all frazzled after this morning with Dad, not . . . not now. Please. Bad enough everything; Tim hated being embarrassed. And this was an embarrassment, all right.

"Why would I do that? I'll meet you up at your house. It shouldn't take me long."

Tim spent the whole walk home trying to think of a way to make it like he'd never opened his mouth. Didn't come up with a thing. Not that he expected to. He'd stuck himself right into one of those Chinese fingertraps, and everything he did only made things worse. When he tried to pull out, the trap got stronger and tighter, and when he went forward he was deeper in.

But forward was the only way he could move, and he sure couldn't sit still.

Maybe he ought to call Grandpa. Let him know they were coming.

Let him know what Tim had done so's to give him a chance to figure out a solution.

Yeah.

Tim looked up, blinked, and realized that he'd walked two lots past his own house.

Turned back and got so caught up in his Chinese puzzle that he almost did the same thing all over again.

Damn damn damn. Which was cursing even if he just thought it instead of saying it, and Tim knew good and well that he was doing entirely too much of it lately.

Into the house where thank God neither Mom nor Dad were home—thank God because Tim wasn't ready to face either one of them yet. Not after this morning.

Straight to the phone where he tapped out Grandpa's number on the dialing pad. Click click hum and the sound that meant the phone was ringing on the other end of the connection.

And ringing.

And ringing.

No answer after seven rings. Nine. Twelve. Fifteen.

Long as Tim let that phone ring Grandpa still wasn't home.

He let the phone ring five more times before he finally gave up. Went to the garage. Got his bike. And rode back to Donny's.

Donny stood waiting for him perched on his bicycle in the front yard. He looked real suspicious.

"You set me up," he said quietly when Tim was close enough to hear. "You made a trap. I know you did."

Tim sighed. "I might if I could've thought of one to make," he said. "If you're afraid we don't have to make this trip."

"I'm not afraid of nothing," Donny told him. But it was plain on his face that he was scared half out of his mind.

"I bet you're not." Donny didn't seem to hear the sarcasm in that—or maybe he didn't hear it at all. Tim had kind of muttered it under his breath. "Come on. Let's go."

They went.

The ride went a lot faster than usual. Well, maybe not that fast. Maybe just too fast. Tim sure wasn't eager to get to Grandpa's big old house that afternoon. No matter how long they'd've taken it wouldn't have been long enough.

All through the ride Tim was thinking, thinking. Which wasn't any use—even at the end he still didn't have the first clue of a plan.

Mr. Johnson (out in his font yard mowing his lawn in midwinter in Florida) waved as they rode up onto Grandpa's driveway. Tim waved back. For half a moment he thought about stalling a moment longer by going over to say hello. But what was the use of that? It would only buy them a minute or two, hardly any more than that. And besides, Mr. Johnson wouldn't be able to hear them without turning off his lawn mower. Tim couldn't think of anything to say to him that would make it worth the trouble.

No car in the driveway. Grandpa wasn't home. No

news there; Tim had known he wouldn't be here even before the unanswered phone call.

Key. The key on his key chain in his pants pocket. For just a moment Tim prayed that he'd forgotten to bring it—but of course he had. He always had his keys. Had to. Mom locked the door at home when she went out in the afternoon.

No way. No way in the world to go anywhere but forward.

Opened the door. Stepped into the parlor all shadowy from the heavy-velvet curtains drawn tight. Turned to grope for the light switch and saw Donny hesitating a good half-dozen feet away from Grandpa's door.

"You're afraid," Tim said. It wasn't a challenge, just an observation. Maybe one he shouldn't have said out loud, since it got Donny all blustery and defensive. "We don't have to do this if you don't want."

Donny spat into the bushes. "The hell you say. This is just another trick. You don't fool me."

Whatever that meant.

"Are you coming in or aren't you?" There it was— there was the light switch. Tim flipped it—

—nothing. The bulb was dead.

Or the socket was empty.

(But who'd have emptied it? Even at the age of fifteen Tim knew what paranoia was. Of course he had the advantage of watching Grandpa anticipate and second-guess people all his life. Grandpa was the kind of man who inspired paranoia.)

Was this Grandpa again, setting him up?

"Grandpa? You here?"

No answer.

"The light's busted, Donny. If you're going to come in you're going to have to walk around here in the dark. You aren't scared of the dark, are you?"

Another stupidly impatient question. If Tim had half a brain in his head he'd've quit egging his friend on.

"*I ain't ascared of no dark!*" And Donny bustled in all blustery tough and hurried. So uncareful that he damn near tripped over the end table there near the door.

"Watch it! You're going to bust Grandpa's favorite lamp."

Donny snorted.

"This way."

Which was straight toward the stairs. Where Tim groped for the switch that controlled the stairwell light, found it, turned it—

—nothing. Nothing but dark.

The power was out. That had to be it; it wasn't like Grandpa to leave two light bulbs untended like this.

"I think there's something wrong with the electricity. I know my way up these stairs well enough that I don't need the light. But you—are you sure you want to—"

"You heard me. I said, 'I ain't ascared of no dark,' and I meant it. You just go ahead, Tim Fischer. I'll follow along behind you."

Tim shrugged, grabbed the banister, and started up the stairs.

They were strange again today. Strange and seductive as they'd been that day way way back when he was six and tiny. When this house had been so enormous and so strange. Like, like—almost like the strangeness was part of the initiation, and Tim was here for Donny's initiation to the Cross, and was that right? Was it really? Grandpa had taken such pains to ensure Tim was alone that first time he saw the Cross. (No, no the Cross itself was the least of it. What Tim saw that morning here at the top of the stairs wasn't just some mouldering ancient fragment of wood: it was the vision. His vision of Our One True Lord Jesus Christ. And now Donny would have that vision—or perhaps he'd have his own vision— and then—and then—)

"I remember this somehow," Donny said, stumbling on the stairs in the dark. "There's something here that someone told me once. . . ."

"If you say so." At the top of the first stairway. Tim groped for the hallway light switch, found it. Pointless; no effect whatever. He should've known, he thought: should've known not to bother. It wasn't light bulbs. There was something wrong with the current everywhere in Grandpa's house. "Be careful," Tim said. "This is the top of the stairs. Up ahead there's a short hallway, then more stairs."

Didn't do any good. Donny got to the last step and tried to step onto another one—Tim could tell by the way his foot stomped down hard, by the scrambling sound he made as he nearly fell on his face. Then Tim heard footsteps as he caught his balance, started walking again.

Dim dim light filtering in around the curtains in Grandpa's room—

Donny gasped.

"It's Him," the other boy said. "It's Jesus. . . ."

And in an instant Tim saw how he'd made that mistake: the great lifelike crucifix that hung above Grandpa's bed. It was the only thing clearly visible in the shadowy filtered light—

"No, that isn't Him. It's only Grandpa's crucifix." Tim started to move on toward the second stairway. And realized after a moment that he was alone, that Donny still stood staring agape at the false sight of the Lord. . . .

"Really, Donny. That's not Jesus. Just wood and metal carved to look like Him. Are you coming or not?"

Snort!

"I'm coming—I'm coming!" And Donny started toward him with a limp. "I ain't afraid the dark and I ain't afraid of none of your tricks either. So there!"

"Whatever you say, Donny. Just don't fall and break your neck. Second stairway starts here."

Donny tripped anyhow. Pretty bad. Not bad enough to break anything, at least. Or maybe it was that bad; what with the dark it was hard to say. But if Donny did hurt himself like that, he didn't let it stop him. Just cursed a couple times and started clambering up the stairs.

To his credit he minded Tim's warning this time, and managed not to stumble at the head of the second stairway. Not that Tim was paying any attention. The door at the end of the hall had already transfixed him by then.

The door that led to the Cross.

All around the edges of that terrible door was light oozing out into the pitch that was the hallway. Light—wondrous, miraculous light like something angels spin with the motion of their wings. Inside the room something went *thud!, thud!* like the sound—

—like the sound of iron, wood, flesh, and bone meeting all at once in some terrible blow—

And blood (just barely visible in the tininess of that miracle light) sprayed out through the cracks at the edges of the door—

And Donny screamed and screamed—

And Tim reached back not even thinking reached back to cover his friend's mouth.

"Stop," he said. "You've got to stop. Something's very wrong, something's wrong and—"

Tim didn't even know *what* was wrong. Didn't understand what was happening, didn't understand if and how it all tied to Donny screaming. He only knew they needed quiet, calm—

And someone screamed inside the room.

Something Someone someone maybe Jesus something screamed inside the room that held the Cross, screamed exactly the scream Donny screamed only a moment before, but louder, deeper; greater and more terrible—

Tim ducked against the wall, pulled Donny with him, held him to protect him not just to keep him quiet—

But there wasn't any need. In a moment the scream went silent, and only quiet weeping came from the room beyond the door.

Donny made a small, shrill noise, and Tim realized that his friend was panting—no, worse than that. Gasping for breath. Tim tried to make out his friend's expression, but there was no way in the gloom. . . . "What's inside there?" Donny asked. "Is it dangerous?"

Tim looked away, back toward the silhouetted door. "I told you," he said. "It's God."

"Then how come he sounds like somebody dying?"

"He just does sometimes, that's all. Sometimes you see Him and He's turning water into wine, and sometimes you see Him and He's walking out onto the water. Or bringing Lazarus back from the dead. Or curing the lame. But most of all you see Him on His Cross, dying, because that's the part of Him—the tiny, tiny part—that bled into the Cross."

"Oh yeah? And what was *that* sound—that sound we just heard?"

"I don't know."

The weeping stopped. Lead-heavy quiet replaced it.

"You still want to go on?"

No bluster now. No rush to answer. When Donny finally did speak he sounded scared out of his mind. "I do," he said. And it seemed to Tim that made him very very brave.

Tim pushed away from the wall. Started toward the door still outline-etched in miracle light.

"You're sure?"

"Yeah."

Step.

Another.

A third, a fourth—and he was there at the door, turning the knob—

"*No—!*"

Too late—

"—Tim don't I've changed my mind—"

Because already the door was partway open, already swinging creaking on its hinges easing open into—

—an empty room.

The same empty room Tim had seen a thousand times: curtainless windows, bare whitewashed walls. The wooden floor sanded smooth but dusty and unfinished.

Plenty of light. So much that it near to blinded Tim—but it was nothing but sunlight streaming in through the curtainless windows. Donny came limping up behind Tim to stand behind him just outside the doorjamb.

"I heard it," Donny said. "I did. I saw that blood,

too—look! There!" His arm snaked out over Tim's shoulder to point—

—to point at the door frame still glistening with a thousand infinitesimal beads of blood.

Tim blinked, looked again. The blood didn't go away.

"Where is He?"

"I don't know."

Tim walked across the room, scanning the floor—useless. The fragment of the Cross was nowhere to be seen. In a moment he stood by the window that faced the backyard. Stared out at the yard, at the woods beyond them. Pine and live oak, here in Florida all grim dark green regardless of the season. Maybe they were thinner now than they were, say, in spring. But not by much.

Way out beyond the woods, barely visible in the tiny spaces between the leaves, the highway—I-75.

"My gramma says that Jesus is everywhere. That all you ever have to do is let Him into your heart, and He'll come."

Tim wanted to argue with that. Not because it was wrong, really, because it was the truth. He wanted to argue because—because he was fifteen and he was good and tired of hearing lectures on the obvious from grown-ups—even secondhand lectures.

No; it wasn't good to vent that. Donny didn't mean any harm, and there was no denying he was right. *Let Him into your heart, and He'll come*—and for just an instant Tim did exactly that, opened himself—

And yes, yes, yes, there it was, Glory Glory Glory Jesus Is Lord; the fulfilling clear powerful Love of the Lord enfolded him made him one O Glory Glory Glory

And somewhere behind him Donny made a sound like he was choking on his food. Tim turned—

To see the Lord Jesus Christ crucified between them. The great, tall, rough-wood Cross with its crude hewn beams. The red-brown half-congealed blood spattered here and there on the wood, some of it oozing down onto the floor. Here from behind Tim could see

*how the nails that pierced the Lord's wrists penetrated
all the way through the beams—*

*All of it, all of it, even from behind Tim could tell
that every last fragment of the vision was identical to the
revelation he'd had that Saturday morning when he was
five—*

*And the strangling Lord lifted himself up to gasp for
breath—*

And Donny James collapsed. Fell writhing and
trembling to the floor.

A seizure. He's having a seizure.

Tim hardly knew anything at all about epilepsy. But
there'd been a girl in his fifth-grade class who'd had two
seizures right there in school, and he remembered what
she'd looked like.

Like Donny did right now.

What was it you were supposed to do when somebody has a seizure? His memory was real vague. Something about a spoon? In his eye socket? In his mouth?
No, no, no—not that. Frankie Munsen had said *Yer
s'posed to stick a spoon in her mouth to keep her from
swallowing her tongue,* and he'd taken a spoon out of his
lunch pail and started down the aisle toward her. The
teacher, Miss Minor, had shouted *Don't you dare—you
stay away from her, Frankie Munson!* and she'd picked
the girl up and held her close and gentle to keep her
from hurting herself. When the fit was over and the
school nurse had taken the girl away to the hospital Miss
Minor had explained how that business with the spoon
was just an old wives' tale, and how if anybody ever
pitched a fit in front of you the only thing you ought to
do is keep them from bashing into something hard and
sharp.

Okay, Tim thought. *I can do that.*

Didn't take much doing. There wasn't anything big
or sharp or dangerous anywhere near Donny, unless you
counted the door—Tim had to reach over and push that
out of the way about halfway through the seizure. Wasn't
hard. (But he looked—looked at the doorjamb for the
blood patina from before. And couldn't find it. The blood
was gone clean as though it'd never been there.)

Then finally Donny went still, so still Tim had to check to make sure he was still breathing which he was. Breathing but still like he was deep asleep or blacked out in a coma or something. Must've been something serious; when Tim tried to wake his friend up Donny just lay there on the floor limp, unmoving like a lump of warm meat or something.

I need to get him out of here. If he wakes up and sees Jesus again. . . . Tim pictured Donny rolling into a fit all over again. Which worried him considerably; he didn't imagine that a body could go through something that intense twice in an hour and still come out whole and hale. *Okay, then. I'll have to carry him.* Easy to think; not so easy to accomplish—Donny was grievously overweight. And he wasn't short, either. Which meant that Tim ended up grabbing him under the arms and dragging him—

—Lights! The lights were back on in the hall!—

—dragging him out of the room with the Cross and down the stairs. Careful, careful with those stairs; lots of opportunities here to stumble backwards and go flying, breaking both their necks. Even easier to bang Donny up on the edge parts of the steps.

There: the last step, and he pulled Donny free from it too. Halfway across the second-floor hall when he realized that he needed a rest—and anyhow what was the harm to stop here? This far from the Cross Donny was safe, wasn't he?

Had to be.

Eased Donny down onto the hallway floor. Leaned back on the wall and took a handful of good deep breaths.

And kept leaning there, and breathing, and staring off into the space between him and the wall opposite. Stood that way for half an hour—maybe longer. Digesting what had just happened; trying to figure out how he was going to get Donny not to blab about it all over hell and creation.

He needn't have worried. Donny woke dizzy and confused, and he remembered nothing—talking to him

Tim realized that Donny's memories stopped somewhere in the second-floor hall.

As though carrying him back here Tim had reversed
the events above them.

"What happened to me? Did I fall or something?"

"You're lucky you didn't break your neck."

"I dreamed somebody loved me."

"I know He does."

Donny turned, caught sight of the massive crucifix
above Grandpa's bed. Seeing it he sneered.

"Is *that* all you were talking about?" He nodded
toward the crucifix. "That isn't God. What're you trying
to do, play some kind of a trick?"

Tim didn't argue the point.

When he woke and saw the light Tim first thought that
the Lord had brought some miracle to bear on him. That
made him very sad, because whatever love he had for
life (and for a truth his love for life was considerable) he
didn't want life extended one moment past his time.
He'd seen that, that light, that hill, that dream; when he
went to it he'd go gladly.

Then it occurred to Tim that the dream light could
well be what he was seeing. And for a moment he was
full of awe. Until he realized that the light about him,
bright faceted and wondrous as it was, was in no special
way divine.

He was alive; there was no arguing. It was firelight
he saw.

How. . . ?

He opened his eyes, tried to wake. It wasn't easy,
even with the boy underneath him, pounding on his
back. Heat, light—all around them the hallway was
afire. Bright as it'd never been since hands had first
erected these walls.

And his chest. Was his chest on fire? No that was
the source of light. Light was at all sides, and above, but
it wasn't upon him.

Then what was the fiery pain in his chest?

His chest had taken the full force of the blast from Gail Benjamin's shotgun.

He winced. Not from the pain—which was intense—but from the image of his chest a gaping cavity open to the world by lead shot, and how was he breathing maybe not through his throat but through the open flesh?

Calm down, damn it.

The wound couldn't be that bad. If it were he wouldn't have lived long enough to wake to this inferno. He craned his neck, reached up terrified to touch—

Wax.

His chest was covered with wax, still congealing, soft, warm. And everywhere the skin burned and welted, but only barely broken there in the very center.

What on earth. . . ?

As though he'd been shot with hot wax instead of buckshot. Shot at such close range that it forced the wind out of him and knocked him out—but not so close that the force of wind and heat would break him open.

He forced himself up, into the heat of the burning. The boy was shouting at him, but Tim didn't hear any of it. He was too busy trying to figure out why the Bleeding Man would have her kill him, and fail. And why all this charade? She could have killed him any time, that night he spent delirious in her bed.

And why would she seem to love him and do this deed?

Or was it that she'd been *meant* to kill him, and constructed this ruse to . . . to what? Tim couldn't begin to guess. It made no sense at all.

"Come *on*, God damn it!" Tim heard it only because it was the Lord's name in vain. "You want to get out of here or you want to burn to death?"

Ah. *That* was what Thomas was shouting about. They did have to get out of here, didn't they? If they didn't leave the boy would burn. That was something to worry about, even when Tim's head insisted on spinning the way it spun now.

All right. He let the boy lead him all the twenty paces to the door. Down hill till they were at the car, where both of them sat on the hood to watch the castle burning.

They stayed there in the rain (that faded slowly to a drizzle) all the while that the castle burned itself to ash.

It took about an hour. Twenty minutes in, the fire trucks arrived, and up above helicopters from the forest service. All worked valiantly to save the strange old place that showed on no map, but even with the help of rain it was no use. The wood inside was too old, too dry; it burned bright and hot like kindling.

Tim didn't let the fire or commotion fluster him. He watched peaceably all the time it burned. A little while after the firemen arrived he went around to the back of the car, opened the trunk. Took out his suitcase and changed his torn, burned, wax-scarred shirt.

More than once Tim saw firemen staring at them. He kept expecting one of them—or someone, anyone—to come up and ask what connection they had to the fire.

But no one did.

When the fire was nothing but ash and smoldering char Tim and Thomas got into the car, and Tim drove the boy home.

Neither of them spoke through the entire drive. Not even when Tim pulled up to the Brady house to let Thomas off. The boy got up, got out, and that was the last Tim heard or saw of him.

It was all but the end of the events in Tennessee.

He almost turned right at the junction in Tylerville.

Almost forgot the last bit of the trip completely.

But didn't: at the last moment his eye caught on the veterinary office, and the instant that it did Tim knew what he had to do. Left, not right, and damn the blinker. Not thirty yards and a right-hand turn into the lot.

Just like it had been early this morning: unmarked sheriff's cruiser and a late-model Toyota in the front lot. It was just a tiny wood-sided building—peculiar looking. Maybe it had been a convenience store somewhere back in the dim past? Tim thought it had.

A small brass plaque, there beside the door: ROBIN SMITH, VETERINARIAN.

Tim turned off the ignition. Sat there for a moment tapping the steering wheel.

It's time. Go in—now. Before it's too late.

Tim couldn't have guessed where the words came from, not on a bet. They were inside his head, and they sounded like his voice. Or did they?

No time for this. Inside, ask—

Ask what?

He was here to ask a question.

Something obvious.

Something important.

The castle. He was here to ask about the castle.

Up, out of the car. Into the veterinary office.

Where the desk in the waiting room was empty. Not that it mattered; a buzzer went off the moment he opened the door, and as he walked though it a woman's voice called him.

"Just a minute," she said. "You've caught us at an awkward moment." Which made Tim think thoughts that made him blush.

And he shouldn't have. No one came out from the back straightening hair or smoothing clothes. In fact, when Tim saw the veterinarian she was wearing a scruffy white lab coat that bespoke anything but romance. Then he saw the small velvet box in her hand, and the glow in her eye, and the proud smile on the face of the sheriff and he knew he'd walked in on something a good deal more personal than an afternoon tryst.

A diamond. There was an enormous diamond in that velvet box. The damned thing was an engagement ring.

And suddenly Tim was embarrassed that he'd come here. He'd interrupted a marriage proposal, for God's sake, and the only thing he could think to do was back quietly out the door.

"I'm sorry," he said. Already he was reaching back for the door handle, reaching to open the door to leave. . . . "I don't mean to interrupt."

"Nonsense." The veterinarian spoke quite forcefully, and she sounded sincere. The deputy, on the other hand, looked a lot less willing to accommodate the interruption. "What can I do for you?"

A northern accent. Midwestern—Tim could almost hear the Rust Belt in her voice. If she wasn't local how could she possibly know about the castle? Thomas had known about it, just barely known about it. Tim was sure that there was nothing she could tell him.

The thing to do was to ask his question and get out; anything else would take longer to explain.

"I came up here looking for a place called Still Ridge," he said. "And when I got there all I found was an old, old house on fire. A friend of mine—told me she'd moved to a town by that name. But when I got there all I found was that one place, burning, and when I asked about it they told me that the place had been abandoned years ago."

The deputy stared at Tim coolly, almost hostile. The veterinarian looked curious.

"This Still Ridge—it's somewhere nearby? I've never heard of it." She frowned. Turned toward her intended. "Mike. . . ?"

The deputy coughed. "Yeah, I know the place. Been on the radio all afternoon, what with the fire and all. If I hadn't known before I would've known by now." Suspicion all over his face. "You wouldn't mind telling me your name, would you? And the name of your friend?"

No!

This was going all out of control, damn it. If Tim wasn't careful he'd find himself in awful trouble. He smiled, stepped forward, held out his hand. "My name is Timothy Fischer. Tim. Pleased to meet you, ah—"

The deputy hesitated before he took Tim's hand. "Peterson. Mike Peterson. I work for the local sheriff."

"Guessed that from your uniform." Waited a beat to let the joke sink in. Which it didn't. "My friend's name is Gail Benjamin. You don't think something's happened to her, do you? When I saw that place she said she was moving to, I thought the worst, I'll tell you."

A beat, two beats, three. And then the tension in the air broke sudden as it'd come on.

"Shit," the deputy said. "What'm I getting all hep

about? It was lightning caused that fire. Nobody hurt. And the place that burned been neglected so long that nobody could remember who to call to tell 'im bout it."

"Who to call. . . ?" How much to ask? How to ask it without raising suspicion? "I don't understand."

The veterinarian: "Still Ridge, Mike? I've never heard of the place. Where is it? What're you talking about?"

"The ridge is a big hill halfway between here and Green Hill. Used to be a little midge of a town up on top of it, back before they put the highway in. And there was the Fischer mansion—weird old place." He turned to Tim. "Fischer. That's you, isn't it? You some sort of a relation or something?"

Tim blinked. "My last name is Fischer, yes. But I don't know of any relatives up in this part of the country. My family's from Florida."

"How 'bout that. Guess the name's common enough. Anyway, Robin, all the little wood places rotted off the face of Still Ridge when my Daddy was still a boy. Weren't nothing but shacks, most of 'em. All that's left up there is the old Fischer place. My Aunt Meg used to work at the bank, and when I was little she told me that the bank sent a caretaker up there to see after the Fischer place twice a year. Some sort of a caretaker thing; I don't rightly understand what business the bank had taking on that kind of work, but I imagine that if they care to it's their own concern.

"Make that cared to. Ain't been no caretakers going up that way since I started working for the sheriff. I'd've noticed it if they had. That road up to the Ridge gets so overgrowed you can see it for weeks when someone takes his car up that way. Till this week there ain't been no one up there in a good five years."

Fischer.

Was it Grandpa they were talking about? Was that possible? Tim tried to imagine his Grandpa in that enormous old nightmare of a mansion. And found that he couldn't. There was no way Grandpa would build anything that . . . warped. Yes, warped was exactly the

word for it. Whoever's house that was was someone with
an unwell mind.

The Bleeding Man. Of course it was his home; who
else?

But why would he use Grandpa's name—Tim's
name? Why would he call himself *Fischer*?

It was a question that could chase itself through his
head for days without finding any sensible answer.
Which was to say that there was no point in thinking
about it.

So Tim didn't think about it.

And that, of course, was a serious mistake.

"Somebody was up on Still Ridge this week? Do you
think that could have been my friend Gail?"

The deputy sheriff shrugged. "I don't imagine so. I
checked with the bank when I saw the way disturbed.
What I heard from them was that old Mr. Fischer had
come back to take up residence in the place. I don't see
how that could be, since he was an old guy when my
grandma knew him. Maybe his son, I don't know.
Grandson, even. Anyhow, fella at the bank told me that
old Mr. Fischer came in, picked up his keys, and said he
was moving back in. You think your friend could've been
moving in there with him? Sounds kind of crazy to me."

Tim frowned. "I guess it does. Do you think the
bank could put me in touch with this Mr. Fischer? Was
he at the fire?"

The deputy shrugged. "I couldn't tell you. Didn't
see him myself. Bank ought to be open; it's right down
the road a ways. Won't hurt no one for you to go and
ask."

Tim didn't stop by the bank on his way out of town.
Maybe he should have. Maybe. Would it have changed
anything if he'd been able to track the Bleeding Man
down to his root? Soon enough, Tim was sure, the
Bleeding Man would find him, attack him. When he did
Tim would ask the question that made him so
uncomfortable—the question about names, and why

Fischer was for both of them. He was beginning to think he didn't want to know the answer.

Maybe. Maybe not.

There was another point, too; one that nagged at Tim has he drove the highway out away from Tylerville into evening. It was the part of him that said: Now, do it now, take the initiative. Strike where he lives. Don't just defend yourself: attack.

But no, he thought. No, the Bleeding Man left this string untied deliberately. Left it four generations back for me to find it here.

And he drove on.

Eventually the sun finished setting and the road grew dark. And Tennessee rolled on and on and on till it turned to Georgia. Where Tim pulled into a rest area—he waited till just before he hit the first Atlanta suburb—pulled into a rest area just to rest his eyes. Three a.m.? Four? Late, anyhow; so late that Tim didn't check his watch because he didn't want to know what it said. He pulled into the rest stop, parked in the first empty slot he saw, killed the engine. Let his head rest on the wheel. Closed his eyes.

Closed his eyes and thought about his daughter who he'd hardly known and never met, and ached, and grieved despite the fact that the night he'd lost her was seven long years in his past. And tried to think of anything, anything else in the world. And failed. . . .

And then it was late morning.

No transition whatsoever.

Steamy, bright-hot sun-warmed car, and if he hadn't had the window wide open the place would've been hot enough to cook him.

Craned his neck. Looked around, remembering where he was—when he slept as deep as he just had it was always hell putting himself back into context. Parking lot. Rest area. Lord Almighty, what had he done to his back, sleeping in that position? His neck, too. Fierce, fierce pain, and all he'd done was turn his head.

Relax. The way around an ache like this was to relax.

And his chest. Blessed be for the antibiotics; if not

for them the burns would already be infected. As it was they'd bled and scab-glued themselves into his clean shirt, and now this one was probably ruined, too. He needed to get a motel room for a few hours, pry this shirt off, get himself clean and showered.

No. The hell with that. The thing to do was to get the car going again. Get home where he could really rest.

Three minutes later he had the car in gear and moving, pulling out onto the highway. Which led him to hours and hours of the dull thrum of tires on the asphalt; steady, easy navigation on roads that led forcefully toward Florida, almost as though they been patterned after a kitchen funnel.

Perhaps they had. There were days when it seemed to Tim that the Florida Tourism Board had had a hand in the creation of many things.

Two hundred miles south of Atlanta Tim pulled off the highway for gas and oil and drive-through hamburgers. It took him a good ten minutes to get back on the road, even though he took the burgers with him to eat as he drove instead of pulling into a parking spot to sit and eat. That was longer than he'd planned, but there wasn't much he could do about it, what with the fellow at the gas station taking so long to check his oil.

The sun was up again, long since, by the time he got to Tampa. And Tim was exhausted by then, so sick of roads and driving that if anyone had asked he'd have said he hoped he'd never see the inside of a car again.

Ha. Some chance of that living in Tampa, with the godawful bus system and no other mass transit to speak of.

Off 295 at the Sulphur Springs exit, down Nebraska out Hillsborough and then up again to his apartment.

Where Walt Fulton was sleeping on his couch. Snoring, too.

It was an awful scare at first. Tim walked in, and there was this stranger on his couch making a godawful racket, and who the hell and what the hell and this was one of the Bleeding Man's people, he had to be had to be—

And right when panic hit its peak Tim realized that the man on the couch looked awful damn familiar. Familiar like a brother, almost. And then he remembered Donny in the bar telling him that Walt was back in town and trying to get ahold of him, and suddenly he recognized the man despite the fact that he hadn't seen him in the twenty years since they'd both been boys—

Tim never found out how the hell he'd gotten a key. Maybe he didn't need one? God only knew. When Tim asked where Walt had been for the last twenty years he got a tale so improbable that it does not bear recounting. Weirder stuff (to Tim's way of thinking) than anything Tim had lived through himself. Aliens, spaceships, dead people. Weird stuff like that.

But the tale didn't come till late that night. Because Tim didn't bother to wake Walt; he saw him on the couch, figured out who he was, said *What the hell. . . ?*, and then shrugged and wandered off to bed. Where he collapsed, still wearing the shirt that had scab-welded itself to his chest.

And woke to the smell of strong Cuban-style coffee and powerful cigars. Was that Walt stinking up the place? Where on earth had he picked up habits like those?

Where on earth indeed.

"If you're going to smoke those things, open a window, huh?—I know the air-conditioning is on. Open a window anyway."

The sound of a window opening. Tim sat up in bed, yawned, rubbed his eyes.

Walt Fulton stood in his doorway. Cigar in one hand, coffee in the other.

A strange sight, Walt was. Very strange indeed.

"Cup of coffee?"

Tim was going to say: *That* shit—are you trying to poison me? Until he started to get out of bed. And his head swam out over the world like a bird swooping around underwater, and he knew he needed the caffeine.

"Yeah. Please."

Lurching up, out of bed, and the scabs pulled against his shirt till Tim howled in pain and surprise. And Walt turned to see him, snapped around like a well-trained Oriental boxer, and from the look in his eye Tim thought his childhood friend would scream and leap—no, no, nothing like that. Soon as Walt saw it was just Tim, Tim and no one but Tim and in some kind of pain he relaxed, relieved. Sighed.

"I thought. . . ." Walt said. But he never said what he thought.

Eventually Tim realized that Walt wasn't going to continue. "Sorry. Scabs stuck to my shirt. Stung something awful when they pulled."

Walt was gaping. "Those are bloodstains," he said. "And that—what did you did to your head?"

Tim shrugged. "It's been a bad week. Somebody keeps trying to kill me."

It was supposed to be a joke. It really was, even if there was a measure of truth in it. Walt didn't take it that way at all.

"Yes," he said. "That makes sense, doesn't it?" He looked away. "I wondered what he meant."

"Who meant?—Let me by, would you? Where's the coffee?" Walt stepped aside; Tim stumbled out into the kitchen, poured himself a cup of vile-smelling coffee. "Who said what?"

Walt frowned. Closed his eyes. His expression—it was the expression of a man reliving something large and unpleasant. It took a long while for the moment to pass, and Walt didn't answer till it did.

"Your Grandpa."

He let that sit there for a moment, heaping tension out over everything. He knew Grandpa was dead, didn't he? He had to know. He wouldn't be saying it with that look on his face if he didn't know.

If he knew Grandpa was dead, why was he saying he'd talked to him? Maybe they'd talked back before Grandpa died?

That was it. Had to be.

"I went to the cemetery—the graveyard where they put me. Back when I was dead. You know they buried my mom in that same place, don't you?" Tim was too dumbstruck to respond. "Guess you don't. Well, they did bury her there. So I'm back home for the first visit since I left way back when, so I go to see my mom. To say hello, good-bye, all that. You know what I mean?— Tim, don't look at me like that. You know damn well I'm not crazy, because I know you're involved in weirder things than I ever had happen to me. I had a good long talk with your Grandpa on my way out. I know all sorts of things that you can't tell a soul."

Tim shook his head. "Go on."

Walt nodded. "Mom wouldn't say a word to me. I think she's still mad at me—I mean, I guess she has to be. So I leave, and as I'm going I hear your Grandpa calling me from way down inside his grave."

"Inside his grave?" Tim tried to reconcile the idea with the image of the hill that had come to him in his death-dream. And failed. "What do you mean?"

Walt shrugged. "Inside his grave is what I mean. In there dead and waiting for the Second Coming." Walt frowned. "Or maybe he just came back to talk to me? Most people wait in their graves for Christ to return. But not all of them—I think your Grandpa's already called on to his reward."

"I don't think . . . I don't think that's what it's like."

"How would *you* know? Have *you* ever been dead?"

Tim frowned. He didn't like talking about stuff like this. He hadn't hardly ever talked to anyone about it before—nobody but Grandpa, at least. Not honestly and openly. "I almost died a couple times. I saw things then."

Walt rolled his eyes. "And you believed them? No, it isn't like that all the time. Won't be till after the Second Coming. Till then when you're dead you're just dead. Trust me; I was dead for a long time when I was little."

Tim wanted to say: no, no, that's not like it is. That's not like it is at all. But he couldn't find the breath to say

it. What came out was something more like a cough, or
a grunt, but not exactly either. It could be Walt wasn't
exactly telling the truth. That was always possible,
wasn't it? But no; Tim knew better than that. His friend
wasn't just being honest with him, but straightforward,
too. However it was that his experience was different—
however that was, Tim didn't know, and didn't have to
know, either.

"What did Grandpa say?"

Walt smiled. Amusement? Or maybe Tim had said
something funny. Or maybe it was good news? It wasn't
a mean smile, anyway. It was, in fact, the first thing
about this new, grown-up Walt that made Tim feel at
ease. "He says you should relax. He says that when
you're ready to find the Cross, it'll find itself for you.
And till then there's no sense you getting all bent out of
shape over it. He also said that you need to stop being
such a cold fish—if you keep yourself all shut down
inside you'll end up serving your enemies." He frowned.
"I'm not sure what he meant by that last part."

And what Tim felt wasn't what he was supposed to
feel at all. He felt as though Walt Fulton violated
something deep and secret and inviolable. He felt
attacked, and hurt, and held up for humiliation in the
scornful light of day. And he looked away, and clenched
his teeth, and felt himself turn red.

Red from anger; red from embarrassment.

"Tim. . . ?"

What could he say? And even if there were anything
to say, how was he to say it, with the blood surging in his
temples and his ears ringing and the breath forcing itself
so hard in and out through his lungs?

Tim held his tongue. Or perhaps it held him.

"Are you okay?"

A deep breath. Another.

"I'm fine."

It wasn't rational to react this way. Why was he so
upset? Why was he so embarrassed? Walt wasn't lying to
him. Nor was he a thing sent by the Bleeding Man. Tim
could be surprised about a thing like that, the way he'd

been with Gail—but only when he didn't bother to ask himself the obvious questions.

And right now he was asking himself every question about Walt Fulton he could imagine. And none of the answers told him anything at all.

"Your Grandpa said you might not take that well." A sigh; a headshake. "He didn't tell me what to say if you got shook up like this."

Sympathy.

Walt was sympathetic, and Tim thought that maybe he really did understand. Which only made things worse—somehow unexplainable. Made Tim want to run out of his own home screaming into the night. He didn't let himself do it, of course. How could he? The thing to do was keep putting one foot in front of the other. Calm; do the duty he owed. (Owed? Owed who? Tim wasn't even sure who he owed it to. He only knew that it was his duty because of who he was and who he'd been born to be, and that nothing he could ever do would release him. Not till the day he died.)

Later, when the responsibilities were done and seen, he could ask himself why he hurt so much to hear Walt say what he did. Right now there wasn't time.

"I'm okay," he said. "Don't worry about me."

Walt was frowning. He didn't believe Tim for a minute. As he shouldn't: Tim was lying. Both of them knew it.

"We could go out to the grave if you want. Maybe—I don't know—I could teach you how to hear them talking. The dead people, I mean. Do you think you want to learn?"

And that was it: the one tiny bit of business that pushed Tim over the edge.

Splat.

Poof.

Bapp.

And he was gone. Just like that.

Not screaming into the night the way he'd expected. Exactly the opposite: Tim went catatonic. Oh, it didn't seem that way from the inside. Didn't seem like much of anything at all from the inside, in fact. Just pulling away from the world, and none of it mattered much at all. Were they going on a trip? Well, they could if that was what Walt wanted. Tim didn't want to go on any trip. He wanted to sit at his kitchen table, and drink a tall-tall mug of coffee. Maybe step out to the corner and buy a paper from the vending machine. Bring it back, tune the radio to that classical station. While away the evening sipping coffee and reading the news.

Someone rang the doorbell. Who would do a thing like that? *Go away*, Tim thought. He didn't want any company right now. He wanted to rest, to hide. To take the time to try to reassemble his life. Reassemble: that was exactly the word. His life was a pile of crumbs, and the mice were nibbling at them. If he was going to survive he had to gather them up and glue them back together while he still could. Like—like a sculpture. Or like a roll of dough shaping into a bread loaf? The metaphors were stupid, weird things his brain cobbled together while he wasn't paying it any attention. But stupid or not, they were true, weren't they?

Too true.

That doorbell again. Why didn't that person go away?

And Walt. What was with Walt, staring at him that way? Looking back and forth at the door, back at Tim, at the door again. Couldn't he make up his mind which way he wanted to look? (There was a joke tucked in there someplace, but Tim wasn't sure he wanted to pry it out of hiding.) Okay, now his mind seemed to be made up. And made against the door: He looked Tim in the eye, put his hands on Tim's shoulders. Pressed him down into one of the kitchen chairs.

"Tim, you've got to pull yourself out of this. What's the matter with you? Is this a medical thing, or are you all worn-out inside?"

Tim heard the question, but it didn't parse. Didn't mean a thing as far as he could see. Really! Worn-out inside! What did Walt want to know about, the in things or the out things? Was he saying Tim was worn in or did he mean that . . . well, Tim didn't know what. He just wished that Walt would speak a little more clearly.

About time for that doorbell to ring, wasn't it? But no, no ring. Only Walt there staring Tim in the eye. Twelve inches away? Six? Eighteen? Real damn close, that was a sure thing. So close that Tim could feel the *weird*ness of Walt's eyes, bearing on him. Weighing him. Touching inside him, almost.

The feel of it was almost erotic. Really was: erotic. And boy was *that* embarrassing; Tim hadn't known there was anything in him that could feel this way because of the closeness-inside-him of a man. Was he ashamed? Was he supposed to be ashamed? He didn't know. It didn't seem like he ought to. But then it wasn't erotic like he wanted to jump in bed and start rubbing around; more like erotic like holding close and the warmness of another body nearby when the weather out was cold cold cold. . . .

It didn't matter, when it got right down to it. It weren't like either one of them was about to do anything about it.

"What's wrong with you, damn it?"

Stars. There were stars in those eyes, Tim thought. Had he seen the hearts of suns? Had he flown in the deep black parts of the universe where the no light yet shines? Of course he had. Tim couldn't imagine how his friend could have reached such a place, but he knew that he'd been there.

Tim was right, too. He was very good at knowing secrets no one ever told.

Bing-bong.

There that doorbell was. A little late, but right where it was supposed to be all the same. Tim was beginning to wonder who it was. So persistent! And persistence is a virtue, isn't it? Hmm. Somehow that doorbell didn't feel virtuous. Tim wondered why.

Rattling the doorknob.

Uh-oh.

Somebody at the door was trying to get in. Just like Walt had last night. It occurred to Tim to wonder whether he'd rented an apartment or a public thoroughfare, what with everybody coming and going on their own, without so much as a by-your-leave.

Harrumph.

Fiddling with the doorknob. Was that the sound of a key, or maybe a lock pick? One or the other. And Walt was turning away, which was an awful shame since Tim was still seeing all sorts of interesting places hiding in his eyes.

"Who's there?" Walt called. "What do you want?"

Good questions, Tim thought. Wish I'd thought of them myself.

No answer from the great outdoors.

No answer, that is, except the sound of the door opening.

Time to get the locks changed. Either his key was making the rounds or the locks themselves were useless.

"Who are you?" Walt asked. "What do you want?"

He had a gun out. A gun! What was he doing carrying that thing around—did he want to kill somebody or something? Really. And such a strange gun, too, like something out of a late-night science fiction movie or something.

The person at the door stopped dead in her tracks.

And turned the question on its ear.

"I should ask you the same thing," she said. "But I don't think I will."

Gail Benjamin's voice.

Gail who he loved who he shouldn't love who tried to kill him.

She was walking into the apartment, ignoring Walt's gun. Coming toward Tim. Was she here to try to kill him again? And had she really tried to kill him at all?—After all, the slug that had hit him was wax. How could you kill anyone with a wax bullet? Surely she must have known he would survive. . . ?

"Tim? Are you okay?"

And why did she want to know the answer to *that* question?

That was when the world came clapping back into focus.

Tim blinked. Turned and looked Gail Benjamin in the eye. "You tried to kill me," he said. "I loved you, and you tried to kill me."

She pursed her lips. Stopped walking toward him. "Are you really sure of that?"

Tim closed his eyes. "You know I'm not." Opened them again.

"I didn't, you know. I was supposed to kill you. That was what my master wanted: wanted the Cross to tip its hand by reaching out to save you. He said he thought that it would have to. You're the last heir in the Stewards' line. But how could I kill you? I can't, you know. I care."

No. Or. . . ?

"He could just as well have sent you here to spy on me. To take my confidence and betray it, the same way you betrayed my affection for you."

She looked hurt. "Could I prove that isn't so? You know there isn't any way." She frowned; shook her head. "That isn't why I'm here. I care for you. I do. But saying it over and over doesn't make it any easier to believe—just the opposite, and you know that as well as I do.

"I came to warn you. My master knows you survived the fire. And he expects to find you here—very soon. You don't want to be here . . . when he comes. You don't want to meet him on the terms he plans."

And she didn't wait for him to answer, but turned and left without another word.

More coffee brewing. Which was a good thing, since the cup here in front of him was burned and blackish-looking from scorching on the warmer.

Walt stood by the sink, waiting impatiently for the brew to finish.

"Do you want," he asked, not bothering to turn around as he spoke, "to go to the cemetery?"

"Have you got a cigarette? Or one of those damned cigars?"

Tim didn't smoke ordinarily. But this was no ordinary time.

Walt turned, fishing into his shirt pocket. Taking out a cigar tube, tossing it to Tim. He had an eyebrow raised.

Tim caught the tube; opened it; grabbed Walt's
ghter from where it sat on the table. Lit that long,
orrible cigar. "I don't think I do. Want to go to the
emetery, I mean."

Walt was walking toward him, toward the table.
Carrying two large coffee mugs. Tim could smell the
offee: the problem with Café Bustello—the trouble with
ll those Cuban coffees—was that it smelled burnt
efore you left it on to scorch. Probably, he thought, it
vas something in the way they roasted it. *Pre-burned
offee. That's the ticket.*

"You're sure?" Something heavy and unsaid hover-
ng in the air. A shift in Walt's expression. (Just as
nreadable as before, but different.) "What's happened
o you? Your Grandpa told me who you are. Who he was.
But the way you act—it doesn't make any sense. Like—
ike someone's been trying to take apart your insides.
And doing it, too. You're a mess, all rattled and broken
nside."

Tim took his coffee mug as Walt sat down. Took a big
wallow of the brackish black scorchy stuff, and damn
ear burned his mouth.

"You tell me first," he said. "Where the hell have
ou been?"

And Walt sighed, as though he knew he wouldn't be
elieved. And he told his tale so remarkable, so unbe-
ievable that it does not bear repetition.

When he was done Tim shook his head. Frowned.
Shrugged.

"Your turn," Walt said. "Where's this Cross?
Who . . . hurt you the way you are?"

"If I knew where it was," Tim said, "no one would
have gotten close enough to hurt me."

"Who? Why?"

"I don't know why. He won't tell me. But who I
know: I saw him in a dream. I've met him, too, but I
knew him before I ever did. He's the man who nailed
Christ to the Cross. The Lord's Blood is on his hands,
and it seeps from his eyes—to this day. The Blood
preserves him against time. He's lived all these centuries

bitter, hating . . . and there's a connection. Somethin
I don't understand. A connection to Grandpa.

"They killed Grandpa. The Bleeding Man, and th
people who work for him. When I went up to Nebrask
to identify his body. . . ."

Tim recounted the events that had led him cross
country twice now, told of all that had happened in th
Midwest, in Tennessee. Of the dream he'd had here i
Tampa. When he was done Walt looked as skeptical a
Tim had felt hearing the bizarre story about Walt and th
aliens and the starships and other things much worse.

"I think what your Grandpa was trying to say," Wal
told him, "is that you should relax and lay low for
while. It sounds to me like this man with the bleedin;
eyes is trying to bust you up inside. Trying to do it, no
letting it happen. I don't know why he'd want to do
thing like that, but it seems to me that if he wants to d
that the best thing you can do is get out of his way. Mak
it hard for him to find you, and he won't be able to hur
you."

Was that really so? Was it really best to run an
hide? Tim felt hesitant, uncertain. Something about th
idea felt . . . wrong. Cowardly? Maybe. Yes. The mor
he thought of it the more it seemed to Tim a vile an
ignoble thing to slink away into the night. . . . And yet
And yet he saw how it was wise; how the worst thing h
could do given the circumstances would be to run full til
into menace.

I will, he thought. *The hell with my pride*. H
looked up at Walt. And when he smiled the smile wa
genuine, and he really did think that he'd found th
means to set things right with the world. "Thanks," h
said. "I really owe you."

Walt shook his head. "You don't. I owe you
Grandpa lots more than that."

That meant something Tim didn't understand, no
even after he'd heard Walt's impossible story
"How. . . ?"

Walt shook his head. "Some other time," he said
"Some other place."

I'm not supposed *to understand,* Tim thought. *If he wanted me to understand, he'd speak more clearly.*

He nodded gravely, serious as though he'd engaged a bond too dear and dire to talk about out loud.

Just as though he understood the Mystery. And maybe, down beneath the noise and nonsense, he did.

"I need to leave," Walt said. "I'm overdue already."

"You need a lift someplace? I wouldn't mind giving you a ride. Even if you need to go out of town a distance."

Walt frowned. "No," he said, "that isn't necessary these days." He stood; a moment later Tim stood up as well.

It was three in the morning. Later than that, maybe; the kitchen clock sometimes lost a few minutes, and when Tim let it go it would fall as much as an hour or two behind.

"Can I walk you out to. . . ." To what? Tim couldn't imagine, and mostly he was glad he couldn't.

Walt shook his head. "It isn't far," he said. "You'll like it better not to know."

Tim hesitated. Puzzled. But what was to know, and did he really want to know it? No. Let it loose. He put out his hand to shake Walt's; clapped his friend on the back. "I owe you," he said. "When the time comes that I can help you, you'll know where to find me."

"It's true," Walt said. And they shook hands, and Walt left.

The moment Walt had closed the door behind him, it occurred to Tim that there was one last thing he had to say—something so desperately important that it couldn't possibly wait the years and years he knew it'd be before he saw his friend again.

But in the time it took Tim to reach the outside hall, Walt disappeared. Tim spent a good twenty minutes looking for him, calling after him all around the apartment complex and even on the shore of the Hillsborough River where it touched the north border of the parking lot. But if Walt was anywhere nearby to hear him shouting, he didn't answer.

Two winos on the far bank of the river called back to

him with rude suggestions just before he gave up
looking. Tim didn't answer them; the offers they made
were nothing that interested him.

When he'd finally given up looking Tim went back to the
apartment, showered, dressed, and left the place behind. For good? Even that was possible. Gail Benjamin
said he should leave, and Walt Fulton as much as said
she was right. The talk with Walt had cleaned something
down inside Tim, made it new again. No—not new. But
newer, more alive. The things that had made him want
to run screaming into the night before . . . now they
were minor terrors, or maybe not terrors at all. They
were things he could cope with. Was he prey of the
hunt? Well then he was prey. It didn't bother him to
hide, and it seemed to him that he would do it well.
Better, he thought, than anyone could follow.

But hiding well (as hunting does) requires fore-
thought. Of which Tim had none; all the time he drove
out Hillsborough Avenue, drove west toward Town and
Country—all that time Tim's mind was blank and clean
as blackboard slate first thing in the morning. And
certainly he'd had no plan before he'd left his home.

So out on the far west edge of Tampa, near where
Hillsborough meets Memorial Highway, Tim pulled off
the road to sit and think. Pulled into the dark deserted
parking lot of a run-down Zayre department store, killed
the headlights, killed the engine. Let his car coast to a
slow stop on the table-flat pavement.

And sat. And thought.

Thought as how hiding required a place to hide that
wasn't his place at all. Someplace that had nothing to do
with him—more than that. A place where no one could
imagine him. Where he wouldn't even imagine himself.

That was what he needed, all right. He needed to
be on the other end of the country, or perhaps on the
other end of the world. In a place where he was alien but
invisible. He could think of a place, he was sure. He
could think of a place if only he relaxed and let his mind
wander long enough.

He would find his hidey-hole, and crawl into it, and pull the top in after him. When the world had changed its name and face, he'd come out again. Time was on his side.

He wasn't altogether certain how long that would be. How long would it take for the Bleeding Man to lose all trace of him, to forget the hunt? Years, at least. Tim would need a rabbit hole that would shield him for years.

And that would be a very deep hole indeed.

He would need a new name. A new identity. Grandpa had taught him the art of making such things years back; Tim could make himself a new man anywhere, and on short notice. (It would cause him trouble accessing his old accounts. But he could do it if he were carefully discreet. The Bleeding Man and his people could watch his bank closely, but Tim could transfer funds by phone. By automatic teller. Even with access to his banking records—assuming they could get it— tracking him down from them would be damn near impossible.

Hide. Change his name. His appearance? Ha. Odds were they'd be expecting him to dye his hair and grow a beard. Take up wearing glasses. So to heck with that. Let his looks be their own camouflage. His features, his hair, his height—all of them were common enough that they'd be hell to track him by.

So where—

The sound of a car door slamming, somewhere right nearby.

That was all the warning he had: the sound of a slamming door in a parking lot that had been dead-empty as an open grave not ten minutes before. No gleam of headlights; no sound of auto engines grinding to a halt.

Just the door slam, and then someone hissing *idiot*, and Tim looked up to see that they were all around him, all outside the car, six, seven, maybe eight of them getting ready to rip him out of his seat—

Fuck that. Fuck *it*.

And something in Tim snapped.

The same something that'd given him composure

just a few moments before: that was the something that broke. And when all the shattered bits of it had fallen away what was left was Tim raw wounded naked of civilization; Tim Fischer in his primal state.

Imagine a knight in armor, trained from birth to fight and kill with honor; to conquer; to quest. Imagine him that he'd been born to be that knight, that nothing life could bring him could possibly alter his true nature. Only mask it. Obscure it.

That was Tim Fischer: knight of the round table born to quest for his own grail, and though time and circumstance conspired to hide his nature from him, from the world, neither one could alter the essence of him.

And at the same time that the knight was Tim, Tim wasn't that knight. For though his Grandpa had trained him carefully and taught him many things, he'd taught him nothing of the art and study of violence. Tim had an enormous talent for fighting, but no knowledge of it whatsoever. And because he was so ignorant, so angry, and so good at breaking bones, he did more uncareful harm to his opponents than any knight ought to have done.

There in the deep black dark of that parking lot everything Tim had ever learned or known—everything that the world had ever taught him—fell away from him. Left him standing wild in the night as though no one had ever tamed him.

And he *was* standing, now. Out of the car, on his feet, in motion. Hearing, feeling, tasting the air and aura that surrounded him. He could feel every weakness in his adversaries; taste the bluster bravado that masked their fear. He could hear the weakness in the beating of their hearts. He grabbed the man nearest him by the throat and the belt. Lifted him up over his head! If there'd been any of the thinking part of Tim awake to see it he would have marveled at his own strength. Lifting a full-grown man over his head! Dear Lord, he couldn't do a thing like that. But he did it still. Adrenaline rage lifted the man high up over Tim's head—

—and threw him thirty feet across the parking lot.

Where he flopped and rolled and tumbled flailing arms like a rag doll's.

Like a broken rag doll.

They were backing away now. All of them come here to menace him were openly afraid. Tim's rage flared—feeding on their fear. Tasted it delicious as the beautiful scent of fresh meat brought home from the hunt.

Three long strides and he had this one, the one with the beard (just barely visible in silhouette against the Arby's sign far, far in the distance) and he grabbed that beard, grabbed and *pulled* the whole head down, down till the face met Tim's rising knee, and then again, and again, and the fourth time there was a sickly crunching sound, the sound of bone breaking. The neck? No, no, it was a bone in the face, a cheek, or maybe the nose. And the bearded man was limp, dead limp but still alive Tim could tell because of the bubbly bloody air that came from his nose as he breathed. He let go the beard. Let the man fall to the pavement.

That was a good thing to do. Necessary, even. Because someone had jumped on Tim's back. And was trying to strangle him.

Maybe succeeding.

Tim grabbed the arm at his throat, yanked it free with all the strength he had. And kept pulling, pulling, pulling the man up and over his shoulder, not just throwing him onto the ground but swinging as the arm wrenched free of its socket, swinging the man like he was a club to hit the others.

Let the force of the swing carry him off in the direction of the storefront.

Four of them, now. Or were there five? Or six? For all Tim could see into the pitch there could be a hundred far out there in the dark. However many they were, it wasn't enough to give them all security; Tim saw one of them turn in the shadows, heard him run, not run toward him, but away out toward the street and that had to mean his fear had broken him—

—someone moved fast off to Tim's left, and there was an eye-searing blue-white flash to show a man standing, firing a gun at the one running for his life, and an explosive blast rang in Tim's ears long and hard as he dove toward the muzzle of the gun, dove to take it before anyone could aim that thing at him—

As the running man died screaming—

As Tim tackled the gunman, brought him down, pounded his head up and down into the blacktop—

As the gun skittered out across the parking lot—

And four were left, and of them two were running, Tim could hear them running as though their lives depended on it, and the other two were on his back, grabbing him by the shoulders, and they had him, had him trapped pinned still standing up and if there'd been more than just those two he'd've been a dead man. But there weren't more, there were only two, and they hardly had the strength to hold him, much less move him, and in a moment

In a moment

In a moment they'd try to bring him up off the ground, and they'd lose him, and that moment was now now now as Tim pulled his arms in, pulled both the men who held him clear off their feet, pushed-threw them *down* and *in*, and their heads met (*thuck!*, that was it, that was the sound they made) just before they reached the ground. One of them must not've been hurt too bad, because right away he tried to get up. Tim kicked him right below the ribs, put a stop to that real quick. He didn't try to get up after that.

An engine starting. Headlights, and Tim looked up to see two men in a car, visible plainly under the dome light on from the open door. The two who had run. It had to be them. Were they going to try to run him over? Tim didn't wait to find out. He ran straight toward the car, ran toward it and if they tried to run him down he'd dive up onto the hood, dive right through that damned windshield. . . .

But the way it turned out there wasn't any point. The one behind the wheel slammed his door, put the Toyota into reverse and floored it, and in a moment they were too far away to be a question, let alone a threat.

Tim was still mad. Furious, in fact. It was time to

leave. Time to get back on the road, find a place to stop and think things through. As he'd meant to do here.

But his blood—his blood would have none of that. It still seethed with the berserk rage that'd come on as these men first approached him.

Rage. And no one standing to vent it at.

And then it occurred to him: *Grandpa's furniture*. These folk knew where it was if anyone did. Not that they were likely to admit to it. . . .

Heh. Heh heh.

He could always convince them to admit to it. Convince them to tell him where the hell it was while he was at it. *I'll have to hog-tie 'em, or they'll throttle me the minute the first of 'em wakes up.* He could do that if he had to. Wouldn't be that hard. *Throw 'em in the car and haul 'em all out to a place where I can get a little privacy while I work on 'em.*

A deep breath as he walked toward the one car of theirs still here in the lot. Another breath; his body was calming. His blood beginning to slow.

He could feel his self returning to his body. No, that wasn't the right metaphor. It was like—like the conscious part of him had been swimming in a deep, deep lake, face up toward the surface. Watching the world through a shimmery unreality.

And now he'd risen up. Broken the surface.

There was blood on his hands. It shamed him: what in God's name had he done? If he hadn't killed one of those men (they were men, too. Not women. It was dark, but not so dark that he couldn't see a man only arms' length away) if he hadn't killed one of those men it was only God's love that had protected him.

Here he was: the station wagon. Ashamed, standing in the dark beside a station wagon that wasn't his, about to rifle it as though he were a thief. Walt Fulton was right—he was too wound up. He needed to get away before he lost himself to anger, rage. . . .

Opened the station wagon's front passenger door. Looked inside—

What he saw pushed away his calm, drowned him in

rage so deep that it was hours and hours before he saw the world clearly again.

Ropes. Clubs. Electric cattle prods, there in the far back. It looked, Tim thought, as though they meant to torture him.

That made him angry, but it wasn't the worst. None of it, in fact, amounted to anything at all when you weighed it against the Bible.

Grandpa's Bible. Plain, pocket-size, leather-bound King James version. Tim would have recognized it anywhere, anyplace; it was peculiar and very very fine.

It didn't come from the house. It couldn't have; Grandpa never left that Bible home when he traveled. Carried it with him—in his breast pocket when he wore a jacket; in his suitcase when he didn't.

Whoever had that took it from Grandpa's body. No way Grandpa could've lost it while he was still alive.

Whoever had it was the one who'd killed Grandpa. Not just one who'd known or helped or ordered the murder, but the one who'd done the deed itself.

Tim reached into the car. Took the Bible from where it sat beside the driver's seat. Put it in the back pocket of his jeans.

And lost himself to rage.

It was a long long time before he saw the world clearly again.

There was plenty enough rope in the station wagon for trussing up the six who had attacked him. Even some left over for the seventh—that first one to bolt and run, the one the gunman shot square in the back. Tim couldn't find any sign of him, though, nothing but a stretch of gritty sand right around the spot where he'd gone down. After a while Tim decided he'd limped away during the fight and gave up looking.

Bad assumption, that one was, but how was Tim to know? With all the rage boiling around inside his skull he didn't have much sense about things. Little things like he would've known with his gut ordinarily—he was blind to them.

And so he missed the fact that the sand wasn't sand at all, but ash like you'd find in a crematorium.

Exactly like you'd find at a crematorium.

Tim parked his car neatly into one of the slots near the store's front entrance. Rolled the windows, locked the doors tight. And left it there.

He found the keys to the station wagon in the pocket of one of the men he'd beaten. Used them to open the car's back hatch. Threw all six of the men into the back—piled them in like so many logs.

And drove off into the woods.

Deep, deep into the woods.

Where trees could fall in the forest. And no one could hear them scream.

It took hours to get there.

No, not hours: an hour and forty-five minutes. Wouldn't have taken that long, but a big piece of the drive was in and around through Lutz on overgrown unpaved roads, and Tim had to slow down to just a couple miles an hour or he'd've bounced the folks in the back hard enough to break a neck or two.

When he found his spot in the deep deep woods there were already hints of dawn down at the edges of the sky. That was bad; the things that Tim had planned were best done under cover of the night. No matter, except on his heart and gut: this place was five miles from the nearest living soul. No one would pass to see what Tim was doing. No one would hear, no matter how hard or long the screams.

He tied each of them to a tree of his own. They were awake now, and they all struggled a little as he fastened and knotted. Didn't do them any good. Tim knew knots; knew binding. Wasn't a one of them getting loose from these ropes, not till Tim was good and ready.

Which he might be, eventually.

And might not. Heh.

Bastards killed *his* Grandpa. Tim'd show *them* a thing or two, all right.

Took a good long while to tie up the lot of them.

Half an hour, maybe? Maybe more than that. However long it was, it was all soft morning light out there in the woods by then, and Tim could see all the men pretty clearly. He went down the line of them, staring each one in the eye. Shoving hard against each chest.

"You," Tim said, "were you there in Tennessee with Gail Benjamin, shooting at me? Shooting at that poor kid?"

By the time he was finished with the question, he was already at the third man.

"Were *you*"—*shove*—"one of the ones who jumped me in the dark, up in Nebraska?"

The fifth, now.

"Are you the one who killed my Grandpa?"

The sixth.

Tim recognized the sixth.

Would have recognized him long before if there'd been light enough.

From Nebraska. The sheriff. Deputy sheriff, actually. The one who'd disappeared as soon as it got obvious he knew something about Grandpa. What was his name? Tim hesitated, fished for it—

Joel Kimball. When Tim thought about it hard enough he could almost see the name as he'd first seen it, engraved on a badge just below the words DEPUTY SHERIFF.

"It is you," Tim said. "It was you who killed him."

Tim was amazed, even confused. Was that how he was supposed to feel? Till this moment he couldn't have admitted it, but now he knew that from the very first Tim had been looking for Grandpa's murderer. Looking for him to—?

To avenge his grandfather, of course. What else?

Vengeance is Mine, sayeth the Lord. Tim knew that good and well. Knew it with his heart. But then and there his heart was the farthest thing in the world, and what he wanted was blood.

He wanted this man to die, and he wanted him to suffer. Wanted him to suffer for the longest time and in the worst possible way. But that was feeling; it wasn't thinking clearly. If he'd been thinking clearly Tim would surely have gone easier on the man. As it was Tim hit him hard, and again and again and again, and if he'd kept at it for as little as five minutes he surely would have been a murderer.

No matter that the man he killed was the one who'd killed Tim's Grandpa. Killed the man in the parking lot the night before, for that matter. Killed his own partner—the man whose corpse Tim had found in the Nebraska woods, half-gnawed by coyotes. Murder is murder, regardless of the victim or the victimizer.

It does not reflect well on Tim that what saved Joel Kimball was not mercy but Kimball's own will to live.

"I—" Kimball said. Tim cut him short with a fist. Not on purpose, really; the fact was that he barely heard the man, and there was no time to stop the blow in the space of a syllable. Kimball gasped, and hurried to speak before Tim could strike him again. "I can tell you where it is," he said. "I can tell you—" And winced, because Tim's fist was coming toward him again. Hard and fast and . . . and Tim managed to stop himself this time. Stop himself and listen. "The old man's furniture. The contents of his home. Let me loose and I'll tell you where it is."

He was bleeding from the mouth. From the nose. And looked terrified as he stared Tim in the eye, but he looked him in the eye just the same. A sidelong glance at his companions, and Tim thought it was possible, just barely possible, that the sight of them scared him more than Tim himself. What would they do to him, Tim wondered, for telling? Even for the offer to tell?

"You've got to set me loose," he said. "You've got to."

Tim ignored that. "What do you know?"

Kimball licked a little of the blood away from his lips. "It's all in a warehouse near downtown Tampa. The Port of Tampa? Near the docks. In my shirt pocket there's a business card with the address. Heh. It's in storage under your own name."

Tim reached into the breast pocket of Kimball's shirt. Sure enough, a business card. For a self-storage warehouse at an address—Tim didn't recognize the address, but he wouldn't have expected to; he didn't know the Port of Tampa.

It's another of these damned tricks. Everything about these people is a trick. Everything. The only way around it was to do exactly what they didn't expect.

Right. And the moment Tim decided to do that they'd be there one step ahead of him, waiting for him to jump left when they said right. And he'd be had either way.

A deep breath. His heart was still racing, but now he could see, just for a moment, see the blood all over everything. The tree, Kimball, Tim's own hands. A little pool of it down there in the pine straw.

And he knew he had to get away before he grew angry again and killed someone.

He didn't hesitate a moment, but turned and left. Without looking back. But he didn't have to look back to hear Kimball calling after him, terrified, screaming to be free. . . .

Tim routed himself by the Zayre's on West Hillsborough, where he traded the run-down station wagon for his own car. While he was there he stopped inside, picked up a Tampa map—he had one at home, but he didn't want to go back for it. He was sure that the Bleeding Man and his people would be there waiting for him. He didn't want that confrontation—not right now.

With the map in hand, he found the warehouse easily enough. Out Hillsborough Avenue to I-275, south, then east on I-4 where the two met up in downtown. Off the interstate in Ybor City, and south on 22nd Street to the Port of Tampa. Right just before the bridge that went out to the middle of nowhere. (He'd driven that bridge once, and regretted it enormously. It was a long, long bridge across the northeasternmost arm of Tampa Bay, and on the other end of it was a long swamp-shouldered stretch of highway that led eventually to US 41, and then on to 301. None of which was anyplace Tim wanted to be.)

Half a mile along a potholed road that reeked of

phosphates, ammonia, and sulfur. And there the warehouse was: PORT OF TAMPA SELPH-STOR. Big big letters,
bright red on the pale-blue aluminum siding. Recognized it right away, *Selph-Stor* not being a name he
could easily forget.

The parking was real convenient, and not near as
badly paved as the road that led up to the lot. Tim put
the car right near the warehouse door, hopped out, went
inside. The clerk at the desk was friendly and helpful; he
took Tim's name, spent two minutes locating his paperwork and reading it against a map of the warehouse.

And then he nodded, and smiled. "This way," he
said. He led Tim five minutes through tidy dim corridors
lined with lockers and larger storage rooms.

And stopped at the sheet metal end of a long, sparse
hall. And unlocked the doors to four enormous storerooms. And smiled, and nodded, and left Tim to his
search.

The rooms were exactly as promised: Grandpa's
furniture—all his worldly goods—lay inside them. Everything but the Bible in Tim's back pocket.

Most of everything was boxed—main exceptions
being the largest pieces of furniture, which were
wrapped in plastic and hemp padding.

Tim looked quickly through each of the rooms.
Listened to his gut as he did, waiting to feel the tug that
would tell him he was in the presence of the Cross.

Nothing. Nothing. Nothing. Nothing.

Nothing in any of the rooms but furniture and books
and boxes of odd things like clothes and kitchen utensils.
Among them the rooms seemed to hold all the contents
of Grandpa's big old house. But the Cross was in none of
them, and Tim knew that even before he began to search
the boxes.

Systematically.

One by one, stack by stack, room by room.

It took hours and hours and hours, but Tim hardly
noticed the time. He was too obsessed, too wrapped up
in the act of searching through every possible nook and
crevice.

And when he was done, late late that evening, Tim had found exactly what he'd known he'd find: nothing.

Nothing at all.

They waited for him outside the warehouse. Not the same ones who'd found him last night, but others recognizably from the same source. A dozen of them this time: eight women, four men. Dressed in rough clothing like you'd expect to see folks wearing down near the docks: cheap advertisement T-shirts; ragged, work-stained denim trousers. Scruffy-looking people. Looked like they'd hardly had one bath among them in the last couple weeks.

The night clerk at the warehouse was staring at them nervously. He started to say something to Tim as he walked by, but hesitated, thought better of opening his mouth, and closed it.

Out beyond the chain-link fence that marked the edge of the parking lot, out there near the water, there were forty, maybe fifty men unloading a ship.

These people here—these folks the Bleeding Man had sent for him—wouldn't have the nerve to jump him in public. Not anyplace *this* public, anyhow; the long-shoremen were too many, and the clerk too near, watching too hard . . . if they had any sense at all they were going to follow him out of here. And wait till he was someplace alone. And Tim didn't want to think what they'd do after that.

For half a moment as he walked toward his car he thought that maybe they were even smarter than he expected them to be, that maybe there were two or even three of them hidden in there waiting for him. Waiting to hold a gun to his head and give him careful clear directions to some abandoned place. And he looked into the car closely and thoroughly. Made certain as he could that no one waited for him inside it.

And no one did.

So Tim climbed in quickly, got the engine running, got the car in gear as fast as he could. Hoping that moving directly enough would get him out of there and

oo far away to follow before any of the lurkers could
atch him. It wasn't any use, of course. He wasn't thirty
eet away from the parking lot before he looked into his
nirror and saw the first of their four cars pull out,
ccelerate to catch him.

No use.

No use at all.

If he was going to lose them, he'd need to be a damn
ight trickier than that.

And thought.

And thought some more, all the while driving
gently, aimlessly except to be certain he kept to popu-
ated places.

North of here, in the projects north of Ybor City,
vere some of the nastiest little streets he'd ever come
cross: twisty little things so narrow there was barely
oom for a wide car, and forget about trying to get a truck
n there because there were these sheer high concrete
urbs, just high enough so that if you rode into them
vrong they'd jam into the place where car tires meet
heir rims. Oh, it wouldn't happen at any reasonable
peed. Those curbs were made like that on purpose,
nade to keep people driving slowly around there with so
nany children running around the place. But if you ran
nto one of those curbs going even as fast as thirty miles
n hour . . . *whoosh!* (or *bang!*, depending how you
it), your wheels'd fall right out from under you. And
here you'd be, one, two, maybe three or four flat tires
roken down in a place where the teenagers would skin
ou alive as soon as look at you. Especially if they saw
ou not in a position to look after yourself.

It was possible, Tim thought, just barely possible he
ould lose these people in there.

Heh.

If he was lucky enough not to get himself stuck. If
ven one of them got stuck, the ones behind it would be
tuck too. If everything went just right he could lose 'em
ll.

Heh.

Fat chance of that.

More likely he'd get himself stuck, and then the lot

of them would be stranded at night in the middle of hell

Considered that for a while, and decided there were worse hells in this life than that one, and that getting stuck there might not be such a bad thing.

And on the other hand it might be worst of all.

Well, hell, Tim thought. And bore north, which was a left turn from here.

Three short blocks later he was at 26th Street and Adamo Drive, and the traffic going by on Adamo was steady and too damned fast. And the traffic light was out of service for the evening.

No way he was going to get across—not without all the luck in the world.

He could turn right. Break in the traffic in the near lane right now, right here—no, too late. That space was gone already.

There were four cars of men and women stacked up behind him. Waiting patiently . . . or maybe not that patiently. Any moment now, Tim thought, there'd be a tap at his window, a hand reaching to open his door and pry him from his seat—no. Too many people here—surely they'd wait till they had him someplace dark and deserted. Still, he shuddered, reached for the door lock to press it home. It was already engaged; the locks on this car caught automatically any time the speedometer went over fifteen miles an hour.

Another opening, a little one. Enough to jump in, but not enough to jump in safely. Tim took his chance while he still could—and made it. Just barely. Not gracefully; two or three car-horns blared at him. Brakes squealed somewhere behind him, and maybe that was on account of him and maybe it wasn't.

His pursuers weren't as lucky. Tim caught sight of them in his rear-view mirror, watched as the first of them bolted out of 26th Street to follow him without checking to be certain there was room. Which was a very bad idea, being as Tim had left no margin for error behind him. *Sqeee-blaaam!*, and the first car was a hood ornament for a semi-trailer. The follower behind him piled into the rear end of the first one—didn't do as much damage as the first collision, but it put that car out of commission all right.

That left two cars to follow him. Number three hesitated, but the fourth honked and pulled around him, right into the flow of traffic.

That was when Tim lost sight of them. Not that they lost sight of him; he knew damn well that they hadn't. They were back there someplace among the headlights. Watching him. The fourth car, and probably the third—odds were the driver had gotten over his paralysis and managed to get onto Adamo behind the fourth car.

As soon as he turned, Tim was sure, he'd see a car turn to follow him. Two, maybe; and even a third was possible if car number two had managed to extract itself from that wreck in running condition. No way he was going to see four, though. He'd *seen* the front end of that first car slide under the tires of that semi.

And he needed to make that turn as soon as he could, too. He needed to be headed north. Adamo was more like a highway than it was a street. Here between the Port of Tampa and Ybor City there were half a dozen streets that crossed it, but if he didn't turn onto one of them real soon he'd be out in the middle of nowhere before there was a chance to turn around.

And that was the last thing he wanted.

He sidled across two lanes of traffic, pissing off several drivers. 28th Street, right here, and if he didn't turn here there was no telling where he'd be before he could turn north, because the road ahead was wide open and empty, no turns, nothing but factories on either side of the road—the turn he had to make was right here and he was moving too damn fast—and he screeched into the turn lane. And heard the sound of colliding cars behind him.

That brought him back to himself just long enough for a pang of conscience: what was he doing, driving so wildly as to cause car wrecks behind him? Tim had things to atone for, and he knew it. Bad things at least, and perhaps things that bordered on evil.

But that was all the time there was for regret, because the traffic in the westbound lane parted just long

enough for Tim to dart across, and once he was moving
once he was on 28th Street, he was moving so fast on
road so rough so potholed that there was no time to d
anything but concentrate on the pavement. If he blinke
for even as much as an instant at that speed Tim woul
have broken an axle. As it was he damn near broke on
anyhow, and more than once.

He'd gone three blocks before he realized what he'
gotten himself into.

The dark, that was what. The dark and alone. 28t
Street wasn't a through street at all, but an access roa
for mouldering dead factories, for night-empty truc
yards, for the railroad that ran parallel to Adamo tha
hardly saw four hours' use in a busy week. At seven a.m
when folks were coming to work here—Tim couldn'
imagine that there were many of them, or someone
would have repaved this road by now, but there'd be
few at least—at seven a.m. there'd be a few folks around
But now it was after ten at night, tired, tired in th
evening.

The last thing Tim wanted to be was alone with
these people following him. But here he was, in the dar
and alone and—

And 28th Street was deserted.

And there were three cars on the road behind him
three steady careful-driving sets of headlights drawing
close and closer now because 28th just dead-ended int
the railroad tracks.

Oh shit. Oh shit. He was done for. He knew it.

Or was he? There—on the left. A road. A road with
even less surface than this one had, like a dirt road
almost, with traces that showed that someone had pave
it once. But it was a road, and it looked like it wen
through to something. . . .   There, there in the dis
tance. Streetlights. It did go through. Or maybe it di
sometimes in this city roads this poor were deliberately
blocked off, with iron posts or oil drums filled with
cement or even once he'd seen a road netted off with
chain-link fence.

No way to tell from here. But what choice did he
have, except to find out? It was either forward into the

dark or back into those headlights. No, he couldn't turn around—they couldn't be stupid enough to let him through. Couldn't be, not even if one of them had been stupid enough to jump into the path of that semi. All they'd have to do was line their cars up to block him off. Even if they were stupid enough to do it, Tim couldn't depend on them to be that stupid. Or wouldn't, anyway, so long as he had a choice.

Eased the car back into gear. Turned; let the car pick up a little velocity when it became clear that this road was a little smoother than 28th Street. What with all the pavement gone, there was nothing but sand and a little of the clay that had once been the road's underpinnings. If it'd been potholed once upon a time, years of rain had worn it irregularly smooth.

Ka-blam! A gun or a backfire or one of those fools had just broke an axle. Did they want to kill him?

(The question sent Tim's mind off on a tangent: He didn't *think* they wanted to kill him. He thought . . . thought that they just wanted to drive him out of his mind. Or maybe they were trying to find the Cross before he did. When he thought about it, he wasn't sure. Wasn't even sure that either one was what motivated them. It was like playing chess with someone who knew what he was doing when Tim hardly knew the game himself. Like everything he did was just a whole new way to play into the Bleeding Man's hands.

(The idea made him dizzy. He thought that what he needed to do was go someplace and hide, and relax, and let himself get quiet inside. But it was possible that even doing that was a way to let the Bleeding Man back him into a corner.)

No more loud noises. And if that was the sound of a gun, wouldn't there have been another shot by now? Backfire from an engine, well, it happened often enough in dirt-poor neighborhoods like this one. But not often enough to allow for the coincidence that it was right here, right now. Tim looked up, checked the rearview— and sure enough, there were only two sets of headlights bouncing along behind him. Another, pointing askew, far behind those. It didn't look like that car was moving, but there was no way to be sure in the moment he had to steal looking back, and even that one moment was too much, because when Tim looked back at the road he was in deep shit all over again, and there was barely time to hit the brakes, much less turn back to avoid the concrete-and-iron fence that rushed toward him.

Nasty-looking fence, too. Chipped, weathered old concrete; crude rusted iron bars strung between the cement posts—the iron looked like the same stuff they use to reinforce concrete pillars. Industrial-grade stuff. Not anything you want to meet up with at fifty miles an hour on a washed-out road.

No sir.

Tim braked and turned simultaneously, and the car began to spin out before it swung up off the road toward the railroad tracks, through the gravel railroad bed, and if he hadn't been real, real lucky—luckier than anyone ever deserved to be—the car would've broken in two when he slammed into the tracks. But the way it happened the tracks didn't do any special harm. Tim hit them in the apex of his spin, front tires first, and they went up and over the near rail, diverting the energy of his momentum, throwing the whole damn car into the air and up, up, up over the tracks. And down again on the other side with all its angular momentum shifted back to forward velocity of about thirty miles an hour.

Tim thanked God for luck, and thanked Him again for automatic seat belts, because if he hadn't had his on he surely would've broken his neck whomping around inside that car.

Not that he had any such trouble; he was on the far side of the railroad bed, easing to a stop, getting ready to turn right on 27th Street. Both of the cars behind him were stuck on the railroad tracks. One of them—the one farther back—looked as though it might eventually work its way free. Eventually. With a lot of push from behind.

Tim'd be long gone by then.

Turned right.

And went on up through Ybor City, up and over dark 27th Street to bright-lit Broadway. Over that to 22nd; and up to I-4.

Where he remembered that he'd left half a dozen men tied to trees in the middle of nowhere. And felt his heart sink through his stomach. How long ago? Twelve hours? Sixteen? He was calmer now than he had been early-early in the morning, and had his conscience back. And when he thought back, remembered everything he'd done and even worse the things he'd nearly done and but for God's Grace would have committed—

He drove a hell of a lot faster than he ought to've. Fast, nearly, as he had last Sunday morning when he'd rushed to Grandpa's to find the Cross. And found nothing.

And maybe, just maybe, the hurry now was more important than the other had been. The Cross was important, and its Stewardship was important. But nothing on this earth, Tim thought as he sped north, nothing on this earth is so important that it weighs against a mortal sin.

And surely what he'd done to those men deep in the woods—surely that was a mortal sin.

A mortal sin.

When Tim thought about it, there were more mortal sins than one behind him these last days.

Many more than one.

The needle on the gas gauge hovered just above the empty mark. How had he let it get so low?—and remembered that the last time he'd bought gas was on the road in north Florida, heading home. Which meant it was a miracle that he hadn't run out of gas already. (Imagined himself running out of gas in the dark place south of the railroad tracks south of Ybor City. And he almost screamed.)

An exit up ahead; Bearss Avenue. How in the hell had he gotten this far this fast? He glanced at his watch, saw it'd been a good half hour since he'd pulled out onto 27th Street. It wasn't that he'd covered the distance quickly, but rather that he was so absorbed in guilt that he'd lost the time.

And knew that guilt was a thing to feel stupid about too.

Pulled off onto Bearss, where the ALL-NIGHT HAN-DEE-

MART waited for him with its cheery orange/yellow/fluorescent green plastic sign all aglow. Tim parked the car beside the self-serve gas pumps, went inside to leave a twenty with the clerk. (Who smiled at him nervously, uneasy because it was late already late at night, and convenience stores are dangerous places for clerks alone late late at night.) Back to the car, where he spent five minutes filling the tank with low-grade gas, then back inside for his change. (Where the clerk looked half relieved that Tim was going away and half terrified that now he'd be alone.) Then out to the car again, and back on the road—

Only before he could get the car in gear, after he'd started the engine, there was a hand on his arm that rested on the rolled-down driver's-side window, and before he looked up—just by touch—Tim knew that that hand meant him to stop.

Meant it *hard*.

Meant it *serious*.

Meant it like Tim didn't dare ignore.

He looked up and saw the Bleeding Man standing beside him.

"The time has come, little fish," the Bleeding Man said, "to reel you in."

No clue anywhere in sight as to how he'd gotten there. No cars but Tim's own and the clerk's beat-up old Escort that'd been there since Tim pulled into the lot. No other cars anywhere, anywhere in sight—none out on Bearss; none even up on the highway overpass.

"No," Tim said. He wanted to scream. He thought that he might at any moment if the Bleeding Man didn't let go of him. But he didn't let go. Didn't speak for a while, either—just stood there in the parking lot, holding Tim's forearm authoritatively. Staring at him. And what was Tim to do? He couldn't scream because his throat was jammed. So he looked up, looked the Bleeding Man in the eye. Saw the blood that leaked steadily from his eyes mingling with beads of night-sweat so easy in the humid Florida air. Saw him staring at Tim with eyes that seemed to—seemed to, hell; they did penetrate his *self*. Tim knew the violation. He understood it

with his heart, just as he understood any true violation of
his soul. . . .

The Bleeding Man laughed at him.

Laughed and laughed and laughed.

"You don't frighten me," Tim told him.

It was a lie.

The Bleeding Man stopped laughing. And he
looked at Tim real close.

And then he smiled.

"You think you're brave, don't you, little man? You
amuse me. Sincerely, you amuse me." He paused, and
Tim could see him thinking, weighing words against
what he could see. It made him uncomfortable, but not
anywhere near as uncomfortable as that other thing he
saw, looking at the Bleeding Man.

"You only think you've got me," Tim said. "You
don't frighten me alone."

Saw a face he recognized. Oh, not recognized
precisely; more it was the recognition of a family resemblance.

The Bleeding Man looked like Grandpa. Looked
like Tim, for that matter; there was a peculiar something
in their features that marked all three of them. Tim
couldn't help but recognize it; he'd seen it in the mirror
all his life.

"Little man, there is nothing you have done in these
last days that I have not seen and known from its
inception. I know where you are, and what you are, and
what you do to its least iteration; and the day will come
soon now when I control those things even as I know
them. And you know this, because you hear my voice.
You will not run. If you did I would have you in a
moment. You will abide me."

That was *supposed* to frighten him, Tim thought.
Maybe some other time it would have, but here and now
it was nothing beside the shock and self-loathing that
came from recognition. Tim looked away from the
Bleeding Man. Let those piercing eyes watch him
without worrying what they might find. And a sudden
impulse found him, and Tim threw the car in gear,
stepped on the gas.

To get himself the hell out of there.

The Bleeding Man still held him by the arm. And he wasn't letting go. Tim would've expected the force of the car's forward surge to drag the Bleeding Man along, the way he gripped Tim. But no; the Bleeding Man stood planted on that ground firm as though he were a tree. It wasn't him that pulled to stretch, but Tim—for a long moment the grip and the car yanked his arm back, back off its perch and out the window, and Tim imagined his arm as a wishbone tine, and the rest of him was the other, and in just a moment his shoulder would split at one side of its socket or the other, and if he didn't make a wish by then it'd all be for nothing—

Then something gave, not the shoulder socket or the arm or even its skin, though nearly that, what came loose was the hair of his forearm, all of it, all of it, coming free big and bloody by the roots, and then he was free no matter how bad he hurt.

A moment later he was back on 275 and driving fast as though his life depended on it.

Which it did.

Till he was away from the highway he was findable. He couldn't relax until he was way up in Lutz and off the highway. Far, far from the highway; this time of night there was so little traffic going north on 275 that every car was findable, none of them anonymous. But once he got away from it he had to be safe, didn't he? Weren't the narrow, winding roads up here as scattered and anonymous as anyplace could be? Weren't they?

Tim hoped they were.

It was a lie, what the Bleeding Man said about knowing everywhere he went, everything he did. It had to be.

He tried to tell himself that he was safe and that the roads were anonymous, but even as he did Tim drove fast and frightened to that empty place deep deep in the woods.

The place where he'd left six men tied to trees.

Drove dangerously fast: even when the roads turned to sifting, overgrown sand he didn't slow as he ought to've. Three times he hit deep ruts and had reason to regret his speed, but that didn't slow him either. Maybe it should've; maybe it was just as well that it did not. Because when he got to the knoll where he'd left the men tied, he found only one of them still tied where Tim had put him.

That was a bad bad thing.

Because the one who was left was the leader of that pack; Joel Kimball, who Tim had met in Running Board, Nebraska. Kimball who Tim had beaten half-senseless; who Tim might've beaten to death if things had happened just a little differently.

Kimball who had told Tim where to find Grandpa's belongings.

There wasn't much left of him when Tim pulled up. Not much but blood and bone and skin: Tim saw the carnage clearly despite the darkness, because he left the car running, left his headlights shining on the tree where Kimball was tied.

Bad bad bad. Very bad, and not pretty at all.

The rest of them were long gone. Of course they were. They'd beaten Kimball, beaten him, and beaten him some more. And then they'd left him here to die alone. Kimball mumbled this and other details as Tim untied him. Carried him back to the car, stretched him across the back seat. How the man could talk all broken like he was Tim couldn't even begin to guess. But he did talk; volunteered all sorts of secrets, in fact. Told Tim precious dangerous things about the Bleeding Man as they drove out through Lutz toward University Community Hospital.

Told him things like how the Bleeding Man could see him, and how he could hide. And how the Bleeding Man didn't have the Cross but planned on using Tim to get it. *Needed* Tim to get it? *Needed* him? Was he really saying that? Yes, he was, he really was.

He spoke all the while Tim drove. Down 275. All the way out Fletcher. Or nearly so. Somewhere around 22nd Street he grew quiet, and Tim thought maybe that was just as well, just as well since it meant he would rest, reserve his strength to get him to the emergency room. . . . And then just after 30th Street, just as he pulled into the emergency-room access drive, there was a sound.

Not talking this time.

A sound like something very very horrible.

Like the sound of a rattlesnake, but long and low and deep like it made a reverberation in the back of his skull, and then there was a horrible horrible stench sulfur everywhere pervasive enveloping cloying clawing down his throat, and before Tim looked back to see he knew that it was too late for the hospital.

The sight of Kimball crumbling crumbling crumbling to dust.

Awful. Flesh flaking away bloodlessly easy as though it were ash but no burning not burned at all more like dry rot taken to its ultimate possibility awful awful already catching in the wind that rushed in through the front window and the ash dust not-ash filled the air to breathe and Tim opened his window wide to suck fresh breath that didn't reek of ancient age-old corpse which only made it worse worse worse.

More wind now. More dust as he pulled away from the hospital, out onto Fletcher again.

A man was dead.

The reason he was dead was because Tim had left him bound and frightened too close to those who meant him harm early this morning. Oh, there were ways Tim could have ducked away from the responsibility for death: it wasn't him who tore Joel Kimball to shreds. He'd hurt the man this morning—but hadn't he stopped before he made a killing blow? And tonight, when he'd found Kimball three-quarters dead in the woods, hadn't he tried to save him? And didn't that make amends for anything he'd done before?

Like hell it did. The good he did was all well and fine, and given who he was good was a thing that obligated him. But the only thing that makes amends for an act is the thing that negates it, and there was nothing Tim could do to negate the man's death. No matter that he'd tried; consequence was on his shoulders because he'd failed to save the man.

Consequence.

He turned right on Nebraska, which was a block and a half before 275. Nebraska Avenue was also US 41, which didn't matter much so long as you were kicking around in Tampa, but up here on the north edge of town it made a difference because 41 went on up into forever, way the hell up into the Upper Peninsula of Michigan, his Dad had told him once. (Dad had gone to college at Michigan State, way the hell north in the middle of nowhere. Tim had never rightly understood why.) Turning onto Nebraska here and now meant that he could drive and drive and then drive some more, and he'd never have to look back or turn or decide where it was he wanted to go next.

That was good, Tim thought. He shifted into the left lane. Farther up 41 would be a two-lane road. But this lane, the center lane, this would be here. He could drive this lane forever.

And tried to.

As the wind whipped through the car, stirring the dust that once was Joel Kimball into the air, into everything. Out the window, most of it. Except what pressed itself into the upholstery, Tim's clothes, Tim's skin. Even his lungs—he couldn't help from breathing the dust. Not without a gas mask. Too fine; too omnipresent.

A *million miles*, he thought. *I could drive a million miles*. It probably wasn't so. He was only up at the Apex, now—up where Florida Avenue merged with Nebraska—he'd hardly gone any distance to speak of and already his eyes were burning itching tearing up from the dust. Caustic stuff. Unpleasant. He blinked it away. Emptied his mind. Stared at the road rolling through his heart.

When he'd gone a long time—maybe that meant an hour; maybe it only meant fifteen minutes—Tim saw a red-neck middle-of-nowhere bar on the roadside, a nasty crowded noisy-looking place with a big violet neon sign that said HELLHOLE, which was its name and its nature, too, and looking at the HELLHOLE Tim knew he had to go inside and get himself a drink.

Maybe more drinks than that, now that he thought about it.

So he went into the bar, and he ordered Maker's Mark straight up. Which wasn't what he wanted or what his mood demanded, but how could he go into a place like this and not drink Maker's Mark? That was a question, all right. Question enough to keep his mind busy all through his first three drinks, and after that he didn't have much mind to worry about, and that was okay.

Okay, hell. Fact was it was pretty fine.

He lost count of the drinks, but there were at least four more before he started choking on his own lungs.

Trying to cough up all the dust he'd breathed as he drove north. His lungs weren't *really* ready to clear themselves, of course—more like they wanted to hack and hack and cough themselves into bits of dry-hack blood.

It was time to get himself some air. Air as in outside and way the hell away from the drooling red-neck over there five seats down who was smoking that drooly half-chewed cigar. Only he wasn't done drinking yet, and that was quite a problem, because the bouncer looked pretty fierce and Tim suspected he wouldn't let him out with a bar glass.

Hell, he thought, *I don't need the glass. Just get the pretty bartender to give me one of them go-cups.* The bartender wasn't nearly so pretty as all that, of course. But in the dark here in the HELLHOLE and under the weight of half a fifth of Maker's Mark she looked a lot prettier than was natural.

While he was getting the go cup, he had her give him a double to go, too, not really planning to drink it 'cause he'd already had so much too much. But maybe maybe he'd feel a yen for that drink a little later, and if he did he had to have it handy tonight because of what he wasn't thinking about.

Toward the back door—only stumbling a little as he walked toward it—where the bouncer looked him up and down real careful, almost like he wasn't going to let Tim out with his drinks in hand.

"You ain't going to drive nowhere with that," the bouncer said. Tim could barely hear him through the noise and alcohol.

"Just going to sit in the car,"—Not *exactly* true, but not really a lie either.

Then the tall muscley man stepped aside, to let Tim by. . . .

Outside. Tepid Florida night air that felt cool and warm both at once. Warm enough to bring up a sweat the moment you moved, but so dense, so moist that it drew Tim's warmth away the moment he stood still. *Screw the air*, Tim thought. He was too drunk to care about the temperature, too drunk to feel discomfort. Or to care about it if he felt it. He stumbled toward his car—and then thought no, no, not the car, not with all that dust. Sitting in that car the way it was now, that was just too much.

So where to go?

The parking lot, here? No. If he sat down here one of the drunks would run him down as he drove away. If the bouncers didn't find him first and do worse. He could lean against the side of the building—but with the urine stains deep into the stucco that was even uglier and more unappealing than the parking lot.

Out beyond the parking lot there were woods. Partly jungle, partly pine. Those woods were probably the last place on earth he ought to go. Look at them— swampy, sulfury. The rot was so intense Tim could feel it from here. If he went in there he'd come out with welts he'd regret for days.

Tim lifted the tall tumbler of whiskey to his mouth. Took a long pull. Let the fiery liquid trickle burning down the soft flesh of his throat.

If he went into the woods, no one would bother him. No one would even notice him.

And what were bug bites? What were welts? Nothing at all, that's what: he was going to be so hung over tomorrow that welts and stings would all be so much background noise.

To hell with it, he thought. And stumbled in through the underbrush and the swamp muck and the

thick roots that wound around his ankles and three times
tried to trip him, send him flying headfirst into the dark
and soft-wet—

But no, he didn't fall, he only tripped, and each
time managed to catch himself and save himself from
falling. And in a moment he'd found a high, dry spot, in
among the roots of a live oak. Where he sat, and rested
his head and back against the tree trunk.

Something under the left cheek of his rump—Tim
reached back, felt around trying to figure out what the
problem was . . . a book.

Grandpa's Bible.

He'd taken it from the seat of the run-down station
wagon two nights ago—and then he'd forgotten about it
completely.

He opened the book. Turned on an intuition to the
end papers.

It was there, just as he'd expected.

Another note from Grandpa.

He read it by the light of the moon. It said:

> *Tim, remember that when you've done a
> thing you regret God does forgive you. He
> loves you. He loves us all.*
>
> *The hard part is remembering to forgive
> yourself.*
>
> *Remember most of all that you have to do
> it. Because if you can't forgive yourself, and if
> you can't love yourself, you can't love anyone
> or anything, not even God Himself.*

And Tim read it, and he knew that Grandpa was
right, and he knew that Grandpa saw this moment
exactly as it was from years and years away, and wrote
that note to try to save Tim from himself.

But even knowing all those things wasn't enough to
save Tim from self-loathing.

And looked up, and stared and stared and stared at
the moon.

The moon.

It was trying to tell him something, wasn't it?

Another long drink of whiskey. And he listened very hard. If he listened hard enough, he thought, the moon would explain things to him. Tell him how he'd come to be here, and why, and explain the way his nightmare was just a part of Our Lord's Great True Design. And maybe it would tell him how to forgive himself for everything he'd done.

But hard as he watched and listened and waited for that great white moon to speak to him, it said nothing.

Or did it? There were no words—not a single solitary one—but as Tim waited willing for command and enlightenment, it occurred to him that there was a good and obvious and sufficient reason why he hadn't found the Cross.

Because he wasn't meant to be the Steward.

Because he wasn't worthy, and underneath duty and commitment wasn't even honestly willing. He was a murderer; a thief; a bully. There was nothing in him that warranted trust, and least of all a sacred trust as dear and holy as the Cross.

And just like that, almost on cue, he blacked out. Drunk, alone, in the woods in the middle of nowhere, his eyes drooped shut while his head rocked prone pointing at the sky.

And woke hung over and still half-drunk early in the morning when the sun got high enough to burn his skin. And he woke knowing he had to give up the quest for the Cross, run as far from it and his life as he could. He wasn't sure he could; the Stewardship was born to him, and the quest came so natural as to be unbidden. But he swore to himself that if he could turn away and run and never look back, that was what he'd do.

He stumbled out of the woods, into his car. And started it despite the fact that he knew he was still too drunk to drive

And drove north into forever.

FOUR

Jill got pregnant in August, just before the start of Tim's senior year in college. Tim turned twenty-two that year. He was due to graduate at the end of the spring term.

It was an awful time to have a child. Tim wasn't half done with being a kid himself yet, and here he was about to be a daddy. Oh, there was abortion, sure. But while Tim wasn't any too certain how he felt about abortion for other folks, he knew for sure that he couldn't see it for any kid of his. No damn way!

Jill, thank the Lord, was inclined to agree with him. And all through September, October, and November Tim and Jill talked babies and plans and even marriage. Which was a pretty extreme step; they'd moved in together back in April, and there were certainly great things about the relationship. But Jill had a wicked, wicked temper, and Tim had realized a long time ago that the relationship wasn't one that could last a lifetime. Too unstable; there were just too damn many opportunities for spontaneous combustion.

But with the baby to worry after Tim knew he couldn't let himself give in to that unease. The baby needed parents. *Would* need parents. Not just a mom, not just a dad, but two-count-'em-two parents. And Tim knew that he'd be there for his daughter (yes, she was a daughter—Tim knew that sometime in early November. Just knew it) knew he'd be there for his daughter no matter what it took to be certain that he could. How could he possibly do anything else?

Besides, that fall waiting for the birth of his first

child there were no special burdens. Jill—always so
eager to pick a fight—was sleepy and sweet-tempered.
School was easy, undemanding; and there were days
when he was sure that he could feel his child growing in
Jill's womb.

It was a good year, and more than that: wondrous
and special and illuminating. Every day brought Tim
some new and special thing, and it seemed to him that
life had taken on some new aspect more important and
fulfilling than anything he'd ever seen or imagined.

And maybe it had. Maybe it's true that God makes
men and women first and foremost to rear and love the
succeeding generations. Maybe it's true that God forges
no greater love than has a parent for a child.

If you had asked Tim that December he would have
told you it was so. (Later he would have looked at you all
broken and confused. And with good reason.)

They went to the Baby Store on the weekend before
Christmas, and they went absolutely ape. The Baby
Store was all the way over in St. Pete, but it was *the*
place to shop for baby stuff. Damn near as big as a
K-Mart. Low prices—well, not that low. A little above
ON SALE! prices the way they'd be anywhere else—but
the thing about ON SALE! the way it works most places is
that some stuff is marked down cheap cheap cheap and
everything else is priced right up there through the roof.
The Baby Store wasn't like that; everything they sold was
at a considerable discount.

And they had everything. Literally everything Tim
could imagine. And a lot of stuff he'd never thought of. It
didn't matter. They bought that stuff, too. Bought and
bought and bought. Spent so much that Tim knew that
when he got to the register he'd actually make a serious
dent in the money he'd made last summer selling
encyclopedias. (Which was a considerable amount. Tim
had a gift for sales, and the Britannica was a product he
believed in. It hadn't been hard at all to make a lot of
money selling it.)

Besides, everywhere Tim had gone to shop for baby

stuff in Tampa he'd found the prices not just high but outrageous. As though the merchants thought their customers too smitten with their children to worry what they paid. And there was something about that particular gouge he found offensive.

So they went to the Baby Store in St. Pete, and they parked four blocks away in a pay-by-the-hour lot because all the nearby parking was full to capacity, and Jill muttered about the pain in her legs all the way to the store.

But her grumbling came to a stop the moment they passed through the door. Jill loved to shop, and she loved shopping on Tim's money even better. Went right to town, she did.

To be fair, Tim went right with her. And with some of the paraphernalia he ran out ahead: it was his idea, not hers, that they buy two of every single type of bottle the store had in stock. After all, he said, how would they know which kind they liked best if they didn't try them all? And once they found what they liked, they'd need more than one, wouldn't they?

Jill rolled her eyes toward the ceiling, shook her head, and laughed. She didn't care, really, one way or the other; she wasn't interested in the small stuff. She had her eye on that row of cribs over there, and he knew she wanted a changing table, and one of those fancy Inglesina strollers, and a bassinet, and wouldn't the baby need a dresser?

And a swing, of course. They'd have to have a swing. One of the battery-operated models that would run for hours at the flip of a switch to keep their child mesmerized and silent.

Tim didn't mean to be uneasy about spending that much money. He really didn't. Buying clothes and furniture and etcetera for their daughter was necessary, and since Jill barely had the money to pay her own tuition the burden fell on Tim. Had to. Where else was it to go? And it wasn't like he couldn't go make more money if he wanted it. Or borrow from Dad or Grandpa—they both had money to spare.

And still it hurt him some. Not because he couldn't

afford it, or because the spending was burdensome; but because she made such a show of *shopping!* on his dime that he felt—used. Dehumanized. Like: wasn't the person he married, or lived with, or whatever it was you wanted to call it—wasn't that person supposed to be a partner? And where was her part?

Well, she was the one having the baby. That was God's Own Truth. Already at five months her body had stretched and wrenched itself in ways that made him ache to see. Oh, a stranger might look right at her and not realize Jill was pregnant. But Tim knew her, and even if he'd been barely an acquaintance he had a careful eye. He could see how the major organs in her body engorged, enlarged themselves to cope with the doubled need. Could see the great muscles that made her abdominal wall bulked and distended to carry the new and coming weight. He tried to imagine her body stretched to term, and the image unnerved him.

Tim worried for Jill a lot.

He worried for the baby a lot more.

Lord but he worried for that baby.

Like now. Jill was hurrying along the aisle toward a big display of playpens. Playpens? Couldn't a playpen wait till they had a little better idea—well, an idea what the baby was like? Didn't different babies need different sorts of things? No, no, Jill said; a playpen is absolutely necessary. Every baby has to have a playpen, even if she hardly ever uses it.

"And here," she went on, "here, look at this. Read all about it. Now *that's* a playpen, isn't it?"

Tim was about to say, *How can I tell when you're standing in front of the label?* when she bent down, as though to point at the writing on the side of the box—but no, no, that's not what she did.

Oh Lord.

She reached down and heaved the box up to eye level.

What was she trying to do, break her back? The doctor had warned both of them that Jill shouldn't do any heavy lifting till long after the baby had come. Said it with a Very Serious Warning in her voice. Something

bout Jill's back, and how it was already stressed too
ar. . . .

"It's okay, Jill," Tim said. "We can get it if you
vant." And he stepped forward, reached to take the box
rom her—

Too late.

Too damned late. Tim watched horrified eighteen
nches away as Jill's expression changed, as she—
ouckled, that was what it looked like. Like a girder
tressed too far collapsing under its burden. He tried to
catch her as she fell, but that damnable playpen was in
he way, now in his arms, and now when he tried to
eave it away he almost hit her with it.

Oh damn damn damn.

And now it was no use anyway because while Tim
ried to figure out what he was supposed to do with the
ooxed playpen at such close quarters, Jill was falling—
not toward him but away onto her back into the
lisplay—

Which wasn't as stable as it really ought to have
oeen—

—and the whole world came crashing down around
heir ears.

No, not the whole world. Just that damned playpen
lisplay, stacked nearly all the way to the top of the
varehouse-high ceiling. Thud and slide and *thwap!*, that
ast some spring-loaded part of something or other
oursting loose and smacking Tim upside the ear.

Which gave him a moment clearing his head. When
t finished the crashing was over and he was half-buried
n baby stuff and there were people rushing toward them
asking if they were all right, but there was no time to
answer them because he had to find Jill to make certain
he was okay, make certain the baby was all right—

—pushing, pushing away boxes and bright padded
cloth-webbed metal frames piled till they were nothing
out debris—

And found her.

And screamed.

He shouldn't have screamed like that. Shouldn't

ever have done it; no one else could possibly know wha he knew looking at her.

Because Jill looked pretty fine.

Oh, she was shaken, and bruised, and much the worse for wear. But look how she pushed the boxes awa from her, how she got to her feet and only winced a little as she did it. No one here would know could know—

They needed an ambulance. They needed an am bulance right now right now right *now*, because if they didn't get to the hospital right away their baby was going to die.

She was. She really was.

"Somebody call a doctor," Tim shouted. If he kicked aside the boxes in front of him, pushed aside the ones that surrounded Jill, lifted her, carried her out the door and screamed till someone brought up an ambulance—i he did that someone would probably try to have him committed.

He knew that.

"It's all right, Tim. I'm okay. Really."

Tim could feel his mouth hang open, could feel his tongue groping in the air for words to respond with. Felt his throat choke shut because there were none, nor could he see any possibility of them.

How could he say that he knew she was wrong? She was her own master. Her body was her own.

"I'm afraid," he said. Tried to say it; what came out was more like a hoarse whisper. "The baby—"

She looked at him impatiently. "It's fine," she said "We'll both be fine."

Right there, right then: something in Tim began to die.

Later he wound the moment back a thousand times trying to find the right thing he should've done. Was it really true that nothing he could've done would have made any difference at all? It may be so. To this day Tim has found no alternative that would have saved his daughter's life. Not medicine; for what doctor in that day could mend the crushed and broken back of a fetus so far from term? Or mend any back at all? There are times he thinks he should have knelt and prayed that the Lord bring down a miracle upon her—but at sober moments he knows that would have been pointless. The Lord Our God does not bring evil down upon us, and if He did no supplication would dissuade Him—for those few times He reaches in to touch the affairs of men are dire indeed, and if His acts pain us it is only to our greater good.

What Tim did do was say, "Trust me, Jill. Please. Call me crazy if you want, but go along: we need to see a doctor right away."

And he said it with such certainty, such assurance that he knew she couldn't deny him.

The baby wasn't dying quickly. Just the opposite—slow, slow; Tim could feel her life leak away so gradually that he knew that there were hours yet left to her.

"All right," she said, "I will if it'll let you relax. But no ambulance. I don't want that much fuss."

Which was a pretty silly thing to say when you considered that the entire store was staring at them. They already had all the fuss and attention they could possibly attract.

That was what Tim wanted to think, anyhow.

Jill was picking her way through the boxes, working her way toward the clear part of the aisle. Once she slipped—predictably, since she was in heels—and Tim nearly had a heart attack before he managed to catch her and keep her from falling all over again.

Out in the clear.

Down the aisle, toward the door. (The store manager stood all but in their way, looking as though he wanted to talk to Tim about the damaged merchandise. Feh. Tim glared at him and just kept walking.)

Out to the sidewalk, where Tim turned to Jill to tell her to wait while he went for the car—

—and saw her doubled over in agony.

No, no, please God no let me try to save her let me try try try—

"Jill—!"

She looked up at him angrily. "Just go get the car, damn it."

And Tim left. Ran. Didn't even bother checking the traffic at any of the four intersections he had to cross.

Which was pretty damn stupid since it nearly got him run over a couple-three times.

Found the car in its lot. Unlocked it, started the engine, pulled out of the lot without pausing even a moment to warm the engine—tore rubber and screeched into the street recklessly and screw these assholes with their horns and their curses and the tractor-trailer that nearly ran him down.

Screw them all.

Ran two red lights—half he hoped he'd get a police car trying to pull him over for the offense, since a police escort might get him to the hospital a moment sooner. But no, all he got from running those lights was damn near into a wreck (again). Oh, and he got half a dozen people mad at him, too—but fuck them all anyway. If they didn't want to get out of his way he'd damn well move them out of it.

Finally, finally at the curb out front of the Baby Store. Took long enough! And there Jill was doubled up on the ground with people crowded all around her, and Tim could see the blood already seeping through her panties through her dress. And when he lifted her up off the sidewalk and set her on the back seat, half a dozen of those fools protested and told him how there was an ambulance coming and he hadn't ought to move her. He didn't even look at them—sure as shit didn't answer. Only set Jill down, and closed the rear door, and grabbed the arm of the nearest little old lady.

"You can tell me how to get to the nearest hospital?" He didn't wait for her to answer; he could see how she was about to give him directions. "No, get in. You can point me there. I got no time to take directions." As he said that he opened the front passenger door, scooted the little old lady into the seat. She didn't protest too much. "I'm much obliged to you, ma'am."

Ten blocks, no more. And they hit every light exactly right. A miracle for sure. Even still the time it took to get there felt like about half a million years, what with Jill groaning as she hemorrhaged in the back, and deep inside her the tiny tiny baby scared witless as she struggled for to keep her hold on life.

She was going to die, Tim thought. Doctors don't do emergency surgery on five-month fetuses. No matter how much their fathers love them.

He parked the car at the lobby entrance to the hospital's emergency room, lifted Jill out of the back seat, carried her inside. Maybe he left the engine running. Almost certainly he left the keys in the ignition. And he sure didn't think to thank the old woman who'd directed him to the hospital. (Later he wondered how she got back home, and he felt very bad about forgetting her.)

Through the electric doors too fast—Jill's left leg smacked ungently into the door on his right. Tim hardly noticed. He was too preoccupied; too intent on the nurse on the far side of the reception desk.

"She's pregnant," Tim said, "she's hemorrhaged." He didn't know what hemorrhage was, except that it had something to do with internal bleeding—maybe it was when a big blood vessel burst? But the nurse saw the blood, and she saw how Jill's skin was all pale and bluish, and people back there started moving loud and fast. Someone shouted something or other about a code—sixteen? seventeen?—Tim didn't hear too clearly, upset as he was.

An orderly wheeled a rolling cot out into the lobby, took her from Tim's arms, turned to push back into the medical area. Tim grabbed his arm before he could go more than a few steps.

"Save her," Tim said. "Save my baby."

The orderly looked away.

"The doctors will do what they can," he said. He sounded frightened. And something else in his voice, too—what? He knew something. Or suspected it.

The same thing Tim knew. Same thing Tim had known since the moment he'd seen Jill all crushed in that mound of boxes.

There's nothing they can do.

He knew it; of course he knew it. But he hid from the words, and refused to admit them. The moment he admitted them he admitted defeat, and, and—

And how could he do that to his daughter?

Never.

Tim followed behind the orderly. Maybe he should have asked permission, and maybe he should've stopped and turned back when the matronly nurse glared at him as he passed through the door. But he couldn't have done either of those things any more than he could've allowed himself. . . . No. He glared back at the cruel-looking nurse, and he thought *Try, lady, try it—you just try to stop me*. She must've gotten the message well enough, because she didn't say a word, but looked away all sullen-like.

People hurrying all over the place, hurrying with scary-looking heavy equipment. There a woman with a bright-red cart that looked vaguely like a chest of drawers—that thing was for cardiac emergencies, wasn't it? Tim thought they'd been when he'd seen them in movies, anyway. Over the intercom someone kept saying those code words, too, and then paging this doctor and that doctor and the other doctor, all of them *stat*. (That one Tim knew from the cold medicine commercial. It meant *right now, damn it*.)

There were several of them there waiting when they pushed Jill's stretcher into its cubicle. Three of them went right to work—one nurse cutting away her clothing, another cleaning away the half-congealed blood. The others, all but one doctor, backed away, and gradually they seemed to become spectators, as though the trouble had somehow become a false alarm for them.

The doctor still close moved up to look at her, and he pushed her legs up into spread-eagle, and he reached in to *touch*. . . .

"She's stopped bleeding," the doctor said. And then something else about effaced or effacing or some such—it made no sense to Tim. Too much doctorese. "Attach the fetal monitor."

Fetal monitor. Did that mean they were going to watch the baby somehow? Or was that monitor as in *heart monitor*, which was another device he'd seen on television lots of times. Yes, yes, that's exactly what it was. Look at the machine there, with its two little video screens. As the nurse strapped that big metal disk to Jill's abdomen (and pasted it down with that stuff that looked like K-Y jelly or Vaseline or something) there on the screen was the same heartbeat display he'd seen on a thousand TV programs. Mostly right before the patient died of heart failure.

The nurse who'd strapped the thing on looked at the doctor. "The heartbeat is weak, and very rapid."

"I can see that."

Tim could feel the baby inside Jill, aching and afraid, dimly aware of the commotion in the world outside. She felt . . . hopeless.

Hopeless.

He wanted to bend down and whisper to it, *I love you, baby girl, love-you love-you love-you. Don't be afraid—Daddy loves you, Mommy loves you, God loves you. It's all going to be all right.* But he knew there was no way she could possibly hear him, or understand him, and he didn't want to interfere with the doctors' work. And too he knew it'd look silly, and this was a very public place.

And worst besides it was a lie: nothing was going to be all right. They were all three of them doomed, and Tim had known it for a long while now.

The doctor looked up at Tim. "How far along is she?"

Tim frowned, tried to think. Usually the answer to that question was right there on the tip of his tongue, but just now he felt cut loose in time, drifting. Uncertain when he was; only half aware of *where*. "Four months? Four and a half?" His tone was as doubtful as he felt.

The doctor nodded. "That's what I thought." He sighed. "I'm going to call in a neonate-specialist. Your wife is miscarrying, but we may be able to save the baby if we're very, very lucky. You want us to try, don't you?"

Outrage: how could he even ask? "Of course I do."

"I thought you would." He nodded, turned toward the older of the two nurses. "Watch her closely. If the bleeding starts again, call me immediately."

And he left. To make a phone call? To see another patient? To play golf? There was no way to know—

except to know that he was gone a long long time. Two hours.

Two damnable hours.

The crowd waiting, watching against the emergency dissipated as soon as the doctor left. After only a few minutes the older nurse left too. And then the younger one mentioned an errand, and told Tim to call out to her if he saw blood—

And they were alone.

Tim was alone, damn near. Jill sure wasn't awake. Not that first hour. All that hour there was nothing for Tim but Jill breathing steadily and ragged, and the faint flickery hum from the fluorescent light on the ceiling of their cubicle—and the baby, distant inside Jill, terrified, fading. Strangling, it seemed to Tim, though that wasn't possible—how could a baby that wasn't yet breathing on its own possibly suffocate? But that was what it felt like.

A little way into the second hour Jill stirred, and opened her eyes, and started to move. Then stopped with a small cry, and Tim had an awful panic while he thought she'd broken something inside her, and thought she'd begin to bleed again—but no, no, she was still and there was no blood. But her eyes were open, and she was watching him. She was awake.

"How do you feel?" he asked her.

She looked as though she were about to cry. "I hurt." She reached out tentatively to take his hand. Her fingers trembled, and Tim saw that they were blanched-white, whiter even than the skin of her face.

He took her hand. *Something's gotten worse*, he thought. *I ought to call the doctor*. Yes, yes, he should. What business did the doctors have leaving them alone here so long, anyway? Had they gone away for lunch to wait for Jill and the baby to die?

"Wait here," he said, "I'll see what I can do." It was a pretty stupid thing to say when you got down to it. Where was she going to go? Jill barely had it in her to open her eyes, let alone climb off her stretcher and head for the door.

Not that she responded that way. She nodded; she

smiled; she asked him to hurry. And closed her eyes to drift away. . . .

Tim pushed away the curtain and scanned the emergency room, looking for familiar faces. Finding none. And scanned again, looking more closely. And again. And again.

No one. A shift change? Had there been a shift change? Everyone here was new to Tim.

Maybe they did *forget us.*

He went to the front desk. "Excuse me. . . ? Ma'am?"

The ER clerk looked up at him not-quite-angry. Very unfriendly. "Yes? Can I help you?" It almost wasn't a question. Almost—almost it was a threat.

"I'm Tim Fischer. With Jill Robbins back there—" he pointed toward their cubicle "—and we've been waiting a long time. Is our doctor coming back? Can you tell me. . . ?" Careful, careful with the words: he didn't want to seem like he was accusing. Probably there was a reason for the wait. Probably these people were busy doing their jobs, and they just hadn't gotten around to letting Tim know what they planned to do. Besides, it wasn't smart to walk in shouting and making demands—if they were doing like they ought to be raising hell would only alienate them. Which was the last thing Tim needed. Or Jill needed. And the baby—Lord in heaven but that baby needed every friend she had.

Down at the bottom of his heart Tim could feel the baby slip a little farther into the pit that was trying to consume her.

The ER clerk finished shuffling her papers. Looked back up at Tim. "Dr. Magee is on her way down from Clearwater," she said. "She's a very important neonatologist. Dr. Smith, the on-duty obstetrician, left word to keep your wife" (the clerk hesitated ever-so-slightly when she said this word) "under close observation till she arrives." She nodded at a tall, severe-looking redhaired woman. "Nurse Robertson has your wife's readings on her desk monitor. If you have any specific questions you should address them to her."

Tim blinked, feeling off-balance. He'd hardly expected any answer at all, and here he had more information than he could cope with. "But shouldn't that doctor—you said her name was Magee?—shouldn't she be here already? It's been hours."

The clerk sighed. Shrugged. "The traffic on US 19 can take hours," she said. "The nurses are watching your wife very carefully. Dr. Smith is in the hospital. If there's a problem she'll be here in a moment."

Off in the distance in the deep Tim thought he could hear his daughter try to scream for fear of her life.

Tim closed his eyes. "There isn't anything I can do, is there?"

Nothing but wait.

"No. There isn't."

Opened his eyes in time to see the clerk turn away. "Can you ask the doctors to hurry?"

She didn't look up. "I'll tell Dr. Smith you want to speak to him. Dr. Magee will be in to see you the moment she arrives."

Tim went back to the cubicle. He hurt inside, and he felt useless, and if desire were all it took to kill a body he'd have curled up on the emergency room floor and left this mortal coil.

But it isn't, and he didn't. He opened the curtain to see Jill—writhing, or maybe not quite writhing because that takes energy and strength and her movements and her body were both much too weak.

The monitor screen beside her was all crazy, wild looking graphs and lines—

"*Help me.*" Quiet quiet just like that, a voice so small Tim almost thought it was the voice of their child. But no; it was Jill, and she *hurt*, and if that damned nurse was watching the screen she wasn't paying any attention.

Then Tim saw the blood all pooled up on the floor around Jill's cot. And he screamed.

"Nurse! Help! Jill in here, she's, she's—" And Tim didn't know how to end that sentence because he didn't know what was wrong, only that things were very very bad. "*Now!* Please come *now!*"

And the red-haired woman looked up from the

papers on her desk, and she looked at Tim, and then back at the monitor above her—

And she looked down through the now-open curtain to see all the blood, not just pooled blood but tracked, too, because Tim had gotten it on his shoes and now he trailed it everywhere—

And it started all over again: the shouting, the codes, the doctors. Emergency carts. And surgery right there in the emergency-room cubicle.

Gruesome, gruesome stuff. Blood all over, and that the least of it: Sounds. Smells. One doctor went in to open up Jill's abdomen, and the tool she used—it looked like a pair of silvery-bright kitchen shears.

Meat shears. The kind of scissors he'd used so many times to cut up chicken before he boiled it to make salad. And that was exactly the sound the scissors made when the doctor cut Jill open: *Snap!*, exactly the *snap!* he heard when his scissors cut through the flesh of the bird.

Snap!, and a spray of blood, and she was wide open like a frog in ninth-grade biology, and there was blood all over everywhere though now controlled because the doctors knew how to keep it in check.

Smells: blood, urine, excrement; faint strange perfumes from the disinfectants that the doctors used for scrubbing.

The baby.

The baby could feel, could hear, could almost see the hands. The tearing flesh sprung free all surrounding her. The hard sharp-bright knife blades that the doctors used to cut, to stretch, to pull her mother's flesh aside and hold it there.

Urea, vomit, dung. Some other scent he could not name but knew, some smell that must have risen up out from his lover's open gut. . . .

Baby could not smell them. She didn't yet breathe, and maybe she never would. *Breathe*, Tim thought. *Please, God, let her breathe.*

But he knew it wouldn't matter what he said, because God leaves most matters of life and death in the hands of the men and women who are His children.

Now the air felt damp, thick-humid with some

disinfectant chemical dissolved into the atmosphere around them.

The light that filled the room was strange, unearthly—or perhaps it only looked that way. Perhaps it was Tim sprung fast (or was it slow?) in time to meet the moment's crisis who saw the light shifted out beyond its ordinary range.

Or maybe it was only that his eyes—bent, pressed, perhaps poisoned by stress—filtered the room in some peculiar fashion.

Perhaps.

But would that explain the brightness? All around them, magical brightness that was neither light nor fire nor any electric thing—and all of those at once, for Tim could feel it, taste it, see and even hear it.

"Forceps," the doctor said. That was Dr. Smith, wasn't it? Yes. Hard to recognize in the gown and cap, wearing that mask. But it was him.

What the nurse-assistant handed him was an awful fright: two great institutional-steel tongs that looked more than anything else like carving tools for Thanksgiving dinner. And he reached down with them, into Jill—

And Tim looked away. He couldn't bear it, not for another moment. Could not bear to know or see or hear—

Not that hiding was any use at all. There was still the strange link between him and the baby, and he could still feel the prodding poking pressure and release as the doctor cut away her caul—

And something sprung loose—

And the baby screamed!

And the pressure that held her abdomen together burst loose to let her die.

The doctors tried to save her. They did, they really did. Part of Tim felt guilty about that—because he never thanked them for their heroic efforts. Heroic efforts in both senses of that term: they put great energy and spirit

into an attempt to take healing out beyond the bound-
aries reason extends it.

And guilty too because the doctors couldn't know
what Tim did, and by rights he should've tried to tell
them—his daughter was dead two long moments before
they first set eyes on her, and no art that they could
know could hope to resurrect her. Tim knew that, and he
knew he should have found a way to ease the guilt that
pushed them to try to start (or perhaps it was restart?—
Tim wasn't sure) her life. But he didn't have the heart to
speak to them, much less find a way to say a thing he
couldn't admit to knowing.

He left them there. And went out to the lobby of
the emergency room, and out beyond that through the
visitors' entrance, where three old men stood smoking
cigarettes and breathing in the sun.

He looked at the oldest of them, thinking that he'd
beg a cigarette and let its acrid smoke burn away
numbness and terror by burning at the flesh of his mouth
and throat and lungs.

But before he could ask the old man offered—held
out his crumpled pack of Camel Filters and said, "You
need this, don't you?" in a thick-thick accent that might
have been Eastern European and might have been
Turkish. And Tim said yes, please, and thank you, or
maybe he only meant to and didn't say any of those
things. Whatever; he took the cigarette, and when the
man held out his disposable lighter Tim took the light.

And then he walked out into the street, across it
into a parklet there in the space between two office
buildings. And he sat on the bench, and stared deep into
the asphalt pavement that made the boulevard.

And died.

Tim didn't really die so's you'd notice, walking along that
wide four-lane avenue in downtown St. Pete—if you
walked directly past him it isn't likely you'd say, *There,
over there on the bench that's a corpse I ought to call the
police*.

And nevertheless the events that day killed him.

They killed some essential, vital part of him—jammed it down into itself until it ached too much to function. And shattered.

Or perhaps withdrew.

Perhaps that says it more exactly: after the things he'd seen and felt and heard in the cubicle in the emergency room, the part of Tim that loved and wept and *wanted* shrunk in on itself and hid from all the world, and if you spoke to him three days later—no, not simply spoke to him, for this part is in no way vital to workaday conversation—if you came to him three days later and told him he was a fiend, he would not grow angry. He would not hurt, or take offense; nothing in him would sting at the assault on his character. Nor would he especially tolerate the attack. But where any ordinary soul might lash out in anger and from injury, or a wise one would hold his anger in abeyance while he acted with an eye toward consequence, Tim would have calmly, coolly exerted pressure on you till you stopped.

There are worse forms of behavior. But few that need more heart.

He didn't yet understand any of this as he walked away from the bench, across the street, through the hospital parking lot. Into the ER lobby. To the desk, where the clerk stared at him blankly, afraid to speak to him—and what was there to do? He went around her, in through the doors that said AUTHORIZED PERSONNEL ONLY. Probably he wasn't authorized, though he'd been through those doors two or three times already today. And he sure wasn't personnel—he didn't work here, he'd never worked here, and odds were he never would.

Screw that anyway, he thought. And walked right through, looking for the doctor or Jill or their cubicle. All he managed to find was that last one: it was their cubicle, all right, but it was clean and empty. No sign anywhere of Jill, her cot, her linen, their child. Nor even the blood that Tim and the doctors had tracked all over the floor.

It's all right, he thought. *Jill's off in the recovery room. That's all.*

Probably it was so—probably she was fine. He could find out easily enough.

"Where is she?" Tim asked. The question wasn't aimed at anyone in particular, but he said the words loudly, and turned to scan the room as he did. Scanning he saw the hard-eyed red-haired nurse. She looked afraid.

She looked as though the question were directed specifically at her, and as though it were a threat.

"Down there," she said. "In the OR wing. In Recovery."

Tim waited for her to go on.

"She'll live," the woman said. There was something else in that sentence—something not-quite-said, hiding down between the words. Tim had a feeling that whatever it was was almost as important as the fact of life. But he couldn't think what it might be.

Or maybe didn't want to.

A long, long corridor lined here and there with stretchers and forbidding medical machinery. Two hundred yards—maybe three. Someone in all that distance should've noticed, Tim thought, that he had no business being there. Sent him out to work his way through proper channels. No one did; Tim looked up to see a door marked RECOVERY, and he went in without thinking.

RECOVERY was a long, wide corridor lined with cots—deliberately made longwise, probably to allow doctors, patients, and equipment to move fast and in quantity. Jill was in the third cot, pale and bandaged. Two IV bags fed down into her arm, one blood, the other some clear fluid.

She looked very, very ill. But when he looked at her Tim was certain that she'd live.

"Can I help you?" Which wasn't a friendly offer. In fact, it sounded threatening. "This isn't a public area. Visitors aren't allowed here."

Tim turned to see a pinch-faced woman dressed all in white. A nurse—weren't the ones in white nurses? Or was it different here in the recovery room?

"I wanted to see my—Jill. Jill Robbins. I want to make sure she's okay."

"You'll have to talk to—" and Tim was sure she was going to say —*talk to your doctor, I'm not authorized to answer your question*. . . . But then she stopped quite suddenly, and stole a glance at Jill. Shrugged before she looked Tim in the eye. "She'll be fine," the woman said. "Her biggest problem is the blood she's lost." Scowl! "Now go! Get out of here before you get us both in trouble."

Tim found his way to the recovery waiting room, where he sat blank-faced for hours staring at the wall.

Early in the evening someone came in to ask him what arrangements he wanted to make for the baby's remains. He didn't answer; he couldn't bring himself to focus on the problem. Eventually the man realized Tim wasn't going to reply, and he went away.

An hour after that the woman from Recovery came in to tell him that they'd moved Jill to Intensive Care, up on the third floor. Tim shook himself for a moment, and thanked her, and made his way up to the ICU waiting lounge.

Another hour, and an hour after that. Someone came out twice to say it wasn't yet time for him to visit, would be soon. Not that it mattered. He was here because Jill might need him; if his visit might interfere with her health that was the last thing he wanted.

Then the phone rang, an hour or so after midnight. Tim reached over to answer it, certain that it was the nurse calling to tell him Jill was well enough to wake and ask for him—

But it wasn't.

It was Grandpa.

"Tim," he said. He paused there a long long time, and Tim kept thinking *How'd he find me, how did he know, how did he even begin to know where to look for me. . . ?* And there was no answer he could imagine, and after a while he decided that he didn't want to know. "I'm sorry, Tim."

At first Tim thought he meant about the baby, and Tim didn't want to think about that. He didn't want to think about his daughter, because the place she'd had in his heart still ached raw like torn flesh with the absence where she'd been. And so long as he looked somewhere else, and kept his heart and mind dead quiet and distracted, the pain was something he could live with.

He sobbed.

He didn't want to. Didn't mean to. But he thought of his daughter, and thought of how much he'd loved her, and the long agonized sob was all he could do, and to hell with his intentions.

After a while the sob wore away, and Grandpa was still on the line, and it finally began to sink through to Tim that there was a reason Grandpa had found him and only called by telephone, and not come to help him cope.

Grandpa knew, of course. If Grandpa had found him here, then he had to know everything that had happened since they'd walked into that shop.

Something even worse. It's something even worse.

And then thought, *No, that's impossible, there's nothing in the world that could be worse.* That certainly was true. But the news was just as bad as it could possibly have been.

"Tell me, Grandpa."

"Your father, Tim. Your mother. There was a fire."

A long silence. Two minutes? Three? Tim could have filled in rest of the sentence if he'd had to.

He knew already—knew everything but the details.

"Is either of them still alive?"

Grandpa's breath, deep in the speaker. "Your mother is. Deep in a coma."

Tim knew—they both knew—that she'd never wake. Till Grandpa'd called he'd been blinded to the truth of it, but now there was no avoiding the knowledge—his sensitivity reached deep down into the hearts of his parents, and if it was numbed to the point where it didn't tell him that he'd lost his father and was soon to lose his mother, looking into it Tim found all the information waiting in the dead chamber of his heart.

After that things grew very, very blurry.

There was the hospital here and the hospital there, and Tim spent all his time in one or the other or on the road between them. The first trip he was alone, driving back to University Community Hospital in Tampa. After that Grandpa was with him.

Three days.

Three days, waiting for Jill to heal; hoping despite the certainty in his gut that Mom would wake and live and survive the horrible burns that covered her body.

Once, late late at night on the Howard Franklin Bridge, Tim looked up at the moon from the passenger seat and said, "Why can't we make a miracle, Grandpa?" But he already knew the answer to that, and Grandpa knew he did. "The Easter Bunny used the Cross to make miracle for himself—why can't we do it, too—just this once?"

And Grandpa said, "Easter Bunny? What're you talking about, Tim?"

Tim thought: *Grandpa doesn't know what happened at Disney World.* And then: *But he knows about that man—the Easter Bunny told all about how he met Grandpa.*

"The man—the workman who fell asleep in the Cross room way back when they were building the bookshelves to your house. The one who got splinters from the Cross in his face? The one who goes around the world doing miracles to make people feel loved?"

Grandpa just stared out at the highway wide-eyed, mouth agape.

"There's no such man, Tim. There never was nor ever will be—the Cross doesn't work that way."

"*Grandpa,* I met him myself, at Disney World, and he told me how you met him too. He said you were the one who woke him up from his nap."

Silence.

"Tim, there was never any workman in that house while the Cross was there. I had it hidden far far away until the place was finished. I never woke anyone sleeping in that room. No one could go in there without making my hair stand on end—no matter how far away I was the moment it happened."

"You never knew when Donny and I went up to see the Cross together back when I was fifteen. I'm sure you didn't. I kept waiting for you to step out from behind a door and give me a lecture, but you never did."

"*What?*"

Tim blinked.

"Grandpa, I was fifteen—it's a little late to get mad at me now, isn't it? I grew up okay enough, didn't I?"

Grandpa winced. "No, Tim, I'm not mad at you." As he said these words his voice was very angry. Or was it frightened? "But something is very wrong. Something important."

"I don't understand."

"I should have known both those things the moment that they happened. If you met the Old Abraham—and who else could it be?—at Disney World, I should have felt the moment it happened. We should have run for our lives that very moment. If you brought a stranger in to see the Cross, I ought to have come running from halfway around the world." He frowned. "Tell me everything about both of these incidents. Everything—try not to leave out a single detail."

And Tim recounted both sequences of events, carefully, slowly—half grateful for the chance to focus on something that wasn't the present.

When he was done they were on the interstate passing over Sulfur Springs. Even by the unsteady light from the highway lamps Tim could tell Grandpa was ghost-white and terrified.

"Go on," he said.

"That's all there is to tell." Or all that Tim remembered, anyhow.

Grandpa shook his head and swore. He glanced at his watch. "We need to eat," he said.

Yes, Tim thought; he was hungry. He couldn't remember when he'd eaten last, but he suspected that it might have been way back before he and Jill had left for St. Pete. If he didn't eat soon he'd make himself ill. But was there time? If they stopped at Denny's would they get to the hospital to find Mom passed on while they unwound?

"You can call the hospital when we get to the restaurant," Grandpa said, "if that'll set your heart at ease."

Maybe it would.

Tim bit his lip. "How long will she live, Grandpa?" Grandpa knew the answer. Tim almost knew it himself—

his heart understood something, he thought, that it didn't want to tell him. Or maybe it was a thing he could not bear to ask?

"She's already dead, Tim," he said. "She was gone from inside before she even reached the hospital."

That was it, wasn't it? That was what he didn't want to know. But now that the words hung in the air around him they didn't seem to hurt especially.

Tomorrow, he thought, *the dead part of me will wake, and there'll be hell to pay.*

But it never did. Not for years. And never entirely. Even to the day Tim went north hiding from the Bleeding Man who was Old Abraham, the greatest part of him lay dead—or perhaps somnolent.

They ate at Lupton's, where the food was as good as it possibly could be. Not that Tim had any pleasure from it. The food came, and he ate it, and by reflex ate more—but his meal was empty of the sensual pleasure he always took from food.

The hospital in Tampa; back to St. Pete. Back and forth and back again. Somewhere in there was Christmas, and interspersed all throughout it were naps and longer sleeps in hospital lounges. Mom waited till the day after Christmas before she let go of the world. Jill woke the day before that, but when she did she didn't want to speak to Tim.

At all.

She never spoke to him again, in fact. Tim was there for her as best he could be, but it made no difference, and after a while she came home, packed her bags, and left him behind forever.

That didn't hurt anywhere near so much as it ought to have.

Grandpa spent almost all of the next few years out away from home. Chasing after—what? "Old Abraham"? That was what he'd said in the car—that was what he'd called the Easter Bunny. Tim couldn't imagine who Old Abraham was, and the honest truth was that it was a long time before he even cared enough to wonder. And then he didn't wonder very long.

• • •

Two months.

Nearly two months Tim held himself hidden in the tiny inn on Narawock Harbor.

Good months; good times. The Rhode Island summer was quietly uneventful, cool. Only the weather stormed and raged all through July as Tim watched fascinated through his great wide window.

Storming seas. Beautifully angry.

Tim didn't watch the storms anywhere near so much as he'd have wanted. There'd been no time—not since his second day here.

That was when he'd remembered the book.

The book Grandpa had shown him. In that dream. How had he managed to forget about it so long? That was the amazing thing. All that time, all those questions—and all along the answers were in his trunk, waiting for him.

The book was infinitely denser than he'd have thought possible. Page-wise, not writing-wise. (Not that the writing wasn't pretty tough going. So many languages! And none of the prose was anything to keep you awake at night, no matter what the language.) The page-density was really weird. Tim had been reading for two months now, reading steadily every day as long as he could keep his eyes open. Hardly even taking time to eat. He must've read—what, two thousand pages? Three thousand? Four? An awful darned lot, that was for sure.

And here he was, almost through the second-to-the-last entry, and even still there was half the book left. All blank pages.

The pages *felt* thick. Real thick—like they were made out of thin, supple leather. But the whole book wasn't more than a couple inches thick.

Weird.

Not as weird as the story, though. Was that the right word? Maybe not. The book sure wasn't a novel. More like a journal, left behind by Grandpa. And Grandpa's Grandpa. And that man's immediate forebear. And that man's great-grandfather back before him . . . every single Steward of the Cross, in fact, had made this book his journal. All but the first, who'd started the book not long before he'd died.

All the way back to the time of Our Lord Jesus Christ.

Tim found himself reading the book all out of order. Starting with Grandpa and working his way back through the centuries; skipping back into the Middle Ages and then jumping forward again to find the resolution of ———

And on like that, back and forth through time.

Soon now Tim would have to start writing in the book himself. Either that or—or what?

What indeed. If he wasn't the Steward of the Cross—and he truly had renounced the Stewardship in that woods back home in Florida—if he wasn't Steward then the very least he owed Grandpa's true heir was to bring him this book.

Maybe he shouldn't even have read it. Who knew? And anyhow there was nothing he could do about that now that he'd all but finished the darned thing.

He hadn't meant to read it. Not at first. He'd just, well, he'd just remembered it, remembered it in the trunk. That was all. And once he'd remembered it there, it weighed on him. Like: how was he supposed to leave that thing in there, there in the trunk of his car where he couldn't even keep an eye on it? Especially when he was holed up here with nothing to do *but* keep an eye on it?

It even didn't seem to him that he was making any sense, but that was how his reasoning went. And it didn't go away, and after a while it seemed easier to go out there and get the damned thing than it was to sit here with nothing to do but think about it.

Once he had it there in the hotel room it only took a couple more hours' rationalization before he had it open. Just to look at, of course. And once it was open how could he *not* read?

Even if that passage was ancient Greek. Hell, Tim could read Greek. Grandpa had taught him—Greek, Latin, early German. Aramaic. All sorts of languages. Till the day he'd opened that book, Tim had thought it was just Grandpa making certain he had a broad, wide education.

But no, that wasn't it: look here. Read these words:

And after a moment the words faded away and there was only story.

Until finally came the day he'd read every entry but those first two. He'd been avoiding them from the first—because even without reading them Tim knew they were something he didn't want to cope with. And the hints and references caught everywhere in the book—odd bits that referred to those seminal events—only served to assure him that there were things at the beginning of the book that he did not want to know.

> *Abraham: My name is Abraham. Fisher for He is my Father and my Lord.*
>
> *Neither is my born name.*
>
> *My time is at an end, and I know that I must leave words behind to give secret history to all of those who follow.*
>
> *I am Steward of the Cross—warden of that fragment of the Lord's True Cross that still remains in this world. I have served so since the days immediately following the passing of Our Lord Jesus Christ, and in the centuries that passed I came to believe that I would serve perpetually into the future. Until these last three days I had no reason to believe I would ever pass from this world, for I have hardly aged in all this time. Even now, now when the sun has fallen away to winter more than three hundred times since the passing of Our Lord— even now I feel scarcely more aged than a man of thirty years. It is a strange thing, to be so old and feel so young and know that my day is nearly done.*
>
> *But know I do, and I have neither fear nor regret as I go to meet the Maker of Us All. I am no perfect man, and I have sinned gravely against the Lord in my day. But as I have spent these long years working to atone for my*

transgressions, I go to Him if not with clean heart at least in good faith.

Last night as I sat in the presence of the Cross, praying as I do every evening, I had a vision. I saw my body lifeless, dead for burial, and before me stood my son who is my heir. Seeing him I knew he was not simply heir to my worldly possessions, but would be the Steward of the One True Cross. How could I fail to know, seeing him? I have lived in the presence of the Cross too long to fail to see its touch.

In my heart, I think, I have known this was to come for a long long time. I hope that I have prepared my son, my Michael, for the days that are to come.

My life began the day our Lord was crucified.

The man I was before that day is none important to me now, nor to anyone else: he was a minor tool in the hand of Caesar. He did precious little but labor as he was directed, and eat, and sleep; and grow logy on days of the feast when he would drink his wine tempered by far too little water.

His work that day—my work that day— was Crucifixion: I was told to nail Our Lord to His Cross. It was a task that weighed little on me. I was no Jew, nor even a Samaritan. I had neither love nor hate for the Prophets of the Jews, whether false (as many then claimed the Lord to be) or true.

As to the grisly nature of the work, it troubled me not at all, for wine and lust and violence had long since blistered, burned, and calloused my heart. I had no love for anyone, and less sympathy still for suffering.

And yet. . . . When I came to Him Who lay already roped and bound to His fate, I found myself agape. I could not act. Even in

*my stupor—and that morning my head
throbbed painfully in the aftermath of wine—
even in my stupor the sight of the Lord was a
revelation to me.*

I would say: Seeing Him I fell to my knees
worshipful and devout to pray Him forgiveness
for my sins. (Not least among those foul acts my
intention to maim Him.) But this is not so.—
The truth is that I hesitated only a moment at
the sight of the Lord. Paused only long enough
to gather awe that I should be the one to begin
the destruction of so magnificent a being.
Gathered my hammer from my belt, took the
long heavy-crude nails from my pouch.

And began my defilement of the Lord.

All the while I pounded that first nail into
Him He watched me, eyes steady, gaze gentle,
and I knew despite the hardness that was my
soul that He loved me no matter what I did, no
matter how I hurt Him. No matter what hateful
thing I could do.

The burden of that love began to weigh on
me after a time.

He did not struggle against me for a
moment. Did not so much as cringe with the
pain I caused Him. Which must have been
considerable. Grown men wither to be crucified. I know this because in my work for
Caesar I crucified many men, and of all those
whose wrists I impaled only the Lord took the
mutilation—as He did. Where most men writhe
and scream in agony or tighten themselves
against the pain to prove their strength, the
Lord remained quiet—and at once not dull nor
resigned. The only sound that escaped Him was
a gentle groan as that first nail pushed through
his wrist—not a groan as a man groans from
pain. More as though the tendons in his newly
ruined wrist had pulled tight involuntarily,
and further tendons connected to them till the
tension forced air up from his lungs.

He watched me carefully, and as He watched I could sense that the only thing that weighed on Him that moment was the sight of me defiling my soul with violence against Him.

He did not scream even when His body betrayed Him: as I began to nail His second wrist to the wooden beam my unease overcame me, and where I should have pierced His right wrist square between two knotlike bones my nail went lower, in through the soft flesh where it ruptured a fast artery, and the blood
  the blood
  the blood
the blood was everywhere jetting up from his wrist in hemorrhage to gush. My eyes! The blood was in my eyes
  lancing through the window to my soul!
I screamed, again and again as the Blood of Our Lord burned into my eyes—and through them deep deep into myself I could feel that blood scoring blistering
  blistering
  infusing
  permeating
  changing
Changing me. The Blood of the Lord touched me where I am.

I could say: His essential nature touched me and altered forever what I was.

But this would be only half a truth. More truly it suffused me, and in its presence I could no longer abide to be the vile creature I had been all my life.

I blinked, blinked, and blinked again, pulled away. Let my hammer fall into the dust. Stood blinded, raised my hands to rub my eyes.

After a moment I had cleared them.

And I knelt to Him, leaned close, to whisper: "Lord, Lord, forgive me for the evil that I am."

He smiled sadly, and I knew that He still

loved me despite all I'd done to Him. "FINISH THE
WORK OUR FATHER SET OUT FOR YOU, ABRAHAM.
THE WORLD DEPENDS ON YOU."

Abraham was not my name—or, more
rightly, till that moment it had not been. Our
Lord Jesus gave me this name there, then, in
that ultimate moment. I have never questioned
it.

In my heart I screamed again for fear of
completing that foul act. But as I did I knew my
Lord was right, that He went to this awful fate
for love of all mankind. And that to veer away
from my duty would be a terrible thing indeed.

I finished the work of crucifixion, and
then let my hammer fall forever to the ground.
Before I ran forever from the life I'd led till
then, I kissed the Lord and begged Him for
forgiveness.

My memory of the three days that followed is vague. I walked hours and hours out
into the desert, paying no attention to my route
or bearing. Sometime in the night I collapsed
onto a rocky ledge as I tried to climb it—and I
slept there until late morning.

When I woke bleeding from my eyes as the
sun blistered my back and neck. And set out to
walk into the horizon.

Three days I spent in this fashion, walking
under the bright hot sun until I would come
apart with exhaustion to sleep in the rock and
sand. On the third day it began to come to me
that I had walked nowhere at all—that hard as
I tried to leave my life behind me and start
anew I had only gone in circles. Here, now: I
was high on the arid plane where days before
I'd helped to kill the Lord Our God.

I did not doubt for a moment that He had
guided me here. Fate Mysterious is no mystery
at all but the Hand of God subtly shepherding
events.

And so indeed it was. For my steps guided me that evening to the very hill I dreaded most: the crucifixion hill.

O Lord.

Even now at the end of my years I grow uneasy to think back on that night. I had not known that hill before that moment. Had not seen nor heard tell of it. Yet still I knew it from the instant I first set eyes on it there in the fading dusk as chill winds blew the first hints of the thunderstorm that was to come.

For half an instant lightning lit the sky to day—and then was gone. It didn't matter. I'd already seen with eyes what my heart had known I would: three crosses high on the hill before me.

Of the three only that in the center stood vacant. Even from the distance where I stood, even in that briefest flash of light, I could see the crow-pecked corpses of the two thieves stretched and sagging from their crucifixes.

He died here, I thought. I did not for a moment doubt it. His empty Cross stood silhouetted high on the hill against the clouds shimmering with fire. Was it his essence trapped inside the wood that made the Cross shine brighter than lightning? Or a trick of some reflected light, come down from the sky? Or was it only my imagination, deceiving me to think. . . ?

How could I know from so far? But I did. Seeing the Cross I knew it, and knew that I had to set hands on it to touch. . . . had to, and so ran through the rain gathering to pour and rage first spatters slapping hard as they fell on and all around me, now bursting, bursting till the torrent opened way. Running drenched and all but blinded by the rain's ferocity; stumbling uphill through the rocks and scrub and mud. Twice before I reached the summit I slipped and fell face-first into the muck. And

*then a third time, near the top, where the fine
wet grainy mud spattered up into my eyes, and
I looked blind up into the sky to clear my
vision, and the mud and the still fresh blood
from my eyes washed down over my lips, and I
tasted it, tasted the Lord's fresh blood, smelled
it deep and bitter mixed with earth, and I
blinked and blinked until my sight cleared to
see—*

—to see—

*—to see the Cross loom up above me, and
lightning everywhere around me, and thunder,
and everywhere it struck—*

(right and left the corpses thieves' corpses made
fresh in the rain, and I could smell them now smell the
death left to rot for days there on the man's shoulder
the dung a crow had left, rolling down rinsing away in
the rain just as in time their flesh would rinse like ashes
sifting down dust to dust)

*—to see blood of the Lord stained but yet
fresh perhaps or perhaps made wet by rain
there the blood of the Lord soaked deep into
the wood, and I thought I see, I see the Lord
My God I can feel Him here in my presence feel
His agony feel how He died here, suffering
struggling to breathe—*

—the lightning—

*And then I had a vision. Gone were the
clouds, the night, the fire in the sky. It was day,
days ago I knew and the Cross still loomed
above me, but now it was not bare.*

*Strangling, strangling, my Lord my Christ
was strangling, and there there look at his
wrists pierced by nails as I pierced them, and
he pulled up against those grievous wounds to
struggle, to lift himself to breathe now gasping
a breath as he raised up on his shoulders pulled
up for air and soon soon I knew he'd be too
weak to lift himself to breathe—*

—my God my God what have I done to You?—

—forgive me, forgive me Jesus Christ I love You—

—God's quiet agony everywhere in the air—

And then abruptly the vision ended, sudden sharp broke clean and now again I lay in mud at night in rain, and lightning flashed struck thundered all around me as though apocalypse had come down all around me and nowhere else.

Perhaps it had.

Perhaps it had.

Or perhaps this was my own private apocalypse, lightning now strike now now strike down to smite me—no not me I was alive untouched it was the Cross the Cross before me burst asunder burst to vapor gone! Gone! Taken away from the world! My Lord my Lord why have You abandoned us?

No not gone the presence of Him wasn't gone still here in that tiny fragment that tiny blood-wet fragment six feet from me on the hill, and I crawled up, up to retrieve it, to save it, to save it for the good of all mankind—

And as I did the Lord was with me.

I was on hands and knees lifting the last fragment of His Cross, thinking to stand to leave to find shelter, noticing the softness of the now-gentler rain, the sky now bright with the fullness of the moon unhidden through the break high among the clouds, feeling the mud rinse away so lightly as I touched the Cross and felt the Lord made whole made real again on earth, and I looked up to see:

Looked up to see the Lord whole alive and real untouched standing beside me, above me.

Whole and hale and healthy, as though I'd never maimed Him. As though He'd never died.

I fell to my knees again to worship Him, prostrate in my love—but He had none of that. He reached down to lift me to my feet; to embrace and hold me.

He did not speak to me now, but in my heart I knew his words:

It is a grave thing you take on yourself and all your sons and daughters. A terrible responsibility. Are you certain you would be Steward of My Cross?

I had no doubt, no indecision.

"Yes, my Lord. I'm certain."

And He was gone. But His Cross and His Love were still with me, as they remain to this very day.

Now my life is over, and I look over the ephemera of three centuries to wonder what it is I have to tell you who follow me. What have I learned, in all my time? What can I say that to know it will make the burden of the years easier to carry?

I have this, at least. It has guided me from there to here; whether it can guide you I am uncertain—

Someday a man will say, God is dead, Glory be, God is dead and we are free, now right and wrong are ours.

He will be wrong.

Nonetheless right and wrong are ours, and always have been and always will be. Though they hardly free us—they are ours because there is nothing we can do to renounce the responsibility for our acts.

God Loves us no matter what we do. To accept that Love into your heart is to know good from evil. That knowledge liberates and binds—because when we know right from wrong no one can absolve us from the sins we know are ours. Nor condemn us for deeds that are no sin.

> *Because right and wrong are a covenant between Our Lord and ourselves:*
>
> *Sin is not an act on a list of things forbidden, but a blemish on our heart, naked and ugly beside the God Who loves us.*

> *I am Michael son of Abraham and today I bore witness to great unspeakable horror.*

Tim leaned closer to read, fascinated at the sudden dramatic turn of tone and event—and suddenly everything changed. No longer did he sit reading in the hotel room on Narawock Harbor; now the world faded out and in around him. . . .

. . . and somehow he is Michael, son of Abraham, standing on a beach where gentle tiny waves lap in across the corpse of his father.

"Father. . . ?" Tim-who-is-Michael hears himself say. Tim feels a strange-and-yet-familiar melange of emotions: grief, disbelief, a cool void that holds the place where something powerful and terrible will soon come to dwell.

He remembers that his father (who is not his father) set out in their fishing boat last night before the storm. Remembers warning his father, begging him not to go. And watching him sail slow and languorous out to sea.

(There, in that memory, see the Bleeding Man in that memory. Look at him closely, through Michael's eyes. Filter away that part of the image that is the father seen through the eyes of the son. . . . There. Closely now. Closer still. It *is* the Bleeding Man—and yet, and yet. . . . There is something about him so starkly different from the Bleeding Man Tim has known. So stark, so different, and at once unnameable. It settles slowly on Tim that he has found a strange, large blind spot in his ability to see into the hearts of men: what is this thing he cannot name? Why is it that as he blinks for a moment he loses the sight of it, and even memory fades all but from his mind. . . ?)

And now it is morning and he is here, here on the beach, and here are his father's remains washed ashore.

He walks to the water's edge, looks closely into the corpse's vacant, bleeding eyes. There is no question: this is the Bleeding Man.

He is Tim's ultimate forebear.

And he is dead.

Plainly dead; there is no questioning this. Look down through those eyes, into its soul—there is no soul inside that corpse. Only cool flesh like meat and the memory of spirit creased deep into the dead folds of the brain.

Tim thinks: no, this can't be. I know the Bleeding Man, I know him and he lives on into my time. This isn't any vision but a lie.

Soon as he thinks those words he knows that they are wrong, that this is indeed a true seeing—truer than the book itself would have been.

And then the world closes down to black.

In the light again Tim can see a funeral. There at the head of the grave stands a priest dressed in a dark robe, reading from a scroll.

It is a eulogy he pronounces.

On a platform near the grave is the shroud-wrapped body of the Bleeding Man who is the father of Michael who is Tim. It is knowable, recognizable even through the shroud because of the eyes—blood still fresh and leaking through the cloth, plain to see. And so much! In another hour that blood would blot the shroud's mask entirely.

Bleeding. Dead and bleeding. Tim has an awful impulse to step over to the corpse and pull back the shroud to see . . . see what?

To see if the Bleeding Man is alive beneath the blood-wet cloth.

And he thought: yes, he's alive, of course he's alive. I know he's alive.

In the past and somewhere far in the future the Bleeding Man lies dead. But now in the here and now and now where Tim lives and breathes he is alive. There is no understanding this, but nonetheless Tim believes that it is true.

Believes it without the slightest doubt.

That is why Tim-who-is-Tim feels no great surprise when the corpse sits up on its platform and peels away its shroud.

He screams despite his foreknowing, of course. His actions, feelings, memories—none of them is his own at this moment. They are the thoughts and feelings of Michael, son of Abraham who was or perhaps was not or perhaps will be the Bleeding Man.

Screams and screams and screams in horror and love and disgust at the apparition that was but is no longer his father.

And even through the eyes of his son, Michael, the Bleeding Man is no longer Abraham, Steward of the Cross. Everything that made him who he was, his heart, his regret, his *soul*—all these things are gone.

He is not a man, but a monster. Where a man has a soul this Bleeding Man reanimated by the still-flowing blood of the Lord has only the hunger for spirit.

Seeing that hunger Michael who knows his father knows that this *thing* will reach immediately for the Cross, will—

—will—

No.

Tim cannot, will not hear it. But he knows no less that it is so.

—*will remake the universe in his own soulless, vacant image*.

Tim tries to imagine it: a world where no man nor woman had love or compassion or regret; only simple hungers and lusts, animal things that even animals transcend; where no meadow would shine with the earth's love for all living things upon it; where no mountain would hold fast to the nest of the eagle that makes it aerie; where no ground would bind to hold tower; where—where nothing would bind, for God's love itself would be void, and God's love ultimately binds all things together.

Michael turns, begins to run from the thing that is

all that remains of his father. But Tim is certain he will need one last glimpse of the Bleeding Man, to see exactly what changes time had wrought upon him. And he forces Michael Abraham's son to pause for the tiniest of instants. . . .

And the Bleeding Man sees him.

Through the vision, through all time. And he looks Tim in the eye. "Yes," he says, "I see you—and I know that you've found my deepest secret. You know that I have no soul." He smiles, then, and it is a thing more terrible than his hate. "But we are not so unlike in this, are we? I lost mine because I've lived beyond my own passing. You've buried yours so deep that it barely lives at all."

Tim's own scream woke him from that vision.

That was when they burst into the room. Hundreds of them, hundreds, breaking through the doors, the windows and more than he could begin to count crowding behind them—

All Tim could think was *They heard me, they heard me, they heard me scream heard me reading heard me just sitting here thinking about him that's how they found me why they're here*—

And he thought: *I've got to run run run*, but already it was too late for that, already they were climbing all over him, pounding him, beating him, and where was the book just a moment ago on the desk in front of him now vanished before the first of the invaders touched him? Was it still here, invisible, disappeared—or was it away? Or had it never been at all—was it just a dream that followed him up from sleep and through the months?

Holding him down, now, a dozen of them held him down thrown out of his chair pinned to the carpet that smelled of sea-salt and mildew, and while those held him others beat and kicked him, angry, furious to kill him held back only in the slightest way. . . .

There was no time to struggle; no time even to react. By the time it dawned on Tim that he needed to fight back he was held too tightly to move his arms or legs. There was barely room to turn his head to see the people above him clear away. . . .

And where they'd been the Bleeding Man stepped forward. And smiled all terrible and frightening just as he'd smiled in Tim's vision. And then he spoke. "Twice, now, boy, I've had to move against you unprepared. You made me pay for that, didn't you? Yes, you did.

"This time I am *not* unprepared. I found you weeks ago, and in the time since then I gathered to me everything and everyone I own. And spent them.—For all it matters. We are at an ending now; tomorrow they are no use to me."

What. . . ?

No sense. No sense at all. "Explain," Tim said. Or tried to say—it was hard to talk with the shoe that pressed down on the side of his mouth. "What are you talking about?"

The Bleeding Man only smiled yet again and turned away. "Beat him senseless," he said. And then he was gone.

Things got vague and bloody then. Ten minutes, fifteen minutes—it was hard to say how long the battering went on. More than one blow hit painfully enough that Tim was sure he'd broken open. But he hadn't; and he didn't. Later, thinking back, it seemed to Tim that the only thing that saved him was that there were so many, so close, that there was no room for any of them to haul off and pound him hard enough to break anything.

So many of them.

The clerk at the hotel desk must've seen them. And if he had any sense he'd called the police.

Police in Narawock Harbor. The local police must have what, three patrol cars? If that. Tim thought he remembered seeing a police car once, but he wasn't sure. They were anything but omnipresent. Three patrol cars wouldn't be a lot of help right now.

A hundred, maybe. But Tim had a hard time imagining that there were a hundred patrol cars in the

entire county. When the first three got here and saw
how outnumbered they were, they'd call every cop in
the county.

Maybe every cop in the state.

But by the time a fraction of them got there, Tim
would be prisoner, or dead, or something.

Now suddenly he was in the hotel room's tiny
bathroom. How had he gotten here? How had so many
of them gotten here, pressing, hitting, kicking from all
sides, and this one with his hands in Tim's hair, pounding
Tim's skull over and over against the rim of the toilet, as
though Tim's head were an egg to be cracked apart and
savored. . . .

And something *did* burst open, deep inside him.
Tim thought of when he was fifteen, when his father beat
him that awful day and like to break his eye open. And
suddenly he was fighting back, and because here in the
bathroom there was no room for two dozen of them to
hold him still—there was room to fight.

Tim yanked his left arm free from under the feet of
the woman who stood on it. Which pulled her off-
balance, sent her thump and *crack* into the bathroom
wall. He reached up, grabbed the collar of the man
about to pound his head into the toilet one more
time—grabbed and pulled and kept on pulling. Pulling
till the bastard went *smack* face-first into the toilet rim,
hit the bridge of his nose right there on the hard sharp
edge where something *crunch*ed, must've been bone
and deeper, softer stuff because of the way blood went all
over everywhere.

Tim thought: *He's not a man he's a spigot.* Which he
knew was silly and brutal and grisly, even dazed and
bruised confused as he was.

The two who held his right arm were trying to get
at him now, but they weren't having much luck on
account of the one on top of Tim. Who'd gone into a
spastic fit because of his nose getting broken, or maybe
because of the blow to his head—Tim'd yanked him up
and down a couple times after he'd broken the nose just
for good measure, and both those times he'd gotten the
guy's forehead bang hard into the toilet bowl.

Tim pushed away the one who was convulsing inches from his face—pushed him into the arms of the two on his right. Pulled his right arm out of their grip as he did it.

And now he had to worry about the two down there by his legs, jumping in to fill the void where the first man had been. Tim pushed up, off the ground, lunged forward to grab the two attacking. One hand into the throat of the man on his right; another into the throat of the man on his left.

Let his fingers dig down into the soft flesh of their throats.

Crushed the throats with the hard grip of his palms.

Amazed him he could fight at all after the beating he'd taken. But here he was, fighting. Praise God for adrenaline.

Looked out the bathroom door over the shoulders of the two gasping for air, trying to fight but too surprised and afraid of strangling to put up a struggle—

And saw the throng that filled his hotel room till there was no room at all between them, filled it pressing lurching tight like carcasses wedged solid for shipment—

And felt himself despair. No matter how he fought there was no chance he could overcome so many. Not even if he had a lifetime to do it.

No way to fight. No way to run unless the outside wall were to collapse of its own accord and free him. Which wouldn't do a damn bit of good even if he could make it happen, because there were more of the folks from out in the living room right outside the tiny bathroom window, trying to climb in. Not that there was room for them to squeeze through the damned thing.

If he could fly up through the ceiling, he could get away like the impossible rabbit did, back when Tim was—what, twelve? Thirteen?

Without meaning to he found himself stealing a glance at the ceiling.

The ceiling.

There in the back left corner of the ceiling, just above the john, was a hatchway—a trapdoor access to the attic.

As hope went, it wasn't much—but it was something.

Tim yanked the two he held by the throat, pulling them forward and out of the swing of the bathroom door. Kicked the door closed in the instant that he had before the horde out in the hotel room could break it down. Which wouldn't be hard. The door was thick solid wood. At least a hundred years old, to judge by the layers of paint caked over it. It wouldn't break so easily as the flimsy-modern outer door—but it wouldn't hold up forever, either.

Tim shoved the man in his left hand headfirst into the door, and then the man in his right—both of them fell stunned to the floor, where their bodies did a little to jam the door shut.

Somewhere in the middle of that the two who'd held his left arm had gotten themselves free of the one who was still convulsing, and they'd grabbed Tim from behind. Lord only knew what they were trying to accomplish, but they weren't making a much better job of it than they had of holding him down. Tim leaned forward and over, tearing away from the one behind his left, taking hold of the hands of the other—hands that were trying to strangle Tim—and pulled her over his shoulder. Flipped her judo-like, so that she slammed flat-back and upside down into the door. Which was a good thing just that moment, since it closed the door which someone outside had managed to push partway open.

Spun around, turned to face the last one still standing.

Who looked afraid.

Who wasn't making like to attack.

Tim thought: *If I leave him standing here he'll come after me the moment my back is turned.*

A punch, two, three, and the man would be senseless and no danger at all. But how could Tim do that to a man who wasn't trying to fight with him?

To hell with him, Tim thought. And he turned away from the man, started to step up onto the toilet seat—

Whap!

Measly little rabbit punch to the side of the head. From behind. Well, so what? It wasn't like Tim couldn't take a measly little rabbit punch.

Someone was actually climbing in through that tiny porthole of a window. And it looked as though he were actually going to manage it, too.

Tim ignored them both.

Climbed up onto the toilet tank.

A kidney punch. Another, and then another—and that third one *hurt*, damn it! Tim couldn't stop himself. He didn't bother to turn around; just kicked his heel back into the face of the jerk—he wasn't exactly sure where the blow connected. But it connected good and hard, and there was this awful soft-wet crunching sound. . . .

No time to think about it. No time at all.

Tim pushed the trapdoor open. Gripped two sides of the frame, hauled himself into the crawl space.

Dark. Dusty. Very, very warm. The slope of the roof cut so close here by the edge of the building that there was hardly room to crawl. Not that there was any choice.

He scrambled crab-style out to the center of the attic, stood where there was room to stand—

Crack!

From back down in the bathroom. It had to mean that the bathroom door downstairs was gone. In a moment they'd be up here through the trap—more of them than he could count. Chasing after him. If he wasn't long gone out of here by then he was had.

Here in the center was a stovepipe chimney that led through the roof to an aluminum dome-fan. Not good, not useful—if he ripped it out of its mooring he'd make a hole not quite wide enough to squeeze his shoulders through.

What else? Slat vents at opposite ends of the building. He could kick them out easily enough. Yes, that was what he had to do—that vent, that one there hung over the low-roofed extension to the inn. Where the office was.

And from there, well, he'd have to figure it from

there. Maybe run out along the coast, or make a dash for his car, or—

There! Kick! There! and the slats were gone, and he could jump the half dozen feet down to the office roof. . . .

As behind him the first of his attackers emerged through the trapdoor.

Damn damn damn damn! His ankle. He landed funny on his ankle, and then worse it slid out from under him in the dried-slick layer of pine straw, and in half a moment the rest of him was flying out into the void after, into the pine limbs thick here over the low roof—

—there. He caught it, caught the pine branch as it flew up into his face. (Or was it his face that flew? It was, Tim thought. Though it didn't seem that way.)

Looked down. And saw that he hung out over the void as the branch bent down by the pull of his weight.

It was a long, long drop: this branch hung out over the edge of the sea-cliff. Sixty feet down to the water where waves crashed over the great rocks at the base of the cliff.

Or three feet, if he could get the branch to swing him back onto the edge. No mean trick. But there was no time to worry how difficult or dangerous—only time to swing out and back and forth again to build momentum, build the arc, and jump. . . !

. . . .jump. . . !

. . . .into the air where he hung long long moments as he saw it, moments so long that he began to grow certain that it wasn't an arc that carried him, not a jump up onto the edge of the cliff but a fall down to the rrocks. . . .

. . . .rocks below him. . . .

. . . .where he'd be sure to shatter into so much disintegrated meat and bone.

But no, no. He was up up here in the air landing on the rocks well in from the edge of the cliff, stumbling slightly as he set foot to earth because he had no balance. Not that it mattered; if he fell here he'd only fall to the ground; the cliff was long feet away from him.

On his feet; catching his balance. Caught. As above

him his pursuers stumbled in the pine straw, just as Tim
had—but their luck was nowhere near as good as Tim's.

Their luck was very bad indeed.

For the branch that Tim had caught to save his life
was still in motion sawing back and forth uncatchable,
and even if a one of them had been able to catch the
thing it could only have saved that one.

If indeed it could have saved her—that one who
nearly did catch hold before she fell screaming to the
rocks.

No time to watch the five who died. (Were there
more than five who followed out through the attic? Did
they stop when they saw it was suicide to follow him down
that roof? It had to be, Tim thought. But there was no way
to know for sure that they hadn't gotten the jump on him,
gone around to meet him here where he was. . . .)

Out and around the office, where he saw hundreds,
maybe thousands, not watching him at all but crowding
into his abandoned room and there in the office he saw
through the window was the clerk blood blood everywhere his throat slit like a pig's arms legs tied to the feet
of his desk to hold him still for the sacrifice like a human
sacrifice that's exactly what it looked like horrible horrible horrible—*moving!*—*moving!*—dear God the man
was still moving still alive holy fucking Christ he was
trying to breathe and as Tim watched blood gushed up
out of his neck—!

As he shuddered, rattled loud enough to hear right
through the glass. And lay dead stock-still, died suffering
desperate to hold his life died awful while Tim watched.

Oh God.

Oh God.

And Tim didn't even notice how horribly he'd
cursed.

He had to go.

Had to move while he still could, before anyone
noticed he was here and free. There was someone, no,
not just someone but half a dozen someones there
waiting on and in his car, which meant that he was
screwed on that account.

Damn.

Motion off to the left and behind him. Had they seen him? Were they coming for him? Tim turned to see—

And saw Gail Benjamin gesturing furiously quietly calling him silently over to the car where she was ducked down barely visible even from this close. He went to her slowly—half cautious, half because he was afraid of her and half because he was still in shock from the chase and worse the sight of the murdered clerk—

"Get *in*, damn you. Before someone sees you."

Tim blinked. Blinked again. *Get in. . . ? Sees me. . . ?* And spent a long numb-dumb moment standing stupid obvious out in the open like an ox chewing hay. And realized where he was and who she was and knew that even if Gail Benjamin was a danger she was the best danger he had available.

And got in the car.

And they drove.

She didn't say anything for the longest while. Tim didn't either, but that wasn't a matter of choice so much, not for him. Not like he was trying to make some kind of statement by putting on a cold aloof face. More like, like—how could he talk? What could he do with words after the way he'd seen the clerk so desperate terrified hungry to live and dying and dead? Gone?

What unfinished business, Tim wondered, did that young man leave behind him with this life?

Then Gail Benjamin said, "I've missed you," and there wasn't any question in Tim's mind about that. He knew that she really meant it, that she loved him. And if it was impossible, well, so what? There wasn't any profit in trying to stop it.

Tim turned to look at her. She took her eyes from the road just long enough to smile at him, and he nodded, smiled back. Tried to smile, anyhow. "I've missed you too."

"It was hard," she said. "We've known where you were for three weeks now. And I couldn't come to see you without making it obvious. . . ."

She didn't finish the sentence. Obvious that what?,

Tim wondered. Obvious that she loved him, that her real allegiances were with him, and not with her fellows?

And were they with him? Tim was certain that they were, but he had no right to be.

"I would've found a way to come to warn you," she said, "but I had a dream the night before we first learned where you were. I dreamed everything that's happened between now and then. Right up through the moment you walked around that corner looking dazed and confused. And because of the dream, I knew I had to be careful. The Master suspects me already. He doesn't know for certain yet that I loaded that gun with a wax cartridge, but he's guessed at it."

"Wax. . . ?"

She bit her lip. Nodded. Kept her eyes focused on the empty highway.

"A wax cartridge. In my shotgun. He wanted me to try to kill you. He said that if I did it would force a miracle—that the Lord would not let you die, because there's no one else who could inherit."

"No," Tim said. "That isn't true. It can't be. He doesn't want to kill me."

Tim looked out the window. Watched the New England scenery rush by. Pine, maple, oak; and now and again the woods would turn to rock shoreline where the sea beat fierce against the mossy stone.

"What do you mean? It isn't a lie I'm telling. My master ordered me to kill you. His instructions were very careful, and I betrayed them."

Tim let his eyes close. Leaned into the afterimage of his dream.

"I think he knew you would," Tim said. "I think he planned every moment of this a long time ago." He frowned. "Maybe even this. Maybe—no. Or. . . ?"

He didn't think she'd accept that right away. People don't generally listen unguardedly when confronted with rupture in their view of the world. But somehow Tim's words went right to Gail Benjamin's heart. In a moment she looked stunned, unsettled—as though he'd pulled away a curtain to show her life was nothing but a soundstage on a movie set.

And maybe Tim had done exactly that.

They drove, quiet for a long time.

Gail looked greyer and greyer as they went on—as though the unsettle and the upset made her progressively more and more ill.

"It doesn't mean we aren't real," he said. "It only means that he knew us very well."

She was crying.

"I love you," she said. "I really, truly, honestly love you."

He wanted to cry himself. Maybe he was crying; his eyes burned bad as though they were teary. But everything hurt right now—the pain could just as easily be dust and stress.

He loved her too, he thought. He'd never meant to feel that way. Never wanted to. But how could he feel anything else? The very fact that she was near him made him all warm and electric down inside, and whether that was God's work or the Bleeding Man's or simple consequence of Tim's nature, it was real.

"I love you too." It made him ache to say it.

Sobbing. She sobbed, quietly, again and again. "We should do something," she said, "something to mark this moment out. Something to let us always remember. . . ." And left the sentence unfinished.

Tim didn't understand.

"Something to celebrate," she said.

"The moment marks itself," Tim said. "If there's something you want to do—do it. We've got a little while, at least."

She frowned, and seeing that expression Tim thought maybe there was something that she hadn't said. If there was, she didn't say it now. After a moment she masked her expression, and something in the atmosphere inside the car grew still. Leaden-still, despite the air that rushed in through the open windows.

They're closer behind us than I thought. That's why she's nervous—we don't have much time, and she still wants to take a moment to. . . .

He let that sift around inside his head for a little while. Maybe it wasn't so bad; maybe it was more important to take a moment to make Gail Benjamin feel like she'd done things right than it was to get every iota of distance between them and their pursuers.

It'll be okay, as long as we don't waste too much time.

As soon as he thought it Tim knew it was the right thing.

Suddenly Gail Benjamin's expression brightened, and Tim knew she'd had a revelation.

"Yes," she said, "that's it exactly."

She pulled the car over to the shoulder of the road—pulled over here where the highway ran close along the sea and waves rushed all violence and froth a dozen feet below them. A heavy white-edged crash, and Tim felt sea-mist puff against his cheek through his open window.

Gail Benjamin engaged the emergency brake, turned, and reached into the back seat. Found a duffel and began to rummage through it.

It took her three or four minutes to find it. Long enough for Tim to get nervous worrying over cars rushing along the highway so close to them, worrying that one would stop—

"*There* it is!" She came forward again, carrying an oblong bundle the size and shape of Tim's forearm—maybe a little smaller.

She leaned close to him, carefully peeling away the chamois wrapping.

"It's the only thing I have," she said, "that's really and truly mine."

Tim looked at her blankly. He couldn't imagine what she meant.

"The only thing I have that's always been mine—the only thing I've always had."

Inside the chamois a fine leather sheath.

Inside the sheath a dagger.

A fine and ancient dagger, beautiful old steel—a simple wooden hilt stained deep brown and rubbed with oil.

That stain. Something about that stain.

And then he recognized it.

Dear Lord.

It wasn't a curse. It was a recognition.

Because the blood that stained the hilt of that dagger was the Blood of Our Lord Jesus Christ Himself. Tim knew that just to see it. And knew just as quickly and easily the provenance of the blood.—It came from the Bleeding Man. That blood, the Lord's blood that leaked from his eyes. . . .

Used now to make this weapon holy. Repellent and Sublime, Tim thought. To bless an instrument of destruction so powerfully. Ultimately. What would that do? What would happen to a man killed with this dagger?

"My mother gave it to me," Gail Benjamin said. "This is my legacy—from St. Helen. Way way back when."

Her legacy. Tim spent a moment wondering exactly what she meant by that. Her legacy was death? A knife to kill made sacred by the Blood of the Lord? The idea made him dizzy.

"I want you to have it," she said. "I know it's not the world's most appropriate gift. But it's important, and there's nothing that I have that's dearer to me."

And he thought: *He would have known this. He would have known she'd offer me this knife.*

If he took it he'd be trapped maybe forever. . . . In what? He tried to clear his head to think.

She's proposing to me, Tim thought. The idea frightened and pleased him both at once. *The dagger is a token meant to seal the betrothal.* It wouldn't matter, except that Tim knew what she was doing. How could they be engaged without both of them consenting and agreeing? Couldn't, of course. But Tim knew, and she was serious as could be.

"All right, then," he said. "I'll marry you." It came out all abrupt and embarrassing, not like Tim meant it to at all. "I mean—"

She smiled, and shook her head to silence him. "I know what you meant," she said. She leaned forward and kissed him all warm moist wonderful. The taste of her lipstick was mysterious and extraordinary. "I'll marry you in a moment, I will."

And the taste of her kiss was nothing beside the wonder and awe he felt just because she was so near him. Like—almost like a holy feeling. Tim thought of the way he'd felt those times he'd stood in the reflected presence of the Lord. It wasn't the same, exactly, but there were powerful similarities between the two sensations.

This isn't real, Tim thought. *In the real world doing things like this so rashly is always a mistake*. And maybe that was true. But looking at Gail Benjamin (staring out at the road all misty-eyed and beautiful, her eyes focused on something a thousand miles away) looking at Gail Benjamin Tim knew his love for her was no mistake.

"Boston," she said.

Tim blinked, confused. "What's that? What about Boston?"

"That's where we need to go. It's close enough to get there quickly. Large enough to hide us—for a day or two. Long enough to marry—"

And then she screamed.

The first thing Tim thought when he heard her scream was that some horrible thing inside her *self* had snapped clear and shot up out through the saner part of her mind. It wasn't a charitable thing to think about a person he loved, and he knew it. And knowing didn't make him proud. But—darn it!—there *was* something off-kilter about her, something alien at least and maybe warped altogether. Something weird about the way he felt about her, for that matter. Oh, he loved her—truly loved her, he knew. There wasn't any mistaking the feeling. And the . . . bond. There was a bond between them, something very strong. Tim knew he hadn't made that bond. He didn't understand it, and he didn't trust it, but he thought that it was possible that he could live long enough to accept it and be comfortable.

But he didn't know her, and he didn't understand her, and then and there it seemed to Tim that he wasn't likely ever to do either.

Anyway, that confusion, that distrust—they were

the reasons that it took Tim three long moments to react when the Bleeding Man came to kill the woman he loved.

When he did turn to see it was an awful, awful shock. The Bleeding Man behind Gail Benjamin, hands around her throat. Choking, strangling—there wasn't any mistaking the bloodlust in his eyes. (And not just bloodlust, but blood, too: sanguine tears in the corners of his eyes, and there on his cheeks Tim could see stains where blood had begun to dry before he'd thought to wipe it away.)

Tim didn't think; he jumped. Jumped at the Bleeding Man, trying to rip those awful hands away from Gail's throat before they could—

Before they could—

So strong!

So strong those hands those arms might just as well be iron statue hands, or bronze or even granite, so stiff that hard as Tim tried to pull them away from Gail's throat he made no difference as she purpled, as her eyes bulged from their sockets. . . .

(If he'd stopped to think, if there'd been anything free in him to think with, Tim would have noticed how the Bleeding Man had just appeared again. No trace of how he'd gotten there. No car, no bike or motorcycle— and those were dress shoes, hardly anything to wear walking end to end a shopping mall. Certainly nothing as would let him walk so fast so far from the hotel. . . .)

The Bleeding Man turned to look Tim in the eye. "You may run," he said, "and my servants will betray me. But no less will I have you, and only moments less soon."

Tim felt an awful wave of panic wash up to engulf him, but he didn't let himself despair again. He didn't dare.

Maybe he couldn't stop the Bleeding Man. But he could still attack him. Gail's neck was large enough to need both his hands, and that left none free to fend away Tim's fists jabbing into his eyes, his throat, and now again into the bridge of his nose and again and again and again with everything he had, all the strength he had intent on breaking bone and breaking gristle away from bone, and strong as Tim was he wasn't strong enough to break—

But no, no, look. Look at the flesh of the Bleeding Man's face begin to give way. Slowly under the weight of blows—bending the way lead gives way, or gold does. Not shattering like bone.

And suddenly he screamed as the bridge of his nose folded inward.

And flailed out at Tim wildly, swatting the way Tim would've swatted at a fly that had grown to be too much an annoyance. But like that fly Tim was elsewhere long before the blow hit home. And unlike, too; because Tim wasn't any fly. He wasn't nearly so strong as the Bleeding Man (the strength in those hands was inhuman, Tim thought—unreal to the point of grotesquerie) but he was more than strong enough to get under him, to get under and lift and *throw* just as he had in that pitch-black parking lot, throw the Bleeding Man off the low cliff down onto the wave-crashing rocks. . . .

Where he crumpled into the foam like melted tin. A breaker; another; and then all trace of him was gone in the sea.

Gail stood beside him, gasping for breath. Both of them stared down into the breaking waves.

"He isn't dead, you know," she said. "Don't let him deceive you. It wasn't him that was here, but . . . his image? His doppelgänger? There's sorcery about him. The blood in his eyes lets him *do* things . . . things like that. Like making a copy of himself.—A puppet? But flesh, not cloth. That's why he was so strong, because he wasn't real.—And even if his image dies because it can't abide salt water, it doesn't hurt him. Doesn't do much but annoy him."

And Tim had a feeling that no matter how strange things seemed, no matter how strange a circumstance Gail Benjamin described, the truth was different and stranger still.

"We need to go," she said. "We need to be far from

here before he can make another. He can find us if we're close enough."

And something clicked, and Tim thought: *Wait a minute*. If that was true, and she knew it was so, and that was how the Bleeding Man found them in the first place. . . .

"Yes," she said. "I knew he could. But I didn't think he knew to look here for us. It takes so long. . . . We need to leave. If we don't run he'll be here in a moment."

And they got into her car, and they left. She drove hard, and fast; but only barely fast enough. As they pulled away Tim looked back to the spot where they'd been, and saw the Bleeding Man on the side of the road.

Running toward them.

And losing ground only very very slowly. If they'd left even a moment sooner, he'd've had them.

They were on Route 1, halfway between Providence and Boston, when she made a small, astonished sound.

"He knows this too," she said. "He knows exactly where we're going."

"He doesn't know me that well," he said. "If he did he would have found me a long time before he did."

She shook her head. "But he knows me. And Boston was my plan—for weeks."

"Maybe it will be better if we didn't go to Boston," he said. "Maybe it will be better if you don't know where we're going."

A mile later they pulled into a supermarket parking lot, and Tim took over the driving.

Gail got in the back, where she lay face up on the seat. And dozed. And woke now and again to watch the sky pass overhead.

She didn't get up for a long, long time. Tim wasn't really certain that was necessary—it seemed to him that once they were enroute she couldn't do much to influence their path. But no, no, she insisted. She didn't want to know where he took them, not till they were there. And maybe not even then.

"Where are we?" she asked—but this was after they'd traveled for a long, long time. They were in the Queens-Midtown Tunnel, coming into New York City.

"You're sure you want to know?" As they passed a sign that read 41ST STREET KEEP RIGHT. "You sure you can't guess?"

She shrugged. "Oh, I could guess. But I'm sure I'd be wrong.—This is where we're going, isn't it? It *feels* like a destination."

WEST SIDE LEFT LANE.

"Huh? How's that?—We're in New York." She looked at him blankly, as though she didn't understand the question. "How did you know this is where we're going?"

Shrug. "I don't know. It just . . . felt that way. You know what I mean, don't you?"

"Sure. It's just—I don't know. What if you knew we were here because he could see here through you? Sounds silly when I say it out loud. What's the word? Paranoid, that's it. Crazy-like."

She nodded gravely. "You could be right," she said. "I hope you aren't." Frown; furrowed brow. For a long moment she looked like she was concentrating. "It never seemed to me that he owned us that way. Oh, we followed him. Because we believed in him—if you know him well, it's hard not to believe in him. He really is wise, you know." She hesitated. "But cold, some ways. There are things he never feels."

Tim asked the question he'd promised he wouldn't ask her: "Is that why you betrayed him? Because he has no heart?"

She winced, but she didn't look away. "I love you," she said. "Beside that there is nothing to betray." Tim heard her sigh; looked into his rearview mirror and saw that she'd let herself fall back against the seat. "It bothers me to betray him. But what else can I do? He means to kill you. I can't help him do that. And I have to stop him if I can."

The tunnel opened out onto a smooth, narrow street in the West Thirties.

She looked flustered, hurt.

"I'm sorry," he said. "I didn't mean to ask."

Horns blaring somewhere a million miles away.

"I've never meant to hurt you."

Then there was a long time where it was quiet in the car—thick quiet like a body hears sometimes when the ears are too full of thunder for sound to penetrate—as they inched north through traffic. It felt to Tim like an hour at least, but the truth was nowhere near so long. Twenty minutes, tops—he checked his watch as he pulled into the parking garage of the Waldorf-Astoria, and he'd checked it just before Gail woke. There'd been scarcely half an hour between those points, and when he allowed for time spent in the tunnel, time before he'd asked that hurtful question. . . .

"The Waldorf? You've got interesting taste in hotels," she said. She didn't look impressed, exactly. It was hard to say what her expression was about.

Tim handed the car keys to the valet, looked over his shoulder to be certain there was no one in earshot. "Oh, it's nowhere near as nice as its reputation. Nice enough, and clean, and there's lots of service—quantity service, not quality service. The rooms are small, though, and the furnishings aren't anything as special as you'd expect."

"I know," she said. "But I don't understand why are we here if you know it too."

Tim shrugged. "I know where this hotel is—know how to get here by car. It's easy to park here, and not hard to get out in a hurry if you have to. All those things are tricky in New York."

Saying the city's name left something stuck in Tim's craw. The superstitious part of him was still sure that saying where they were would draw the Bleeding Man down on them.

Maybe it would. It was a sure thing that sooner or later something would bring him down on them; or that they'd come to a place where he sat waiting for them; or that. . . .

Or that they'd confront him.

Maybe that was it, Tim thought. Maybe the thing to do was take the hunt to his doorstep.

The elevator door opened into the hotel lobby. Where no one waited for them but the clerks and baggage handlers.

"I want to marry you today," he said when they were alone in their room. It was possible—barely possible— that they could manage it. The time was still morning; getting marriage papers would take hours, but there were hours yet left in the day.

The hotel room was as small and as prettily uncomfortable as the room he'd had the other time he'd been here.

"If you want," she said. "But it seems to me we're already married in the eyes of the Lord. If both of us say it, doesn't that make it so?"

"I. . . ." Tim wasn't sure—wasn't sure what he thought of the idea, what to say about it, why his head throbbed at the idea. "I'd rather do it by the law," he said. "I really would."

"Then we will."

And that was all the discussion there was on the issue. Half a dozen phone calls later they were in the Lexington Avenue subway, headed for the city offices downtown.

By late afternoon they'd finally gotten all their papers.

At five they found a judge with a spare moment who agreed to perform the ceremony—but only if they'd hurry; he had a bus to catch at six and the terminal was in midtown.

At seven they were in a restaurant not far from the hotel—the Brasserie, on 53rd, which is very nice and kind of special but not so especially nice that it meant they had to get dressed for the occasion. (Which would've been considerable trouble, being as Tim had left the hotel in Rhode Island without taking along his luggage. He could've shopped, sure; and Manhattan is a good place for that. But Tim's gangly long arms made it hard

for him to buy clothes that fit, and there was enough
already in this day without another ordeal.)

Gail ordered champagne when the waiter asked
them what they'd like to drink, and they sat sipping and
smiling and reading the paisley-bordered menus for
most of twenty minutes. After a while the waiter brought
bread—hardcrusted yeastsour white rolls—and butter.
Eventually Gail looked up from her menu, and she asked
him if he knew what he wanted to order. Which he
didn't. He hadn't begun to make a decision. But he
nodded anyway because it was time to get on with
things, and she called the waiter over and told him that
she wanted the salmon with scallions, and Tim said he'd
have the steak very rare because he didn't know what
else to do.

When the food came it was just this side of wonderful. Which was what Tim expected; the food here was
exactly that good when he and Grandpa had spent the
summer in New York the year after Mom and Dad had
died.

They ate quietly, savoring the glow of one another's
company all through appetizers, salad, and the main
course. Then, during dessert, Tim looked up and saw
her staring at him, smiling wide and beautiful and
unguarded, and all of a sudden both of them were
breaking out into uncontrollable giggles. Probably because of the champagne (they were almost done with the
second bottle) but because of other things, too.

And giggled and giggled and giggled. And eventually Tim knew that there wasn't any way they'd
straighten up enough to finish dessert, and he took four
large bills from his wallet and left them on the table to
cover the bill and the tip, and he took Gail by the arm
and led her upstairs out the door into the stifling warm
night.

It was late, and they were drunk, and New York
being an unfriendly place it was a miracle that no one
molested them during the four or five blocks they
walked from restaurant to hotel. But no one did, and
soon enough they were together alone in the pretty room
that no longer seemed so uncomfortable as it once had.

Tim thought that it'd get a little awkward then, because the first times were always a little awkward. But Gail *knew* something about how to be a woman and how to reach a man, and Tim was like clay in her hands; malleable, make-able; completely hers because she knew a powerful craft.

Through all of this he never doubted that she loved him.

In the dark part of the morning she woke him and took him again, wild, aggressive taking that left him dizzy with her love. When she was done they sat in bed for long moments staring out at New York through the high window of their room.

As they sat it finally came through to Tim what his heart had known since the moment he'd first seen her as a silhouette in that parking lot in Kansas.

"'Gail' wasn't your name when you were born, was it?—I remember now. I've known you almost all my life."

Her breast moved gently with her breath in the city light reflected through the hotel window. She was beautiful—perfect as the most flawless statue any master could ever conceive. In the light and dark she was a sculpture cut from onyx and white alabaster, and he wanted to take her and have her all over again. But how could he now so dizzy with the aftermath of love?

"Yes," she said. "I've known you for a long, long time."

"You were Erica. Erica Skolner." It wasn't a question; he knew the answer. She looked out the window for a time. Looked back at him.

"I was born to love you," she said, and they both knew she meant it literally. "I am what I was meant to be—and even if I was meant to be your undoing, it doesn't mean that I don't love you. And it doesn't mean that you're undone."

Tim smiled; he felt confident, and he knew that the feeling was surer to betray him than Gail could ever be. "I know," he said. "I love you too."

• • •

He woke again two hours before dawn in a dead quiet room lit bright by the left-on bedside lamp.

Quiet. The quiet was strange, striking; peculiar and notable even through the low din of his throbbing head. It was in no wise a function of the aftereffect of champagne—he knew his hangovers. No hangover he'd ever survived had turned quiet into this . . . menacing. That was what it was; unearthly and menacing. What evil. . . ?

And thought: *Something in me has turned paranoid, that's all this is. What's to be afraid of in the quiet of the night?*

The question struck him as so reasonable that for a moment Tim put aside his unease. It was back on him in a moment, rushing in like water to fill the void of fear displaced.

Something was wrong.

Tim leaned over to kiss his new-wed wife on the cheek, pushed his blankets aside. Got up from the bed and went to his window.

Which faced west, toward Times Square and Broadway.

He stared out into the Manhattan night for the longest time, watching cabs whiz by down below him on Park Avenue; watching a helicopter with police markings push through the air above Fifth Avenue, scoring the city with the beam of its searchlight; watching tiny bright-white flashes in the dark distance that Tim thought had to be gunfire—

That was when it settled through to him that the unnatural thing about the silence in this room was the fact it was there at all. New York is a city where there is no quiet, not even in the deep dark of the night, and not even this high room in this thick-walled hotel was an exception. Tim could remember falling asleep to the sound of the half-muffled din; could remember it surrounding them at close range all yesterday. And looking at the traffic outside below him, Tim knew that it ought to be here and now as well.

But it wasn't. There was no sound in this room; not even sound for the faint noise of his breathing. Nor Gail's.

And it came to him then that the room where he stood was not the place he'd rented the morning before, but no real place at all. He stood in a vision that waited only for him to admit it.

And turned away from the window—away from the eerie image of the thriving silent city—and found himself facing his own nightmare. Made real and whole and flesh.

The Lord Jesus Christ, nailed to His Cross.

Less exhausted, here, than He'd been most all the times Tim had seen Him. As though . . . as though this were a vision from a moment much earlier in His Ordeal than any Tim had seen before.

He was watching. Watching Tim very deliberately, and Tim thought that at any moment He would speak.

And all Tim could think was *No no no no not me O Lord not me I'm unworthy I'm a menace to the world please please please O Lord leave me to my life*, and Tim knew that the Lord could hear him think it, feel it, but still He didn't respond.

He only watched Tim patiently. Quietly.

And Tim thought: *I am the lurking menace, I am the evil that waits just inside the glass*.

And said, "O Lord O Lord forgive me for I've sinned against You, against those I love, against all mankind." And the air cried out empty waiting for him to finish out his thought with words he'd tried to leave unsaid. "I've tried to take responsibility for what I was born to do, Lord. Honestly and truly I have. But it's always just outside my reach, hiding from me, and as time goes on I come to see that I do more evil than good for this world. I understand now that it's best not to try to answer an obligation I'm not large enough to meet."

Jesus only hung bleeding on His Cross, watching Tim with His eyes so full of patience, tolerance, and love. He said nothing. But Tim heard his own words as he said them out loud, and the moment that he did he knew that they were a lie.

An awful and all but deliberate untruth. A lie told not just to himself but to his God.

I've been hiding, haven't I?

A part of him—a great, enormous mass of his self—shrieked silently at the very idea. He wanted to run and hide and pull the world in after him—

And just like that he was in the dark not nearly silent hotel room in Manhattan.

He closed his eyes. Forced himself to try to face his responsibility.

When Tim opened his eyes again it was broad daylight and he was alone in that empty room at the top of Grandpa's stair—transported by what device for what purpose he did not know.

It's not that I couldn't see the Cross, Tim thought. *It's that I didn't want to.*

And suddenly there in the middle of the empty floor, there among the cobwebs and the footprints on the dusty floor—there was the Cross.

Plain worn wood, just a shattered fragment of the Cross that once was. But there was no mistaking its majesty, its presence; no one could see it and mistake those dry brown stains that was the age-old blood of the Lord spattered along the high edge of the broken beam; no man nor woman could bask in the Holy Holy Holy Light the Cross exuded and fail to Know His Truth.

For a moment Tim's heart tried again to deny that Truth, and the vision of the Cross began to fade from his sight. But he knew the cowardice in his heart, and admitting to it he could no longer harbor it; and as he gave it up the sight of the One True Cross came back to him.

"I love You, Lord," he said aloud. And he went to the Cross, and took it from the spot where it had sat all these years since Grandpa had first set it there long before Tim's birth. And he clutched it to his heart, and made to leave the now-empty house of his grandfather behind.

He didn't get far. Which was a bad thing indeed, for the moment Tim lifted the Cross from its place his vision had ceased to be a vision, and turned real; he now stood—really, truly, honest-in-the-flesh stood—in that room at the top of Grandpa's house.

And he wasn't alone.

Out in the hall, out on the stair stood the Bleeding Man and at least two hundred of his servants. Waiting. Watching wide-eyed and amazed—all of them but the Bleeding Man. He wasn't surprised; wasn't mystified. Rather his expression was malevolent and hungry, and Tim thought he looked about to swallow him whole.

Perhaps he was.

Tim turned, tried to dive for the window off to his left. But as he launched himself toward it the Bleeding Man grabbed him by the neck, and pulled him up short. When Tim struggled against him the Bleeding Man clouted him over the head, and the world began to grey . . .

The knife. The knife Gail gave him two days ago. He thought of it, and the moment he did it was in his hands magically—as though the Blood that set it out from ordinary weapons had brought it to him. And maybe it did; there was no time to ask, no time even to think of it. Only time to strike out, to stab the Bleeding Man. Up, through his diaphragm, into his heart—

And the Bleeding Man screamed, screamed mortal terror frustrated afraid to die after a life that stretched two thousand years—

Tim thought of the clerk in the hotel dying scared out of his mind—

And the Bleeding Man's knees began to sag, and Tim felt his feet touch ground, and he began to struggle to get free—

And then the screaming stopped. And the Bleeding Man reached for the knife, took the hilt in his hand, and pulled it free. Black ichorous bilge gushed out through the wound, blood nothing like the stuff that oozed from his eyes. But it made no difference. The Bleeding Man stood straight, furious, and lifted Tim back up off his feet.

And he laughed.

When Tim began to struggle again, rattled and afraid and desperate to get away, the Bleeding Man heaved back and threw him against the wall.

Tim felt the impact, and then everything went still.

FIVE

Tim woke tied to an altar in the burned-out husk of the castle in Tennessee. He didn't know how he'd gotten there; didn't know how long he'd been unconscious to get here; didn't know how the Bleeding Man could've kept him out that long. But he did know this place. Even blinded Tim would have known where he was—the strangeness in the atmosphere, the odd half-sulfury scent of the stone flowers, the subtle electricity that made the hair on the back of his neck stand on end—every little thing about this place was graven somewhere deep in Tim's hindbrain. There was no mistaking it.

The great ballroom—this is all that's left of it now. Three roofless crumbling walls. Ash and charred wood piled everywhere ankle-deep. Blurry in the moonlight.

Everything was wrong. Everything. There was something he still had to learn, something he still had to do, and he knew that as he woke struggling groggy drugged against the ropes that bound him to the altar. But what could he do? How could he learn when there was no time?

The Bleeding Man, standing dressed in shimmery silk robes watching in the moonbright dark, saw Tim wake and smiled at him. It was a terrifying sight, it was; all hungry and threatening.

"What are you doing?" Tim asked.

The Bleeding Man made no answer.

That was when Tim noticed the last remaining fragment of the Cross—the Cross he'd been born and bred to ward—bound to his chest with the same strong thin rope that held him.

"Why have you brought me here? Why am I bound?"

The Bleeding Man smiled again, this time a smile more predatory than any Tim had seen before.

"The world is mine," the Bleeding Man said. "Mine to destroy and recreate. As I now will."

Vain, vain, vain. Vanity at its ultimate extension.

He's going to remake the world in his own image.

"You're out of your mind," Tim said.

And something else: something that the Bleeding Man had just said was an outright lie. Tim could hear it, tell its untruth.

The Bleeding Man laughed. "No," he said. "You're out of my mind."

And the moon went dim.

A hundred people stepped out of the shadows in unison, and they hummed all in time:

hmmm, *hmm*-hmm *hmm*-hmm *hmmm*

Over and over and over again, so many voices so tight in sync that what should have been a quiet hum was thunderous throbbing in his ears—

Headlights on the hill in the distance.

hmmm, *hmm*-hmm *hmm*-hmm *hmmm*

All of them dressed just as the ghosts who'd haunted Tim on his first visit to this unreal place. Stepping closer and closer each time on the final beat. Soon enough they'd crush so close as to crowd out everything but the sky with its dim grey moon.

Knife.

The Bleeding Man had a knife in his hand, and he was coming closer. Even before he came near enough for certainty Tim knew in his heart which knife that was.

It was the knife he'd used when he'd tried to kill the Bleeding Man. The same one Gail had given him as a token of her love. She'd called it her heritage, hadn't she? Tim thought that was what he remembered.

Her heritage from St. Helen.

He still wondered what she meant by that. He didn't think he'd live long enough to find out.

hmmm, *hmm*-hmm *hmm*-hmm *hmmm*

The Bleeding Man, coming toward him. Knife held
igh as though to—

—*as though he meant to cut Tim open.*

hmmm, *hmm*-hmm *hmm*-hmm *hmmm*

Light flashed against one wall like lightning though
he night was cloudless. Which seemed so natural here
nd now that it took Tim a moment to remember the car
.eadlights he'd seen only a moment before. The sound
f car tires pushing through the hill of hard-glass flowers,
,arely audible beneath the all-encompassing hum.

hmmm, *hmm*-hmm *hmm*-hmm *hmmm*

If the Bleeding Man and his people heard the car
Irive up into the ruined ballroom, there was no sign of
t in their faces. No reaction of any kind at all, despite
he crashing sound that came when a big section of the
ballroom floor collapsed from under the car's front tires.

Tim noticed, of course. Whatever drug-dream held
he Bleeding Man and his servants, it didn't hold him.
Ie watched the car as best he could through the bodies
·rowding constantly closer around him. When Gail
·limbed out of the driver's seat holding a machine gun,
Tim saw her. When she began shooting he heard the
.ound of gunfire; saw the bodies of the Bleeding Man's
.ervants rock and sag to the ground.

And one part of him thought *I'm saved I'm saved*
·*he's the cavalry come over the hill to save me* and
.nother part of him knew that it was only evil that could
:ome from so much killing, and no matter how well
neant, no matter how much she loved him, this was just
o much more of the Bleeding Man's plan—

"No! Gail, *no!*" But how could she hear over the
;ound from her gun? There was no way. It was hopeless,
.nd they were dying all of them dying none standing
1ow but the Bleeding Man who stood riddled with
;unfire laughing as she still shot at him, laughing,
.aughing—

—black ichor everywhere—

And now collapsing because the bullets had torn
.way too much of his torso to leave him standing—

Collapsing onto Tim, still holding the knife high in his left hand—

And the Bleeding Man and the blade came down both at once. And when the impact and the confusion were over the Bleeding Man lay slumped across Tim' chest above the Cross, and his dead black blood gushing everywhere on Tim—

And the knife had pierced Tim's arm, run clean through it into the altar below him, and his blood flowed red and free to mix with the black plasm of his ultimate forebear.

And still the Bleeding Man laughed. Laughed and laughed and laughed.

All around them the bleeding shuddering corpses of the ghost-dressed servants caught fire and began to burn with impossible blue flames. And the world shuddered with an earthquake that went infinitely deeper than the center of the earth.

Gail was with them now, kicking away the burning corpses, pushing away the animated corpse of the Bleeding Man, trying to untie Tim. It didn't matter, didn' matter at all. Already it was much, much too late.

Because the heavens themselves were disintegrating.

All around them suddenly the burning corpse flared and then went dim; and Tim saw that there was no trace of any of them left.

The walls around them faded, shimmered into irreality as the world shook and shook itself apart; and beyond the walls beyond the world the fabric of the universe too crumbled into the dark. Stars above them shimmered, twinkled, nova'd, and went still, and Tim watched terrified and stunned as the dark invisible husks drew close to form an implosion too bright to bear to see—

—as the walls, the world, the moon, and the dead-cold husk that was the sun ripped away to fall into the primordial egg—

And when it was done three long moments later all that was left outside the infinite thing at the center of all that thing shining darkness visible, the thing that was

he universe or might be or would be—all that was left of
he world that was real and not just a possibility to
ome—all there was was the Cross.

And Tim.

And Gail still struggling to free him.

And the Bleeding Man, who was a broken laughing
orpse here beside them.

The blood still endured, as well; Tim's, foul black
tuff from the Bleeding Man, and blood of the Lord still
eaking gently from the Bleeding Man's eyes. But there
vere no walls, no world, no floor beneath them. Nor
·ven gravity to bind them in one place, and Tim realized
vith a start that there was no longer any altar, either,
nd he was no longer bound. And he put one arm tight
round the Cross to hold it with all he had. Grabbed
Gail's arm with another. And *kicked* at the Bleeding
Man, to push them away away away

It didn't slow the Bleeding Man's laughter. If any-
hing the uproar intensified.

*Night. All around them Night so deep so intense like
un ice-cold weight on his heart. Primordial Night, Night
us it was before the dawn of the Lord's Creation.* . . .

"Watch," the Bleeding Man said. "Watch as I re-
nake this world."

And Tim was very, very afraid. And he thought,
*Lord, Lord, where are You? It's time to save the world,
Lord, time to save us save us all—*

There was no answer. But there was the touch of
His presence; quiet, watching, loving. Not like the touch
of Him that was everywhere in the world, nor the sense
Tim felt when he stood (as now) in the presence of the
Cross. This was different somehow—as though He
watched now with all His attention, no matter that He
still refused to interfere in the affairs of our world.

*Please, Lord, please: there's nothing I can do. The
universe crumbles around me, and I'm only man unable
to stop it.*

The Bleeding Man pointed at the great universal
egg in the distance before them, and as he did the egg
exploded with an act of new creation. . . .

And Tim felt something down inside him like a hand

reaching up through his bowels to rip away his heart a
terrified and frozen. . . .

And the Word Was—

And the new universe perverted to the needs an
means of evil bloomed out into the void—

In a moment he stood on impossible alien so
holding Gail, clutching the Cross helpless as all aroun
them a world began to materialize around them a worl
warped subtly, perverted to the wants and needs of
madman. Ghostly faint at first, now firmer, realer, reale
still.

Colors no eye had ever seen; sounds and scent
unsettling and strange. A spice in the air like somethin
from a crypt, but green/not-green and growing. Noise
out beyond the range of human hearing and still clearl
audible because the fundamental rules that made th
physical world were like nothing Tim had ever live
before.

A taste on his tongue like suspicion and some nev
original sin. A touch from the air like sandpaper thoug
the atmosphere was free from dust.

It was an evil place, Tim thought. A foul place lik
the inside of a madman's skull. And evil more than that
evil and empty of—

Empty of something powerful and important tha
for the longest moment Tim could not name. And then i
dawned on him, and as it did he felt shamed that h
hadn't realized it sooner.

*God's love. God's love is what binds all thing
together, and it isn't here in this creation.*

Almost on cue the horrible new world began t
disintegrate. Gravity failed first: Tim felt himself begi
to drift away from the foul ground, once more weightles
in the not-yet-void. Then small joined things, like th
leaves (arcane unleaf shapes of mysterious color sprun
from thorny hard-edged wild-limb thing—but it was
tree, Tim knew) and their branches disintegrating on
from the other, and then larger things like the sheer roc
wall that stood where once had stood the yonder hill
Great sanguine bloody bloody rocks came to hang in th
sky like vultures above them.

And the new green sun distorted like some rotting melon: fell in on itself and died.

And the Bleeding Man screamed. Tim saw him scream, saw him scream there in that infinite Night only because the light of God's love made a luminance around the lot of them, the Bleeding Man included.

And as he screamed the Bleeding Man pointed again at the egg that was the All, and again the One Thing spun out in an endless explosion of light and matter to make the universe—

And again the sensation, like a hand reaching up through Tim, up, up, into his heart—no. Not into his heart. Into the Cross. It was the Cross that allowed the Bleeding Man to make the world—but in all this time Tim had never seen the Bleeding Man lay hand on it.

And it finally occurred to him to wonder why it was that the Bleeding Man had even let him live.

He needs me, Tim thought. *He needs me to touch the Cross.*

And he thought: everything he's ever done to touch my life was meant to make me hide from what I knew I had to face.

To hide from the world.

To hide from the Stewardship of the Cross, which was his so long as he should live, whether he wanted it or not.

Suddenly everything around them—*everything*— changed. For the Bleeding Man, dead, soulless, all essential part of him that once was Steward long since passed to eternity—the Bleeding Man could not command the Cross unless he worked through Tim. As Tim was blind to the Cross until this moment, blind to his own authority and responsibility, the Bleeding Man could act through Tim unhampered.

But now that changed: Tim opened himself up, opened up to the Cross and to the world, to the universe crumbling and rebuilding all around them—

"Too late," the Bleeding Man said when Tim finally rose to face the world. "My Will is done. I am the Word."

But out in the void the shooting stars that were or would be the world stood still.

It was silent in the emptiness between Tim and the Bleeding Man. No laugh; no scream; not even the fainter sounds of breathing.

"This isn't you," Tim said. "God is the word. Not you."

There was something desperate in the Bleeding Man's eye. He didn't say a word, but he didn't have to. Tim knew what it was he wouldn't say.

And something in that desperation that reminded of the archetypes that came to him a vision on the roadside when he lay broken late at night so long ago/not long ago at all.

I am to be, Tim thought: *I am to be him.* That was the choice that weighed before him now, wasn't it? The Bleeding Man and how Tim answered him were a challenge, and the manner in which he answered the challenge would mark him and shape him forever.

What he did now would shape his Stewardship irrevocably.

Now Tim could feel the Cross and how it touched inside him; could feel the Bleeding Man and the deep bond there was between them—a bond made of blood and commonality and the werebind that comes of the responsibility both of them had borne.

Tim could *feel* the Bleeding Man reaching through that bond toward Tim's heart, to capture him, to take him, to—

To take the Cross again.

This will always be the way, Tim thought. *So long as we both shall live, he will haunt me, and seek me, and live to steal the Cross to steal the world.*

That was the challenge. That was the trouble that lay on him.

What came to him now was the memory of the dream, and the realization that how he answers the challenge will make him forever into the Steward he would be. Some choices would make Tim into the model of his grandfather—so like the Wise Man Who Loves, wise and aware and careful of the hearts of all who find him. Others might create him the Blind Keeper of the

Grail, ignorant to the world deliberately, strong with softness of sand that cannot break.

Still other choices would grow him into the bond that tied him to the Bleeding Man; for his eye could indeed grow careful and sensitive where his heart grew hard.

A terrible thing, and Tim knew it. Because he had his soul it was in him to be a greater deeper wider threat to all the world than ever the Bleeding Man could be.

I could kill him, Tim thought. *If I kill him he will never threaten me again, and the bond between us dies, and I don't have to worry.* What did it matter, after all, to kill a man who had no soul? He died two thousand years ago.

It would be easy, Tim can feel that through the awareness of that Cross the burns in him. All he had to do was draw the Blood Flame that burned in Old Abraham's eyes though the bond that tied them—and then press it out through the Cross.

Tim could do it now, in a moment. He was certain of that.

And still he hesitated; there was something wrong here. He couldn't be the first Steward to realize that Old Abraham lived only because the Stewardship allows it. But then why was the Bleeding Man still alive, these two thousand years?

The answer came to him with a chill current in his blood: To use the Cross to kill Old Abraham was to *become* Old Abraham. Because his spirit trapped in the Cross would change Tim and the Cross forever? Because to use the Cross to kill would lead inevitably toward the archetype that was the Bleeding Man? Tim wasn't certain how or why, not yet; but he knew with all his heart that he dare not kill this man who'd tried so hard to break him.

What, then, was he to do? Spend his life hiding from Old Abraham, the way Grandpa did? For all the good it did him: Grandpa died because he'd hidden. And left Tim to inherit his mistake.

I could ignore him, Tim thought. *Let him try to*

come for me: I'm stronger than he is. There's no reason to be afraid of him.

That would lead in time toward the archetype that was the Blind Keeper of the Grail. He would grow stronger and stronger inside himself, but in the end his life would be to no effect—for the nature of that archetype was the nature of a mountain: it does not *do*, but *is*.

Almost as though he were a monument to himself.

Then it comes to him that there is another path—one that leads in none of the archetypic directions he has foreseen.

Embrace him.

Love him.

Reach in through the bridge between them, and set his strange soulless heart to rest.

"Forget," Tim said. And he held the Cross up so that they both could see it—

—and stood in the burned-out ballroom of the mansion in Tennessee. Gail stood beside him staring wide-eyed, terrified, amazed. Everywhere were charred corpses dressed in smouldering cowled robes unburned by the flames.

And the Bleeding Man stood before them, waiting furious and terrible—

And he screamed—

—*and he leaped*—

And then Gail was out in front of Tim, holding the dagger that was her heritage, and it was plain that she meant to kill him before he could set hands on either one of them—

"No," Tim said. He reached forward to take Gail's shoulder and pull her back. Stepped out to meet the Bleeding Man, to take the hand that shot clawlike out to steal Tim's eyes. "Forget," he said. "Close your eyes. Forget. And sleep."

And as the blank expression formed on Old Abraham's face, as his legs sagged out from under him, Tim reached out to take him in his arms, lower him gently lovingly to the ground.

They backed away after a moment, and left him to wake when he was ready.

After a while Tim and Gail got into her car and drove away.

There are other things to tell: how Tim and Gail, Steward of the Cross and Daughter of St. Helen, united their lines, bringing round and whole a circle that had opened two thousand years before; and how their sons and daughters. . . . But so easily we outreach the scope of the tale at hand, and that's no virtue. Leave it at this: They lived a happy, rocky life (what else of two willful folk?) for many many years, and in their time were buried side by side. Perhaps they've gone on to some reward; perhaps they wait the Second Coming resting in the arms of the earth.

A NOTE FROM ALAN RODGERS
ON HIS FORTHCOMING NOVEL, *PANDORA*

Three AM in our fourth-floor tenement apartment in New York City.

They don't call them tenement apartments any more. But they haven't changed in any special way since immigrant families crowded themselves into them. Their misery seeps from the floorboards.

Barry Farber is on the radio, taking calls from America-at-large.

A man calls, and he says, "They're wrong, you know. About those aliens in the hangar on the air base in Ohio. There aren't three of them."

I can almost picture Barry raising one eyebrow. "Oh?"

"Yes," the caller says, "there are three and a half."

* * *

I step back a moment, I listen to them again in my head—this time from a distance. I try to forget everything I know about UFO aliens, science fiction, B-movies from the fifties, and *listen*.

The two men on the radio are passing folklore. The aliens in hangar thirteen aren't deranged sf; they're a modern myth, and the fact that we tell of them speaks more of us than it does of them.

This was the fall just after I started work on *Night*.

A lot of what horror is about is being an ordinary person in an extraordinary situation. About coping with a world bigger than you can ever hope to be. Sure, it's about scariness—of course it is. Any place as big, as merciless, as extraordinary as the world we live in is bound to be terrifying. How could it be otherwise?

And folklore: a lot of what it's about is folklore.

Certainly many well-known horrors come directly from traditional sources—vampires, werewolves. Ghosts. Zombies.

What sort of monsters, I wondered, are we breeding with out modern myth? What stories will our children tell their children, and what will those stories say of us?

Are we breeding monsters at all—or do we make something even more frightening?

Two, three months I let folklore, tradition, urban legendry, and Space Aliens from *the Weekly World News* stew in the recesses of my brain. And then I did the first sketch of the book I'm working on now: *Pandora*.

It's a different kind of book. I can tell that even now, looking at the corner of it I've finished. And at the same it's part of a very long tradition.

You'll see.

Look for *Pandora* in August 1992 from Bantam Spectra.